Jay Kristoff grew up in the most isolated capital city on earth and fled at his earliest convenience. He worked in 'creative advertising' for eleven years and has won several awards that nobody outside the advertising industry gives a tinker's cuss about. He is 6'7", has approximately 13,870 days to live, and can demand whiskey in almost a dozen European languages. He lives in Melbourne with his wife and the world's laziest Jack Russell.

Kinslayer is second novel in his The Lotus War series, following on from *Stormdancer*.

By Jay Kristoff

Stormdancer
Kinslayer

JAY KRISTOFF

Kinslayer

The Lotus War: Book Two

TOR

First published 2013 by Tor

This edition published 2014 by Tor
an imprint of Pan Macmillan, a division of Macmillan Publishers Limited
Pan Macmillan, 20 New Wharf Road, London N1 9RR
Basingstoke and Oxford
Associated companies throughout the world
www.panmacmillan.com

ISBN 978-1-4472-0050-5

1 3 5 7 9 8 6 4 2

A CIP catalogue record for this book is available from the British Library.

Typeset by Ellipsis Digital Limited, Glasgow
Printed and bound by CPI Group (UK) Ltd, Croydon, CR0 4YY

Visit **www.panmacmillan.com** to read more about all our books
and to buy them. You will also find features, author interviews and
news of any author events, and you can sign up for e-newsletters
so that you're always first to hear about our new releases.

For Kath and Tony.
Words fail.

Mons of the Shima Imperium

Tiger Clan (Tora)

Fox Clan (Kitsune)

Dragon Clan (Ryu)

Phoenix Clan (Fushicho)

The Lotus Guild

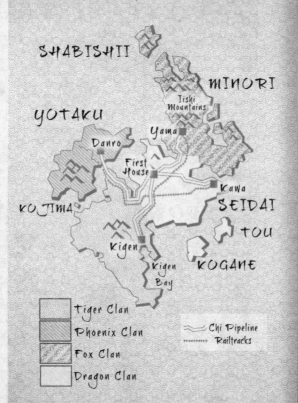

THE SHIMA ISLES

SHABISHII

MINORI

YOTAKU

Iishi
Mountains

Yama

Danro

First
House

Kawa

SEIDAI

KO JIMA

TOU

Kigen

KOGANE

Kigen
Bay

▢	Tiger Clan
▨	Phoenix Clan
▧	Fox Clan
▢	Dragon Clan

〜〜	Chi Pipeline
┄┄	Railtracks

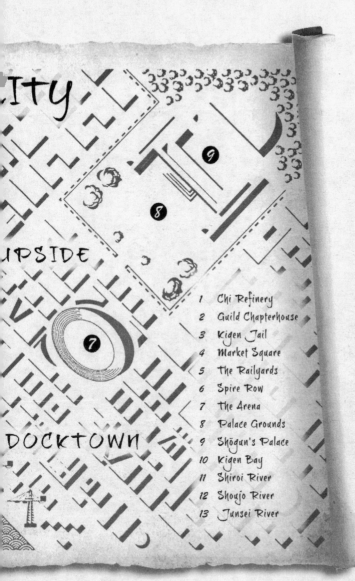

ITY

UPSIDE

DOCKTOWN

Your anger is a gift.

Aristotle

Lotus War character refresher –
Who the hells are all these people?

Yukiko – A young girl with the ability to speak telepathically to animals (a gift called 'the Kenning'). Commanded to capture a legendary thunder tiger by Shima's cruel Shōgun, Yukiko ended up forging a powerful bond with the beast, whom she named Buruu. While lost in the wilderness, she joined the ranks of a guerrilla rebellion, known as the Kagé (meaning 'Shadows') and decided to take retribution on the Shōgun for his crimes against her family.

Last known whereabouts: after murdering Shōgun Yoritomo, Yukiko fled Kigen city. She returned forty-nine days later and delivered an impassioned speech, urging the populace to rise against the government and the Lotus Guild.

Buruu – A thunder tiger (aka arashitora). Yukiko's best friend and loyal companion. Buruu is the last of his race in Shima. His feathers were clipped by Shōgun Yoritomo, and until he molts again, he cannot fly without the aid of mechanical wings built for him by the Guild Artificer, Kin.

Last known whereabouts: with Yukiko.

Kin – An Artificer (engineer) of the Lotus Guild who crashed with Yukiko in the Iishi Mountains. In defiance of all he had been raised to believe, Kin built mechanical wings for Buruu, allowing the thunder tiger and Yukiko to escape the Shōgun's clutches.

Last known whereabouts: surrounded by guards in Kigen city as Yukiko flew to freedom.

Masaru – aka 'The Black Fox of Shima.' Hunt Master of the Imperial Court. Yukiko's father. Drunkard. Gambler. Lotus-addict. But he turned out to be a decent fellow, underneath it all.

Last known whereabouts: Masaru was shot and killed by Yoritomo-no-miya during a showdown in Kigen's Market Square.

Kasumi – Hunter of the Imperial Court. Masaru's lover.

Last known whereabouts: Kasumi was killed during Masaru's jailbreak. She died in his arms.

Akihito – A hunter of the Imperial Court. Masaru's right-hand man, and Yukiko's friend since childhood. His leg was badly wounded during Masaru's jailbreak.

Last known whereabouts: limping to Kigen docks with Michi in order to flee the city after the Shōgun's assassination.

Yoritomo-no-miya – Shōgun of Shima. Daimyo of the Tiger clan. Last son of the Kazumitsu Dynasty, a familial line that has ruled the Shima Imperium for two centuries. A lunatic who came too young to power, and was ultimately consumed by it.

Last known whereabouts: Yoritomo was slain telepathically by Yukiko and Masaru during their showdown in the Market Square.

Aisha – Yoritomo's sister. Last daughter of the Kazumitsu Dynasty. Secret ally of the Kagé rebellion (a fact discovered by Yoritomo before his death).

Last known whereabouts: Yoritomo alluded to a grim fate for his beloved sibling, but whether Aisha survived his retribution remains unknown.

Michi – A maidservant of the Lady Aisha. Secret member of the Kagé rebellion. Swordmaster.

Last known whereabouts: making her way to Kigen docks with Akihito in order to flee the city after the Shōgun's assassination.

Hiro – aka 'The Boy with the Sea-Green Eyes.' Iron Samurai. Member of the Kazumitsu Elite (the Shōgun's personal bodyguard). Hiro formed a romantic relationship with Yukiko while she was resident in the Shōgun's palace, but ultimately betrayed her when he discovered she was plotting against his lord and master, Yoritomo.

Last known whereabouts: During a bloody battle in Kigen arena, Buruu tore Hiro's arm off and Yukiko stabbed him in the chest. He was left for dead on the arena floor.

Hideo – Imperial Spymaster, master of intrigue in the Shōgun's court. Hiro's uncle.

Last known whereabouts: Hideo was eaten by rats during Masaru's jailbreak.

Daichi – Leader of the Kagé rebellion. A former member of the Kazumitsu Elite who rebelled against the Shōgunate after Yoritomo mutilated his daughter, Kaori. While in Yoritomo's service, Daichi murdered Yukiko's mother – a warning to Masaru when he refused to obey the Shōgun's will.

Last known whereabouts: the Kagé stronghold in the Iishi Mountains.

Kaori – Lieutenant of the Kagé rebellion. Daichi's daughter. She bears an awful knife scar on her face, courtesy of Yoritomo-no-miya.

Last known whereabouts: the Kagé stronghold in the Iishi Mountains.

Kensai – Second Bloom of the Lotus Guild, and Voice of the Guild in Kigen city. One of the most powerful and influential Guildsmen alive. Kin's adoptive uncle.

Last known whereabouts: Lotus Guild Chapterhouse in Kigen city.

Isao – A young member of the Kagé rebellion. He spied on Yukiko while bathing, discovering she bore the tattoo of the Shōgun on her arm.

Last known whereabouts: the Kagé stronghold in the Iishi Mountains.

Atsushi – A young member of the Kagé rebellion. Isao's partner in crime during the 'Affair of the Bathhouse Wall.'

Last known whereabouts: Kagé stronghold in the Iishi Mountains.

Skin

'The prelude was Void,
And unto Void they return. Black as mother's womb.'
So spoke he the first; holy Lord Izanagi, Maker and Father,
Unto the second; great Lady Izanami, Mother of All Things,
Not his to foresee, the doom of all mortal men,
Would also be hers.

The Book of Ten Thousand Days

Prologue

Now witness the end of the beginning.

A ghost-pale girl, sixteen years old, wisps of dark hair and warm scarlet scrawled across her face. A smiling tyrant, stained with his own sister's blood, a smoking iron-thrower in a white-knuckle grip. The pair standing in the crowded Market Square as children's ashes swirl and dance in the gulf between them. And she stretches out her hand, and opens her mouth, and speaks the last words the tyrant will ever hear.

'Let me show you what one little girl can do.'

Fifty-five days ago. Almost two months since the last son of the Kazumitsu Dynasty perished at her hands. So much chaos since then. The earth shifting beneath our feet. The threads beginning to unravel. One by one by one.

Our war of conquest against the round-eyed gaijin collapsed as news of the Shōgun's death spread, the threat and promise of a now-empty throne coalescing in every clanlord's mind. And as the shadow of civil war reared over the Seven Isles, the Lotus Guild urged only calm. Obeisance to their puppets in the Tiger clan. Threatening embargoes of their precious fuel – the blood-red chi driving the Shōgunate's iron heart – to any who disobeyed their will.

Then came the truth of how that fuel was made.

The words that would begin the avalanche were transmitted over the pirate radio frequencies of the Kagé rebels. The Shadows revealed that inochi – the wondrous fertilizer used on blood lotus fields across the Seven Isles – had been manufactured with the remains of gaijin prisoners of war. And Shima's people awoke to the horror that the Imperium, the technology driving it, their entire way of life – all had been watered with innocent blood.

Like flames on long-dead leaves after a breathless summer, or ripples on still water after rain's first falling, the riots took seed and spread. Outraged. Bloody. But brief. Brutally suppressed beneath the heels of Iron Samurai still loyal to the vacant throne. Uneasy peace settled over the clan metropolises, broken glass crunching underfoot, as the forty-nine days of official mourning passed in shivering, breathless silence.

Until she returned.

Yukiko. Arashi-no-odoriko. Stormdancer. Astride the mighty thunder tiger Buruu, fire in her eyes, lightning crawling along his clockwork wings. Flying to every capital, from the Floating Palace in Danro to the Market Square in Kigen city. Her voice a clarion call. Urging the people to open their eyes and open their minds and close the fingers on their hands.

How I wish I could have been there.

How I wish I could have heard her speak. But since the moment Yoritomo's corpse hit the cobbles, I have been running. Fleeing Kigen in a trail of blue-white flame. Abandoning the burnished brass I had worn all my life in some fallow field, my touch lingering on its surface as if I were saying farewell to my oldest friend. Long miles of empty road under my bleeding feet, endless skies of bloody red before my burning eyes, flesh hardened and torn from the weeks it has taken to make it back to the Iishi wilds.

Back to her.

And here I am. Almost there, now. The Lotus Guildsman who betrayed all he knew, all he was. Who gifted a crippled thunder tiger with metal wings to bear him from his prison. Who helped a lone girl slay the Kazumitsu Dynasty's last son and plunge this nation into the tempest. Traitor is the name I will wear in the histories. Kioshi was the name I inherited after my father died.

But in truth, my name is Kin.

I remember what it was to be encased in metal skin. To see the world through blood-red glass. To stand apart and above and beyond and wonder if there was nothing more. And even now, here in the depths of Shima's last wilderness, the dogs closing in around me, I can hear the whispers of the mechabacus in my head, feel the phantom weight of that skin on my back and on my bones, and part of me misses it so badly it makes my chest hurt.

I remember the night I learned the truth of myself – my future laid bare in the Chamber of Smoke. I remember the Inquisitors coming for me, swathed in black and soundless as cats, telling me it was time to see my What Will Be. And even as the screams of those brethren who failed the Awakening echoed in my head, I felt no fear. I clenched my fists, thought of my father, and vowed I would make him proud. That I would Wake.

Thirteen years old and they call you a man.

I had never watched the sun kiss the horizon, setting the sky on fire as it sank below the lip of the world. Never felt the whisper-gentle press of a night wind on my face. Never known what it was to belong or betray. To refuse or resist. To love or to lose.

But I knew who I was. I knew who I was supposed to be.

Skin was strong.
Flesh was weak.
I wonder now, how that boy could have been so blind.

1

The Girl all Guildsmen Fear

Three Guild warships rumbled across a blood-red sky with all the finesse of fat drunkards lunging towards the privy. They were capital warships of the 'ironclad' series; the heaviest dreadnoughts constructed in the Midland yards. Balloons the colour of flame, shuriken-thrower turrets studding their inflatables, vomiting black exhaust into opiate skies.

The flagship leading the trio was a hundred feet long, three red banners embroidered with lotus blooms trailing at her stern. Her name flowed down her bow in broad, bold kanji – a warning to any fool who would stand in her way.

LADY IZANAMI'S HUNGER.

If Brother Jubei felt any trepidation about serving on a ship named for the Dark Mother's appetites, he hid it well. He stood at the stern, warm inside the brass shell of his atmos-suit despite the freezing wind. Trying to still the butterflies in his stomach, quiet his pounding heart. Repeating the mantra: 'skin is strong, flesh is weak, skin is strong, flesh is weak,' seeking his centre. Yet try as he might, he couldn't still the discontent ringing inside his head.

The fleet's captain stood at the railing, surveying the Iishi Mountains below. His atmos-suit was decorated with ornate designs, brass fixtures and pistons embossed with steel-grey filigree. A mechabacus clicked and chittered on his chest; a device of counting beads and vacuum tubes, singing the tuneless song of windup insects. A dozen desiccated tiger tails hung from the spaulders covering the captain's shoulders. They were rumoured to have been a gift from the great Fleetmaster of the Tora Chapterhouse, Old Kioshi himself.

The captain's name was Montaro, though his crew preferred to call him 'Scourge of the Gaijin.' He was a veteran of the Morcheba invasion, had commanded the Guild fleet supporting Shōgunate ground troops against the round-eye barbarians across the Eastborne Sea. But when the war effort had begun disintegrating in the wake of the Shōgun's assassination, Chapterhouse Kigen had recalled the captain and set him tracking a new foe, back on Shiman shores. To Brother Jubei's great pride, of all the newly Awakened Shatei in Kigen, Second Bloom Kensai had selected *him* to serve as the Scourge's new aide.

'Do you require anything, Captain?' Jubei stood at the Scourge's back, a respectful distance away, eyes downcast.

'A sniff of our quarry would suffice.' Faint annoyance in the crackling buzz that passed for the captain's voice. 'Other than that, this weak flesh abides.' He touched a switch, spoke into his wrist. 'Do you see anything up there, Shatei Masaki?'

'No movement, Captain.' The lookout's reply was faint, despite him being perched only thirty feet above their heads. 'But this forest canopy is thick as fog. Even with telescopics, we're hard-pressed to pierce it.'

'Clever rabbit,' the Scourge hissed. 'He's heard our engines and gone to ground.'

Jubei watched a spire of rock drift past their starboard; a black iceberg in a sea of maple and cedar. Thin cloud clung to the mountaintops, peaks crusted in snow, the rumble of engines and heavy *thupthupthup* of propellers echoing in the forest beneath them. Autumn cupped the Iishi Mountains at the edge of a cold embrace, the colours of rust waiting at the edge of the stage.

The Scourge sighed, hollow and metallic.

'I know it to be the impulse of my weak flesh, but I confess I missed these skies.'

Jubei blinked back his surprise, wondering if he should engage his commanding officer in idle chatter. After long empty moments, the young Guildsman decided it would be impolite not to respond, speaking with hesitation.

'. . . How long were you stationed in Morcheba, Captain?'

'Eight years. Eight years with nothing but blood-drinkers and skinthieves for prey.'

'Is it true the skies above the round-eye lands are blue?'

'No.' The Scourge shook his head. 'Not anymore. Closer to mauve now.'

'I would enjoy seeing them one day.'

'Well, the sooner we butcher our rabbit, the sooner we get back there.' Gauntleted fingers drummed the wooden railing. 'I'd hoped to run him down before he reached the Iishi. But he's resourceful, this one.'

Jubei looked at the ships around them, bristling with weaponry and mercenary marines. The discontent rapped at the inside of his teeth, demanding to be let out for air.

'Forgive me, Captain,' he ventured. 'I know Old Kioshi's son is a traitor. I know he must be punished for crafting the thunder tiger's wings, aiding in its escape. But this fleet . . . all this effort to kill one boy seems . . .'

'Excessive?'

'Hai.' A slow nod. 'I have heard rumour that Old Kioshi and Second Bloom Kensai were as brothers. That Kensai-sama raised the traitor as his own son. But, forgive my temerity – does it not seem to you there is more important prey for us to be hunting?'

'You speak of Yoritomo's assassin.'

'And the Kagé rebels who shelter her.'

The Scourge glanced at him, grim amusement in his voice.

'Shelter her? She is not exactly hiding from us, young brother. Visiting all four clan capitals in the past fortnight. Bringing the skinless to the edge of outright rebellion. Slaying the Shōgun of this nation simply by *looking* at him.'

'All the more reason to hunt her down, surely?' Jubei felt righteous anger curdle his voice. 'The citizenry say we in the Lotus Guild are *afraid* of her. A slip of a girl. A *child*. Do you know what they call her, Captain? The skinless, gathered in their filthy gambling pits and smoke houses? Do you know the name they give her?'

'Stormdancer,' the Scourge replied.

'Worse,' Jubei spat. 'They call her "the girl all Guildsmen fear."'

A hollow chuckle echoed inside the Scourge's helm. 'Not this Guildsman.'

Jubei lost his voice, stared at his feet, wondering if he had spoken out of turn. The Scourge glanced at one of their support vessels, the *Lotus Wind,* rumbling a mile off their stern, twin trails of blue-black exhaust spewing from the ironclad's engines. He touched a switch at his chest, spoke again into his wrist, iron in his voice.

'Captain Hikita, report.'

'. . . o sign,' came the faint reply, almost inaudible through the static. '. . . ut we are almost directly abov . . . site where the *Resplendent Glory* picked . . . tsune girl last summer . . . ronghold should be . . . rby.'

'He cannot be far,' the Scourge growled. 'He left the river only last night, and on foot. Have your munitioneers prepare a fire barrage. Five-hundred-foot spread from the water's edge. Time to flush this rabbit from his hole.'

Confirmation crackled down the comms channels, tinged with reverb.

The *Lotus Wind* banked ponderously and trekked back south, the drone of its propellers smudged across the sky. Jubei saw fire crews swarming over the decks like tiny armoured ants, loading incendiary barrels, setting ignition charges. He was scanning the forest canopy when the *Wind*'s captain signalled the barrage was finally primed and ready. The Scourge's voice hissed down the all-comms frequency.

'Lookouts, eyes open. Captain Hikita, commence bombardment.'

Jubei saw a cluster of black shapes fall from the *Wind*'s belly, tumble down into the autumn shroud below. A second later, all peace shattered, a series of dull whumping booms accompanying the blossoms of flame bursting amidst the trees, unfurling a hundred feet into the air and buffeting the *Hunger* like a child's toy. Faint vibrations pressed against Jubei's metal skin as the *Wind* cruised the shuddering riverbank, setting huge swathes of the forest ablaze.

The flames caught and spread, licking autumn leaves with fevered tongues, a curtain of choking soot and char drifting through the woods on blackened feet. Off the starboard side, their second escort, *Void's Truth* dumped a second cluster of firebombs amidst the ancient trees, trembling reverb echoing down the river valley. Flocks of shrieking birds took to the wing, animals of all shapes and sizes fleeing north through the undergrowth, away from the grasping flames. Jubei watched it all unfold with a kind of fascination – the power of his Guild's technology obliterating what had taken centuries to grow in a matter of moments.

'Any sign?' the Scourge asked over all-comms.

'Negative,' reported the *Wind*'s lookouts.

'No sign,' from the *Hunger*'s eyes above.

The *Truth*'s reply popped with faint static. 'We have contact. Three hundred yards, north-northeast. Acknowledge?'

'I have him,' reported the *Hunger*'s lookout. 'Seventy degrees starboard.'

The *Hunger*'s pilot kicked the engines to full burn, the propellers' song rising an octave as they swung about to begin pursuit. Jubei engaged his telescopics, scanning the shifting chinks in the forest canopy as a sudden sweat burned his eyes. The vista below crackling sharp in his vision. Smoke coiled amidst moss-encrusted giants. Falling leaves and fleeing birds. An empire of bark and stone. But at last, yes, he saw him, he *saw* him – a thin figure in dirty grey, darting between two gnarled and looming maples.

'There!' Jubei cried. 'There he is!'

Short dark hair. Pale skin. Gone.

'Ground crews, prepare for pursuit.' The Scourge's command was calm as millpond water. '''Thrower teams full alert. Second Bloom has ordered us to liquidate target on sight.'

The *Truth*'s shuriken-throwers opened up, followed by the *Hunger*'s; twin batteries of razor-sharp stars spraying from their flanks and shredding the curtain of curling leaves below. Severed branches crashed earthwards, the *chug!chug!chug!chug!* of the 'throwers ringing over the rush of starving flames. Jubei thought he saw their quarry flitting amidst the undergrowth, a hail of gleaming death raining all around him. The *Hunger*'s marines were performing final weapons checks, readying to drop into the woods below. Flames to the south. Troops and spinning death from above. Ironclads overhead.

Jubei smiled to himself, surging flames reflected on metal skin. The rabbit had led them on a long chase, to be sure. But at last, his luck had come to an end.

The Scourge turned from the railing, grim satisfaction in his voice. 'You may get to see Morcheba sooner than you—'

A flash of light.

Searing. Magnesium-white. It took a split second for the shock wave to catch up to the flare. Jubei saw the air around him grow brighter, highlights glinting on brass skin. And then came thunder – a shuddering, bone-shaking report sending *Lady Izanami's Hunger* skidding sideways across the sky, engines wailing in soot-smeared protest. Jubei lost his balance, and to his shame, clutched the Scourge's arm to stop himself falling.

A rush of superheated air. Tortured metal screaming, the hollow thudding booms of secondary explosions. Jubei turned, breath catching in his lungs, unable to comprehend what he was seeing.

The ironclad off their starboard. *Void's Truth*. A complement of twenty Guild marines, twelve Lotusmen, four Artificers, six officers and thirty crew. All of them.

They were falling from the sky.

The inflatable was simply gone, a long, ragged fireball swelling within a blackened exoskeleton, great flaming hands reaching down to incinerate anything on her deck. Cables snapping, motors whining as she reared up under unrestrained thrust, bow pointing into the sky even as they plummeted earthwards. The comms system was filled with screaming; tiny burning figures spilling over the railings and tumbling towards maws of rock hundreds of feet below. Jubei could see a few crewmen struggling with the aft lifeboat, bent low in terror. Another deafening explosion sounded as the *Truth*'s chi reserves ignited, her backside blew apart in a shower of blazing shrapnel, and she spun end over end towards her grave.

'What in the First Bloom's name?' the Scourge bellowed into the comms system. 'What hit us? Report!'

The *Hunger*'s crew was in chaos. Marines scrambling for the secondary shuriken-throwers. Shouted orders. Running feet. Fire teams on the dirigible yelling for target coordinates, lookouts aiming their telescopics through the billowing smoke, ashes falling like rain. Jubei saw the blue-white flare of rocket-trails through the haze off the starboard side; brothers who had survived the explosion and managed to engage their jet packs.

'There!' he yelled. 'Survivors!'

The closest Shatei was forty feet from the *Hunger*'s railing when it took him. A flash of white amidst the smoke, the squealing crunch of ruptured metal, a strangled shout. And then Jubei saw the rocket pack flare and die, a haze of red, and the brother tumbled from the sky, the top half of his body struggling to keep pace with his legs.

'First Bloom, save us,' he whispered.

Jubei felt the *Hunger* shudder, heard a bass-thick crackling across blood-red skies. A sound that shivered the flesh inside his skin, rivets squealing, deck trembling under his feet like a child beneath his sheets in the thick, dead of night. The unmistakable roar of thunder. And yet, aside from the smoke, the skies around them were clear as polished glass . . .

'Battle stations!' the Scourge roared. 'Battle stations!'

Jubei heard the shuriken-throwers arcing up again; a heavy *chug!chug!chug!chug!,* the hiss of pressurized gas, the clunking clatter of feeder belts. The sky around them sparkled with shards of razored steel, withering death sprayed blindly into the smoke. The mechabacus upon his chest spat a chattering spiel, confirmation requests from Chapterhouse Kigen flooding his inputs. His hands were shaking too hard to respond.

Screams again. Cries of 'Contact! Contact!' A pinprick of flame off the stern. Jubei looked behind in time to see that same white silhouette skirting the *Lotus Wind*'s inflatable, talons rending the reinforced canvas of their sister ship like damp rice-paper.

The world held still for a fleeting second, the deathly hush between one heartbeat and the next. Jubei looked across the space between him and that white blur, a sky of spinning steel and acrid smoke, and in that tiny, fragile moment, he saw her: a black shape, long hair whipping in an ember wind, crouched between two metal wings on the back of an absolute impossibility. And as its long and terrible talons ripped the *Wind*'s inflatable asunder, he saw a flash of orange light in the girl's hand, a tiny flame at the end of a handheld flare, tumbling from her fingertips towards the escaping hydrogen.

And then light. Rippling, deafening light.

The explosion rocked the *Hunger* onto her starboard, the shock wave sending four marines over the side and into the abyss. Fire blossomed, the *Wind*'s inflatable tearing apart like an overfull bladder, timbers snapping, choking smoke. The Scourge bellowing, the chatter of shuriken fire, the roar of wounded engines, the ironclad spinning like a child's toy as the white shape swooped around and down the port side amidst a hail of 'thrower fire, taking the *Wind*'s engine off at her shoulder.

So fast. So impossibly fast.

'Concentrate fire! All 'throwers fire! FIRE!'

The shape wheeled away, keeping the *Wind*'s tumbling corpse between itself and the *Hunger* until it was well out of range, diving behind a towering knuckle of black mountain stone. Jubei heard a rumbling crash as the *Wind* hit bottom, flaring like a second sun as her chi tanks exploded, setting the autumn valley ablaze. The pilot was spinning the wheel beside him, the *Hunger*'s nose swinging towards their quarry. Jubei saw several rocket packs flaring, heard the rush of wings, lonely, awful screams out in the smoke. Bursts of shuriken fire. Metal thudding on wood. The Scourge shouting orders to the radio operator to report contact, request backup, a tumult of voices over the open frequency.

'*Did you see it?*'

'*Report position!*'

'*What was it?*'

'*Need ammunition. 'Thrower four, twenty per cent.*'

''*Thrower seven, fifteen per cent!*'

'*Eyes high! They came from above!*'

'*Do you see anything?*'

'*Arashitora!*'

'This is Captain Montaro!' The Scourge's roar cut through the babble like a chainkatana. 'Clear comms of unnecessary chatter now! The next brother who speaks out of turn is headed straight for the inochi pits!'

Silence rang out, tinged with frightened static.

'Munitions, get those 'throwers restocked. I want extra eyes on the inflatable, compensators on, maximum contrast. Helm, get us out of this accursed smoke. Hard to port. Engines full. Ascend one hundred feet.'

The Scourge walked to the edge of the pilot's deck where

his crew could see him. The engines' volume increased, a deep shuddering whine, *thupthupthupping* prop-blades. The smoke thinned, ashes coating the deck like flurries of grey snow.

'I know you, brothers. We've served together on this ship for years. The gaijin speak of *Izanami's Hunger* with fear for a reason. A terror of the skies. Undefeated in battle. And I tell you now we will *not* quail before this—'

'Contact high! Port side!'

'Out of the sun! They're coming at us out—'

'FIRE!'

Jubei heard it again. That awful thunder, turning his gut to water. The *Hunger* dropped thirty feet as if slapped out of the sky by the hands of angry gods. His legs were jelly-soft, mouth dry as ashes, gripping the rails so hard his gauntlets scored the wood. He longed to rip the helmet from his head, paw the salt burn from his eyes. For one moment of blessed relief.

He thought of his Awakening, the blurred and tumbling visions of his What Will Be, the destiny that could be his if only he had the strength to seize it. The Chamber of Smoke had showed him precious little of his future to make sense of, but he'd seen nothing about burning to death on this ship, being crushed to pulp on teeth of stone a hundred miles from the place he called home. And as the shuriken fire began again, as panic gripped their lookouts and that shape plummeted towards them out of the blinding sun, Jubei felt himself break. Red fear rising up and strangling reason, all the mantras and doctrine fleeing his mind, leaving him with a single truth burning bright before dilating pupils.

He was not meant to die here.

The terrified Lotusman ran to the bow's edge, ignoring the Scourge's bellowed order, fumbling with the ignition switches on his wrist. His boots scraped against the railing as he leapt up and over, snatched from gravity's pull by blue-white flame. The rockets' vibration shook his flesh, overshadowed by a spear of bright light at his back, the thunderous resonance of the *Hunger's* inflatable bursting apart. His comms rig was filled with the screams of dying marines, the conflagration's roar, the agony of flame on naked flesh. He switched it off, left with the frantic high-frequency data streams from his mechabacus, demands for someone – anyone – to report.

He set his pack to full burn, rocketing away from the *Hunger's* death throes, the echoing crash of her ruin on the mountainside behind him. He could see the shape clearly in his mind's eye, a lithograph etched in sweating fear and sour-tongue adrenaline. Wings twenty-five-feet wide, clad in iridescent metal. Sleek feathers at its head, eyes like molten amber, forelegs of iron-grey. Snow-white fur on its hindquarters, rippling stripes of pitch-black, long tail lashing like a whip behind it. Muscle and beak and claw; a creature from impossible fictions sprung inexplicably to life and spattered red with the blood of his brothers.

He prayed. For the first time he could remember, he prayed. To gods he knew weren't there, who couldn't listen. Figments of the imagination, crutches for the skinless and the ignorant, a superstition no Guildsman he knew really believed in. And yet he prayed with a fervour that would shame a priest. That his pack would fly him faster, get him out, away, his pulse rushing so hard he feared his veins would burst. If his heart were an engine, he would have thrashed it to breaking. If his blood were chi, he would have opened his veins and poured every last drop into his fuel tanks to fly just one foot farther.

And still, they caught him.

A rush of wind behind, the thunder of beating drums. He

glanced over his shoulder and they hit him in a shower of sparks and flame. He bucked in the thing's grip, arms pinned, his skin screeching like a wounded corpse-rat. Throat torn raw, spittle-flecked lips, screaming until at last he realized that, though he hung in those talons like a gaijin corpse above the inochi pits, completely at their mercy, the death blow hadn't fallen.

They hadn't killed him.

They flew for what seemed like years, south over the sky-clad ranges. A sweeping ocean turning slowly to the colour of flame, an undulating carpet of whispering trees and frost-clad teeth that seemed to go on forever. Finally they descended, circling above a flattened spur of rock and snow. A sheer cliff face dropping down onto grey foothills below. The very edge of the Iishi.

Twenty feet from the cliff top, they dropped him. He fell with a crash, sparks and grinding metal, skull cracking against the inside of his helm, biting hard on his tongue. Skin squealing across the plateau, he skidded to a halt two feet shy of the precipice.

And he lay there, too terrified to move.

He heard them land behind him, the crunch of claw on frost, a thumping wind. He rolled over and saw the beast; a looming hunk of beak and talons and snow-white fur, spattered with thick sprays of crimson. Kioshi's son – the rabbit they had chased across the entire country – was slumped on its shoulders, clutching a bloody wound on his arm, pale and sweat-slicked, but still very much alive. Grubby grey cloth, short, dark stubble on his scalp, knife-bright eyes. The boy did not look like much. Not the kind to raise his fist in defiance of all he'd been raised to believe. Not the kind a fleet should die for.

But Jubei's gaze was pulled to her, the girl (just a *girl*) slipping down off the beast's shoulders, light as feathers. She was clad in loose black cotton, long dark hair flowing around her shoulders, pale skin dusted with ash and daubed with blood. Polarized goggles covered her eyes, an old-fashioned katana strapped at her back, the obi about her waist stuffed with hand flares. She was slender, pretty, impossibly young.

'Take that off.' She gestured to his helmet, her voice cold. 'I want to see your face.'

Jubei complied, fumbling with the latches at his throat. He pulled the helmet from his head, felt icy wind on his flesh. Licking his lips, he spat blood onto the snow between his feet. The world was garish, horribly bright, the sun scalding his eyes.

She drew her katana, the blade singing as it slipped from its scabbard. Marching over to him, she sat on his chest. The arashitora growled in warning, long and deep, setting the plates of his skin squealing. The girl pulled down her goggles so he could see her eyes; flat black glass, bloodshot with rage. She pressed her blade to his throat.

'You know who I am,' she said.

'. . . Hai.'

'You've seen what I can do.'

'H-hai.'

'Run back to your masters. Tell them what you saw here. And you tell them the next time they send a sky-ship *near* the Iishi Mountains, I'm going to carve my father's name into her captain's chest before I paint the sky with his insides. Do you understand me?'

Jubei nodded. 'I do . . .'

She pressed on his neck, her blade sinking a little farther in. Jubei gasped, not daring to move, blood welling and running down his throat. For an awful, terrifying moment, he could see it in her face; the desire to simply open him up, ear to ear, to bathe in the spray of his carotid and jugular, lathering the bloody froth from his windpipe on her hands. Her lips peeled back from her teeth, blade twitching in his flesh, looming over him like a terror from some children's story, some nightmare sprung inexplicably to life.

The girl all Guildsmen fear.

'Please,' he whispered. 'Please . . .'

The wind was a lonely, howling voice between teeth of stone, a threadbare wail singing of death and the hunger of wolves. In it, he could hear the voices of his dying brothers. In her eyes, he could see an ending. The ending of all things. And he was afraid.

The boy on the thunder tiger's back finally spoke, voice soft with concern.

'Yukiko?' he said.

The girl narrowed her eyes, still fixed on Jubei's, hissing through clenched teeth.

'His name was Masaru.'

She smeared blood across her cheek with the back of one hand.

'My father's name was Masaru.'

And then she stood, chest heaving, breathless. Knuckles white on her katana's grip, she thrust it into the ground beside his head, left it quivering point-first in the snow. Without another word, she turned and stalked back to the beast, leaping onto his shoulders, her hair a long ribbon of black. The rabbit put his arms around her waist, leaned against her back. And with a rush of wind and that awful sound of breaking thunder, they dropped out into the void, soaring away on sweeping thermals, a swirling trail of ashes in their wake.

Jubei watched the three of them fly away, growing smaller and smaller on the smoke-stained horizon. And when they had disappeared from sight, when all he could see was red sky and grey cloud and distant fumes, he glanced at the sword beside his head, a faint smear of his own blood running down the steel.

He closed his eyes.

Lowered his head into his hands.

And he wept.

2

Drowning

Slow flames danced in the light's decline.

Her tantō rested near the fire pit's edge, thrust tip-first into burning embers. Dark ripples coiling across the metal gave the impression of the grain in polished wood, or whorls at a finger's tip. The blade was not blackened or smoking, nor incandescent with a forge's heat. But a wise man might have noticed the way the air about it rippled, and like any man once burned, he would have left well enough alone.

Yukiko had watched the blade waiting on the glowing coals, no light in her eyes. The cedar logs crackled and sighed, oppressive heat smothering the air; a weight in her chest to match the one on her shoulders. She'd seen the air shivering around the steel and realized she was almost looking forward to it. To feeling again.

To feeling something.

'You do not have to do this yet.'

Daichi had watched her across the fire pit, eyes underscored by the flames.

'If not here, then where?' she asked. 'If not now, then when?'

The old man's skin was worn; leather browned too long

beneath a scalding sun, his biceps a patchwork of burns. Long moustache, close-cropped hair, just a blue-grey shadow upon a scalp crisscrossed with scars.

'You should sleep. Tomorrow will be a hard day.' Daichi groped for the words. 'Watching your father put to the pyre . . .'

'What makes you believe I'll watch?'

The old man blinked. 'Yukiko, you should attend his funeral. You should say good-bye.'

'It took us five days to fly here from Kigen. Do you know what this heat does to a body after five days, Daichi-sama?'

'I have a notion.'

'Then you know what you burn tomorrow is not my father.'

Daichi sighed. 'Yukiko, go and sleep, I beg you.'

'I'm not tired.'

The old man folded his arms, his voice as hard as the steel gleaming on the embers.

'I will not do this.'

'After all I've done for you. After all you took from me.'

She'd glanced up then, and her expression had made the old man flinch.

'You owe me, Daichi.'

The Kagé leader had hung his head. Breathing deep, he coughed, once, twice, wincing as he swallowed. She could see it in his eyes as he stared at the calloused hands in his lap. The blood that would never wash away. The stain of the child forever unborn. The mark of the mother who would never again hold her daughter in her arms. Her mother.

He spoke as if the word was bile in his mouth.

'. . . Hai.'

Daichi had picked up the jug of red saké beside him, rose

like a man on his way to the executioner. Kneeling beside her, he retrieved the tantō from the flames.

Yukiko hadn't looked up from the fire. She loosened the sash at her waist, shrugged her uwagi tunic off her shoulders, covering her breasts with her palms. Her irezumi gleamed in the firelight; the beautiful nine-tailed fox tattooed upon her right shoulder to mark her clan, the imperial sun across her left marking her as the Shōgun's servant. She'd tossed her head, flicked her hair away from Yoritomo's mark. A few stray strands still clung to damp flesh.

As he held the knife up, the air between them had rippled.

'Are you certain?'

'No lord.' She swallowed. 'No master.'

He placed the saké jug on the floor between them.

'Do you want something to—'

'Daichi. Just do it.'

The old man had breathed deep, and without another word pressed the tantō to the ink.

Every muscle in her body seized tight as the blade touched her skin. The air was filled with the spittle-hiss of fresh fish upon a skillet, the sizzling tang of blackening meat and salt overpowering the scent of burning cedar. A long moan shuddered over her teeth and she closed her eyes, fighting the scream seething in her chest. She could smell herself burning.

Searing.

Charring.

She'd reached out with her mind, to the flood of warmth waiting just outside the door. Feather and fur and talons, wide amber eyes, his growl shaking the floorboards beneath him. The thunder tiger she'd found amidst storm-torn clouds, and now loved more dearly than anything beneath the sky.

Buruu . . .

YUKIKO.

Gods, it hurts, brother . . .

HOLD ONTO ME.

She'd clung to his thoughts; a mountain of cool stone amidst a flaming sea. Daichi peeled the steel from her shoulder, bringing ashen layers of tattooed skin with it. The blade that had killed her lover, Hiro. The blade that had been in her hands as she ended Shōgun Yoritomo, as the shot rang out and took her father away. Five days and a thousand years ago. She'd gasped as the agony receded to a dull ebb, and for a second, the urge to turn to Daichi and beg him to stop was almost overpowering. But she set her back against the thunder tiger's strength, forced it down, far easier to swallow than the thought of that bastard's mark still inked on her skin.

Anything was better than that.

She looked at the saké bottle on the floor beside her. Buruu's thoughts washed over her like a summer breeze.

YOU HAVE BEEN STRONG ENOUGH FOR ONE DAY, SISTER.

Reaching for the bottle with trembling fingers, she gulped a mouthful of liquid fire, cooler than the steel in Daichi's hand. The liquor rushed down her throat, burning her tongue, promising a return to the oblivion she'd been so eager to escape just moments before. The choice between agony and emptiness. Between living or existing.

It had been no choice at all on a night that dark.

'Do you want me to stop?' Daichi had asked.

She'd swallowed another mouthful, blinking back her tears.

'Get it off me,' she whispered. 'Take all of it away.'

*

Yukiko closed her eyes, bloodshot and throbbing in their sockets.

The ground was a blur beneath them, falling leaves filling the spaces between each beat of Buruu's wings. The air had the vaguest hint of chill, autumn's pallid touch creeping through the Iishi wilds. The towering trees around them were fading; a subtle shift from gowns of dazzling emerald to a brief and brittle lime, their hems beginning to curl and rust.

They flew above it all. The pale girl swathed in mourning black, long hair flowing in the piercing wind. The boy with his dirty rags and dark, knowing eyes. The majestic beast beneath them, twenty-five feet of clockwork wings, cutting effortlessly through the sky.

Kin was perched behind her on Buruu's back, one arm wrapped about her waist, the other hanging bloody at his side. He was obviously exhausted, shoulders slumped, head hung low. Yukiko could feel the heat of him through their clothing, hear the faint catch in his breath. Her mouth dry, stomach curdling with fading adrenaline. It'd been nearly two months since she'd seen him last – this boy who'd saved her life, who'd given up everything he was to see Buruu freed. In the chaos after Yoritomo's death, the riots, her speeches, the threat of civil war, she'd spent every spare moment searching for him; urging the Kagé city cells to be on the lookout, patrolling the Iishi's edge for hours on end in the hope of catching a glimpse. They'd owed him that much. That much and more. And now, to find him at last . . .

'Are you sure you're all right, Kin-san?'

Yukiko spoke over her shoulder, concerned eyes hidden by polarized glass.

'Well enough,' he breathed. 'My arm is bleeding . . .'

'We're still an hour or so from the village. Can you hold on until then?'

A slow nod. 'It took me over a month to get this far. A few more minutes won't kill me.'

'Wandering the Iishi alone might have, though,' Yukiko said. 'You were travelling the wrong way. Headed right towards Black Temple. You could have run into an oni, or gods know what else. The Kagé village is northeast of here.'

'I know,' he nodded. 'Once I realized the ironclads were on my trail, I tried leading them away from the stronghold. I didn't want to put anyone else in danger.'

Yukiko smiled, reached down and squeezed Kin's hand. She should have known. Just as selfless as always. His own safety ever a distant second. Her thoughts were all a-tumble, emotions jostling for position in her chest; joy they'd found him, guilt it had taken so long, genuine fear at how close he'd come to death. Underscoring it all, the feel of his body pressed against hers, his hand about her waist, the tumult of confusion and adrenaline and Buruu's fading bloodlust thudding in time with her own racing pulse.

She drew one shuddering breath, let it out slow.

'Try to get some rest, Kin-san. You're safe now.'

They flew on towards the Kagé village, the smoke of the ironclads they'd torn from the sky still hanging in their wake. Kin rested his head against her back and closed his eyes, his breath slowing, exhaustion getting the better of him. Buruu's muscles seethed beneath them, his eyes narrowed, amber and gold, glittering like embers in a forge's belly. Sleek feathers and thick fur, the colour of melting snow on the Iishi's highest peaks, his hindquarters wrapped in long, snaking bands of deepest jet. Thunder tiger. Arashitora. The last of his kind in all of Shima.

His thoughts were intertwined with hers, images echoing in each other's skulls, the pair of them linked by a bond deeper than blood. Yukiko and Buruu. Buruu and Yukiko. Harder and harder to tell where one ended and the other began these days. The ability to speak to the minds of beasts was called the Kenning in old folklore, but to even give it a name seemed to lessen it now. The truth was, it was more than a thing of weak and clumsy words. It was her father's legacy, his gift to her, forging a friendship that had defied a Shōgun, ended an empire.

It was a reminder. A birthright. A blessing.

A curse?

THE BOY IS LUCKY WE FOUND HIM BEFORE ANY DEMONS DID.

She winced as Buruu's thoughts filled her own, just a touch louder than they'd ever been before. The sky seemed a little too bright. Her skull a fraction too small.

I know. The western slopes are crawling with them lately.

FOOLISH OF HIM. STILL, I AM GLAD HE IS SAFE.

You must be. You didn't even call him 'monkey-child.'

WELL, DO NOT TELL HIM THAT. I HAVE A GRUFF DEMEANOUR TO MAINTAIN.

Laughter died on her lips almost as soon as it had begun. Yukiko pushed up her goggles, pressed her fingers into her eyes. Pain throbbed at the base of her skull, the echoes of Buruu's thoughts sending barbed tendrils up and across her temples. Ice-cold and burning.

YOUR HEAD STILL HURTS?

Only a little.

YOU ARE A TERRIBLE LIAR, GIRL.

There are worse character flaws. All things considered.

THIS PAIN HAS LINGERED FOR WEEKS. THIS IS NOT NORMAL.

I have more important things to worry about than headaches, Buruu.

FORTUNATE THEN, THAT I DO NOT.

You fret too much.

AND YOU NEVER ENOUGH.

You know what they say. Kitsune looks after his own.

Yukiko pressed against the mighty beast beneath her, felt the blood-red percussion of his pulse, the smooth motion of his flight. She ran her hands through the arashitora's feathers, following the glass-smooth lines down his shoulders until her fingertips brushed the metal framing his crippled wings. The feathers clipped by a madman, barely a month in his grave.

At least now Kin is back and he can adjust your wings for you. This contraption looks ready to fall apart. How long until you molt?

YOU CHANGE THE SUBJECT AS ARTFULLY AS YOU LIE.

You're becoming quite the master at avoiding questions, though.

The thunder tiger growled in the back of his throat.

I WILL HAVE NO NEW PLUMAGE FOR MONTHS. NOT UNTIL MY WINTER COAT GROWS IN.

Yukiko curled her fingers through sleek feathers, right where neck and shoulder met. His favourite spot.

And then what?

I DO NOT TAKE YOUR MEANING.

I mean what will you do after you can fly again under your own power?

WHAT DO YOU EXPECT ME TO DO?

I don't know. Go home, maybe? Leave this place behind.

LEAVE YOU, IS YOUR MEANING.

. . . Yes.

AFTER ALL WE HAVE BEEN THROUGH?

This isn't your fight. This isn't your home. You could fly away right now and forget any of this ever happened.

YOU KNOW THAT IS A LIE.

Do I?

YOU KNOW ME. AS YOU KNOW YOURSELF.

I don't know anything, Buruu.

THEN KNOW THIS. BETWEEN AND BENEATH AND BEYOND ANYTHING ELSE I MAY BE, I AM YOURS. I WILL NEVER LEAVE YOU. NEVER FORSAKE YOU. YOU MAY RELY UPON ME AS YOU RELY UPON SUN TO RISE AND MOON TO FALL. FOR YOU ARE THE HEART OF ME.

She rested her head on his neck, wrapped her arms around him and breathed. The burn scar on her shoulder was a distant, nagging ache. The last few weeks with Buruu had been like something from a dream – flying to the clan capitals and speaking to the people, watching the fire grow in their eyes as she spoke. In Kigen, the citizens had laid out hundreds of spirit stones in the place where her father died. In the Dragon capital of Kawa, their arrival had kicked off five days of rioting. In Yama city, home of her own clan, the Kitsune, they had been treated like heroes. The whole country felt ready to rise. To throw off the shackles of the old Imperium and forge something new.

And still, the memory remained. Grief turning to slow and smouldering rage. Her father's death. His blood on her hands. Dying in her arms. She hadn't attended his funeral pyre. Hadn't watched the flames consume the swollen, bloated thing his body had become. Hadn't visited his grave in the days since, to burn incense or pray or fall to her knees and weep.

She hadn't shed a tear since the day he died.

She glanced over her shoulder at the boy pressed against her, his breath soft, eyelashes fluttering against smooth cheeks.

One hand seeking his, the other pressed to Buruu's feathers. Surrounded by those who cared for her. And still . . .

And still . . .

Part of me feels like I'm still trapped in Kigen, you know. I can see Yoritomo looking at me over the barrel of that iron-thrower. Hands stained with his own sister's blood. It makes me want to scream. To reach inside his head and kill him all over again.

YORITOMO CAN HURT NO ONE NOW. HE IS DEAD. GONE.

He's still all around us. In red skies and black rivers. In soldiers' graves and blood lotus fields and dying soil. The Kazumitsu Dynasty is shattered, but even without a Shōgun, there's still the Lotus Guild. They're the cancer at this nation's heart.

She shook her head, felt the warm swell of rage in her breast. Sudden and seething, curling her hands to fists. Remembering the heat of conflagration on her skin, the screams of dying Guildsmen as the sky rained ironclads. Because of them. Because of her.

And it felt *right*.

Daichi and the Kagé speak the truth. The Guild needs to be burned away.

AND YOU WILL BE THE SPARK? A HANDFUL OF WEEKS AGO, THE ACT OF TAKING A SINGLE LIFE WAS UNTHINKABLE FOR YOU. AND NOW—

A handful of weeks ago, my father was still alive.

THERE IS BLOOD DOWN THIS ROAD, SISTER. BLOOD LIKE A RIVER. AND THOUGH I SWIM IT GLADLY, I DO NOT WISH TO SEE YOU DROWN.

He bled out into my arms, Buruu. You don't know what that's like.

I KNOW THE SHAPE OF LOSS, YUKIKO. ALL TOO WELL.

Then you know what I have to do.

The thunder tiger sighed. His stare fixed on the ancient forest below, glazed and distant, staring into a future stained a deeper scarlet than the poisoned sky above.

WHAT WE HAVE TO DO.

We?

ALWAYS.

Buruu banked down into murmuring gloom.

ALWAYS.

*

Her bedroom trembled in the midnight hush, candles flickering on the walls like dawn through rippling autumn leaves. Yukiko watched the shadows play through the blur of her lashes, eyelids made of lead, the same blood-drenched pain that had plagued her for weeks pounding inside her skull. Fists to temples, breathing deep. Teeth clenched, focusing on the aching scar at her shoulder to stop her mind drifting back into the dark. The place where her father lay, cold and dead, the ashes of his funeral offerings caked on his face. The place where she was helpless. The little one. The frightened one.

She drew the back of her fist across her mouth.

Never again.

Buruu's low growl dragged Yukiko from the throb inside her head, the ache in her body. She closed her eyes, tried to look through the Kenning to see what he was grumbling about. But as she reached inside his head, the world flared bright and loud, screeching and clawing – the thoughts of a hundred tiny lives out in the gloom flooding her skull. An owl soaring through the velvet dark (*seekkilleatseekkilleat*), a tiny furtive thing of fur and pounding heart hiding in long shadows (*stillstillbestill*), mockingbirds curled in their nests (*warmandsafesafeandwarm*), a lone monkey howling (*hungreeeeeeee*). So many. Too many. Never in her life so impossibly loud. Gasping, she closed off the Kenning, as if locking a disobedient child in an empty room in her mind. Breathing hard, she dragged her eyelids open, squinting out to the landing.

A figure stood in the shadows.

High cheekbones and steel-grey eyes. Dressed in dappled forest-green. An elegant, old-fashioned wakizashi sword at her waist, a scabbard embossed with golden cranes in flight. A long, black fringe cut to fall over one side of her face, almost concealing the jagged diagonal knife scar running from forehead to chin.

Another of Yoritomo's legacies.

'Kaori.'

Daichi's daughter lurked in the near darkness, wary eyes locked on the thunder tiger.

'He won't hurt you,' Yukiko said. 'Come in.'

Kaori hovered for a few uncertain moments, then slipped past Buruu as quickly as she could. The arashitora watched her, amber stare glittering. His metal-clad wings twitched, and he lay his head back down with a sigh and a hiss of pistons, tail sweeping in broad, lazy arcs.

The bedroom was ten feet square, unvarnished wood, wide windows looking out into a sea of night. The perfume of dried wisteria mingled with sweet candle smoke, doing their best to banish the pulsing ache at Yukiko's temples. She lay back in her unmade bed with a sigh.

'The lookouts told me you had returned,' Kaori said.

'I'm sorry I didn't come see you and Daichi-sama. I was tired.'

The woman looked her over with a critical eye, lips pressed tightly together. Her stare lingered on the empty saké bottle at the foot of the bed.

'You look awful. Are you unwell?'

'The Guild ships are dealt with.' Yukiko's arm was slung over her face, words muffled in her sleeve. 'They're no threat to us anymore.'

'Your Guildsman is resting. He is torn. Bruised. But Old Mari says he will recover.'

'He's not *my* Guildsman. He's not a Guildsman anymore at all.'

'Indeed.'

'My thanks, anyway.' Her tone softened. 'Your father honours me with his trust. I know what it means to have Kin here.'

'I sincerely doubt that, Stormdancer.'

'Don't call me that.'

Uncomfortable silence fell between them, broken only by the whisper of dry leaves, the thunder-rumble breath of the arashitora outside. Yukiko kept her arm over her eyes, hoping to hear Kaori's retreating footsteps. But the woman simply hovered, like dragonflies in the bamboo valley where Yukiko had spent her childhood. Poised. Motionless.

Finally, Yukiko dragged herself upright with an exasperated sigh. Pain flared at the base of her skull, claws curling up through her spinal cord.

'I'm tired, Kaori-san.'

'Thirsty too, no doubt.' Steel-grey eyes flickered to the empty saké bottle. 'But we have news from our agents in Kigen city.'

She sensed the hesitation in Kaori's scorn. The weight.

'Is Akihito all right?'

'Well enough. He cannot escape Kigen while rail and sky-ship traffic is locked down. But the local cell is looking after him.' Kaori walked to the window, avoided her reflection in the dark glass. 'The city is in chaos. The Tiger bushimen can barely maintain the peace. We get new recruits every day. Talk of war is everywhere.'

'That's what you wanted, isn't it? The body thrashing without its head.'

'The Guild seek to grow it a new one.'

Yukiko blinked through the headache blur. 'Meaning what?'

The woman sighed, clawing her fringe over her face, kohl-rimmed eyes downcast.

'I take little pleasure in telling you this . . .'

'Telling me what, Kaori?'

The woman looked at her palms, licked her lips. 'Lord Hiro is alive.'

Yukiko felt the words as a blow to her stomach, a cold fist of dread knocking the wind from her lungs. She felt the room spin, the floor fall away into a beckoning nothing. And yet somehow, she managed to sway to her feet, to hold her centre and pretend she didn't feel like a stranger clawing at the insides of someone else's skin.

She could see him in her memory, lying on sweat-stained sheets, the light of a choking moon playing on planes of smooth skin and taut muscle. His lips, soft as clouds and tasting of salt, pressed against hers in midnight's hush. Peeled back from his teeth as she drove her blade into his chest, as Buruu's beak sheared his right arm from his shoulder in a spray of hot crimson.

How could it be? He was dead. They killed him.

I killed him.

'Gods,' she whispered. 'My gods . . .'

'I am sorry,' Kaori said, still staring into the dark. 'We hear but whispers. We only have one operative left who can move freely within the palace grounds. But we know Hiro is one of three seeking the title of Daimyo. Rumour tells he has the full backing of the Lotus Guild. Once he secures position as clanlord, he will claim the Shōgun's throne.'

'But that's madness.' Yukiko tried to swallow, her mouth dry as desert dust. 'Why would any of the other clanlords support him?'

'Their oaths of fealty bind them to the Kazumitsu Dynasty.'

'But Hiro is not of Kazumitsu's blood. The dynasty died with Yoritomo.'

'There is one of Kazumitsu's line who still lives.'

Yukiko frowned, trying to clear her thoughts. To focus. Buruu was on his feet, growling, his heat echoing through the corridors of her mind. She could feel the nightbirds beyond the window glass. Monkeys flitting across the trees. Tiny lives and tiny heartbeats – hundreds of them, bright and burning in the Kenning. So hard to think. To shut them out. To breathe.

'I don't . . .'

'Aisha lives.'

A flash of memory in her mind's eye. Yoritomo in Kigen arena. His eyes dancing with hate. Wiping his hand across the bleeding gouges on his cheek.

'No, my sister refused to betray you. And still she dared to beg me for mercy.'

Yukiko bent double, hands on her knees.

'She found none.'

Black flowers bloomed in her eyes, unfurling in time with the strobing pain in her skull.

YUKIKO?

'Hiro will cement his claim by joining the dynastic bloodline through its last surviving daughter.' Kaori spoke as if her words were a eulogy. 'He and Aisha are to be wed.'

The dark fell still. Sudden and silent as death. No nightsong.

No wind. A wet thump rang out in the room and Kaori flinched, squinting through the bedroom window to the black beyond. A small splash of blood was smeared on the glass. Another thump, against the far wall. Another.

And another.

She turned towards the girl, saw her doubled over in pain.

'Yukiko?'

YUKIKO!

A sparrow smashed itself against the window, colliding headfirst and dashing its skull open against the glass. Another bird followed, another, as dozens upon dozens of tiny bodies slammed into the bedroom walls, the ceiling, the glass. Kaori drew her wakizashi, blade gleaming in the candlelight, turning in circles, her face thin with fear as the pounding of flesh against wood became thunderous. A rain of soft, breathing bodies and brittle bones.

'Maker's breath, what is this devilry?'

Yukiko was on her knees, hands pressed to her temples, forehead to the floor. Eyes shut tight, features twisted, teeth bared. She could hear them all – a thousand heartbeats out in the dark, a thousand lives, a thousand fires, hotter than the sun. Their voices in her skull, nausea rising black and greasy in the pit of her stomach, overlaid with the taste of his lips, the bitter words he had spoken right before she killed him, she killed him, gods, I *killed* him.

'Good-bye Hiro . . .'

SISTER.

Buruu. Make them stop.

THEM? IT IS YOU. THIS IS YOU.

Me?

YOU ARE SCREAMING. STOP SCREAMING.

'Stop it,' she breathed.

Kaori took hold of her shoulder, squeezed tight. 'Yukiko, what is happening?'

Hearts beating in thin, feathered chests. Blood pumping beneath fur and skin. Smashing themselves against the walls, falling broken and bloodied towards a grave of fallen leaves. Eyes burning bright, teeth gnashing, the girl inside their head screaming and screaming and screaming and they had to make it stop because it hurt what does she want why won't she stop make her stop *make her stop*.

'Yukiko, stop it.'

SISTER, STOP IT.

Knuckles and pulses and a thousand, thousand sparks.

'*Stop it!*'

Her scream rang out in the darkness, her eyes wide and bloodshot, hair splayed in dark tendrils across her face. Silence fell like a hammer, broken only by the sound of small, still-warm bodies tumbling down into the darkness below. Bright spots of red spattered on the boards between her knees. She reached up to her nose, felt sticky warmth smeared down her lips. Pulse throbbing in her temples in time to the song of her heart, Buruu's thoughts cupping her and holding tight, the Kenning's heat receding like floodwaters out into a cold and empty black.

Kaori knelt beside her, blade still clutched in one trembling fist.

'Yukiko, are you all right?'

She dragged herself to her feet, smudged blood across her mouth with the back of one hand. Stumbling out the door, she wrapped her arms around Buruu's neck. Sinking to her knees again, him beside her, wrapping her beneath his clockwork wings. Salty warmth on her lips, clogging her nose. Echoes bouncing inside her skull. The sparks of every animal out in the forest, out there in the dark, flaring brighter than she could ever remember.

'*Good-bye Hiro . . .*'

She could feel everything.

'Gods, what's happening to me?'

3

The First and Only Reason

Yukiko's dreams were of burning ironclads.

A golden throne and a boy with sea-green eyes.

Smiling at her.

Her sunlit hours were all motion. Visiting Kin in the infirmary. Speaking with the Kagé council about the ironclad attack. Talks of Hiro's wedding. Concern over the flurry of small, warm bodies that had dashed themselves to dying against her bedroom walls. Halfhearted assurances that all was well. Disbelieving stares.

The ache in her skull swelled by the day – the thoughts of the surrounding wildlife encroaching just a fraction further, a thousand splinters digging ever deeper. But every night, she made it stop, reaching for the saké bottle to dull it all. A blunt force trauma knocking her wonderfully senseless, burning mouthfuls submerging her beneath a merciful, velvet silence.

She would sit with the bottle in her hands, fighting the urge to hurl it into the wall. To watch it shatter into a thousand pieces. To ruin something beyond repair.

To unmake.

Buruu's concern was a constant white noise inside her skull.

But if he thought less of her as he watched her retching up the dregs every morning, she felt no trace of it inside his mind.

Hauling herself from her bed in the splintering light of the third day, the ache flared inside her head; an old friend waiting in the wings with open arms. Liquor dregs sloshed inside her empty innards, hangover fingers buried in her skull all the way to the knuckles. She sat at breakfast with the rest of the village, avoiding Daichi's watchful stare, swallowing her puke like medicine. It was almost midday before she made it to the infirmary, asked Old Mari if Kin would be well enough to take a walk with her.

She'd been putting this off for far too long.

The graveyard stood in a quiet clearing, guarded by ancient sugi trees. The sparks of a hundred tiny lives burned around her, the heat and pulse of Buruu beside her so overpowering it was almost nauseating. The forest was a smudge against sleep-gummed lashes, eyelids made of sand, pickaxes in her throbbing skull. She remembered the saké blurring the pain as Daichi burned away her tattoo, sensation fading to oblivion. She remembered her father, drowning his own gift in smoke and drink.

Don't want it.

A sigh.

Just need it.

She looked down at the marker at her feet, at his name carved deep into the gravestone.

I think I understand you more and more each day, Father.

Her mouth was dry, tongue like ash. The Kenning burned in her mind alongside the memory of dozens of small, broken bodies scattered around the tree cradling her room. Wind moaned through the fading green, the Thunder God Raijin pounding on his drums above the gentle rain. Incense smouldered in the shrine, thin smoke weaving towards the heavens.

'Do you want to talk about it?'

Kin stood a few paces away, knife-bright eyes locked on hers, rain beading upon his lashes. He was clad in grey, his feet and arm wrapped in fresh bandages, fading burn scars etched on his throat and chin. She saw his flight from Kigen had taken its toll, turned him lean and hard, tanned his sun-starved skin. His once-shaved skull was now covered in dark stubble, short sleeves showing taut muscle and the strange metallic bayonet fixtures studding his flesh. Yukiko remembered unplugging him from his atmos-suit after he'd been burned, pulling black, snaking cables from his flesh, the plugs gaping like hungry mouths. All that remained of his suit now was a brass belt around his waist, stuffed with an assortment of tools and instrumentation – the only component he'd salvaged from the metal skin he'd worn for most of his life.

'No,' she said. 'Thank you.'

'Your father loved you, Yukiko. And he knew you loved him before the end.'

'That won't bring him back.'

'No. It won't. But you can make his death mean something anyway.'

'I said I don't want to talk about it, Kin. Please.'

He chewed his lip, eyes to the floor. 'You seem . . . different somehow. Changed. What you did to those ships the other day . . .'

'I don't really want to talk about that either.'

She knelt near the grave, dug her fingers into the soil. Dark earth on pale skin, rain rolling down her cheeks instead of the tears she should be crying. She could see Yoritomo's face, eyes narrowed above the iron-thrower, hear his voice ringing inside her head.

'All you possess, I allow you to have. All you are, I allow you to be.'

Her hands curled into fists, eyes closed tight. She stood, face to the sky, cool rain on her cheeks washing none of it away. Buruu stretched his wings, shook himself like a soggy hound. His thoughts were so loud they made her wince.

YOU MUST LET HIM GO, YUKIKO.

I can't just forget what's happened, Buruu.

I FEEL THE RAGE IN YOU. GROWING BY THE DAY. IF YOU ALLOW IT, IT WILL BURN EVERYTHING AROUND YOU TO ASHES. EVERYTHING.

Am I supposed to be weeping? Crying for my da like some frightened little girl?

IT TAKES COURAGE TO SAY GOOD-BYE. TO STARE AT A THING LOST AND KNOW IT IS GONE FOREVER. SOME TEARS ARE IRON-FORGED.

She stared at the grave, sighed like the wind through the trees.

'Hiro is alive.'

'What?' Kin whispered, eyes growing wide.

'The Guild is backing him as Daimyo of the Tora clan. He's going to marry Lady Aisha. Claim the Shōgun's throne. We have to stop him.'

'Hiro.' Kin swallowed. 'As Shōgun . . .'

She pictured a boy with sea-green eyes, remembered the way her stomach tumbled upwards into the clouds when he smiled. All the sweet nothings he'd whispered in the long hours between dusk and dawn, touching her in ways and places no one ever had before. Holding her close, arm wrapped around her naked shoulders. That same arm they'd torn from his body, those beautiful eyes staring up at her in disbelief as she lay him on the stone, her tantō in his ribs.

If only she'd twisted it.

If only she'd torn it loose and opened up the smooth skin at his throat . . .

'Do you still love him?'

Yukiko blinked in surprise. Kin was watching her closely, eyes clothed in shadow. His fingers strayed to his wrist, fidgeted with the metal input stud in his flesh. She was reminded of the day they first met on the *Thunder Child*. The night they'd stood on the prow and breathed in the storm, let the rain wash their fear away.

'Hiro?'

'Hiro.'

'Of course I don't, Kin. I thought I killed that bastard. I wish I had.'

'I . . .' His fingers twitched, and he stuffed his hands into his tool belt, scuffing dead leaves beneath his feet. 'Never mind. It doesn't matter.'

Yukiko heaved an impatient sigh. The headache squeezed tight, the pulse of the lives around her was thunder in her ears. Soaking wet. Miserable. And he wants to play games?

'Kin, say what you mean, godsdammit.'

'I'm going to sound like an idiot. I'm no good at this.' He waved at the spirit stones around them. 'And a graveyard probably isn't the best place for this conversation.'

'Izanagi's balls, what conversation?'

He sucked his lip, looked into her eyes. She could see the words welling up in his throat, a flood pressing at a crumbling levy, bursting over in a tumble.

'Travelling here after Yoritomo died . . . on a road that long, you have a lot of time to think about what matters to you. And I know everyone is looking to you now. This war isn't over, and I understand that. I don't know how any of this is supposed to work. I spent my whole life in the Guild. I don't know what . . . happens between men and women . . .'

Yukiko raised an eyebrow.

'I mean, I know what *happens* happens,' Kin added hastily. 'I mean, I know what goes where and that there's supposed to be flowers, and poetry fits in somehow too, but . . .'

Yukiko pressed her lips together, trying to smother a smile that somehow felt traitorous and out of place. She felt a lightness in her chest, breathing just a tiny bit easier. The simplicity of it. The sweet and awkward stumbling of it. The beauty of it.

She remembered.

The boy ran his hand across his scalp, threw a pleading glance to the heavens.

'I told you I'd sound like an idiot . . .'

'No, you don't.'

YES, HE DOES.

Hush.

THIS IS MY HELL, I SWEAR IT. WHEN I PASS INTO THE AFTERLIFE AND AM PUNISHED FOR MY SINS, THIS WILL BE MY TORMENT. SURROUNDED BY A SEA OF MOONING, ADOLESCENT MONKEY-BOYS. MUDDLING ABOUT IN PUDDLES OF THEIR OWN DRIBBLE.

Her smile emerged, bright in its victory.

Kin was looking into her eyes. A soft stare full of silent hope. A hope that had made him betray everything he was – his family, his Guild, his way of life. A hope that had bid him gift Buruu with mechanical wings, that had freed them both from their prisons.

Without him, Buruu would still be Yoritomo's slave. Without him, she'd probably be dead. What had it taken, for him to throw everything he was away? To cast aside the metal he'd worn his entire life, trek all the way here just to find her? Not just hope.

Courage.

'I just want you to know . . .'

Strength.

'. . . I missed you.'

Love?

Yukiko blinked, opened her mouth to speak. She felt rooted to the spot, stomach lurching, heart thundering in her chest and echoing the storm above.

With a small huffing sound, Buruu stalked off into the forest.

'Kin, I . . .'

'It's all right. There's no rule saying you need to feel the same way I do.'

'. . . I don't know how I feel. I haven't had time to even think about it.'

'If you felt something, you'd know it. You wouldn't need to think.'

'Kin, the last person I thought I loved tried to *murder* me.' The words tasted copperish, the bleed of an old wound reopening. The first boy she'd ever loved. The first she'd ever . . .

'I'd never hurt you,' he said. 'Never betray you. Never.'

'I know that.'

'I'm sorry. I didn't mean to pressure you. I just . . . wanted you to know.'

'I care about you.' She took his hands, stared until he met her eyes. 'I really do, Kin. I worried about you. We looked for you, every chance we got. And you being here now . . . it helps me breathe. You can't know how much.'

'I know it.' He squeezed her fingers so hard it hurt. 'You mean everything to me. Everything I've done. All of it. You're the reason. The first and only reason.'

The forest seethed about them as they stood, fingers entwined. She could feel the heat of his skin radiating through rain-soaked cloth, the strength in his hands. He ran his thumbs across her knuckles, and some part of her wanted to feel those hands on her, to feel a warm body pressed against her again, to feel something other than the pain and hate growing inside her like a cancer. Butterflies lurched about her stomach, tongue dry, palms slick. His lips were parted, short, shallow breaths, water beading on his skin. He moved, almost imperceptibly closer, and she felt the uncertainty inside slip for just a second, washed away by gentle rain. The noise of the world felt a thousand miles away.

She moved to meet him, closed her eyes.

His lips were soft, a feather-light brush against her own, gentle as falling petals. She sighed as they touched hers, lighting a fire inside her, surging bright. He was wonderfully clumsy, hands fluttering at his sides like wounded birds, almost losing his balance as she pressed tight against him. She could feel the pulse inside his chest, his mouth opening to hers, breathing in her sighs. Her body waking as if from a dreamless sleep, frissons of light tingling across her skin. Feeling for the first time in weeks. Feeling.

Alive.

She pressed his hands against her, taut muscle beneath her fingertips. Something prowled behind her eyes, something forged in lightning and blinding rain, hungry and hot, bidding her dig her fingers into his skin, to bite at his lip. Her heartbeat was thunder, her blood rising like a tide, the uncertainty, the anger, the voices of the forest, all of it at last falling still—

'Stormdancer!'

The cry was high-pitched, urgent, shattering the moment into a thousand glittering pieces. She blinked, pulled away, trying to catch her fleeing breath. Looked towards the voice, the tempo of feet pounding dead leaves.

'Stormdancer!'

A boy dashed into the graveyard, almost slipping in his haste, red-faced and breathless. Stopping before her, he bent double, gasping, pawing the sweat from his eyes. He was a few years older than she, heavyset, an askew jaw and mincemeat face, as if someone had tried to bash it in when he was a child.

'Takeshi?' Yukiko put a hand on the boy's shoulder. 'What is it?'

The boy shook his head, hands on his knees as he gasped like a landed fish. It took a few moments to regain breath enough to talk. He looked as if he'd been running from Lady Izanami, the Dark Mother herself.

'Scouts on the western rise . . . One of the pit traps . . .'

Yukiko felt dread stab her gut. As if bidden, Buruu crashed into the clearing in a flurry of dead leaves, hackles raised, the air filled with static electricity. His eyes were bright, pupils dilated around slivers of gleaming amber. The western rise was close to the Black Temple, where she and the arashitora had fought a legion of pit demons in the summer. If the creatures were probing the rise near the pit traps, that meant they were creeping closer to the village, and just one of the Dark Mother's children loose in the lower woods . . .

'Gods, they caught an oni?' Yukiko asked.

'No. Worse than a demon.'

Takeshi spit on the dead leaves at his feet, shaking his head. 'Another Guildsman.'

*

She was conscious of Kin's arms about her waist for the entire flight, strong hands and gentle grip. Soft breath tickling her neck. Warm as firelight. Her headache returning like a faithful hound, broken glass grinding at the base of her skull.

Clasping Buruu's neck, she tried to ignore Kin's hands on her hips, the play of muscle across his chest as he leaned against her. She entwined her fingers in the arashitora's feathers, felt for the heat of his mind, growing more jagged and bright with each passing moment.

You're awfully quiet.

ABOUT WHAT?

Don't play coy with me.

YOU CHIDE ME FOR PLAYING COY. AFTER TELLING THE BOY YOU DO NOT KNOW HOW YOU FEEL, THEN LUNGING FOR HIS TONSILS A HEARTBEAT LATER.

I . . . He makes me feel something, Buruu. Something I think I need right now.

MMN.

Well, go on then. Get it off your chest.

The thunder tiger tossed his head, swooped around a castle of tangled sugi trees, wisps of lightning crackling at his wingtips. She could feel him in her mind, loud as the thunderstorm gathering overhead, stubborn as the mountains around them, reminding her so much of her father she could almost smell pipe smoke. She remembered the beast she'd roamed the Iishi with, the arrogance and pride, the fury coiled inside him. He'd been an animal then. Clever, yes, but still driven by instinct rather than conscious thought. Now he was more; ferocious cunning layered with human faculties for judgement. And she could feel the urge to speak his piece bubbling inside him like a wellspring, until finally he couldn't stop himself.

I DO NOT UNDERSTAND YOUR KIND. WITH ARASHITORA, THE FEMALE CHOOSES THE MATE WITH THE STRONGEST WINGS, THE SHARPEST CLAWS. THE MALE HAS NO CHOICE AT ALL. HE IS SIMPLY A SLAVE TO INSTINCT AND THE FEMALE'S SCENT.

Well, that sounds awful.

IT IS SIMPLE. YOU HUMANS. ALL THIS SIGHING AND SPITTLE SWAPPING. YOUR COUPLING IS COMPLICATED BEYOND ALL NEED OR REASON.

Gods, please don't use that word . . .

MY OTHER OPTIONS ARE LESS POLITE.

Because you're usually a paragon of courtly manners?

The thunder tiger harrumphed, swooped lower so his belly brushed the tree line. Gentle rain began falling from the storm-washed skies.

TELL ME. THE MASHING OF YOUR FACES TOGETHER . . .

Kissing.

IT DEMONSTRATES AFFECTION.

Yes.

AND THE TONGUES?

. . . What?

HONESTLY, WHAT PURPOSE DOES THAT SERVE?

How under heaven did you . . .

SISTER, YOU WERE PROJECTING YOUR THOUGHTS OVER THE ENTIRE FOREST. IT WAS LIKE HIGH SPRING OUT THERE. A SWEATY TIDAL WAVE OF BARELY REPRESSED ADOLESCENT LUST DROWNING ALL BEFORE IT.

Gods, really?

THE MONKEYS IN PARTICULAR SEEMED . . . EXCITED.

She pressed her fists to her temples, glanced over her shoulder at Kin.

WELL, PERHAPS EXCITED IS THE WRONG WORD . . .
Yes, Buruu, I understand. Thank you.
TITILLATED?
Buruu . . .
ENGORGED, PERHAPS?
Oh my GODS, stop!

The treetops parted like water as they descended through the canopy, showers of severed green tumbling earthwards in their wake. Away from the glare of the garish day, Yukiko pulled her goggles down around her throat, ran her hand across her eyes.

You could really hear what I was feeling?
LOUD AS THUNDER. AS IF I FELT IT MYSELF.

She chewed her lip, listening to the faint cacophony on the edge of her subconscious.

The Kenning has never been like this before, Buruu. Your thoughts are louder than I've ever heard. If I listen, I can hear every animal for miles. All those impulses and lives stacked atop one another. It's deafening.

YOUR FATHER NEVER SPOKE TO YOU OF THIS?

He never even told me he had the gift. But, he drowned his Kenning in liquor and smoke. Maybe this is why? Maybe as we get older, it gets louder? Or maybe breaking Yoritomo's mind did something to break mine?

She sighed, ran her fingers through his feathers.

I don't understand any of this, brother . . .

They circled past a copse of maidenhairs, knotted branches and shovel-tip leaves laden with rain. The soft scent of green rot entwined with the perfume of deepening autumn, the leaden smell of the storm above. Thunder rumbled somewhere distant, as if the clouds were great ironclads, splitting and burning and tumbling from the skies. Yukiko could hear the echoes of old screams, faint and metallic, somewhere inside her head. The humidity was unbearable, her body aching, sweat mixing with rain on her skin and stinging at the corners of her eyes.

'There they are,' Kin said.

Two young men around her age stood about the edge of a broad pit trap. Buruu spread his pinions and reared back, cruising in to land as gracefully as he could on the broken ground. Yukiko and Kin slipped from his shoulders and made their way across snarled roots and green-clawed scrub, Buruu prowling behind, tail stretched like a whip.

Yukiko recognized the pair with an inward groan; Isao and Atsushi. The former had long dark hair drawn back into a topknot, angular features, chin shadowed with fuzz too soft to really be called whiskers. The latter was small and wiry, light-fingered, dark hair drawn back in braids, one hand on the haft of a long spear with a single-edged, curving blade.

The pair covered their fists and bowed.

'Hello, gentlemen,' she muttered. 'Strange seeing you all the way out here.'

'We were scouting, Stormdancer,' Isao said.

'Scouting? Don't you two usually do that through a hole in the bathroom wall?'

The pair looked at each other, then glanced at Buruu's razored talons. The thunder tiger growled long and low, staring at each boy in turn, but his laughter was warm in Yukiko's mind.

YOU ARE MERCILESS.

So I should be. They've seen me naked.

DO YOU PLAN TO TORTURE THEM FOREVER?

A few more years ought to cover it.

'W-we were looking for oni,' Atsushi stammered. 'As Daichi-sama bid us. There have been reports of the demons moving in the deep woods. Their numbers are growing again.'

'They know nothing but hatred for our kind,' Isao said. 'The children of the Endsinger do not sleep, Stormdancer.'

'Why do you call her that?' Kin scowled at the boys. 'She has a name.'

Isao drummed his fingers on his war club, a studded tetsubo of solid oak, haft wrapped in bands of old, river-smooth leather. He glanced over briefly as Kin spoke, but dismissed the boy's words without reply. Atsushi kept his eyes on Yukiko as if Kin hadn't spoken at all.

Yukiko glanced at the pit trap. The hole was twenty feet cubed; big enough for an oni to fall into. It had been covered by a layer of foliage, concealed from anyone who wouldn't recognize the warning markers around it. Judging from the hole in the covering, whatever had plunged through wasn't much bigger than a man.

'We found it an hour ago.' Isao pointed to the trap with his war club. 'It must have fallen in last night. Tracks came from the south.'

'Did you speak to it?'

'No.' Isao shook his head. 'We saw it looked like Guild, so we sent Takeshi to find you and Daichi-sama. I'll not speak to any bastard Lotusman. Their kind are poison.'

Yukiko saw the boy shoot a brief, venomous glance at Kin.

How did it find us?

PERHAPS YOU COULD USE YOUR TONGUE FOR ITS INTENDED PURPOSE AND ASK?

Yukiko poked out the aforementioned tongue and rolled her eyes.

Hilarious, you.

Buruu prowled to the lip of the pit, peeked over the edge, wings spread. He snorted, amber eyes narrowed to knife-cuts. His tail swept from side to side in swift, agitated arcs.

INTERESTING.

Yukiko crept up beside him, put her arm around his neck and looked into the hole. Two bulbous red eyes stared back at her. She saw a humanoid figure, wasp-waisted, a featureless face. It was covered head to foot in some kind of skin-tight membrane, earth-brown, slick and glistening. A cluster of eight chromed arms uncurled from a melon-sized orb on its back, as if some eyeless metal spider were fused with its flesh.

Yukiko's hand went reflexively to the tantō at her back, her voice dripping revulsion.

'What the hells is that?'

4

Doppelganger

The slap was perfect. Hard enough to rock the girl's head back on her shoulders, bring tears to already red and swollen eyes. But not so hard as to split her lip, to leave a mark that wouldn't set to fading after an hour or so. Spittle sprayed her face as the warden bellowed.

'Answer me, you little bitch!'

The girl hung her head, weeping, face hidden by a curtain of tangled hair. Her sobbing echoed off the damp stone of the prison cell, lank straw strewn underfoot. Manacled wrists, long knife wounds scabbed down her forearms. A cracked and swollen cheek healing slowly. Bare and bruised legs dotted with fresh lesions. A perceptive man might have noted the wounds were shaped like rat bites.

The warden's patience had frayed to a few lonely threads over the past week. Each maidservant in his custody was technically nobility; in theory they had families to press the Tora Daimyo for their return – presuming a new clanlord was ever chosen, of course. Even after they'd been arrested, no official accusation was levelled by the disintegrating judiciary. And thus the warden was placed in the unenviable position of having to 'make inquiries' of his prisoners without the burning iron or water torture usually employed during interrogations in Kigen jail.

It was enough to drive a fellow to drink.

The warden seized the girl's throat, forced her head back so she could see his eyes. He saw naked fear, pupils dilated, discoloured cheek wet with tears.

'You served Lady Aisha.' The girl gurgled as he tightened his grip. 'Your mistress spent hours with the Kitsune girl, plotting her brother's assassination. You were privy to all of it!'

'She always . . . sent us . . . out.' A croak through a cinched windpipe. 'Always—'

'You are a Kagé spy! I want names, I want—'

'Warden!'

The shout rang out in the cell's confines, taut with command. The warden turned and saw two bushimen in black-banded armour outside the cell, flanking a third man in a tailored kimono of rich scarlet.

The man's hair was drawn back in an elaborate braid, pierced with golden pins. He was a good-looking fellow with a studious air; a handsome face with perpetually narrowed eyes, as if he spent too much time reading by lamplight. A chainkatana and wakizashi were crossed at his waist – the chainsaw daishō marking a nobleborn member of the military caste. He clutched a beautifully crafted iron fan in one hand. Smooth shaven, sharp jaw covered by an expensive clockwork breather. He was in his early twenties at most, but his rank was that of a man two decades older.

'Magistrate Ichizo.' The warden released the girl and bowed. 'Your visit was unannounced.'

'Obviously.' The man's eyes flickered to the girl crumpled on the stone. 'This is how you treat your wards? Ladies of court? You disgrace yourself and dishonour our Lord, Warden.'

'Forgiveness, honourable Magistrate.' The warden bowed. 'But I was commanded to uncover any Kagé operatives—'

'And you believe torturing handmaidens will bring you closer to them?'

'Each one of these girls served the traitor whore, Lady Aish—'

The blow was so swift, the warden almost couldn't track it. Ichizo's iron fan caught him full in the face, hard enough to open a small cut across his cheek. The crack of metal upon flesh faded, a stone-heavy silence in its wake, broken only by the girl's quiet sobs.

'You speak of the last daughter of Kazumitsu's line,' Ichizo hissed. 'The blood of the first Shōgun flows in her veins, and the next heir to this empire will grow in her womb.' He slipped the fan into his sleeve. 'Mind. Your. Tongue.'

The warden pawed the cut on his cheek, lowered his eyes.

'Forgiveness, Magistrate. But the Chief Treasurer demanded—'

'Chief Treasurer Nagahara resigned from office two hours ago. The stresses of public life have extracted a grievous toll upon his health. He has retired to his country estates with the blessings of our Lord, Daimyo Hiro.'

The warden sighed inwardly.

So. Another power shift.

At last count, three nobles had claimed leadership of the Tora zaibatsu; two senior ministers and the young Iron Samurai who had lost his arm (and very nearly his life) defending Yoritomo-no-miya from his assassin. Now it seemed the time for diplomacy was ending. Hiro's faction had assassinated four high-ranking ministers in the last two weeks – courtly machinations turning inevitably towards the politics of the duelist's katana and the assassin's blade. Swordmen like the warden were caught in between – bound by oaths to the Daimyo, but unsure who the hells the Daimyo even *was*.

'This barbarism will end.' The magistrate's gaze roamed the cell. 'Lady Aisha's handmaidens will be escorted to the palace and placed under house arrest. I will speak to each girl personally regarding their treatment whilst in your care.'

'This one was injured when she came in,' the warden mumbled. 'I had the apothecary tend her wounds to ensure she wouldn't fall to infection.'

'And the rat bites?'

'I—'

'I know the nature of her injuries, Warden. I have read the report. Multiple knife wounds. Beaten bloody, cheek cracked, comatose for days. Lucky to escape the Stormdancer with her life. Yet you believe she was in collusion with the Kitsune girl?'

'There were many secrets in the wh . . .' the warden cleared his throat, '. . . in the Lady Aisha's chambers. Some of these maidens must have been privy to them.'

'This girl is barely seventeen years old.'

'All due respect, Magistrate, but Yoritomo-no-miya's assassin was sixteen.'

'And you thought to beat the insurgency's secrets out of a girl that *same assassin* had already beaten near to death?'

'I was commanded to investigate all—'

'Your loyalty is admirable, Warden. But your confusion about where to place it is of grave concern. You should invest thought in your future.' The magistrate's eyes glittered above his breather. 'My noble cousin, Daimyo Hiro, would be disappointed to learn you had also been . . . retired for the sake of your health.'

'I understand, Lord Magistrate,' he nodded. 'My thanks for your wisdom.'

'Unchain her at once.'

The warden unlocked the girl's manacles, blanching as he noted the raw bruises on her wrists. Ichizo shouldered him aside, throwing his robe around her to preserve her modesty. The magistrate tut-tutted as he assisted her from the cell.

'It is over, my dear.' His voice was soft as feather down. 'It is all over now.'

The girl continued crying, hugging herself as the magistrate escorted her down the stone corridor. The warden heard the sound of heavy boots: more bushimen marching into the prison, barking orders at his men to release the other maidens. He could feel it all around him – the entire country teetering on a knife edge. The promise of bloody conflict looming among the clans. Kagé insurgents infecting the city like a cancer. Samurai thrashing about like spoiled children, concerned with nothing but carving paths towards the throne.

The warden sighed again, wished for a return to simpler days. Days when a soldier knew where his allegiances lay. Days before the Stormdancer had taken his world away.

Then he clomped out of the cell and went in search of that drink.

*

'Your suite, I believe.'

They stood in a wide palace hallway, flanked by four bushimen, the stink of their motor-rickshaw journey still clinging to her skin. The girl had stared out the window as they drove from the jail, forehead pressed to glass as Kigen city brushed past in all its misery. Market stalls standing empty and abandoned, broken glass crunching under their wheels. People in rich garments scurrying to and fro, hunched shoulders, nervous glances behind custom goggles. Past the empty, bloodstained arena, through the tall iron gates of the palace grounds. Stunted gardens behind high walls; grey stone with a broken-bottle crust. Autumn had finally broken the awful summer heat, and yet everywhere she looked, she could see the colour of flame. Smell the tinder, waiting for the spark.

Waiting to burn.

Magistrate Ichizo slid the door to her suite open, and she stared into the small, familiar room. Unmade bed, drawers upended, clothes strewn over the floor. She could see the congealed bloodstain on the wicker matting, reached up to touch the scab at her cheek, the memory of the knife strikes on her forearms, the blow to her face, fresh and real in her mind.

'You will forgive the state of things.' Ichizo's tone was apologetic. 'Another minister must have ordered your possessions searched. The past month has been . . . turbulent. I am sure it will not take long to put all back in order.'

'My thanks, my Lord.'

'You . . . do not remember me, do you?'

A shake of her head. 'Forgive me, my Lord.'

'We met last spring festival.' A gentle smile in his voice. 'The Seii Taishōgun's banquet. We spoke about poetry. The strengths of Hamada over Noritoshi. I recall that evening fondly . . .'

She looked up at him then, still clutching his robe about her shoulders, and her face crumpled like candlewax in a burning fireplace. She threw her arms around him and sobbed, pressing herself into his chest to muffle her wails. The magistrate was taken aback, unsure whether to embrace her or push her away. He nodded to the bushimen flanking him, and they retreated to spare her further loss of face.

'Come now, my dear.' He patted her awkwardly on her shoulder. 'You shame yourself.'

'It was so awful.' Hot tears soaked into scarlet silk. 'The l-last thing I remember was the Kitsune girl h-hitting me. Then I woke in that cell and they were screaming at me, calling me a tr-traitor. My gods, there was no servant more loyal to Yoritomo-no-miya than I . . .'

'Hush now.' He tried to hug and push her away simultaneously, failing on both counts. 'They will not hurt you again. You may not leave these rooms unattended, but you will suffer no more ill-treatment. Upon my honour, I vow it.'

'Thank you, Lord Ichizo. Bless you.'

She stood on tiptoes and kissed him, soft as summer showers down his cheek, until at last she reached his lips. And there she pressed herself, just a little longer, pushing her body against his. He broke away with a nervous smile, extricating himself and straightening his kimono.

'Very good, very good.' A small cough. 'Duty well served.'

She was ushered inside, tear-soaked, pawing her eyes with her sleeve. Ichizo bowed and backed out of the room, shutting and locking the door behind him, his cheeks a subtle shade of rose. She stood amidst the flotsam and jetsam and continued sobbing, just loud enough to be heard through the walls. As their footsteps faded across the polished boards, she counted one hundred heartbeats, weeping still. And finally, she dropped her hands away from her face and the tears stopped as if someone had choked them.

She stared into the warm void on the back of her eyelids, listening to the emptiness inside her head. Still and mute in the free air. Finally, she moved, stalking towards the washroom, towards clean water and sweet-smelling soap, intent on scrubbing the prison from her skin.

She glanced at the looking glass as she passed by, caught a glimpse of her reflection. For a terrifying moment, she was seized by the unshakable sensation that a stranger stared back at her. Oh, the long dark hair, the slender body, the plump, pouting lips were all hers. But the face belonged to someone else entirely; a girl she didn't know, and didn't care to. A weakling whose skin she wore.

She stripped the rags and robe from her shoulders, stared at her body in the mirror. The stain of false tears on skin she had pinched until it was red and swollen. The knife wounds she had carved into her own arms. The cheek she had slammed against the corner of her own dresser. Remembering the rats squealing and flailing in her hands as she pressed them to her flesh. Anything, everything to evoke pity, to soften the hearts she longed to tear still-beating from their chests.

The urge to smash the reflection burned bright in her mind. She stared at her doppelganger, the tiny, broken girl she pretended to be, hands curling into fists.

'You are death,' she whispered. 'Cold as winter dawn. Merciless as Lady Sun. Play the role. Play it so well you could fool yourself. But never forget who you are. What you are.'

She pointed at the glass, and her whisper was sharp as knives.

'You are Kagé Michi.'

5

Chrysalis

Cold nausea in her belly, bubbling past her lungs to the tip of her tongue.

Blood-red eyes stared at Yukiko from the pit trap's gloom – polished glass affixed in a bone-smooth, mouthless face. The membrane covering the figure's body was brown as old leather, glossy and supple, creased at the joints. A transistor-studded mechabacus on its chest and the cables snaking around it body marked it as Guild, the cluster of thin, chromed limbs at its back completing the horrific, arachnoid portrait.

'What the hells *is* that?' she breathed.

'A False-Lifer.' Kin frowned, pawing at his stubble.

'A what?'

Yukiko glanced at the boy beside her, hand still on her tantō hilt. Buruu loomed near her shoulder, watching the pit with narrowed eyes. The warmth radiating from his fur gave her goosebumps, that now-familiar scent of ozone and musk filling the air, flecked with electricity.

'They create the flesh-automata for the Guild.' Kin shrugged. 'The servitors that work in the chapterhouses. The city criers that trundle about calling the hour. They conduct surgical procedures, install implants into newborns, that kind of thing.'

Four sets of eyes looked at him as if he were speaking gaijin.

'They build machines that emulate life.' He waved one hand in the air. 'False. Lifer.'

'Gods above,' Atsushi breathed.

'What's it doing here?' Isao demanded.

'Do I look like a mind reader?' Kin asked.

Isao glanced at Yukiko. 'If we were alone, I'd tell you exactly what you look like, Guildsman.'

Kin blinked, opened his mouth to retort when a gravelled, sibilant rasp drifted up from the pit. Half statement, half question, retched from the belly of some rusted metal serpent.

'Guildsman?' The thing tilted its head, looking at Kin. 'You are Kioshi?'

The name sparked a chill in Yukiko's gut, slick and oily. An unwelcome reminder of who and what Kin had been in days past. The name of a father long dead, a Lotusman of station and esteem, passed to his only son as Guild custom bid. The name Kin had called himself, encased in that metal skin. The name of the stranger. The enemy. Before she'd discover the boy beneath the brass. Before he'd . . .

'Shut up!' Isao raised his tetsubo, apparently amazed to hear the thing speak. 'Shut your mouth or I'll cave your skull in, bastard.'

The False-Lifer raised its hands. Seven of its metallic arms lifted up in unison. The eighth spat a shower of blue sparks and twitched, dangling beside the Guildsman's leg.

'I mean no harm to any of you,' it hissed. 'By the First Bloom, I vow it.'

'What the hells is a First Bloom?' Isao spat.

Jay Kristoff

'The leader of the Lotus Guild,' Kin said. 'The Second Bloom of every chapterhouse reports to him.'

'And you people swear by him like he's a god?'

Kin stared at the boy for an empty moment, then turned back to the thing in the pit.

'What are you doing here?' he asked.

'Looking for you, Kioshi-san.'

Looking for him?

'My name is Kin.'

'You . . . no longer bear your father's name?'

'His name is none of your business.' Yukiko spoke through clenched teeth. 'I'd stop asking questions and start answering them if I were you.'

The False-Lifer averted its smooth, glass eyes. Yukiko could have sworn it cringed.

'Forgiveness, Stormdancer.'

'What the hells are you doing here? What do you want?'

A small, helpless gesture, silver arms rippling. 'To join you.'

'Join us?' she scoffed.

'Kiosh—' A pause. '*Kin*-san is not the only one who dreamed of escaping the Guild's control. There are many of us within chapterhouses all over Shima, harbouring secret thoughts of rebellion. But none thought it was possible. None were brave enough to risk it.' The thing looked at Kin, admiration in its voice. 'Until he did.'

'We should kill it, Stormdancer.' Atsushi pointed his spear into the pit, rain running down its razored edge. 'We can't trust it.'

'Please . . .' the False-Lifer whispered. 'I've come so far . . .'

Kin glared at Atsushi. 'When a Guildsman's skin suffers catastrophic damage, the mechabacus sends a distress beacon. The Guild will know *exactly* where we are.'

66

'Can you disable the beacon?' Yukiko pointed to the brass tool belt slung about his waist.

'I could.' Kin frowned. 'But you're not going to— '

Yukiko turned to Isao.

'Get it out of the pit.'

They tossed a rope down, Yukiko watching in disgust as the Guildsman crawled twenty feet up into the light. The arms on its back made a skittering, clicking noise as they moved, as if a hive of scuttling insects were housed in each limb. Glowing eyes lent a blood-soaked tinge to its glistening shell. Though the skin looked moist, dirt or dust didn't cling to it at all.

As the Guildsman reached the pit's edge, Yukiko realized it was wearing a long, buckle-studded apron, making it difficult to clear the lip of the trap. Isao seized one of its humanoid arms, dragged it out and dumped it without ceremony on the ground. Atsushi levelled his naginata at the thing's throat. Yukiko stood back, well out of reach of the spider limbs, but the Guildsman made no threatening gestures, merely raised all its arms amidst more of that horrid clicking and slowly rose to its feet. Eyes averted. Shivering. Its mechabacus was silent, implanted over the swell of its . . .

Gods above.

'It's a girl.' Yukiko frowned at Kin. 'She's a girl.'

Kin shrugged. 'All False-Lifers are.'

'I didn't think there were any women in the Guild.'

'Where do you think little Guildsmen come from?' A small, embarrassed smile.

Yukiko's scowl grew darker still, and she gestured towards the False-Lifer's mechabacus. The device chattered, counting beads clicking back and forth across a surface of relays, heat-sinks and glowing transistors.

'Disable it.'

Kin stepped forward, uncertain, drawing a screwdriver and pliers from his work belt. Looking a little awkward, he placed his hands on the Guildswoman's chest. It kept its eyes downturned as he loosened a handful of screws. Dozens of insulated wires spilled out as he peeled the faceplate away.

'Um.' He held up the covering. 'Can you hold this, please?'

The False-Lifer mutely complied, spider arms shuddering as its real hands cupped the metal. Yukiko felt her stomach turn, swallowing hard, mouth tasting of vomit. Her legs were trembling. Eyes watering. Sparrows called in the distance, the sound closer to screaming than singing. Three monkeys gathered in the trees overhead, roaring and shaking the branches. Heat all around her. Hands in fists.

ARE YOU WELL, SISTER?

I'm fine.

'What's your name?' Kin said.

'Kin, don't talk to it,' Yukiko growled.

He glanced over his shoulder. 'Isn't that the point of this exercise?'

Yukiko glared, scraped rain-slicked hair from her eyes. Kin turned back to the False-Lifer, unspooled several leads from its mechabacus, began tinkering in the machine's guts. He offered an apologetic glance as he touched its breast again.

'What's your name?' he repeated.

'. . . My mother's name was Kei. Gifted to me when she died, as custom bids.'

He paused, looked into featureless glass eyes. 'But what's *your* name?'

A long silence. Yukiko ground her teeth. She could hear the sounds of a thousand gaijin children, sobbing as they were marched to slaughter inside the greasy yellow innards of the chapterhouses. High-pitched screaming amidst the crackling pyres around the Burning Stones. People like her, people with the Kenning, put to the torch for the sake of the Guild's ridiculous 'Way of Purity.' The False-Lifer's reply sounded like a nest of spitting vipers.

'Ayane.'

'What chapterhouse are you from?'

'Yama.'

'Fox lands are a long walk from here.' Kin raised an eyebrow and went to work with a pair of wire snips. 'How did you make it all the way? False-Lifers can't fly.'

'I stole aboard a Guild liner in Yama harbour and fired the escape pod.' The spider limbs flexed, a ripple of silver in the air around it. 'I flew as far as I could. Then I walked.'

'How did you know our direction?' Kin looked up from the innards, eyes illuminated by a burst of sparks.

'The Guild has known the general location of the Kagé stronghold since they rescued the two of you from the *Thunder Child*'s ruins. Since then, they have set up triangulation towers around the Iishi. Every time the Kagé transmit a radio signal, they zero closer.'

'If they know that much, why haven't they massed their fleet to burn this forest down?' Yukiko snapped.

The False-Lifer turned her gaze to the earth, steadfastly refusing to meet Yukiko's eyes.

'Much of the fleet is still overseeing the retreat in Morcheba. But the Guildsman you spared made it back to Yama with your message, Arashi-no-odoriko. The loss of three heavy ships was enough to give the Upper Blooms pause. The captain you killed was a war hero, you know. Kigen's Third Bloom. Master of their fleet.'

'So?'

'So they are afraid of you.' It swallowed. 'You and your thunder tiger.'

Kin was staring at her, the memory of a hundred dead Guildsmen swimming unspoken in his eyes. Yukiko licked her lips, feeling her skin crawl as the False-Lifer's limbs shivered. She ran one hand along Buruu's neck, fingers deep in feathers' warmth.

I don't trust her.

SENSIBLE.

It's too good to be true that there would be more like Kin.

IN ALL HONESTY, THAT PART OF HER TALE IS EASY TO BELIEVE.

A rebellion inside the Guild? No, they're just telling us what we want to hear.

THOSE OF THE GUILD ARE BORN TO IT. NO CHOICE. NO CONTROL. NOT SO HARD TO IMAGINE SOME WOULD RESENT THAT YOKE.

I don't believe one of them would just tiptoe out of a chapterhouse and come all this way to find Kin. It's probably just a survivor from the fleet we burned. Lying to save its skin.

WE LEFT ONLY ONE ALIVE, YUKIKO. YOU KNOW THAT.

This doesn't make any godsdamned sense. It's lying.

YOU MEAN 'SHE' IS LYING.

I mean 'it.'

She eyed the False-Lifer up and down, lip curling.

'Is that why your leaders are backing Hiro? Because they're too spineless to come here themselves now? They'd rather risk men with wives and children in the battle to bring me down, right? Better to see them die than more of their precious Shatei?'

'I am from Yama.' All nine of its functional arms rippled, and

Yukiko was appalled to recognize the gesture as a shrug. 'I do not know the politics of First House, or why the First Bloom bids Shateigashira Kensai to support the Tora boy. But I know seventy per cent of our Munitions Sect were requisitioned by Kigen four weeks ago.'

Yukiko stared blankly.

'The Munitions Sect build machines that require human control,' Kin offered. 'Motor-rickshaw, shreddermen, sky-ship engines and so on. Like I used to.'

Yukiko narrowed her eyes. 'What are they working on?'

'I do not know, Stormdancer.' Another grotesque, multi-armed shrug.

'Don't call her that.' Kin plucked three transistors from the mechabacus. 'Her name is Yukiko.'

The boy snipped a final set of wires, gathered up the contraption's guts and stuffed them back into its housing. Sealing the device closed with a few hasty screws, he stepped back.

'Done.'

The False-Lifer looked at Atsushi's blade poised against its throat. The boy shifted his grip, one word from a bloodbath. Kin was watching her with pleading eyes. Yukiko stared for a pregnant moment, arms folded, eyes narrowed. The rain was falling harder, fat, clear droplets pounding the leaves around them and soaking everyone to the bones.

Everyone except the False-Lifer, of course.

'I have never seen rain that was not black before.' It turned its palms to the sky, droplets pattering upon its body, beading and running like quicksilver. 'It is beautiful.'

Yukiko's eyes were on the blade gleaming in Atsushi's hand. The raindrops glittering on the steel like polished jewels.

We should just get everything we can from her, then bury her.

Buruu growled.

WHAT IF SHE SPEAKS TRUTH? WHAT IF SHE IS WHAT SHE SAYS?

No one leaves the Guild. Everyone knows that.

EXCEPT YOUR KIN.

Don't call him that.

I DID NOT TRUST HIM EITHER, REMEMBER? YET WITHOUT HIM, NEITHER OF US WOULD BE HERE.

I know that.

THEN YOU KNOW WE CANNOT END THIS GIRL ON MERE SUSPICION.

Yukiko hissed, rubbed her eyes with balled fists. The Kenning headache was slinking forward on fox-light feet. The noise. The heat. Lurking in the back of her skull with leaden hands and bated breath.

'Take off your skin,' she said.

'What?' Kin raised an eyebrow. 'What for?'

'If we're taking it back, we're not bringing a tracking device with us. It takes its skin and mechabacus off and we bury them here.'

'The mechabacus won't work anym—'

'That's the bargain, Kin. We bury its skin, or we bury *it*.'

'She's not an "it."' Kin frowned. 'Her name is Ayane.'

Isao scowled, shook his head. Yukiko turned to the False-Lifer, eyes and voice cold.

'Your choice. And I don't mean to sound cruel, but I could sleep either way.'

The False-Lifer glanced at Atsushi's blade, then to Kin. Without a word, it began twisting the wing-nut bolts studding its suit. Reaching back with its humanoid arms, it tinkered with the silver orb on its spine; the melon-sized hub from which the spider limbs sprang. It fumbled around for a moment, hissing softly.

'Can you help please, Kin-san? It is difficult to do this alone.'

Hesitantly, Kin stepped behind it, twisting each bolt dotting its spine, working several clasps under the False-Lifer's direction. Yukiko heard a faint series of popping sounds, all over the grease-slick, gleaming body, followed by the wet sucking of air rushing into vacuum. The skin slackened, as if it were now a size too big. The thing tugged a zip cord running up to the base of its skull, another down to the small of its back. As Atsushi and Isao watched, revolted and fascinated, the False-Lifer bent double, and like a butterfly emerging from its cocoon, chrysalis to imago, sloughed off its outer shell.

She was clad in a membrane of pale webbing beneath. Skin so pallid it was almost translucent. Her head utterly hairless; no eyelashes, eyebrows, nothing. Long slender limbs and tapered fingers, smooth curves studded with bayonet fixtures of black, gleaming metal. Seventeen, perhaps eighteen years old at most. Her lips were full and pouting, as if she'd been stung by something venomous, her features fragile and perfect; a porcelain doll on its first day in the sun. She narrowed her eyes, held one hand up against the light.

Inexplicably, Yukiko felt her heart sink.

She's beautiful.

Kin scowled at the gawping boys and removed his uwagi, slipped it around the pale girl's shoulders. Yukiko could see the same bayonet fixtures in *his* flesh, ruining smooth lines of lean muscle, fixed in the exact same location: wrists, shoulders, chest, collarbone, spine. The silver orb sat affixed to the girl's back, spider limbs rippling, still making that horrid, inhuman noise. Yukiko pointed.

'Take those off too.'

'I cannot.' The girl's voice sounded soft and sweet now that she was outside her skin, underscored with a thin, trembling fear. 'They are part of me. Rooted in my spinal column.'

'Don't lie to me.'

'Please, I am not lying.' The girl wrung her hands, still squinting. Her eyes were a rich, earthen brown, pupils contracting to pinpricks. 'I could just as easily take off my legs.'

ONE WITH THE MACHINE. SUCH MADNESS.

Yukiko scowled at the rippling silver fingers, needle-sharp, swollen-knuckled and gleaming with rain. She looked down at the False-Lifer's toes, pressed into dark, wet earth, sick to her stomach. The headache slipped towards her temples, tightening at the base of her skull. A whisper. A promise.

'Bind her arms.' She glanced at Atsushi. 'All of them.'

Kin looked vaguely hurt by the suggestion. 'Yukiko, you don't need to do that.'

'Please don't tell me what I need, Kin.'

The girl folded her metallic arms at her back; functional limbs curling up like the legs of a dying spider, the broken one hanging near her shin, limp as a dead fish. Atsushi bound her with rope, wrapping it around her torso and pinning all her arms. Drawing a deep breath, steeling herself, the girl raised her eyes and looked at Yukiko for the first time. Her voice was almost lost beneath the whispering rain.

'Thank you for trusting me,' she said.

'I don't trust you.'

'Then . . . thank you for not killing me.'

'Let's get her back.' Yukiko motioned to the boys. 'Isao, bury the skin deep as you can. Atsushi, come with us. I need to speak to Daichi.'

Isao nodded, started clearing a space of dead leaves. Atsushi poked the girl in the back with his nagamaki, hard enough for her to stumble. Kin reached out, caught her before she fell.

'Move,' Atsushi growled.

Yukiko moved off into the undergrowth with Buruu, skin prickling, head throbbing. Looking back, she saw Kin had placed a steadying hand on the knots at Ayane's back, helping her navigate the uneven ground. Atsushi tromped along behind, a dark scowl on his face.

Ayane kept her eyes downcast, voice low. But she was speaking. Furtive and clearly afraid. Stretching out into the minds of the forest around them, inundating herself in a cascading pain, Yukiko could hear every word the False-Lifer spoke. See her through a hundred pairs of eyes, feel the pulse of a hundred heartbeats.

Blood began dripping from her nose.

'Thank you, Kin-san,' Ayane was whispering.

'You have nothing to thank me for.' The boy shook his head. 'We do what's right up here. Yukiko's a good person. She's just suspicious of the Guild. She lost a lot because of them and the government. Most people here have.'

'Her father.'

'Friends too.'

'Are they going to hate me? The Kagé, I mean?'

'Probably.' Kin glanced back at Atsushi and his nagamaki. 'They don't trust our kind . . . I mean, the kind we used to be.'

'Then why do you stay?'

It was a long time before Kin answered; a wordless space filled by faint rain drumming on the canopy, as if a distant army were pounding earth with hollow bamboo. Yukiko could see him watching her, walking there in front of him, Buruu beside

75

her. He looked at the forest, slowly turning the colour of rust, cupped in the palms of autumn's chill. And finally, he shrugged.

'Because there are things here I love. Because I'm part of this world, and I've sat by and watched it falling away for far too long, hoping someone else will save it.'

'So now you will save it, Kin-san? All by yourself?'

'Not by myself.' He shook his head. 'We're all in this together. We need more people to realize that. More people willing to stand up and say "enough." No matter what it costs.'

The girl glanced at Kin and smiled, and her eyes sparkled like dew on polished stone. Beneath the fear, there was a strength in her voice, old as the mountains looming around them, deep as the earth beneath their feet.

'Enough,' she said.

The pain crested and swelled, hot and sharp, too much, too harsh. Yukiko broke away, slipped back into her own thoughts like a thief, wiping the blood from her lips. Buruu cast her a sideways glance, saying nothing, saying everything. She sniffed thickly, spat salty scarlet into the underbrush.

Hundreds of eyes followed them as they walked away.

6

Downside Up

The other servants never called her by name.

The girl was short for her eighteen years, famine-thin, her impish face set with hollow cheeks and pointed chin. Raven-black hair was cut in a messy bob, damp with sweat. Her right eye was covered with a patch of dark leather, the faint stippling of scar tissue in her cheek, a deep hairless gouge bisecting her eyebrow. Her good eye was large, almost too round, so dark as to be nearly black.

A visitor to the Shōgun's palace would have taken one look at her winter-pale complexion and wagered the girl was Kitsune-born – pasty as all the Fox clan were. But a glance beneath the cotton covering her right shoulder would have revealed no clan ink on her skin; shown her to be a lowborn mongrel, unfit for all but the most menial and unclean of labours.

Hence her nickname.

'You!' a voice called. 'Shit Girl!'

The girl stopped in her tracks, sandals scuffing on polished floorboards. She turned to face the approaching house mistress, her gaze downcast, hands clasped together. As the plump, over-powdered woman stopped before her, the girl focused on the floor between her toes. Night was falling out in the palace grounds, but she could hear a lone sparrow singing – choking, really – its lungs full of oily lotus haze. The leaves in the wretched gardens were failing, autumn creeping into Kigen city and painting all with grey and rust-red during the sunlit hours. But the Shit Girl only roamed the palace after dark – the less seen of her in the harsh light of day, the better.

'My Lady?' she said.

'Where are you going?'

'The servant's wing, my Lady.'

'The chamber pots in the guest wing need emptying when you're done.'

She bowed. 'Hai.'

'Go on then,' the woman waved. 'And bathe tomorrow, for the Maker's sake. There may be no Shōgun, but this is still the Shōgun's palace. Serving here is an honour. Especially for one of your breed.'

'I will, my Lady. Thank you, my Lady.'

Bowing low, the girl waited for the mistress to retreat before continuing on her way. She shuffled to the servants' quarters, the loose boards of the nightingale floor chirping and squeaking beneath her feet. Outside each door, a chamber pot awaited – black kiln-fired clay, a little smaller than an armful, with gifts inside just for her. She would carry each pot to a night soil drain at the rear of the grounds and dump the reeking contents. Wash them out and trudge back though the palace. Watching the slow, orchestrated chaos around her, ministers and soldiers and magistrates, scrabbling for power and gathering in tiny, muttering knots.

And she, beneath it all.

The house mistress had spoken truth – serving in the palace was an honour few lowborns ever enjoyed. Burakumin like her were the bottom of the barrel in Shima's caste system, only employed at tasks regular citizens found unwholesome. Male clanless could join the army, of course, serve out a ten-year stint in exchange for genuine clan ink at the end of his tour. But that wasn't an option for the Shit Girl, even if she felt the suicidal urge to serve as fodder for the gaijin lightning cannon. Besides, that plan hadn't worked out so well for her father . . .

So here she was, slinging chamber pots in the Shōgun's palace. Derided. Shunned. Constantly reminded she was un-worthy of the honour. But lowborn or no, in the two years she'd worked those opulent halls, she'd learned a simple truth she'd suspected her entire life – no matter how honourable the backside producing it, shit never fails to stink.

Making her way back to the servant's wing, she would slip the chamber pot through a slot in the bedroom doors, working her way down the row. Each room was sealed with a shiny new lock – Lady Aisha's maidservants were all under house arrest, recently moved from Kigen jail. In fact, more than a few of the palace serving staff had been imprisoned after Shōgun Yoritomo's death, suspected of either assisting the plot, or failing to stop it. But the Shit Girl? The clanless, worthless, bloodless mongrel wrapped in third-hand servant's clothes? She swam as she always did. Beneath their contempt. Beneath their notice.

It had worked out well, all things considered.

She knelt by the final door in the row, reached inside her servant's kimono and retrieved a small pad of rice-paper, a stick of charcoal. Glancing up and down the darkened corridor, she scrawled some hasty kanji on the paper, slipped it through the door slot.

Jay Kristoff

'*Daiyakawa,*' it said.

The name of a little-known village somewhere in the northern Tora provinces, where years ago, a peasant uprising had been quietly quashed by Shōgunate troops. To most, the name would mean nothing. To the girl imprisoned within the room, everything.

Moments later, a note was slipped back through the slot, kanji marked in lipstick.

'*Who are you?*'

And so it began. Paper slipping into the hall, her eye scanning the notes, replies marked on the flip side. Listening for approaching footsteps as the girl imprisoned within the room scratched a new message, passed it through the space between door frame and nightingale floor.

'*Call me No One, Michi-chan. Kaori sends regards.*'

'*Do I know you?*' came Michi's response.

'*Have served in palace two years, but you would not know me. Joined local Kagé a few weeks ago.*'

'*Why join now?*'

'*Saw Stormdancer speak in Market Square. Told me to raise my fist. So here I am.*'

A small pause.

'*And here I am.*'

'*Can you escape room?*'

'*Tried. Ceiling panels bolted in place. Window barred.*'

'*Why return here after Yoritomo died? Must have known you would be arrested.*'

'*Could not leave Aisha behind.*'

'*Brave.*'

'*Overheard rumours. Wedding? Lord Hiro?*'

'*True. Invitations sent to clanlords. Date set. Three weeks.*'

'Aisha would never agree.'

'No choice.'

'Can speak to her?'

'Royal wing guarded like prison. Aisha never leaves rooms.'

'I must get out of here.'

'Magistrate Ichizo has only key.'

Another pause.

'Not for long.'

No One heard creaking footsteps, the low murmurs of two approaching bushimen.

'Must go. Light red candle in window when free to speak.'

Standing quickly, the girl scooped up the chamber pot and shuffled down the corridor, heart pounding in her chest. She forced her hands to be still, her breath to slow. But the guards gave her and her stinking armload a wide berth, neither of them sparing her a glance. Everyone knew who she was. Everyone knew to ignore her. This was the fate of the clanless in Shima – to be treated as less than a person. All her life, she'd been a walking, breathing absentee. Seldom spoken to. Never touched. For all intents and purposes, invisible.

It had worked out well, all things considered.

*

When she was a little girl, No One thought the smokestacks made the clouds. She remembered playing around the walls of Yama refinery with her brother, watching filthy children tramp in and out of wrought-iron gates to a steam whistle tune, jealous they got to work in a place so magical. Trudging home through the wretched streets of Downside, she felt a pang of remorse for that childish ignorance.

The chi refinery grew like a tumour off Kigen Bay; a tangled briar of swollen pipes and bloated tanks, glowering over the labyrinthine alleys with grubby glass eyes. Chimneys dotted with burning floodlights spattered the sky with tar, smothering the broken-back tumbledowns about it in a blanket of choking vapour. A corroded pipeline as tall as houses wormed out of the refinery's bowels, north across the sluggish black depths of the Junsei River. Ramshackle apartment stacks and crumbling lean-tos lined the oil-slick streets of Downside – the cheapest and meanest stretch of broken cobbles in all of Kigen. A body had to be poor or desperate to even consider hanging her hat there.

Truth was, she'd spent eighteen years being both.

A threadbare cloak was slung around her servant's clothes, grubby kerchief over her face, a broad straw hat pulled low over her good eye, narrowed against the rising sun. As she rounded the corner to her tenement tower, a figure prowled out of the gloom to meet her, quiet as final breath. A hulking shape, almost toddler-sized, missing both ears and half its tail, blue-black as lotus smoke. It had a mangled, snaggletoothed face, patchy fur stretched over crisscrossed scars. Its kind were rare as diamonds in Kigen these nights. Its eyes were the colour of piss on fresh snow.

A cat. A demon-born bastard of a tomcat.

She knelt on the cobbles, scratched the creature behind one of its missing ears.

'Hello, Daken. Miss me?'

'*Mreowwwwl,*' he said, purring like a chainblade.

No One stomped up the tenement's narrow stairwell, Daken trailing behind. The walls were plastered with posters for the Kigen army, slapped up just days after Yoritomo-no-miya died; a recruitment drive targeting the city's poor and clanless, promising three squares a day, a clean bed, and a chance to die defending an empty chair.

Out onto the fourth-floor landing, she stepped over a crack-thin, crumpled figure, passed out in a puddle of his own waste. Grey skin, lotus-red eyes rolled back into his skull. It amazed her to think some fiends were still smoking now everybody knew how blood lotus was grown. Without sparing the wretch a glance, she unlocked her door and slipped inside.

'Sis.' Yoshi looked up from his card game. 'How do?'

Her brother sat on the floor beside a low table scattered with cards and coins. His hair was tied in rows of elaborate braids, spilling around his shoulders in black, knotted ripples. He was terribly pale, sharp-edged and handsome, the same pointed chin and dark, round eyes as his sister, glittering like shuriken beneath his brows. The shadows of his first whiskers were a pale dusting on his upper lip and cheeks. He was grubby as a cloudwalker, clothed in dirty rags. A conical straw hat with a jagged tear through the brim sat crooked on his head. One year older than she, but still a youth – gutter-lean, hard muscle and long-limbs, slowly filling out into the man beneath his surface.

'I'm all right,' she sighed. 'Can't believe you're still awake . . .'

'You're not so old I can't wait up for you, girl.' Yoshi hefted the bottle of cheap rice wine from the table. 'Besides, there's still a third left.'

She made a face, turned to the other boy. 'You winning, Jurou?'

Jurou glanced up from the other side of the table, fingers hovering close to his stack of copper bits. He was around Yoshi's age, shorter, darker in complexion. Softly curling bangs of black hair hung about shadowy eyes, cheeks flushed with wine. An empty smoking pipe dangled from pursed lips. A beautiful tiger tattoo coiled around a well-muscled arm; the kind you didn't usually see in Downside unless it was attached to a corpse with very empty pockets.

'Winning? Always.' Jurou shot her his heartbreaker smile, turned over a maple card and flicked the straw brim back from Yoshi's eyes. 'Lucky hat my ass.'

Yoshi swore and pushed across his coin. The flat was claustrophobic, furnished with a low table and mouldy cushions, dirty light guttering from a tungsten globe. A soundbox sat on the floor beside the boys; cheap tin and tangled copper wires, stolen from some peddler's wagon last winter. A tiny window ushered in the pitiful breeze, the sounds of the rising dawn outside: the city stretching its limbs, automated criers trawling the streets, steam whistles from the distant refinery.

No One splashed a handful of copper kouka on the table amidst the playing cards. The coins were rectangular, two strips of plaited metal, dulled from the press of a thousand fingers.

Jurou whistled. 'Izanagi's balls. A month of slinging brown for that pittance? You'd be better off begging in the street, girl.'

'I'd be better off pimping you down at the sky-docks, too, if you're that worried about it.'

'And we'd retire rich as lords in a fortnight.'

She laughed, and Jurou grinned around his empty pipe – the boy had quit smoking lotus once the origins of inochi fertilizer had broken, but chewing the stem had proven an unbreakable habit.

'Forgetting something?' Yoshi asked, raising a lazy eyebrow.

No One sighed, sinking down onto her haunches and scratching at the stippled scar below her eyepatch. She slipped a chunk of metal from inside her kimono, hefted it in her hand. The lump was snub-nosed with a thumb-broad barrel, matte-black and ugly as a copper-kouka whore. There was no symmetry to the design; it was all pipes and rivets and leaden menace. The handle was polished oak, inlaid with golden tigers, a deep scar in the wood from where its former owner had dropped it onto the cobbles at her feet as he died.

Shōgun Yoritomo's iron-thrower.

It was heavy in her hand, seemingly cold and dead. But she'd been there in the Market Square when its trigger was pulled on the Black Fox of Shima. She'd seen what it could do. What one little girl could do, too.

That was where it had started.

'Give it here,' Yoshi said. 'You'll blow your foot off.'

She passed the weapon back with a scowl, mumbled a threat about Yoshi's privates.

'Not sure why you insist on carrying that thing around with you,' Jurou mused.

'You try being a girl walking alone in this city at night,' she replied.

'We should sell it. Make a fortune.'

'There's fortunes to be made without selling anything.' Yoshi fixed Jurou in a pointed stare. 'Besides, what pawnman would be crazed enough to turn grist on the Shōgun's property?'

Her brother took a long pull from the bottle, glanced at her.

'So how was work?'

'Talk of clan war is all over the kitchens,' she shrugged. 'Dragon clan are gearing up to attack the Foxes. Rumour has it the local bushimen are going to kick out all the gaijin merchants in Docktown today. Tell the round-eyes to sail back to Morcheba or have their ships burned into the bay.'

'Do you do anything in that place beside gossip?' Jurou smiled.

'I don't gossip,' she pouted. 'I just listen.'

Daken prowled up to the table, sharing his evil, piss-eyed glare with both boys, lamplight glittering in dirty yellow. The cat sniffed, as if objecting to the smell of the booze, then jumped up on the window ledge to stare out at the dawn, half-tail swishing.

Jurou held out the bottle; a lethal brand of brown rice wine the locals affectionately called 'seppuku.'

'Drink?'

'You know that won't happen.'

The boy shrugged, placed the bottle back on the table. In the distance, the trio heard six tolls upon an iron bell; an automated Guild crier trundling the streets on rubber tank tracks and ringing in the Hour of the Phoenix. No One leaned down and turned on their little soundbox, started trawling the shortwave frequencies.

'Izanagi's balls, not the Kagé again . . .' Yoshi moaned.

'They transmit once an hour, one day a week,' she growled. 'And I have to listen to your serial melodramas every other day, so up with the shut.'

Yoshi adopted a mocking tone, spoke into his fist. 'You're on *rrrrr*radio Kagé. We'll be telling you how wonderful your lives are now the Shōgun's dead for the next five minutes, or until the Guild kicks in our door and we scatter like fleas when the dog comes scratching. Thanks for listen*iiiing*.'

'Least they're doing something,' she muttered. 'At least they *stand* for something. They're fighting to change the world, Yoshi.'

'Girl, if you were any more full of shit, your eye would be brown.'

'I'm supposed to point out my eye *is* brown now, right?'

'Oh my gods, when did that happen?'

She met his lopsided grin with a sour glare.

'Oh, come on now, sister mine.' Yoshi leaned over and gave her a hug, planted a noisy kiss on her cheek. 'You know it's just in fun.'

Jurou took the bottle from Yoshi. 'Seriously, girl. The way you glue your ears to those broadcasts . . . You'll be telling us you're joining up with those fools next . . .'

'Mad though she is, she's not *quite* mad enough for that,' Yoshi smirked.

No One pursed her lips, said nothing. After a long search on the radio, she found a scrabbling snatch of low-fidelity static. Eye narrowed with concentration, she adjusted the dial in tiny increments until she latched onto the signal.

The transmission was distorted, awash with faint white noise. Turning the volume down, she leaned close to the speaker. She didn't recognize the voice – truthfully she hadn't been with the Kagé long enough for introductions to more than a few members, the one safe house on Kuro Street. Less risk that way. For them and her. None of the local cell even knew each other by name – everyone went by some kind of handle to lessen damage in the event of a capture. When Grey Wolf had asked her what she wanted to be called, she'd considered something romantic – something exotic or dangerous sounding. The name of a hero from some childhood story. But in the end, 'No One' seemed to fit best.

She licked at dry lips, listened hard to the tiny voice.

'. . . *curfew still in effect eight weeks after Yoritomo's death. How long will this government continue to make its citizens prisoners in their own homes? Do they beat children and old women caught after dark without permits for the sake of your safety? Or because their slave state is crumbling? Because their fear of their own people is at last justified?*

'*Even now the Stormdancer is in council with Kagé leadership, planning their next strike against the murderous regime that has strangled this nation for two centuries. She is the tempest to wash away the dregs of the Kazumitsu Dynasty, and give birth to a shining new . . .'*

The sound of heavy iron boots and screams in the street outside made her flinch, and she turned the volume down to a whisper. Orders to halt in the name of the Daimyo were followed by scuffling and a wet crunch on cobblestones. A sharp cry of pain.

'Might want to turn that off for a bit,' Yoshi said. 'Unless you want to invite the bushi' up here for a drink?'

No One sighed, flipped a small switch and silenced the soundbox. She settled herself on the cushion next to her brother and Daken jumped down into her lap. The girl ran her fingers through the big tom's smoky fur, across the nubs where his ears used to be, the scars crisscrossing his body. The cat closed his eyes and purred like a motor-rickshaw.

'He stinks of dead rat,' Yoshi scowled.

'Funny that.' She gave the cat an experimental sniff.

'He shit in our bed again last night.'

The girl laughed. 'I know.'

Yoshi brandished the iron-thrower. 'He does it again, he might find himself divorced of more than ears.'

'Don't even joke like that.' She scowled daggers, held the cat close to her thin breast. Daken opened his eyes, stared directly at the boy. A low feline growl rumbled in his chest.

'You don't scare me, friend.' Yoshi waggled the weapon under the tom's nose.

She made a face. 'Little boy with his big toy.'

'Been telling stories about me again, Jurou?' Yoshi raised an eyebrow at the other boy, took another belt of rice wine. No One watched her brother drink, lips pressed shut, radiating faint disapproval. Even with one eye, she could stare down with the best of them, and Yoshi avoided her gaze. Draping Daken over her shoulder, she stood with a sigh.

'I'm going to bed.'

'What?' Jurou cried. 'You just got in!'

'I'd rather sleep than watch you two get drunk and slobber over each other.'

'Well, you should go out and find yourself a pretty man.' Jurou waggled his eyebrows. 'Slobber over him instead.'

'I've already got a man, don't I, Daken?' She planted a kiss on the cat's cheek, shuffled towards her room. 'Yes, I do, my big brave man.'

'*Mreoooowl*,' Daken said.

Yoshi stared at her back, a sour look on his face.

'Makes a fellow ponder gouging his eyes out just thinking on it.' He scowled at the cat flopped over his sister's shoulder, waved the bottle in his direction. 'I mean it, you little bastard. You shit our bed again, I'll feed you to the corpse-rats.'

The big tom blinked once, a broken-glass glint dancing in his eyes. His thoughts were a purr inside the siblings' heads, the whisper of black velvet on silken sheets.

. . . would not sleep with your mouth open tonight if i were you . . .

7
A Pale Inferno

Whether it's a reeking pit in the heart of Kigen city, or a comfortable house with barred windows amidst the branches of an ancient sugi tree, a prison is a prison is a prison.

The room was divided down the centre, thick bamboo bars separating the jailed from the jailers. Ayane sat against the far wall, her spine curved to accommodate the silver orb affixed between her shoulder blades. The long, thin spider legs sprouting from the bulbous hub were curled up against her back, motionless save for the broken limb trailing on the floor beside her. It had stopped spitting sparks once they'd come in from the rain, but still twitched occasionally, like a gutter-child stricken with palsy.

'I'm sorry.'

Kin stood outside the cell, hands wrapped around the bars. The forest air was cloying, sweat gleaming on his body. Ayane still wore the uwagi he'd given her, though she'd torn a hole in the back to accommodate her extra limbs. Someone had fished out a pair of oversized hakama to cover her legs, grubby and threadbare. Her feet were filthy, toes curling against the floorboards. The rain drummed insistent upon the ceiling.

'You need not apologize, Kin-san.' Ayane smiled despite her grim surroundings. 'You cannot blame them for being suspicious. If I were a Kagé who had turned myself over to the Guild, the Inquisition would have arranged far less comfortable accommodations.'

'The Inquisition.' Kin sighed. 'I haven't thought about them in a long time.'

'Do you still dream?' Ayane's eyes were wide. 'Your Awakening, I mean?'

'Every night since I was thirteen.'

Ayane sighed, stared at the floor.

'I hoped . . . once I unplugged . . .' She ran a hand over her bare scalp. 'It might stop.'

'What do you see?' Kin's voice was soft as smoke.

She shook her head. 'I do not want to talk about that.'

'Your What Will Be can't be any worse than mine.'

She looked up at him again, and he saw sorrow welling in her eyes.

'There are secrets, and then there are secrets, Kin-san.'

Ayane drew her knees up to her chest and hugged them tight. The delicate limbs at her back unfurled, one pair at a time, folding around her, cocooning her in five-feet lengths of sharpened chrome. The clicking of a hundred wet mandibles filled the air, cutting through the chilled hum of the wind amidst the trees, the paper-dry conversations of falling leaves. The broken limb twitched, illuminating her face with faint bursts of blue-white.

'It feels so strange to be out of my skin.' She rubbed her knees as if savouring the sensation. 'And First Bloom help me, the *smells*. I used to get skinless alone in my habitat, of course, but it was nothing like this . . .'

'Can you . . . feel them?' Kin pointed to the spider limbs. 'Like your flesh?'

'No.' She shook her head. 'But I feel them in my mind.'

'Does the broken one hurt?'

'It is giving me a headache.' A rippling shrug. 'But I will have to live with it.'

Kin looked around the tiny cell, the moisture beading on her skin, slick upon the iron padlock. He remembered his own time in here, the agony of his burns with no anesthetic to numb him; fear and uncertainty intensified by physical pain. Empty hours alone, listening to the sound of his own breathing and counting the endless minutes in his head.

'I've got a tool kit here.' He pointed at his belt. 'I could try fixing it?'

'Will that not get you in trouble?'

'They said you weren't to leave the cell. You're not.'

'Kin-san, I do not wish to cause you grief . . .'

Kin was already selecting tools from his belt. He gave her a small smile, held up a screwdriver. 'Turn around. Let's see what we can see.'

They sat together, her within the bars, him without, the hushed metallic tones of the tools and metal between them. As his fingers flitted over intricate clockwork, he realized how much he'd missed it – the language of the machine. The poetry of it. The absoluteness of it. A world governed by laws, immutable, unchangeable. A world of mass and force, equations and calibrations. So much simpler than a world of flesh, with all its chaos and complexity.

He murmured around the four screws pursed in his lips. 'It feels good to be working with my hands again.'

'I am surprised they are not worked to the bone.'

'What do you mean?'

'. . . Forgiveness.' The girl shook her head. 'I speak out of turn. It is not my place.'

Kin pulled the screws from his mouth, frowning. 'No, Ayane. Say what you think.'

'It is just . . . your knowledge could make life up here so much easier . . .' The girl shivered, shook her head. 'But no. I am a guest here. I do not understand their ways. I will be silent.'

Kin's frown deepened. 'Ayane, the Guild can't hurt you here. There are no Inquisitors waiting in the shadows, no Kyodai to punish you, no Blooms to answer to. You're your own person. Your choices are your own, too.'

'Then it is my right to choose to remain silent, is it not?'

'But why? You're free now. What's to be afraid of?'

Ayane glanced over her shoulder, spider limbs rippling.

'The girl all Guildsmen fear.'

*

Kaori's glare was the colour of water on polished steel, sharp at the edges.

'I cannot believe you brought it here.'

Four figures knelt in a semicircle around the fire pit in Daichi's dwelling, lit by crackling flame. The assembled faces belonged to the Kagé military council; hard eyes, cool expressions, sword-grip callouses on every hand. There was Kaori, of course, fringe draped over her face, clad in simple clothing of dappled green. Maro and Ryusaki sat together – broad, flat faces, nut-brown skin, deeply lidded eyes that seemed almost closed even when they were fully awake. Ryusaki had a shaved head, a long plaited moustache, his occasional smiles revealing gums bereft of most of his front teeth. Maro's hair was bound in warrior's braids and he was missing an eye, the left lens on the goggles slung about his neck painted black. The brothers were former samurai who'd served under Daichi's command, following him from Kigen city into the wilderness. Maro usually led the arson crew attacks on the southern lotus fields, and seemed perpetually wreathed in smoke. Ryusaki was a swordmaster, Michi's sensei, and the man had been teaching Yukiko some bladework in the few moments she found spare.

Daichi himself knelt in the centre, a cup of tea before him, fists on his knees. He ran his hand down through his long faded moustache, eyes the same blue-grey as his daughter's. His old-fashioned katana rested in an alcove at his back, sibling to the wakizashi Kaori carried – a scabbard of black enamel, embossed with golden cranes.

Yukiko put her palm to her brow, headache digging its boots into the back of her eyeballs. Sickness swelled in her stomach, the floor of Daichi's house rolling like the deck of a sky-ship in a storm. She'd tried to close off the Kenning, but could still feel Buruu waiting on the landing outside – a pale inferno burning in her mind's eye.

'It was either bring her with us or kill her, Kaori.'

'So kill her,' the woman snapped. 'Where is the issue?'

'I don't kill helpless girls with their hands bound at their sides.'

'She's not a girl,' Kaori growled. 'She's a godsdamn Guildsman.'

Peppermint tea. Burning cedar. Old leather, sword oil and dry flowers. A perfume filling Daichi's sitting room, filling her lungs and head, too much input, sharp and pointed inside her skull. She fancied she could still smell charring meat, hear the sizzle of her skin as Daichi pressed the burning blade to her tattoo.

Yukiko stood and walked to the window. The laughing fire

spread awful warmth into every corner, snapping blackened logs between its fingers and breathing smoke up through a beaten brass flue. She pushed the shutters aside, gulping down lungfuls of fresh, rain-sweet air.

Daichi watched Yukiko carefully, faint concern in his eyes.

'Nobody in this room has more reason to hate the Guild than me, Kaori.' Yukiko turned from the window, stared at the council. 'But I'm not certain I want to be a butcher.'

'The crews of those ironclads you destroyed might say otherwise,' Kaori said.

'Oh, you fuc— '

'We all do what needs to be done, Stormdancer,' Kaori snapped. 'You included. We will all turn the waters red when we bathe once this is finished. The lotus must burn.'

Yukiko looked to Daichi, waiting for him to weigh in, but the old man was staring at his hands, uncharacteristically silent.

'I wanted to check with you all before I did anything final.' Yukiko wiped sweat-soaked palms on her hakama legs. 'It's safe to bring her here. Kin assured me there's no way for the Guild to track her out of her skin.'

'And you trust him?' Maro scoffed.

'Of course I trust him.' Yukiko's voice was cold as winter morning. 'He saved my life. I trust him more than I trust you.'

'Be it made of scales or brass, a snake who sheds his skin is still a snake.'

'There is no steel in that boy,' Kaori said. 'No fire. Only treachery.'

'How can you say that?' Yukiko felt heat in her cheeks, memories of his lips rushing beneath her skin. 'He gave up everything to be here with us.'

'He gave up everything to be here with *you*,' Kaori said.

'He cares nothing for the revolution. If you left us, he'd be gone tomorrow. You are the reason he is here, Stormdancer. Open your eyes.'

Yukiko drew breath to reply, but found no words.

'You're the reason. The first and only reason.'

'This is not about the boy.' Sensei Ryusaki's low growl cut through the tension. 'This is about the Guildsman, and what we do with it.'

'Kill it,' Maro said flatly. 'Their kind are poison. The lotus must burn.'

'I agree,' Yukiko nodded. 'We'd be fools to trust it.'

She looked amongst the council, noted the surprise on their faces.

'Look, I know that might make me a bitch, but at least I'm not a *stupid* bitch.'

'What if this girl speaks the truth?' Daichi's voice cut the air like a knife. 'What if there are more like her in the Guild?'

'Impossible,' Kaori said.

'Arashitora were impossible too, a few months ago.' Daichi's voice was rough as bluestone gravel. 'Now look at the magnificence outside this room.'

The council looked out through the open doorway at the thunder tiger sprawled upon the deck. Buruu was stretched out in the rain, idly tearing up talonfuls of planking. His yawn sent tremors through the floor.

TELL THEM IT IS RUDE TO STARE. EVEN AT MAGNIFICENCE.

Hush! Gods, you're too loud. Go back to sleep.

She felt the thunder tiger trying to hold himself back, aware of her pain, allowing only a sliver of himself to creep across the bond between them. And though his thoughts were tinged with bright, crackling feedback, at least the volume receded to a tolerable level.

HOW CAN I SLEEP WITH YOUR MIND SO FULL OF NOISE?

I suppose you want to venture an opinion on all this?

YES. BUT I AM STILL BASKING IN THE 'MAG-NIFICENT' COMMENT. GIVE ME A MOMENT . . .

'Father, you cannot mean to trust it.' Kaori placed her hand on the old man's knee.

Daichi sipped his tea, cleared his throat. 'All I say is consider if she speaks truth. Think of what it would gain us to start a rebellion within the Guild. Think of the damage we could do. This girl could be the secret to bringing down the chi-mongers once and for all.'

Yukiko met the old man's gaze. 'I don't think we can trust her.'

'Can we not, Stormdancer? Yet in the same breath, you would tell us to treat your Kin as one of our own?'

AH, THERE IT IS.

Yukiko winced, turned her head aside as if from an incoming slap.

Too loud!

Buruu pulled himself back again, curling inward until only a splinter remained.

I AM SORRY. I NEED NOT SHARE MY THOUGHTS WHEN THIS OLD MAN SPEAKS THEM FOR ME. I WILL REMAIN MAGNIFICENTLY SILENT.

'I wish you wouldn't call me that.' Yukiko folded her arms, ignoring Buruu's smug, self-satisfied warmth.

'Stormdancer?' Daichi's eyebrows were raised over the rim of his teacup.

'It's not my name.'

'It is what you are.'

'The way you all look at me . . . it's like you expect to see lightning coming out of my hands, or flowers blooming wherever I walk. I haven't done anything yet, and you act like I've saved the world.'

'You have given people hope,' Daichi said. 'That is a precious thing.'

'It's a dangerous thing.'

'No more dangerous than executing this girl for the sin of what she used to be.'

'Gods, Daichi, when we first came here you were willing to murder Kin on exactly the same suspicion. You were willing to kill me over a tattoo.'

'Perhaps I have learned a few lessons since then. From a new sensei.' Daichi smiled. 'And you say you haven't done anything yet.'

Yukiko stared at the old man, mute and still. It wasn't so long ago she was standing over him in this very room, knife at his throat while he demanded she kill him. But it seemed every time Daichi spoke, some new facet of him came to light. His hatred of the Guild and government was tempered by steady hands and a fierce, calculating mind. She could see why the Kagé followed him. Why they were willing to risk their lives for his vision.

The truth was, he was a natural leader – the leader she feared she'd never be. All she had was the desire for revenge. The memory of her father's death, his blood warm and sticky on her hands, bubbling on his lips as he died. The thought of it threatened to overwhelm her, pulsing in time with the headache splitting the bone at the base of her skull.

'It seems somehow out of balance, does it not?' Daichi

coughed hard, cleared his throat as he looked around the council. 'To spare the boy and end the girl?'

'We can always kill them both,' Kaori said.

Yukiko rubbed her pounding temples, closed her bloodshot eyes. She could feel the forest all around her, the myriad lives just beyond the window, the heat and chatter of their minds rising in her own. A barrage. A bedlam. Concussive and sickening, pouring over her like scalding water. And as she closed her eyes, tried to stifle the fires burning in her head, to her amazement, her absolute horror, she realized she could sense other pulses within the Kenning. Something beyond the fluttering thoughts of birds, the faint and furtive impulses of small warm things, the boiling heartbeat of the thunder tiger just outside the door.

She could feel the Kagé too.

Blurry and indistinct, all heat and light, alien shapes and impossible tangles of emotion. Everywhere. Like the answer to a perception puzzle that, once seen, can never be missed. She remembered reaching out to Yoritomo's mind in the Market Square, trying to hold on to him like a handful of sand. But now, effortlessly, she could feel every person in the village. A low-level hum stacked upon itself, one person at a time, until the entire world was shapeless noise. She bent double, blinking hard, Buruu rising to his feet and whining.

SISTER?

Daichi took another sip of tea, his voice a dry whisper.

'Are you well, Stormdancer?'

She smoothed the hair from her brow, the sensation of her fingertips like sledgehammers across her skin. She tried to close herself off, to force the noise and heat away, curling up inside herself and closing down the Kenning completely.

Gods, what's wrong with me?

'Yukiko,' Daichi said. 'Are you well?'

She took a deep breath, exhaled slow. The world had fallen quiet, and yet she could still feel it, just outside her skull. The tide of it rushing back out to sea before its next surge, a tsunami rising to blot out the sun. She in its shadow, standing an insect high.

'I have a headache, Daichi-sama.'

'Perhaps you should rest?' Kaori asked.

'How can I rest?' She blinked at the older woman, out of breath as if she'd been sprinting. 'The Lotus Guild is trying to reforge Kazumitsu's Dynasty and you're talking about killing Kin? We should be talking about Hiro. The wedding. What are we doing to stop it?'

'The Kuro Street cell are already at work,' Kaori said. 'We have an operative inside the palace walls. The ceremony is weeks away. Calm yourself.'

'I am calm!'

'Yukiko . . .' Daichi said.

SISTER.

'No, godsdammit!' she shouted. 'The whole nation was ready to rise a few days ago, and now you're sitting on your hands while it all slips—'

'Yukiko!'

Daichi shouted this time, gravelled voice like a slap on her skin. She forced herself to be still, caught her breath, felt Buruu's concern flooding her receptors. The world pulsing, the thoughts of everyone in the room building against her crumbling little dam as the whole earth beneath her swayed.

'What?' she hissed.

'Your ears are bleeding,' Daichi said.

She reached up to her head, felt the flood of thick warmth

down the sides of her neck, spattering on the floor. Black suns imploded in her vision, tiny singularities folding in upon themselves and drawing her with them. Buruu was at the doorway, his thoughts a storm in her skull, the crunch and crumble of thunder interspersed with white strobes of crackling lightning. She fought for breath, for space, for a moment's silence inside her head.

The tide came rolling in.

The walls trembling, the floor beneath her rolling. She sank to her knees, clutching her temples, heard the clatter of the tiny ornaments on Daichi's shelves, chess pieces tumbling and falling. People on their feet, shouting, their thoughts impossible to keep at bay, flooding into her and out of her nostrils in scarlet floods. A teacup smashing on the boards. Daichi's sword falling from the wall. Cries of alarm from the villagers outside as the trees literally trembled in their roots, and in her head a tangle, a briar, thorned and tearing, all of their thoughts, their hopes, their fear (gods, their fear), everything they were and could have been and wanted to be filling her up and pulling her down to the dark beneath her feet.

YUKIKO!

Buruu, help me!

WHAT ARE YOU DOING?

I can't keep it out!

It rose up on black wings, like some forgotten beast beneath the bed in the days when blankets were armour and her father's voice the only sword she needed to keep the dark at bay. But he was gone, gone to his pyre, gone to the great judge Enma-ō. She could see him now; the ashes of offerings daubed on his face, cadaverous skin hanging loose from his bones, black blood still leaking from the hole in his throat. Her hands on the wound, trying to stop the flow, but it was too much, too deep, too late. Heat and thoughts and screams and floods, and as it rose up to swallow her, she felt Buruu in the black, groping towards her, burning in her mind.

HOLD ONTO ME.

Buruu!

HOLD ONTO ME, SISTER.

A tracery of blood vessels pulsing across the backs of her eyelids, strobing light beyond.

Reaching for him, her rock, her anchor, all that held her still in that gnashing swell.

His wings about her, ozone and feathers and warmth, soft as pillows.

And into the dark, she fell.

8

No One

No matter the shape of the shoreline, or the colour of the horizon, there are three breeds of drunk to be found beneath the rising and setting of the sun.

There's the jovial kind who takes to the bottle when he has cause to celebrate, who has a few too many at festival feasts and revels in the rush of blood to his cheeks. He slurs his songs and argues with his friends about the gaijin war or the last arena match, grinning to the eyeteeth all the while. And though he might swim deep in the bottle, he doesn't drown, and when he looks at the bottom he can still see his own reflection and smile.

Then there's the kind who drinks like it's his calling. Hunched silent over his glass, charging headlong towards stupor as fast as lips and throat can take him. He takes no joy in the journey, nor solace in company upon the road, but he keens for his destination with an intensity that leaves shadows under his eyes. Oblivion. A sleep where the dreams are so far submerged beneath Forgetting's warm embrace that their voices are a vibration rather than a sound, like a mother's lullaby in the blurred days before words had shape or meaning.

And then, there was No One's father.

Seven shades mean, the kind who saw the bottle as a doorway to the black inside. A solvent to peel the paint from his mask, the luster of bone and blood beneath. A mumbled excuse for what had happened the last time, and the unspoken promise why it would happen the next.

The bottle's lips pressed against his own like a mistress, a balm discovered in empty days after he returned from the war overseas. A tranquilizer to silence the cries of the gaijin that still haunted his dreams, numb the pain of the parts he was missing. And though he was a gambler too, hopeless and helpless, the bottle was his first and truest love.

But he loved her too, in his own stumbling, ugly way. He called their mother 'bitch,' her brother 'bastard.' But his daughter? His dearest? His flower? Even at his worst, he still called her by name.

Hana.

Her earliest memories of her mother were of tears spilling from swollen eyes, irises of gleaming blue. Of slumped shoulders, trembling hands and broken fingers. Of screamed abuse. Open palms and bloody lips and spitting teeth. Long days without a crumb to eat. Brief periods of plenty, of laden tables and tiny toys (dolls for her, soldiers for her brother) that he would give them with his broad, broken-toothed smile, and hock to the pawnman a few weeks later.

Running in the gutters of Yama city with other orphans of the bottle or the smoke or the war, she and Yoshi, both harder than a Lotusman's skin by the time she was six. Violence and grime and bloody knuckles, wrapped in the stink of chi and shit. Fistfights. Broken glass. Blacklung beggars rotting in drains, or coughing their last in the squeezeways where the children played and laughed and forgot, if only for a moment. But through it all, they had each other. At least she and Yoshi had each other.

Blood is blood.

And then Father bought the farm. Literally. A tiny crop of lotus near Kigen city, snatched on a triple-nine hand in some yakuza smoke house. War hero turned man of the land. And so they left Yama, caught an airship south to Kigen; the first and only time in her life she'd ever flown. The engines were a thrum in her bones, and the wind a shower of gentle kisses on her cheeks, and she stood at the prow and watched the world sailing away beneath them, wishing they would never, ever have to come down from the clouds.

Yoshi hated him. Hated him like poison. But even when the beatings became too numerous to count, when the bottle had stolen all he was and would ever be, she loved him. She loved him with all her heart.

She couldn't help it.

He was her da.

*

She'd rolled out of bed before the sunset and dragged on her servant's clothes, the taste of stale exhaust buttered on her tongue. Washing her face in their bucket of tepid water, she felt at her cheek, her eyebrow, the scar tissue smooth beneath her fingers. Her memory awash with the gleam of candlelight on broken glass. Spit and blood. She straightened the patch over her eye, smoothed her unruly bob down as best she could and prepared to inhale her night. A glance into Yoshi and Jurou's bedroom showed both boys asleep, sprawled across grubby sheets, mercifully free of cat excrement.

Bye, Daken.

The tom was sitting at the windowsill, a black silhouette against the slowly darkening sky, watching her with piss-coloured eyes.

. . . careful . . .

No One picked up the iron-thrower, lying amidst the empty bottles and scattered playing cards. She slipped the weight into a hidden pocket beneath her shoulder, patted its bulk.

I'm always careful. See you tonight.

. . . will see you first . . .

Out the door and down the stairs into dirty streets and long shadows, hundreds of people scurrying about their business before the nighttime curfew fell. The city's stink was waiting for her – human waste, black seawater and chi fumes. Autumn's chill was a welcome relief after the blistering summer, but the scarlet sunset was still bright as a blast furnace, and she slipped her decrepit goggles over her eye to spare it the burn.

She could feel the noise pressing on her skin, the bustle and murmur of people hurrying to end their day, the hum of motor-rickshaw, generator growls. Beneath it all, more a vibration than a sound, she could sense the subtle ring of discontent. Of anger. Broken glass crunching underfoot, the straw-dry crackle of tinder, ready to ignite. Graffiti splashed over army recruitment posters; the same message on almost every street.

ARASHI-NO-ODORIKO COMES.

She walked over the tar-black Shoujo and Shiroi rivers, into the cramped symmetry of Upside. Here the mood shifted; neo-chōnin merchants scurrying about, hunched shoulders and nervous glances, market stalls standing empty. The sun was kissing the horizon by the time she made it to the palace grounds, bowing low before the gate guards, proffering her permit with downcast gaze. The lowly Shit Girl was unworthy of evening salutations, of course, and the men simply opened the gate and stood aside. The thought of speaking to a Burakumin would no more have crossed their minds than the thought of addressing raw sewage floating in the gutter.

Courtiers gathered in multicoloured knots, murmurs hidden behind breather and fluttering fan, watchful eyes narrowed to paper cuts as she made her way to the royal wing to begin her nightly duties. A trio of wretchedly thin tigers strained against their chains in the gloom-soaked courtyard, wheezing in the poisoned air. Once she entered the Daimyo's wing, everywhere she walked, the chirp and skritch and creak of nightingale floors followed like a shadow.

If the floors were not enough to dissuade potential assassins, the Guild had released a swarm of what were apparently called 'spider-drones' inside the palace a week ago. The devices were fist-sized, set with a windup key and eight segmented legs, needle-sharp. They crawled the halls, the ceilings, delicate clockwork innards *tick-tick-ticking*. She'd picked one up out of curiosity when they first appeared, and it had vibrated in her hand and sang *tang!tang!tang!* until she put it down again. A fellow servant had warned her the devices transmitted everything they saw to their Guild masters, and from that day forth, No One had been looking over her shoulder for the accursed little machines. Between the floors and the Guild's eyes, Lord Hiro's claim to the throne was looking more secure by the day.

Stopping outside the Daimyo's suite, she bowed low to the Iron Samurai guarding his door. Their golden tabards declared them members of the Kazumitsu Elite – the guardians of the royal line, wreathed in the shame of failure after the Shōgun's assassination. They stood seven feet tall in their suits of ō-yoroi armour, all pistons and clockwork and roof-broad spaulders, chainsaw katana and wakizashi crossed at their waists. In the days before Yoritomo's death, their suits had been enamelled black, but now the armour was painted bone-white; the colour of death daubed onto living men.

She'd heard rumours about the night of the Inochi Riots, when news of the Guild's atrocities against gaijin war prisoners had first broken over the wireless. Stories about a legion of pale ghosts issuing forth from the royal palace to crush the uprising into the dust. A young captain leading their charge, flames glinting in eyes as green as hellsfire.

An almost imperceptible nod told No One she was allowed inside. Bowing low, she pulled aside the double doors, gaze downturned, shoulders hunched.

'Try now,' said a metallic, sibilant voice.

She stepped into the room, taking in the lantern-light scene before dropping to her knees and pressing forehead to floorboard. Three Guildsmen were gathered around a hospice chair. The first pair were indistinguishable; vaguely feminine in form, clad in skintight, earth-brown membranes and long, buckle-studded aprons. Silver orbs were affixed to their spines, eight long, gleaming limbs unfolding in a razor-sharp halo about them. They had featureless faces and bulbous eyes, glowing heartsblood red.

She recognized the third Guildsman immediately – Kensai, Second Bloom of Chapterhouse Kigen, voice of the Guild in the Tiger capital. A hulking figure over six feet tall, muscular lines shaped into the atmos-suit of burnished brass covering his flesh. Eyes aglow. Mechabacus on his chest, stuttering and chattering the indecipherable language of the machine. Disconcertingly, the face molded into the Second Bloom's helm was that of a perfect, beautiful boy, segmented iron piping spilling from a mouth frozen in a perpetual scream. As always, the sight of him unleashed a slick of cold fear in the girl's belly.

'Lord Hiro, please.' Kensai's voice was an iron rasp. 'Try again.'

No One glanced up swiftly, focused on the figure reclining in the hospice chair. Long dark hair and a pointed goatee. Piercing green eyes, like Kitsune jade. High cheekbones and smooth skin, bronzed and well-muscled, six small hills on an abdomen that seemed carved of kiri wood. She thought he could have been handsome in a different place, a different time. But sleepless nights had drawn grey circles around those beautiful eyes, and lack of appetite (she'd noted his meals were always untouched) had left him gaunt and stretched.

Lord Hiro lifted his right arm, frown darkening his brow, closing his fingers one by one.

No matter how many times she saw it, she had to admire the artistry. The ball-joint digits with their case-hardened tendons. The intricate lace of machinery, at once awful and beautiful. A hissing, whirring construct, cogs and interlocking teeth, crafted of dull, grey iron.

A clockwork arm.

'Excellent,' Kensai breathed. 'Your response speed is most promising.'

'Will I be able to wield a sword soon?' Lord Hiro's voice came from far away.

'Certainly.' A spider-woman nodded, silver limbs flexing. 'The prosthetic is far stronger than mere meat and bone. But the finesse with which you wield a weapon is up to you. Practise, Hiro-sama. Skin is strong. Flesh is weak.'

'The lotus must bloom,' Kensai murmured.

The Tiger Daimyo stood slowly, flexing the arm amidst the hiss of pistons and small bursts of chi exhaust. An iron cuff sleeved his shoulder, hiding the junction where metal ended and meat began. His other shoulder was tattooed with the imperial sun, burning across sculpted muscle, a newly inked cluster of lotus blooms beneath indicating his rank as a clanlord. A Daimyo. Master of the Tiger zaibatsu.

Impressive work for an eighteen-year-old.

Slipping on a loose, silken robe, he finally spotted No One kneeling on the floor, caught her in the midst of one furtive glance. Blanching, she pressed her head back to the boards, heart pounding in her chest. She should have waited until they were gone. Should have started with the ministerial chambers instead of coming here, falling under those bloody stares—

'Be about your business, girl,' the Tiger Lord said.

'Great Lord.'

She stood swiftly, making her way into the dim bedchamber beyond. Kneeling by the chamber pot, listening to the drone of the Second Boom's voice.

'The Phoenix clanlords have accepted invitation to your wedding, great Lord. The *Floating Palace* is already on its way here. We have it on good authority the Dragons will soon follow. With Ryu and Fushicho ratifying your claim, the Kitsune will soon fall into line. If not, any thoughts of rebellion will be crushed once the Foxes set eyes on your wedding gift.'

'Wedding gift?'

'Hai. I will take you to Jukai province for an inspection. A week or so from now.'

'I have never been fond of surprises, Kensai.'

'Then this will be a first, great Lord.'

No One stood slowly, frowning, chamber pot in hand.

Wedding gift? What in the Maker's name . . . ?

She'd lingered too long for answers. Slipping from the bedchamber, gaze downturned, she carried her clay burden across the room. The assemblage paid her no more attention than a stain on the floor. The spider-women were packing away their tools, the Tiger Lord standing on the balcony, staring out over his city as evening smothered it into silence. The Second

Bloom loomed at his back, the smell of grease and chi thick in the air.

'Now,' Kensai said. 'We must speak of these . . . funerary theatrics among you and the other Kazumitsu Elite . . .'

Out the door, ducking between the two towering hulks of death-white iron standing vigil. Her mind awhirl. She had to get to the Kuro Street safe house, report to Grey Wolf. But to avoid suspicion, she'd have to work her full shift, straight-faced, no pace in her step, no fear in her eye. The girl nobody wanted, nobody knew. An insignificance in human guise, no more worthy of concern or notice than a cockroach crawling in the cracks.

Forcing those cracks wider by the day.

I am nothing.

I am No One.

*

The earthquake struck soon afterwards – a thirty-second tremor shaking the palace walls, vases tumbling from their perches and tapestries from their hooks. The fitful tremblings of the ground beneath their feet provided momentary distraction amidst the mounting courtly intrigue, but of course, it was left to the servants to clear up the mess afterwards. The house mistress was furious and No One, being who she was, wore the worst of her temper.

Lady Sun was perhaps half an hour from waking by the time No One escaped the palace. The girl walked slowly, straw hat pulled down low, through the grounds and out into the predawn still. She saw a beggar on an empty street corner, walking in circles, claiming the quake was proof of Lord Izanagi's displeasure at the impending royal wedding. As she watched, the poor wretch was beset by fresh-faced bushimen in Hiro's colours and treated to an impromptu boot party. When pressed by their captain, she showed her permit, and hurried on her way.

Across the river to Downside, daylight still an empty vow on the eastern horizon. Daken met her in his usual spot, slinking from the alley mouth like a blade from its sheath, the scent of freshly murdered corpse-rat smeared on his muzzle as he purred and pressed his face to hers.

. . . saw you first . . .

Clever. You want to keep lookout for me again?

. . . we go to thin house . . ?

Just for a little while. I need to see my friends.

. . . Yoshi come . . ?

No, Daken. Yoshi can't know about them. My friends are a secret, remember?

. . . many secrets . . .

You won't tell him, will you?

. . . have not told you his, have i . . ?

The tom gifted her with a smug gaze, turned and dashed off into the gloom. For all his size, Daken moved like a shadow, silent as tombstones. From the tumbledown rooftops, he could see for miles – better than anyone who might follow her through the twisted labyrinth into Docktown. Hands hidden in her sleeves, the comforting weight of the iron-thrower beneath her arm, No One set off through the sprawl towards the bitter reek of Kigen Bay.

Doubling back. Checking at corners. Watching reflections in dirty shop-front glass. Just like they'd taught her. Her induction into the Kagé had been swift; need dictating pace. After witnessing Yoritomo's death at the Stormdancer's hands, a tiny spark had flared inside her, dimly illuminating a formerly lightless corner of her mind. The notion of rebelling – of not only standing apart but working *against* the government – it simply wasn't something she'd ever considered possible. But it was surprising how the pillars of an unshakable worldview could be reduced to rubble when a sixteen-year-old girl murders the Lord of the Imperium right in front of you. Impossible notions become plausible in the face of an event that tectonic.

The problem being, of course, she had no way of tracking the Kagé down. No ingress through the doors of the cabal. The spark inside her flickered and dimmed, no kindling to help it flourish. Yoshi kept her clear of the Inochi Riots – told her flatly the systematic murder of thousands of gaijin prisoners for the sake of a flower crop was none of their business. But when the Stormdancer returned and made her speech in the Market Square during Yoritomo's funeral, when the girl had looked into the crowd and stared right at *her*, No One had felt the spark burst into ravenous flame. As the Stormdancer had taken to the sky, despite the risks, despite knowing it was foolish, No One had found her fist in the air and tears in her eye and known, simply *known* she had to do something more.

The very next day, she'd been approached by Grey Wolf.

The safe house was an unassuming building, crammed between two warehouses, close to the towering sky-spires. Kuro Street was narrow, stubborn weeds struggling through the cracks into a life of suffocating exhaust. Boarded windows. Street courtesans beneath paper parasols stained grey by the toxic rain. Gutters overflowing with garbage, lotus fiends and blacklung beggars – just another stretch of Docktown real estate to any without eyes to see the truth of it.

No One nodded to one of the Kagé lookouts (a twelve-year-old girl inexplicably named 'Butcher,' who had the most astonishingly foul mouth she'd ever heard) and walked up to the safe house's narrow facade. Knocking four times, waiting until a thin elderly woman opened the door. She was dressed in dark cloth, silver hair in a single braid, mouth covered by a black kerchief. Her back bent, fingers worn, old lines deepened by hardship at the corners of her eyes.

'Grey Wolf.' No One bowed.

The old woman motioned with her head. 'Come in.'

They walked past a narrow dining area, descending creaking stairs into a dingy cellar. The walls had been knocked out, connecting the basements of the neighbouring buildings into one large room, multiple stairwells leading up into the adjacent structures. An impressive collection of radio equipment was arranged on a long table, maps of Kigen on the walls. A young woman with sleepy eyes was bent over the rig, at work with a soldering iron. A few others were scattered around the room, falling still as she entered. The biggest of them – a towering lump of muscle with shovel-broad hands – regarded her with an even stare.

'Who's this?'

'Our friend in the palace,' Grey Wolf said. 'Now come and say hello, you rude sod. You're not so big I can't take to you with the wooden spoon.'

The man smiled, and favouring his right leg, limped over and offered a bow. He stood a good foot taller than No One. Strong jaw, thick neck, cheeks that hadn't felt a razor's touch in weeks. His right shoulder was tattooed with a beautiful phoenix, his left with the Imperial Sun (she'd learned quickly that city operatives didn't burn off their ink). He had a handsome face framed by tight braids, hard eyes ringed in shadow. A kusarigama hung from his obi, the sickle blade almost hidden by the folds of his grubby trousers.

'No One,' Grey Wolf said. 'We call this unshaven lump the Huntsman.'

No One bowed. 'Forgive my rudeness, but I have news.'

The Grey Wolf's matronly smile evaporated. 'What is it, child?'

'The Fushicho clanlords have thrown in with Lord Hiro. They will attend his wedding, and almost certainly support him as Shōgun. The Ryu are apparently set to roll over and ask to have their bellies scratched too.'

Grey Wolf sighed, shook her head. 'So easily. I had hoped . . .'

'Their oaths bind them to the Kazumitsu,' the big man said. 'If the dynasty lives, so does their obligation. But without the wedding, there's no way in hells the Dragons would bow to someone like Hiro. Their army is huge. And the Phoenix hate bowing to anyone.'

'The Kitsune still have not answered. Perhaps the Foxes will choose—'

'Forgiveness, please,' No One interrupted. 'But there is more. The Second Bloom was speaking of a wedding gift for Lord Hiro. An inspection tour in Jukai province.'

The Huntsman raised one eyebrow. 'What kind of gift?'

'I don't know. Maybe they're building something? A weapon?'

Grey Wolf turned to one of the men by the radio rig. 'Sparrow, send word to the Iishi. Ask if the Stormdancer's Guildsman knows anything about this business.'

'How's Michi?' the Huntsman asked. 'Have you spoken to her?'

'Still under house arrest. All of Aisha's maidservants are. Lord Hiro has appointed his cousin as Lord Magistrate, a man named Ichizo. He's questioning the girls personally.'

'At least she's out of Kigen jail,' the big man sighed. 'I told her not to go back there . . .'

'She said she couldn't abandon—'

. . . beware . . .

Daken's thoughts flared in the Kenning, dulled with distance, sharp with urgency. She could feel him prowling rooftops to the north, caught a glimpse of the jagged skyline through his eyes, the sun just beginning to crest the horizon as a cruel stink drifted in off the bay.

What's wrong?

. . . men coming iron clothes many . . .

Soldiers?

. . . yes . . .

'Gods.' No One glanced around the room, palms sweating. 'We have to go.'

'What?' Grey Wolf frowned. 'What do you —'

'There are bushimen coming. Lots of them. We have to get out of here. Now.'

'I didn't hear any lookout sig—'

A brief whistle sounded in the streets above, two notes, faint and sharp. The signal was repeated, closer, drifting down the narrow stairwell.

'Dawn raid . . .' the old woman whispered.

It seemed to No One the next moment stretched for an age. Grey Wolf and the Huntsman exchanging glances. Faces paling ever so slightly, eyes growing wide. Daken's urgent thoughts pressing on her own – the image of bushimen in blood-red tabards pouring through the alleyways towards the safe house. And all at once, everyone in the basement was moving; snatching up weapons and radio equipment, tearing maps from walls. The Huntsman grabbed No One's arm, looked her hard in the eye.

'Were you followed?'

'Of course not!'

'Are you certain?'

'My lookout saw them before yours did!'

Grey Wolf was directing the other Kagé, the old woman's voice calm as a millpond, hard as folded steel. 'You all know the protocols. Check your drop boxes for word, speak to nobody until you hear from us. Move, move!'

Kagé were already scattering up the different stairwells into the neighbouring buildings, a few casting baleful glares at No One as they left. The big man was still in her face, anger plain in his eyes. Grey Wolf poked him in the chest to get his attention.

'I said get out. Go! Take No One with you!'

'Are you mad?' the Huntsman growled. 'I'm not taking her anywhere.'

'Wait, you think I sold you out?' No One was incredulous. 'This raid is coincidence, then?'

'If I wanted to give away the safe house, I could have just told the bushi' where you were! I'd have to be an idiot to come here on the day they raided you!'

'Maybe you *are* an idiot,' the big man said.

A defiant scowl. 'Pardon me, Huntsman-sama, but maybe you can kiss my—'

A cry of pain from upstairs, the percussion of running feet. Blades being drawn. Steel on steel. Roared commands to halt in the Daimyo's name. A flurry of multicoloured profanity from Butcher. Grey Wolf slapped the big man on the arm.

'I said get out right now!'

'What about you?'

'I can take care of myself,' the old woman said. 'This girl is our only road into the palace. We need her. Make sure she gets away safely, Huntsman.'

The big man cursed, glancing up at the crash of splintering wood, heavy footsteps on the floorboards. Struggling bodies and defiant curses. 'All right, come on.'

He grabbed her hand before she could protest, dragged her up the left-hand stairwell and into an abandoned warehouse. Hauling her fast as his limp could take him, through the back door and out into the glare of a rear squeezeway. No One heard breaking glass behind, hoarse screams, a flare of sunburnt light. She felt Daken in her mind, flitting across the rooftops, closing her eye and seeing through his. Bushimen closing in from all directions. Bodies prostrate in the street outside; some lying obediently with their hands on their heads, others bleeding quietly onto broken cobbles. The Huntsman dragged her west along the squeezeway, but she pulled back sharply, shaking her head.

'Not that way.'

'What?'

'There's too many. Come on.'

The big man paused, reluctant and glacial. But pulling insistently on his wrist, she tugged him back along the thin alley, shrouded in the stink of rat urine. Sleek, furred shapes slunk away at their approach. Empty bottles, human waste, crumpled newssheets. They cut down the crowded brickway, the Huntsman limping hard, No One's heart slapping the inside of her rib cage as she pulled up her goggles against spears of rusted daylight. Army recruitment posters smeared with white paint; a defiant warning in tall, bold kanji.

ARASHI-NO-ODORIKO COMES.

Out onto a main street, a limping dash across open ground into another alley. Squeezing through the narrow space, knee-deep in refuse, her grip on the Huntsman's fingers slippery with sweat. Distant shouts. The tune of clashing steel, the thunder of iron-shod boots.

'How do you know where you're going?' he gasped.

'Trust me.'

On they ran, or ran as best they could with the big man's limp. His face was twisted, sweat-slick. One hand wrapped in hers, the other pressed to his right thigh, blood seeping through his pants leg. Two blocks later, No One was beginning to think they were in the clear when she heard Daken whisper a warning from above. Moments later, shouts echoed up the street, heavy tread ringing on the cobbles, citizens around them scattering. Two bushimen were charging, naginata spears outthrust, roaring 'Halt in the Daimyo's name!'

The Huntsman cursed, shoulders slumping, pulling his hand from her grip.

'This bastard leg . . .' he sighed. Unslinging the kusarigama from his waist, he hefted the sickle-shaped blade in one massive fist and nodded to her. 'Go on, girl. Best keep running. If you're the one who sold us out, I pray that Enma-ō feeds you to the hungry dead when you die.'

The big man turned to face the charging soldiers, letting his kusarigama's chain slip through his fingers, swinging it around his head. With luck he'd take down one soldier before the second skewered him – but there was no chance he'd be walking away alive. No One blinked away the sweat, saw the inevitable outcome in her mind's eye. The Huntsman sinking to the floor, chest punctured, ribs broken. Running back to her little hovel and little life, cut off from the Kagé as events spiralled out of control . . .

She squinted at the oncoming soldiers, realized they were raw recruits only a few years older than she. Scarlet tabards over banded breastplates, embroidered tigers, new kerchiefs. Young men, probably brought up on these same narrow streets, drafted into the military with the promise of regular meals and a place to belong.

The Huntsman threw his kusarigama, the weapon wrapping itself around an oncoming spear. The big man jerked the chain, pulling the wielder off balance and into an elbow that landed like falling concrete, snapping the boy's jaw loose. Swinging the sickle blade, the Huntsman buried it in the bushiman's neck, sent the soldier spinning away in a spray of red. His comrade roared, furious, thrusting his blade straight towards the big man's heart.

No One raised a fistful of iron.

The shot was impossibly loud, recoil kicking up her forearm, knocking a frightened cry from her lips. The bushiman clutched his neck, a sticky red flower blooming in his fingers as he spun on the spot, gasping, scarlet gushing as he collapsed on the road in ruins.

The Huntsman was staring at her dumbfounded, a thin wisp of smoke rising from the iron-thrower's barrel into the breathless space between them.

'If the Great Judge sends the hungry dead anywhere near me,' she gasped, 'I'll kick his privates so hard his throat will have three lumps.'

'Where the hells did you get that?'

. . . more coming go go . . .

'Later,' she said. 'We have to move.'

The giant stooped, pulled his blade loose with a grunt, wiped the spatter of red from his face on his sleeve.

. . . friend . . ?

No One looked to the rooftop overhead. She could see Daken's silhouette against the bloody sky, a black shadow upon the eave, peering down to the drenched cobbles below. He saw the dead bushimen and licked his jowls.

Maybe . . .

'Huntsman, we need to go . . .'

'I have a flat, north of Downside.' The big man wrapped his kusarigama back around his waist. 'It's a trek, but we can lay low there for a while.'

No One eyed his leg, the bloodstain seeping through the fabric of his hakama. 'My place is much closer. Easier to get to.'

'Is it safe?'

'Safer than being out here in broad daylight.'

The Huntsman looked around the street, down at the cooling meat at his feet.

. . . they coming . . .

'We need to go,' she said. 'If you still think I brought the bushi' here, ask yourself why I just shot one of them right in front of you. Ask yourself why I don't blow out your kneecaps now and wait for more to arrive.'

He licked the sweat from his lips. Stared into her eye. Nodded slow.

'All right, then.'

'My name is Hana,' she said. 'My real name, I mean.'

In the distance, they could hear running feet. Cries of alarm. The ringing of an iron bell. The big man sniffed, pulled his hat farther down over his face.

'Akihito,' he said. 'My friends called me Akihito.'

9

A Heart Exhausted

There weren't tears enough for her grief.

All around her, she could hear the voices of the bamboo kami, the spirits in the stalks swaying with the gentle wind. The little girl stood by her brother's grave, bloodshot eyes and sodden cheeks, Lady Sun filling the clearing with hateful, dappled light. The spirit stone on his burial plot was marked with his name, the day of his death and the day of his birth – the same day as hers.

Nine years ago that day.

'Happy birthday, Satoru,' Yukiko whispered.

It had been three months since the snake-strike. Three months since her twin died in her arms. It felt as if a part of her was missing – as if the gods had broken off a piece of her and left it bleeding on the floor. Her mother was lost in grief. Her father in guilt. But Yukiko? She was lost in the enormity of it all. A world too vast and lonely now that her brother wasn't there to share it. An emptiness never filled. A hand never held. A question never answered.

'Ichigo.'

Her father's voice, behind her, calling her by his pet name. She did not turn, simply stared through the tears at the bed where her brother would lay forever.

He knelt beside her on the warm ground, his long hair caught in the breeze and tickling her tear-stained cheeks. He touched her hand, gentle as snowflakes. She turned to look at him then, this man she called father that in truth she barely knew. A tanned and weatherworn face, roguish and handsome. Long moustache and dark hair, just beginning to grey at the temples. Dark, sparkling eyes, always searching.

He'd never been there when they were growing up, forever off on his grand hunts at the Shōgun's behest. He would return to their little valley every once in a while, spoil them for a day or two, then disappear for months at a time. But he always brought the twins presents. He could always make her smile. And when he would lift her on his shoulders and carry her through the bamboo forest, it made her feel as tall as giants. Fierce as dragons.

'Have you finished packing your things?' he asked.

She blinked, avoided his gaze. She didn't think it had been settled. She didn't think her mother would ever agree to it. She thought maybe after her brother . . .

'We are still going to the Shōgun's court then?'

'We must, Ichigo. My Lord commands and I obey.'

'But what about Satoru?' she whispered. 'He'll be all alo—'

The sentence cracked along with her voice and she turned her eyes to the grave at her feet. Tears swelled inside her, a choking ball of heat creeping up her throat. The empty yawned all about her, the world too big for her alone.

'I got you something,' her father said. 'For your birthday.'

He held up a white box, tied with black ribbon. And if the sight of the sun gleaming on that dark silk made her heart beat a little faster, if thoughts of the countless mysteries that might lay within *that box stilled the thoughts of her brother for a moment, she was only nine, after all.*

She was only little.

She took the box in her hands, surprised at its weight.

'Open it,' he said.

She pulled at the ribbon, watching the bow fold in upon itself and fall open. Inside the box waited a gift so pretty it stole the breath from between her lips. A scabbard of lacquered wood, black as her father's eyes, smooth as cat's claws. Beside it, a six-inch length of folded steel, gleaming in the sun, so sharp it might cut the day in half.

'A knife?'

'A tantō,' he said. 'All ladies of court carry one.'

'What do I need it for?'

'It will protect you.' He took the scabbard from the box, sheathed the blade and tucked it into her obi at the small of her back. 'In the times when I cannot. And even when I'm not there, I will be with you.'

She felt strong arms around her then, lifting her off the ground, drawing her up into the sky. He said nothing at all, simply held her, rocked her back and forth and let her cry. She put her arms around his neck and held tight, as if he were the only thing to keep her from going under, falling away into the cold and black.

He pressed his lips against her cheek. His whiskers tickled her skin.

'I will be with you,' he said.

He could always make her smile.

*

A softness to her edges, satin weight on her eyelids. Her tongue too big for her mouth. The world swaying to a tune she couldn't quite hear. The room spinning as she opened her eyes.

'You wake,' Daichi said.

Wind kami called down timeworn mountainsides, the spirits playing in the branches of the treetop village outside, bringing the brittle-crisp promise of winter to come. Yukiko sat up slowly, groaning and squeezing her eyes shut once more. The pulse of the entire world beat beneath her skin, the thoughts of every beast, man, woman and child around her, layered upon one another in a shapeless cacophony. She pawed blindly beside her bed, seized the half-empty saké jug, upending it into her mouth. Daichi murmured concern, tried to take the bottle from her hands but she pushed him away, molten fire pouring down her throat, rushing to fill the void inside her.

'Yukiko—'

'Stop, please,' she begged, curling into a ball with her fists to her temples. 'Give me a minute. Just one minute.'

The old man sat in silence, legs crossed, palms upturned on his knees. He seemed a statue of some bygone warrior, katana slung across his back – a glacial stillness in contrast to the seething shift inside her head.

To even glance into the Kenning was to look at the sun. To make cinders of her eyes. But she could feel Buruu in there, rumbling beneath it all like thunder on a distant horizon. She reached for him, synapses ablaze – just a touch to let him know she was awake. The saké did its work; black velvet thrown over her head and smothering the noise and heat of the world. She felt it flow her to her edges, a beautiful gravity filling her to her fingernails, dragging the Kenning to some quiet corner in her mind and choking until it could barely breathe.

She didn't know how long she lay there, curled like a babe in lightless, amniotic warmth. But finally she opened her eyes a sliver, saw the old man still seated at the edge of her bed, concern plain in those steel-grey eyes. He coughed once, twice, as if he'd been struggling to remain silent, wiping his knuckles across his lips. And finally he met her gaze.

'What is happening to you, Yukiko?'

His voice was gravelled. Rusted. The muddy rasp of a pipe-fiend, so akin to her father's for a moment she thought she was dreaming.

'I don't know.' She shook her head, tongue numb. 'I can hear everything. Animals. People. Everyone. Inside my head.'

The old man frowned. 'Their thoughts?'

'Hai. But it's like everyone shouting . . . all at once. It's deafening.'

He stroked his moustache, slow and thoughtful. 'The cause?'

'I don't know. My father never told me about this. No one told me anything.'

'I do not mean to cause you alarm . . .' the old man paused, licked his lips, 'but I think you caused an earthquake today.'

She stared at him, jaw slightly agape, blinking slow.

'Do you not remember the ground shaking?' Daichi asked. 'Trees shivering like frightened children as you fell to your knees?'

'No.' A hollow whisper. 'Gods . . .'

'Can you not hold it at bay? Control it?'

Yukiko fixed the old man in a bleary stare. The saké was heat in her veins and in her cheeks, pulling her eyelids closed. Legs trembling. Mouth dry. 'My father . . . I think perhaps he smoked lotus to keep it quiet. Liquor seems to dull it, too.'

'That seems a dangerous road to walk. One that does not end in answers.'

'I know it,' she sighed, her tongue clumsy on her teeth. 'Truly, I do. I don't want to hide in the bottom of a bottle.'

'Kaori told me of the birds. The ones who killed themselves against your bedroom walls.'

'Buruu said it was because I was screaming. Inside their heads.'

'And now you say you can hear not just the thoughts of beasts, but of people too?'

Yukiko remained silent, awful certainty of Daichi's destination building in her gut.

'Leave aside the earthquake for a moment,' he said. 'The fact you may shake the very island beneath our feet when you get upset. Think for a moment what else might happen if you lose control again.'

'Are you saying—'

'I say nothing. I simply wonder if next time, it is not birds trying to silence your screams, but people.' The old man gestured around him. 'Us.'

'Gods . . .'

'Indeed.'

Yukiko blinked, cold dread in her belly. She hadn't even considered the thought . . .

'I don't know what to do, Daichi,' she breathed, dragging her fingers through her hair. 'I have nobody to ask how to control this thing. No teacher. No father. Nothing.'

Daichi steepled his hands beneath his chin, brows drawn together in thought. A long silence passed, his frown growing darker as moments turned to minutes.

'I did not wish to tell you this,' he finally said. 'I should have spoken of it after the incident with the birds, but I hoped the matter not as grave as now I know it to be. And in truth, we cannot afford to lose you, Yukiko.'

'I don't understand . . .'

'I know where you can find your answers. If answers exist to be found anywhere at all.' The old man coughed, wiped his mouth on his sleeve with a grimace. 'A monastery on the isle of Shabishii, far north of here, near the Imperium's edge. It was said the monks there kept the mysteries of the world inked on their flesh.'

'To keep them secret?'

'To keep them safe. Their order began with the rise of the Tenma Emperors, when the Imperial Censors first started burning 'indecent' literature. The monks tattooed themselves with ancient arts and the deepest secrets, that they would not be lost to the Imperium's hubris. Much harder to kill a living man than incinerate a paper scroll.'

Yukiko raised an eyebrow. 'But what happened when a monk died?'

'I do not know.' Daichi coughed again, rubbed at his throat as if pained. 'I do not even know if the monastery still stands. I have heard rumour it was destroyed. Others say it is cursed.'

'People say the same about these mountains.'

'Precisely,' Daichi smiled. 'I am hoping the Painted Brotherhood may encourage those rumours for the same reason we do. To keep away unwanted eyes.'

'Painted Brotherhood . . .'

'So they were named.'

Yukiko drew a deep, shivering breath, dragged her knuckles across her mouth. Beyond the saké blur, deep through the haze she'd plunged herself into, she could still hear it. The cacophony. The inferno waiting inside her head.

'But the wedding . . .' she said. 'Aisha. The dynasty . . . I can't leave now.'

'You see our dilemma. We need you and Buruu more than

ever. And in truth, if all that was at stake were a few more birds, I could risk your presence here. But the people of this village . . . the wives and daughters and husbands and sons . . .'

'I'm a danger to them.'

The old man sighed, staring at empty palms as if they might hold the answers he sought.

'Hai.'

'So risk flying north on what might be a fool's errand, or stay here and risk the entire village? Those are my options?'

A faint smile. 'Nobody said being the Stormdancer would be easy.'

Yukiko pressed her knuckles to her temples, the throb pulsing just below the saké lull. Misery and pain and the swelling tide, pushing them all back with the simple, undeniable truth – that the choice Daichi presented was no choice at all. The path was clear. She need only start walking. And every second she wasted was another second the wedding drew closer. But still . . .

But still . . .

'We'll be swift,' she said. 'Fly to Shabishii as fast as we can, find what truths we may. At the very least, it'll be a lot quieter in the sky.'

Daichi nodded. 'You will be back in time to stop Aisha's wedding, with a little luck.'

'You know what they say.' A tired, colourless smile. 'Kitsune looks after his own . . .'

'So I will pray.'

Daichi reached out and took her hand. His fingers were calloused, faint liver spots and wrinkles decades deep. She met his eyes, and for a moment, she saw past the mask he wore, the iron he encased his soul inside. He seemed terribly old, bent beneath his burdens, tired beyond all want of sleep. His smile was frayed at the hem.

'I know what it is we are asking of you, Yukiko. I see the toll it takes.'

She looked into his eyes, searching for a hint of scorn and finding none. The words inside her were like living things, bubbling in her throat, demanding to be aired. She forced her lips together, fighting a losing battle to keep them at bay. When finally they spilled forth, they were a whisper muffled by the curtain of her hair.

'It's all weighing too heavy, Daichi.' She took a shuddering breath, sighed. 'Being this thing. This Stormdancer. I feel like an utter fraud. A little girl stamping her feet and screaming life isn't fair.'

'You give people hope, Yukiko. The strength at the heart of all strength. The steps you take now, the first steps – they are always the hardest. But the footprints you leave in the earth behind you will be followed by *thousands*.'

'I'm so afraid sometimes. I think about my father . . .' She shook her head. 'I haven't shed a single tear for him, did you know that? He's dead and I can't even bring myself to cry.'

'It is not fear that chases away your tears, Yukiko-chan.' Daichi's voice was low, tinged at the edges with a charcoal rasp. 'It is rage.'

'Buruu says the same. He says it will burn me up inside.'

'No.' Daichi leaned forward, pinned her in his stare. 'No, you listen to me, girl. Look around you. At this world they have left you. Red skies. Black rivers. Mountains of bones. You *should* be angry. You should be *furious*.'

He took hold of her hand, squeezed it so tight her knuckles hurt.

'The time for fear is long since gone. It died with the last phoenix, the last butterfly. It died when we traded the ease of the machine for the grace of our souls. Nothing will change if we cherish our fear as if it were a blessing. If we are afraid to tear down the old, and lose what we may in that unmaking, we will never build the new.'

'I'm not sure I can be what you want me to be, Daichi.'

The old man sat up straight, released his grip on her hands.

'*I* am sure,' he said.

Reaching behind him, he lifted the ancient katana from his back, held it out on upturned palms. Yukiko caught her breath, eyes roaming the lacquer scabbard, the golden cranes embossed into gleaming wood. The words he spoke danced like static electricity upon her skin.

'I wielded this blade through many battles, none so great as the one before us. And so I give it to you, who need it now more than I.'

'Gods,' she breathed. 'I can't accept this, Daichi . . .'

'You can.' He ran his hand across the hilt, a lingering caress of farewell. 'And as I give you this gift, I give it a name. I name this blade "Yofun."'

'"Anger,"' she whispered.

'My gift to you, Yukiko-chan.' He nodded. 'Use it to cut away your fear, and leave nothing in its wake. Cherish it. And cherish this truth I speak to you now, if no other before or after: The greatest tempest Shima has ever known waits in the wings for you to call its name. Your anger can topple mountains. Crush empires. Change the very shape of the world.'

He pressed the blade into her hand, watched her with cool eyes the colour of steel.

'Your anger is a gift.'

*

Jay Kristoff

Kin sat alone on the rope bridge, feet dangling over the precipice, listening to the fading day. The transition never failed to fascinate him; the light's slow descent from copper to auburn, through dried blood and onto tar black. Tiny noises that would be lost in garish daylight, sharp and clear under the blanket of night.

When he was younger, locked inside his skin, the entire world was muted beneath the metal, the ever-turning chatter of his mechabacus. Chapterhouse Kigen had no windows, no way to tell night from day. The glow of cutting torches had been his dawn, flickering disks of halogen his stars. He was fourteen years old before he saw his first sunset, on the deck of the *Thunder Child* as they sailed from Kigen Bay. Even now, he could recall the tightness in his chest as that blinding globe sank towards the horizon, setting the entire island ablaze. All was flame and taut, black shadows, reaching out to him like the hands of old, forgotten friends. His breath had caught so completely in his lungs that for a terrifying moment, he thought the bellows in his skin had failed. That he was suffocating.

But in the Iishi, he could hear a thousand tiny voices amongst the whispering leaves. The wood beneath him sighing and shifting, the cries of night birds in search of prey, the song of insects amidst gentle fingers of wisteria vines. The soft beat of approaching footsteps.

He shot to his feet, heart in his throat. 'Yukiko?'

'Hello, Kin.'

He reached out to her, awkward and stumbling and feeling entirely idiotic, gifting her a clumsy hug. She pressed her head against his chest and sighed.

'I was worried about you,' he breathed.

As she turned her face up to his and smiled, he smelled something sharp and poisonous on her breath. Noticed a vacant glaze in her eyes. 'I'm all right.'

Reluctantly he released his hold, sat down on the footbridge again. Yukiko sat beside him, dangling her feet over the edge and swinging them back and forth like a child, eyes shining with the light of a falling sun. He saw her cheeks were slightly flushed, noticed she was carrying a bottle of saké in her hand. He tried not to stare at the katana strapped to her back.

'I thought you'd want to know.' She took a pull from the bottle, closed her eyes. When she spoke again, her voice was strained. 'Daichi and the council have voted. The False-Lifer will be kept alive. Locked up, of course. But they're not going to kill her.'

'That's good.' He glanced at the liquor again. 'I'm glad.'

Sparrows sang to each other in the gloom, calling their good nights as the dark crept closer on velvet-quiet feet.

'Where's Buruu?' he asked.

'Fishing.' She gifted him with a small smile. 'Gorging himself before we leave. He eats like a lotus fiend on a comedown. I hope we can get off the ground.'

'Before you leave? Where are you going?'

'North. Shabishii Island.'

'Can I . . . come with you?'

She sighed, ran her knuckles across her brow. 'I don't think so. Your thoughts are like a tangle of thorns inside my head.' She held up the bottle, saké sloshing inside. 'This is all that's keeping them quiet.'

'My . . . thoughts?'

'Not just you.' She waved the bottle across the village. 'Everyone. All of you. I can't shut you out. So I'm just not sure it's a wonderful idea for me to be around people right now.'

'That's . . .' He floundered for the words, shaking his head. 'That's just . . .'

'Unbelievable?' she sighed. 'Terrifying?'

'What's causing it?'

'That's what I'm hoping to find out in Shabishii. I have to control this power, Kin. I have to master it before it masters me. If I don't, I'm a danger to everyone around me.' She touched his hand. 'Including you.'

'Am I hurting you now? I mean . . . do you want me to go?'

'No.' Her finger trailed across his skin, goosebumps rising. 'Not yet . . .'

Silence fell then. Crushing and empty. All the things he thought he should say sounded hollow in his head. The memory of her lips stirred in his blood, the thought of her body pressed against him echoed in his veins. It felt like she was running away from him. It felt like . . .

'Well, at least I'll have something to do when you're gone,' he shrugged.

She offered a teasing smile. 'Miss me terribly?'

'I mean aside from that.' He gave her hand a shy squeeze. 'I'm thinking about planting some blood lotus.'

'Lotus?' She blinked. 'What for?'

'Experiment with it in a controlled environment. Maybe I can figure out a way to stop it killing the soil it grows in.'

'Why would you want to do that?'

'To save what's left of Shima, of course.' He could feel the warmth radiating from her skin. 'Aside from the Iishi, everything is lotus fields or poisoned deadlands.'

'We won't save Shima by planting more lotus, Kin.'

'Then how will we save it?'

She looked at him strangely then, and her voice was that of a parent talking to an infant.

'We incinerate the fields. So there's nothing left but ashes.'

'You want to light the whole island on fire?'

'The lotus must burn, Kin. The Guild along with it.'

'But what about afterwards? When all this is done?'

'Don't you think you're putting the rickshaw before the runner? Instead of worrying about what we do after the war is over, maybe you should think of ways to help us win it?'

He watched her, silent and still. She stared out into the dark, took another pull from the saké bottle. Pale skin, shadows smudged under her eyes. She looked sick, as if she hadn't eaten or slept properly in days. Oily fingers of anxiety wormed their way into his guts.

'Well, I was thinking about that too,' he said. 'I thought we could salvage the ruins of those ironclads. There's bound to be all kinds of scrap to make the village more defensible. Shuriken-throwers. Armour plating. There are pit traps on the western rise, of course, but everyone around her keeps talking about how there are more oni moving through the lower woods. Old Mari told me they usually get restless after an earthquake, and the one this morning was the worst anyone around here can remember. If they came down in force . . .'

She sighed, glanced at him in the deepening dark. 'They're not going to let you build anything that runs on chi, Kin.'

'No, we can do it without combustion. I can set up the 'thrower feeders so they're hand-cranked. They'll be slower to fire, but it's gas pressure that does most of the work.' Excitement in his gut, voice running quicker at the thought of building, of *creating* something again. 'I can see it in my head. I was talking about it with Ayane and—'

'Ayane?' Yukiko frowned. 'When did you talk to her?'

He blinked, confused. 'This afternoon. In the prison.'

'Kin, you shouldn't do that. The Kagé don't trust it . . . I mean 'her.' If you spend time with her, they're not going to trust you either.'

'You heard Atsushi and Isao at the pit trap this morning.' He tried to keep the bitterness from his voice. 'None of them trust me anyway.'

'All the more reason to stay away from her.'

'She came all this way to find us. Do you realize what she's given up to be here?'

'I don't care what—'

'She's alone, Yukiko. For the first time since her Awakening, she's unplugged from the mechabacus. She can't hear the voice of the Guild anymore, can't feel them inside her head. Imagine spending years by the hearth of an Upside bedhouse. Everything is light and voices and song. And then one day you get thrown into the dark. You've never even seen night before. Never felt cold. But now it's everywhere. That's what she's feeling right now, locked in that cell. That's what she chose when she decided to come here.'

'We don't know she *chose* anything. They could have *sent her here,* Kin—'

'Did you know every female born in the Guild becomes a False-Lifer?' He felt anger creeping into his voice, turning it hard and ugly and cold. 'They don't get a say in what they want to be. Don't get to decide who they're paired with, or when it's time to breed. They don't even get to meet the father of their children. Just another False-Lifer with an inseminator tube and a bottle of lubricant.'

'Gods, Kin—'

'So don't shit on the choices she's made, Yukiko.' He snatched his hand from hers. 'It's the first thing she's decided for herself in her entire life. Not everyone gets a thunder tiger to help them out of their mistakes, you know. Some people risk everything they have alone.'

'Kin, I'm sorry . . .'

He climbed to his feet, and she lurched up after him, knocking the saké bottle onto its side. Rose-coloured liquid spilled from the neck, soaking the boards at their feet. Kin turned to leave but she grabbed his hand again, pulled him around to face her.

'Don't leave like this. Please.'

She was standing just inches away, fingers entwined in his own, lips parted ever so slightly. The world swayed beneath his feet, heart pounding against his ribs like a steamhammer. He was conscious of nothing in the world except her. The scent of her hair entwined in liquor perfume. Her skin radiating the warmth of a kiln, melting his insides. His mouth was suddenly dry, palms soaked. And though he tried, he felt as though he would never catch his breath again.

'Don't be angry with me, Kin.' She inched closer. 'I don't want to fight with you.'

'What *do* you want from me, Yukiko?'

'It might be weeks before we see each other again.' Her eyes searched his face, lingered on his lips. 'But we have an hour or so until Buruu comes back . . .'

She pressed against him, hands parting the cloth on his chest, trailing along his skin, white hot. He glanced at the spilled liquor around their feet, the tide of blood staining her cheeks and lips the colour of roses.

'Kiss me,' she breathed.

She stood on tiptoes, arms slipping around his neck, mouth drifting towards his.

'Kiss me . . .'

She was like gravity, pulling him closer, heavy as the earth beneath him. No noise. No light. Only motion, only the pull of her, down, down to a place he wanted so badly he could taste it, feel it singing inside his chest. A place he would kill for. A place he could happily die inside.

But not like this.

Not like this.

'No.' He took hold of her shoulders, eased her away. 'No.'

'Kin—'

'This isn't you, Yukiko.'

'Not me?' she frowned. 'Who am I then?'

'I'm not sure I know.' He gestured to the saké bottle on the floor. 'Perhaps you find out when you get to the bottom?'

She remained herself for just a tiny moment longer, plain behind her eyes, wounded and sad and desperately alone. The girl he loved. The girl he would do anything for. And then she was gone. Wiped away in a rush of heat, pupils flashing, leaving the rage behind. The stranger who lived inside her skin. What had Ayane called her?

'The girl all Guildsmen fear.'

'You don't get to judge me, Kin.'

'Godsdammit, I'm not judging you. I care about you! And I see you turning into this . . . *thing*, this Stormdancer, and piece by piece I see the Yukiko I know falling away.' He sighed, dragging a hand across his scalp. 'I mean . . . you *killed* those Guildsmen, Yukiko. Three ironclads full. Over a hundred people. And you *killed* them.'

'I let one of them live.' Her stare was cold. Defiant. 'But maybe I should have let them firebomb the forest? Maybe I should have let them kill *you*?'

'Since when were you a mass murderer?'

'Don't you *dare.*' A low growl, eyes wide. 'You stood by while *thousands* died—'

The words were a slap to his face, rocking him back on his heels. The memory of pale-skinned women and children, row upon row of gaijin shuffling meekly to meet their boiling end. Rendered down into fertilizer, reborn in some far-flung field as beautiful, blood-red flowers. He knew it was true. Everything she said. But to hear her say it . . .

He blinked at her. Speechless. Senseless.

'I shouldn't have said that,' she sighed. 'I'm sorry.'

Yukiko breathed deep, clawed away her hair. He could see it written on her face. Boiling inside her. Curling her fingers into fists, her lips to a grimace. When she spoke again, her voice was soft with it, trembling at the outskirts.

'I know it wasn't your fault, Kin. The gaijin. Inochi. All of it. I know there was nothing you could do to stop it. Kaori and the others say otherwise. They say there's no steel in you, but I know helping me in Kigen took more courage than most could ever dream.

'But this is war, Kin. The Yukiko you knew? That frightened little girl in the Shōgun's palace? She's gone.' Fire in her eyes. 'She's dead.'

'No steel in me . . .' he whispered, lips twisting in a bitter smile.

'It's bullshit, Kin.' She took his hand, entwined her fingers with his own. 'Don't you believe it. Any of it. But know you have enemies here. People who see you as Guild first and everything else second. Stay close to Daichi while I'm gone. And stay as far from Ayane as you can. Don't give them a reason to doubt you.'

'Why would I bother?' he spat. 'They're doing perfectly well without one . . .'

'Kin—'

'I hope you find the answers you seek.' He pulled his hand away, let it drop to his side. 'I know Buruu will keep you safe.'

Hurt in her eyes as she chewed her lip, searched the dark for the right words to say.

'Kiss me good-bye?'

Hovering uncertain. Wanting it more than he could say. Pride and anger shushing want, leaving it alone and friendless. All he'd given, all he'd sacrificed, and this was the life he'd purchased. Watching her fly away. Leaving him, just like she'd left him in Kigen. Alone.

Again.

He put his hands to her cheeks, feeling the satin warmth of her skin, the sensation of it beneath his tingling fingertips almost crushing his resolve to powder. But in the end, tilting her head up to his, her lips parting ever so softly, he leaned down and kissed her gently on the brow.

'Good-bye Stormdancer,' he said.

And then he turned and walked away.

Part of him screamed he was an idiot. That he would regret it. But anger and pride urged him on, the burning fuel of the indignant fool, and he stalked off into the dark with the waterfall of his blood thrashing in his ears. She called his name again, just once. But he didn't stop. Didn't turn his head. And somewhere deep in the back of his mind, a tiny thought found its voice for the first time; a whisper almost too faint to hear.

It kept him awake most of the night, belly-up on his mattress of straw, staring at the ceiling with sandbag eyes. Breathing. Listening. The limbo of insomnia, grey and bottomless as the hours dragged on forever, leaving him in the muddy dawn with a heart exhausted and seven words lodged in his mind like a handful of splinters.

The same question.

Over and over again.

What the hells are you doing here?

10

Salt and Copper

Yoshi's lashes fluttered against his cheeks as he stole along fly-blown gutters on four feather-light feet. Towers of fetid waste looming all around him, nostrils filled with rot and fresh death, blood leaking from a broken skull onto cracked cobbles. He skulked past a snarling brood – a sleek and fearsome bunch, fourteen strong – scratching and fighting as they tore strips from the new bones. Squealing and spitting at him as he scampered by. A warning. A challenge. First spoils to the finders. Leavings to the rest. Our meat. Our alley. Our dirt.

He could smell salt and sweet copper, his stomach growled for the slippery, lovely wanting of it, warm and sticky-lush. But on he scampered, up through the spindly broken-leg alleys, a stale ocean of refuse in which to swim. Whiskers twitching. Mangy hide inflamed from the furious worrying of a dozen fat, black fleas. Pausing to scratch with scabrous little claws, delighting in the bloody relief.

Stopping in the alley mouth across from the whorehouse, blinking with eyes as dark as river water, his tail twitching. Rough-looking men were gathered in the stoop, arms inked from shoulder to wrist, speaking in hushed, lotus-scarred voices. No clan tattoos on their shoulders, no, just floral patterns and geisha girls and interlocking scorpions marking them as Burakumin. Lowborns all – turned to the shadow trade calling every man birthed in Kigen's gutters. The fist and the fade. The smoke and the skin. A den of them. A seething, sweltering nest of them.

Yakuza.

Minutes passed. Hours. The Moon God Tsukiyomi rode low in the sky behind a choking veil of fumes. More painted men strolled up to the stoop, ushered inside with gap-toothed smiles. And finally, as the hours wore on and the Goddess Amaterasu was just beginning to lighten the eastern skies, two men exited the building. The first, a skulking knife-thin bastard, yellowed teeth like broken stumps in dark gums. The second, a short, broad lump with piggy eyes and cauliflower ears. On their shoulders, each gangster carried a small beaten satchel, filled with the clink of muffled coin. Yoshi felt his whiskers curl, yellow teeth bared in what might have been a smile, and he whispered thanks to the body he rode and stole on back to his own.

He opened his eyes
the room throbbing and all
a-shudder flexed inside long limbs and hairless
flesh and grubby cloth the body he'd lived most of his
life inside feeling
for just a moment
longer
like something utterly
repulsively
wrong.

Jurou was sitting across from him as his vision came into shuddering focus. Dark bangs hanging in dew-moist eyes, empty lotus pipe utterly wasted on those perfect lips.

'Well?' he said.

'Same time. Every morning just before the dawn,' Yoshi smiled. 'It's a money-house for certain.'

'Who runs it?'

'Scorpion Children. Biggest yakuza crew in Downside.'

'You sure you want to start that heavy?'

'You recall a time old Yoshi ever did things by halves, Princess?'

'I'm just not—'

Yoshi put his finger to Jurou's lips, frowning towards the door. 'Daken's back. Hana too.'

Yoshi arranged himself on a pile of cushions in the corner, Jurou leaning against his bare chest. He sipped the dregs of their rice wine, felt the big tom drawing closer, the way a magnet must feel as iron draws near. Slouching on his cushion, legs askew, hand snagged in Jurou's hair as Hana's key twisted in the lock. Tipping his split-brimmed hat away from his eyes, he aimed a crooked smile at his little sister.

'This is the part where I juggle some comedy about what the cat dragged—'

Hana stole into the room, looking paler than usual, skin filmed in a sheen of fresh sweat. Behind her loomed one of the biggest men Yoshi had ever raised an eyebrow at. A straw hat pulled down low over his brow, ragged black cloak over street-worn thread. Door-broad shoulders, a jaw you could break your knuckles on, a few steps on the right side of handsome, truth be told – at least from what Yoshi could see. He walked with a pronounced limp.

'Well, well,' Jurou smiled. 'Took my advice, girl?'

Hana muttered a mouthful, looking embarrassed. Shuffling before the pair like a disobedient child before the Great Judge, she gestured feebly to the giant still looming in the doorway. She spoke so fast her words tripped over each other in the rush to her teeth.

'AkihitothisismybrotherYoshiandhisfriendJurou.'

Jurou's grin was all Kitsune-in-the-henhouse, aimed squarely at Hana, but he spared a glance for the newcomer. 'How do?'

Yoshi's eyes hadn't left the big man. He nodded once. Slow as centuries.

'Akihito-san is going to be staying here for a few days,' Hana said.

'Do tell,' Yoshi frowned.

'Only a few.'

'Not like you to have houseguests, sister-mine.' His eyes shifted to the big man. 'Can he cook? Doesn't look much of a dancer.'

Her voice was soft, expression pleading. 'Yoshi, please . . .'

Who the fuck is this, Daken?

The tomcat had assumed his usual perch on the windowsill, cleaning his paws with a tongue as rough as an iron file. His thoughts were velvet-smooth by contrast, a whispered purr rolling through Yoshi's mind like sugared smoke.

. . . friend . . .

Yoshi sniffed. Squinted. Trying hard to find fault with it and coming up empty. She'd never brought anyone home before, but Hana was a big girl now. What she did, *who* she did, was her business. He leaned down, kissed Jurou on the forehead and shrugged.

'All good, sister-mine.'

She turned, gestured to the big fellow. 'Come on.'

With a guilty nod aimed Yoshi's way, the big man limped past the pair and into Hana's bedroom. Hana was on her way to join him when Yoshi softly cleared his throat.

'Forgetting something?'

Hana made a face, reached inside her servant's kimono, drew out the iron-thrower. Leaning down, she placed it in Yoshi's open palm, whispered for his ears only.

'Explanations later.'

He glanced at Daken, now sawing away at his nethers with his long, pink tongue.

. . . don't ask hers won't tell yours . . .

'As you say.' He waved the 'thrower. 'By the by, you can't take this to work with you tonight. We need it.'

'What for?'

'Explanations later.'

The curiosity gleaming in Hana's eye retreated with reluctance. She gave him a small nod, slipped into her bedroom. Daken prowled inside behind her and she quietly closed the door. Jurou had a grin on his face like *he* was the one about to do the mattress bounce. He leaned over and switched on the soundbox, turned up the volume to bestow some privacy, looking ready to turn a cartwheel.

'Good for her,' he grinned.

Yoshi lifted the iron-thrower and sniffed. A burned chemical smell, like generator oil and refinery stink wafting from the barrel. It felt just a touch lighter than it had yesterday. Just a little less death inside.

He pulled his lucky hat down over his eyes.

'Doubtless . . .'

*

Akihito perched by the window, peering out through dirty glass as Hana shut the bedroom door with a whispering click. The flat was four floors up, commanding a decent view of the street below; claustrophobic and wreathed in exhaust. But even with an elevated vantage point, he still felt utterly naked, shaking with nervous energy, belly doing cartwheels. His thoughts went to Grey Wolf, to Butcher and the others. Praying they'd gotten away safe or died fighting. He'd seen enough of Kigen jail to know it was no fit place for anyone to end.

Poor Kasumi . . .

Reaching inside a pouch on his obi, he retrieved an old chisel and a pinewood block, began whittling at the surface, his eyes still on the street below. No sign of bushi' out there; just a few street urchins running dice on a corner, two lotusfiends playing pass the pipe. And still his nerves were bunched tighter than overwound clock springs, the chisel's handle slippery in sweat-slick fingers.

'That's pretty,' the girl said, gesturing to his carving. 'What is it?'

'Present,' he muttered. 'For a friend.'

'So what do you think happened? How did they find us?'

Akihito glanced to the doorway, the boys in the living room beyond. The beautiful tones of shamisen players were spilling from the soundbox, slightly muffled by the two inches of cracking plaster between them. He couldn't shake the feeling of wrongness. Of being watched. Vulnerable. 'It's not safe to talk in here. We could be overheard.'

'It's just my brother and his boyfriend.'

'And your neighbours? I've met blacklung beggars who weren't as thin as these walls.'

The girl pouted, blew a stray lock from her eye. He sized her up with a slow stare – waif-thin, pointed chin, an old scar gouged down her brow and cheek, leather eyepatch hiding the worst of it. An unruly bob of straw-dry hair, black as cuttlefish ink. Hard, he decided. The kind of hard bought on broken concrete with an empty belly and bleeding fists. Smart? Smart enough for this whole thing to be a long game? Was she playing him?

Doesn't make a lot of sense. But maybe . . .

She sat down in the middle of her grubby mattress. Glancing at the door. At him. Back to the door. The hint of a crooked smile curling her lips.

'Ohhhh,' she sighed, shivering.

Akihito frowned, hands falling still at his carving. He drew breath to speak when another low moan from the girl killed the words on his lips.

'Ohhhhhh, *gods.*'

The big man sat a little straighter, slightly disconcerted, jaw hanging loose. He watched the girl pull herself up on all fours, prowling across the sheets. Searching the room for somewhere else to look, he found the tomcat sitting at his feet, head tilted, staring at him with wide, pus-yellow eyes.

Blink. Blink.

Leaning up against the bedroom door, the girl groaned, throaty and breathless, as if in the throes of first-night passion. She slapped one hand against the door frame, thumping her heels against the floorboards.

'Ohhh,' she purred. 'Ohh, *please.*'

'What the hells—'

She held up a finger, silenced his protest, continued her performance against the wafer-thin wood. Her brother's muffled curse seeped under the door – a plea to the great and beneficent Lord Izanagi to strike him deaf as stone, or failing that, for a quick and merciful death. Akihito heard what sounded like laughter and applause from the other boy.

'Oh. My. *Go-o-o-o-ods,*' Hana groaned.

The soundbox squealed in the room beyond, cranked to full

over Yoshi's prayers, the tiny speakers now strained and crackling under the increase in volume. Loud enough to drown out the girl's groans. Loud enough to drown out her screams, truth be told. Hana plopped herself back down on the mattress, tucked her feet beneath her with a satisfied smile.

'Safe enough now?'

Akihito couldn't help but chuckle. 'Nice.'

'You'll have to forgive my brother.' Hana began running fingers through her badly cut bob of raven hair. 'I don't usually have friends . . . stay over.'

'Has he always been like that?'

'You mean a smart-mouthed little bastard?' Hana laughed. 'Always.'

'No, I mean like *that*.'

Hana blinked, taking a few moments to process.

'Ohhhh . . . You mean has he always liked boys?'

Akihito muttered a series of incomprehensible words.

'Why?' An eyebrow crept towards the girl's hairline. 'What do you care?'

'I don't.' Akihito seemed mortified at the suggestion. 'I'm just, well . . .'

'Not used to that sort of thing.'

'No.'

'Well, don't fret.' Hana smiled lopsided, began tying her hair into braids. 'You're definitely not his type. *Far* too old.'

Akihito felt his cheeks flush. The girl's laughter rang out on the walls, the empty beach glass eyes staring onto smog-choked streets. The straining soundbox filled the void, drowning the murmur and hum outside. Hana watched him for a long time, saying nothing, working plaits across her scalp.

'So,' she finally said. 'How did they find us?'

'Hells if I know,' he sighed, pulling off his hat and running one hand over his braids. 'Trailed someone. Caught someone and made them sing. I'm still not one hundred per cent sure you didn't set us up, truth be told.'

The tomcat jumped into his lap without warning, and Akihito gasped as its claws sank into his flesh. Using his leg as a springboard, the cat vaulted up onto the windowsill and began licking at its nethers like they were made of sugar-rock. The big man winced, whispered a curse, massaged the old wound and new claw marks in his thigh.

The girl nodded to his bloodstained hakama. 'How's the leg by the way?'

'Hurts like a bastard,' Akihito murmured, still kneading the flesh.

'What happened to it?'

'You ask a lot of questions.'

'So?'

'So how would you feel if I asked what happened to your eye?' He gestured to the leather patch.

'I'd tell you my father was a mean drunk.' A small shrug.

'Izanagi's balls . . .' Sudden guilt slapped him across the mouth. 'I'm sorry.'

'Don't be. So how'd you hurt it?'

It had been over a month since the bloodbath during Masaru's rescue from Kigen jail, but the sword-blow wasn't healing well. Akihito knew he should have been resting, changing his dressings more often, but circumstances being what they were, he was just glad it hadn't gone gangrenous. When Michi had gone back to the palace in search of Lady Aisha after the jailbreak went sour, she'd abandoned him with nothing but a tourniquet and vague directions to the sky-ship that was supposed to ferry everyone out of the city. Akihito hadn't even limped halfway to Spire Row before the bushi' locked Kigen down, sky-spires, railyards and all. He'd returned to the Kagé safe house he'd sheltered in before the prison break, hooking up with Grey Wolf and other members of the city cell. His thinking was simple enough – if he couldn't get to Yukiko, he'd do his best to help her from where he was.

Masaru would have wanted it that way.

Kasumi too.

'Just . . . helping a friend,' he said.

She nodded. 'Well, I'll see if I can find some bandages at the palace tomorrow.'

He scowled, turned his eyes back to the wood in his hand, carved off another chunk. A Guild sky-ship cut through the smog overhead, its engines rattling the windows. He thought of the ambush in Kigen jail, Kasumi's blood glistening on the floor. The betrayal that had killed her. Killed Masaru. Almost killed him too.

'How did you know those bushi' were coming tonight, Hana? You said your lookout spotted them before ours did, but who was your lookout? How did he get word to you?'

The girl peered at him, one dark eye gleaming between disobedient locks of hair. Standing slowly, she padded across the room to tug the window open. A faintly toxic breeze drifted inside, the bustling city song beyond nearly drowned by the soundbox wail. The girl stood back, folded her arms, staring at the cat perched on the windowsill above. For his part, the big tom seemed too intent on his not-so-privates to notice.

'Go on!' the girl finally yelled. 'Get!'

The cat unfolded himself from his knot, made something close to a huffing sound and dropped to the lower sill. After a languorous stretch, he spared Hana a dagger-sharp stare, and finally slipped into the daylight. The girl slunk back to her mattress, her tread soundless. Sinking down with crossed legs and a challenging stare, she continued braiding her hair.

'How long have you been with the Kagé?' he frowned.

'Two weeks.'

'What made you join?'

'The Stormdancer.'

'Stormdancer?'

The girl looked at him as if he were a simpleton.

'The girl who tamed the thunder tiger? Brought it back from the Iishi single-handed? You must have heard of her. She's all over the Kagé broadcasts. Someone's even written a kabuki play about her; I saw it outside a brothel in Ibitsu Street last week, before the bushi' started cracking skulls.'

'Oh, I've heard of her,' Akihito nodded. 'I'm still just getting used to the name, to be honest. I always called her Yukiko.'

Hana's eye narrowed. 'You know her?'

Akihito considered the girl staring at him. Defiance. Suspicion. She was so wretchedly thin; fingers almost skeletal, pale skin covered in grime. He focused on that single dark eye, almost too large in her emaciated face. He wanted to trust her, but couldn't quite fathom why. Was it because she was somehow familiar? Female? Young? How old could she be, anyway? Seventeen? Eighteen?

Almost the same age as . . .

'I hunted with her father, Kitsune Masaru.'

'The Black Fox of Shima?' Hana's voice was awed, and she leaned forward, braids forgotten. 'People lay spirit tablets for him near the Burning Stones!'

The big man held up the wood he'd been carving. 'Who do you think started putting them there?'

'My gods, you *knew* them?' Hana breathed. 'Did you meet her thunder tiger?'

'Meet it?' Akihito's chest puffed out a little. 'I helped catch the bloody thing.'

'Oh my *gods*!' Hana was back on her feet, hands over her mouth. 'So help me, if you're talking out of your—'

'I helped catch it. On the sky-ship *Thunder Child*, neck-deep in the worst storm I've ever seen.' The big man's eyes shone. 'Ryu Yamagata knew how to fly a ship, for godsdamn certain. He was a good man.' The light in his eyes dwindled and died. 'They were all good men.'

'What's she like?' Hana's eye was bright, her imagination afire. 'The Stormdancer?'

'A clever girl.' Akihito nodded. 'Strong. Hellsborn stubborn. But sugar-sweet. Truth be told, she's a lot like you, Hana-chan.' He glanced up at the windowsill where the tomcat had been perched a few minutes before, scratched the whiskers on his chin.

'She's an awful lot like you.'

11

Desolation's Edge

Yukiko had forgotten how beautiful the world could be.

Towering mountains beneath them, ancient and unchangeable. Making her feel like a brief and tiny thing; a spark escaping the rush of a twilight fire, speeding into the sky even as it burned away to nothing. Trees arrayed in gowns of bloody scarlet and shining gold, of bright rust and fading rose, like dancers awaiting the moment autumn's music would falter. And then they would shed their finery in a flurry, sleep naked in winter's arms, and wait for spring to wake them with warm and gentle kisses in all their softest places.

Yukiko rested her head against Buruu's neck and watched it all grow smaller and smaller. She'd closed herself off from the Kenning, just she and the wind in her hair, the world diminishing beyond lenses of polarized glass.

Yofun lay strapped across her spine with a length of braided cord. She'd found the katana clapped and scraped against the tantō at the small of her back, threatening to ruin the lacquer on both. Deciding the knife and sword made an argumentative pair, she'd stuffed her tantō into the bottom of one of Buruu's satchels, melancholy thoughts of her father with it.

The saké had worn off, the memory of Kin's cold farewell a hollow ache inside her. She reached out to Buruu, eyebrows knitted together, opening herself up just a hair's breadth. A burst of heat, blinding, pulses in the forest below flaring bright – lives she'd never have been able to feel at this distance just a month ago.

She clenched her teeth, tried to make the Kenning contract, like an iris as the sun crests the horizon. Trying to build a wall of herself, brick by brick. A bulwark of will to hold the fire at bay, something stronger than the insubstantial numbness granted by a gutful of liquor. Images of her childhood. Memories and moments – anything that would tether her, anchor her, shield her from the inferno waiting beyond. Her breath came shorter, headache cinching tight.

Can you hear me, brother?

YES.

His voice was tiny, as if he stood on a distant mountaintop and called across a valley of burning red.

Don't hold back. Speak like you would normally.

I DO NOT WANT TO HURT YOU.

No, I need to control this. I need your help. Please, Buruu. Do as I ask.

VERY WELL.

She hissed in pain, wincing, slumping forward across his shoulders. Her grip faltered as his thoughts crashed inside her skull, smashing her wall to splinters, her whole body aching. Buruu whined, holding his wings steady so as not to throw her from his back. Blood dripped from her nose, bright and gleaming, smeared through his feathers and upon her cheek.

It's all right . . . I'm all right . . .

She felt him pull himself back, whispering across the link binding them together.

SMALL STEPS FIRST, AGREED?

She wiped the blood from her nose, a slick of crimson on her knuckles. She sniffed hard and spat, salty, bright red.

All right, agreed. Small steps first.

GOOD.

The thunder tiger nodded.

EVEN STORMDANCERS MUST WALK BEFORE THEY FLY.

They ascended, clouds rolling back across a bloody grey sky. The sun was a harsh glint on the edges of her goggles, sharp enough to cut her eyes from her head. The forest pulse receded as they rose above it all, the island shrinking beneath them as the air grew thin and brittle, blood-red ocean stretching all the way to the horizon.

Looking far behind them, miles upon miles to the south, she could see the Iishi Mountains melting into low foothills. And beyond them? Blood lotus. Everywhere. The blooms had been plucked as summer died, red fields stripped to undergarments of miserable green. The weed with a hundred uses, or so the Guild claimed. Proof the gods existed. But squinting across endless fields rippling in the toxic wind, Yukiko only saw proof of her people's greed.

Deadlands. Great, smoking tracts of earth, stripped of life by the poison in the lotus roots – an infection spreading across Shima's flesh. From this altitude, they could see how bad it had become, how far the soil-death had spread. Countless miles of ashen earth, rent with fissures as if the island was bursting; some sepsis forcing its way up through a broken crust. Dark mist drifted snot-thick over the deadlands, never straying far from the desolation's edge.

Yukiko found herself wondering if Kin was right. If there was anything they could do to save the land. Some way to undo all the damage they'd wrought . . .

Buruu lurked behind her eyes, a gentle, cotton-pawed prowl. Feline grace, even in his thoughts, trying his best not to awaken the pain he could feel coiled and ready. She nodded to the southern fields, blurred by smog and distance.

That's Kitsune country. My homeland. The valley I grew up in was filled with bamboo once. Bamboo and butterflies. And now it's nothing but that accursed weed.

WHERE WILL YOUR PEOPLE GO, WHEN ALL THEIR SOIL IS ASHES?

Over the oceans. To steal others' lands with the power chi gives them.

AND WHEN THOSE LANDS ARE ASH? WHEN EVERYTHING BENEATH THE RED SUN IS GONE TO DUST?

Unless we put an end to it? They'll go to the hells, Buruu. And all of us with them. That's why we must be swift. Hiro cannot marry Aisha. The dynasty cannot be reforged.

MY KIND WERE RIGHT TO LEAVE THIS PLACE. TO GO WHERE YOUR KIND CANNOT FOLLOW.

North?

He nodded.

EVERSTORM.

Everstorm?

THAT IS WHAT WE CALL IT.

What's it like?

BEAUTIFUL. I WISH YOU COULD SEE IT.

Will you take me there one day? When all this is done?

She felt sadness in him then, a hint of something usually buried in the darkest corners of his mind. A glimpse was all she saw with the Kenning's new strength, the shadow of something vast, some leviathan moving beneath black waters. And just as quickly, it was gone.

NO.

He sighed.

NO, I WILL NOT.

*

North across the Iishi wilderness, the sawtoothed peak and drop of the mountain range, turning to slow gold in autumn's grip. They cleared the coast of Seidai Island, and she could see Shabishii in the distance; sheer granite cliffs rising like broken teeth from the bloody sea. The storm grew in ferocity, thunder rocking her bones. They slept as night fell, Yukiko's arms bound around Buruu's neck, the thunder tiger falling into a trancelike state; the not-quite unconsciousness of migratory birds who spend months with nothing but the sea for company.

By morning they were floating high above the water, the isle of Shabishii looming out of the mist. The ocean wandered away below them, getting lost before it reached the horizon and melting into the sky. She had never seen the sea before, save the black scum of Kigen Bay. It was nothing like the old paintings; not the colour of deep forest or Kitsune jade or even the eyes of a samurai boy whose smile had filled her stomach with butterflies. It was red as blood, a seething swell reflecting the crimson sky above. And before it filled her heart with aching and she turned from the thought, she realized how childish it had been; to love a boy she didn't even know. To name the shade of his eyes after a colour she'd never seen. And how long ago it all seemed.

She thought of Kin. Eyes closed. Sighing. Running her fingers across her lips, the memory of his kiss lingering like the—

YOU ARE DOING IT AGAIN.

What?

I AM GOING TO START COMPOSING BAD POETRY SOON.

Gods, I'm sorry . . .

A GOOD THING THERE ARE NO MONKEYS AROUND.

They'd begun to find a balance between them: Buruu holding himself back enough that his thoughts didn't make her headaches worse, but loud enough to constantly test her control. She still worked at the wall inside her head, pushing the pieces of herself into place like masonry onto budding ramparts, a dam to bear the brunt of the Kenning's noise and heat. But her grip would often falter, bricks cracking and splintering, his words squealing inside her head like a feedback loop, her nose spitting blood. She felt the Kenning growing stronger; a tide swelling behind her eyes, dashing itself over and over against her slender defences. And still, she had no answers why.

Circling for endless hours around Shabishii island, she finally spied the place she might find them. Glowering upon a natural plateau, rooted so well in the stone it was difficult to tell where the brickwork began and nature's work ended. A skulking cluster of ancient buildings, sheltered against a sheer cliff face, outer walls dropping into the raging sea. Broad curving roofs, like decapitated pyramids stacked atop one another. Dark brick and black tiles.

The Monastery of the Painted Brethren.

No light gleaming in thin windows, no movement on high walls. The buildings were intact but overgrown, long vines working their way decade by dusty decade through the brick. The storm swelled overhead, a splinter of lightning stabbing the horizon, thrust blade-first into that blood-red sea as thunder broke the sky.

Can you see anyone?

NOT A SOUL.

Closer?

They circled. Lower. Nearer. She could see tangled fields in a vast quadrangle, what might have been food crops now trying to run wild in the vaguely poisoned air. A rope and pulley hung forlorn over a natural harbour, gnawed and slapped by the swell.

How the hells did they build this place?

They landed in the overgrown courtyard, cobbles choked by weeds, rain flooding in cackling waterfalls over the battlements. There was no sign of struggle – the outer doors were still whole and barred, the stonework unmarred by siege or fire. But slipping lightly off Buruu's back and surveying the surroundings, Yukiko's heart sank. Whoever lived here had done so long ago. Nobody builds a fortress in climes so inhospitable and then lets nature reclaim it.

Buruu surveyed the surrounds with unblinking, molten eyes, head tilted, puzzlement in his gaze. With a faint disquiet, Yukiko realized the world inside her head was almost completely silent. No blazing tangle of human thoughts, not even the burning sparks of birds or beasts. A few lonely gulls wailed at the very edges of her senses, but that was all. The monastery, the scrub-brushed cliffs, the entire vista felt almost entirely bereft of life. The storm was the only sound, the shushing of constant rain, a whip-crack of thunder setting Buruu to purring, thin fingers of lightning racing each other across the clouds.

I SMELL NOTHING.

Yukiko winced, flinching as if Buruu's thoughts were a solid hook to her temple. Another inexplicable surge of power, always when she was least prepared, her wall dashed to pieces. Breathing ragged, body sore, suddenly and terribly tired of this; her closest friend in the world being the source of almost constant pain.

She fought the welling frustration, knowing it would only make things worse, send the Kenning spiralling out of control. Towards what? Another earthquake? Her skull splitting open, brain flopping about at her feet like some drowning fish?

She pressed her hands to her brow, squeezed her eyes shut.

You're so loud, brother . . .

I AM SORRY. I HATE TO HURT YOU.

Anger flared then, despite her best efforts to press it back. The Kenning had always simply *been*, never changing, never failing; taken for granted as thoughtlessly as talking or breathing. It was as if her legs had suddenly betrayed her, sending her skipping when she wanted to stand still, tripping her onto her face when she wanted to run. For the first time in her life, she was *afraid* of it. Truly afraid of who and what she was.

She looked up to the monastery's silhouette, charcoal-etched against the lightning sky.

I hope we find our answers here, Buruu.

I DO NOT LIKE THIS, SISTER.

We've flown all this way. It seems foolish to stop at the threshold.

I THINK FOOLISH MAY BE BECOMING OUR SPECIALTY.

Thunder crashed again, rain falling like tiny hammers. Though part of her (part of him?) longed to be up in the clouds, her human side was shivering cold, drenched to her bones, the ever-increasing downpour doing little to ease the nagging ache at the base of her skull. She felt exhausted, sore from the flight, thirsty and miserable. A few moments out of the elements would be a welcome change, if nothing else.

We'll find no answers out here in the rain, brother. And every moment we waste is another moment Hiro's wedding draws closer.

A low growl, tail lashing. His volume receding slowly, not unlike an ebbing tide.

AS YOU WISH.

Tall double doors barred entry to the main building, heavy oak shod with iron. She lifted the knocker, rust flaking beneath her grip, pounding it against the wood. Waiting interminable minutes, pounding again, dragging rain-soaked hair from her eyes. She blinked up at empty windows, lighting reflected on cloudy, dust-dark glass.

Nobody home.

STAND ASIDE.

Yukiko backed well away, Buruu lowering his head, talons scarring the flagstones. She could feel it gathering around him – a whisper-rush of static charge, the hair on her arms standing tall, ozone thickening in the air. The thunder tiger spread his wings, pistons on his false-pinions creaking, shuddering, tiny wisps of lightning trickling across his sheared feathertips. The world fell still as he reared up on his hind legs, Yukiko clenching her teeth, covering her ears as Buruu clapped his wings together, giving birth to a deafening peal of Raijin Song.

It was written in the old legends that arashitora were children of the Thunder God, Raijin. That to mark them as his own, their father had gifted their wings some measure of his power. Yukiko had thought the tales a myth until she'd seen it with her own eyes – the night Buruu had almost blasted the *Thunder Child* from the skies.

A thunderous boom rocked the courtyard; the crack of a thousand bullwhips splitting the air in two, the shivering walls bleeding mortar. Flagstones burst skyward as if black powder were being ignited underground, rainwater vaporizing as the shock wave collided with the ancient wooden doors and sheared them to splinters. Iron buckled, rivets popped, hinges squealed as the doors burst inward. One was blasted clear of its moorings, the other hanging from a single stubborn hinge, swinging like a broken jaw.

Dust in the hallway beyond danced briefly in the calamity, echoes dying with reluctance.

Yukiko brought her hands away from her ears, a smile curling her lips. She put her arms around Buruu's neck, stood on tiptoes and kissed his cheek. His purr set the broken stones at their feet trembling anew.

You are *a little magnificent, you know.*

ONLY A LITTLE?

Gasping, hand to her brow as his thoughts bounced like boulders around her skull. Slamming the door on the Kenning again; a recalcitrant child marched off to its bedroom to ponder its wrongdoings. Buruu whined, stepped away, tail tucked. Yukiko could sense he wanted to apologize, but without the bridge of thought between them, he had no way to do so. She wondered what it must feel like for him when she closed off her power completely – to be locked in the cold outside her head, just as alone as she was. Reaching out, she ran her hand down his throat, curling her fingers through whisper-soft feathers, giving him the only comfort she could. As she kissed him again, she saw she'd left a smear of scarlet on his cheek.

Wiping one hand across her nose, she brought it away gleaming and bloody. And with a grim nod to the arashitora, the pair stepped across the shattered threshold and walked inside.

12

Acres of Skin

Skin prickling. Flinching at shadows. Teeth clenched so tight they ached.

A wide hallway stretched out before them into sodden-blanket gloom. Choked daylight streamed through filthy windows, leaking into the corridor as mud-bright stains. The wind was a hungry ghost, chilled fingers scrabbling at the shutters, moaning as it shambled about the halls. The timbers creaked like old men's bones, walls shifting as if the monastery were some slumbering giant, lost in nightmares and praying for dawn.

Yukiko reached into the satchels over Buruu's back, fetched a paper lantern and a wallet of matches. The crackling flare illuminated dozens of old tapestries, faded through the passing of years and the sea's corrosive breath. Bitter cold winds howled through the blasted doors and set the talismans trembling on their hooks.

Buruu was all tingling spine and dilating eyes, wingtips scraping the walls. Brushing the feathers at his throat, her fingertips crackled with static electricity. His talons gouged the stone as they prowled into the dark, ears straining for lifesound. But there were only the tapestries whispering in the gloom, the blustering storm and their own synchronized heartbeats.

They searched every room, found nothing and no one. Dust-cloaked furniture, fabric slowly rotting, lanterns unlit for an age. The sea howling below, rainsong on the tiles above.

At the end of the hall they found an empty doorway, spitting a flight of stairs down into a gloom-soaked room. Yukiko stood on the landing, candle held high, feeble light trickling into a stubborn dark. Down the twisting stairs, she could see a vast chamber, lined with row upon row of dusty shelves. Buruu loomed behind, too big to fit through the narrow space, growling his displeasure, his nostrils filled with the pungent reek of old decay.

Bracing herself, she opened the Kenning again, reached for the thunder tiger's mind. His warmth was sullen, distant, as if oppressed by the deafening silence around them. She could feel nothing but the two of them – no rats, mice, birds. Not a single spark of life. After weeks inundated in the Iishi, the hush should have been a blessing. Instead it planted the seeds of a slow dread in her belly, cold and deep, spreading through her insides with slick tendrils.

It looks like . . . a library.

YOU INTEND TO GO DOWN THERE?

If there are answers in this place, I'm guessing that's where we'll find them.

IT STINKS OF DEATH. THIS IS AN ASTONISHINGLY BAD IDEA.

This place has been deserted for decades, Buruu.

I WISH I HAD EYEBROWS, SO I COULD SCOWL AT YOU.

I can't sense anything. There's nobody here.

I WISH I HAD HANDS, SO I COULD WRITE A HISTORY OF YOUR EXPLOITS AND NAME THIS CHAPTER 'THE WORST IDEA SHE EVER HAD.'

Gods, so just blast the wall with Raijin Song and come with me, then.

THE WALL IS SOLID GRANITE. WE WOULD HAVE BETTER LUCK KNOCKING HOLES IN IT WITH YOUR THICK HEAD.

Maybe you could just sarcasm it to death?

Buruu growled, fell into a moody silence. She could sense the worry in him, the affection clothed in sullen, sulky aggression. But beneath that, the pain was blooming again, the *lubdub* of her pulse like tiny hammer blows in the back of her head. Another surge was building, another squeal of psychic static to paint her lips crimson and make her ears bleed. She was tired of it. Tired of not knowing why.

I'll be back soon, brother. Wait for me here.

Buruu sighed from the tip of his tail.

ALWAYS.

She turned and crept down the stairwell, the stone slick beneath her split-toed boots. Lantern light flickered on granite walls, diminishing the farther she descended. The temperature was chill, a faint smell of oil overlaid with subtle decay. Soft thunder rolled through the tiles overhead, long shadows dancing amongst tall rafters.

The shelves stood ten feet high, crisscrossing planks forming diamond-shaped partitions. Her heart beat faster as she saw the alcoves were piled with scrolls – hundreds upon hundreds, stacked one atop another, running the length of the room.

Daichi said these monks tattooed their secrets on their flesh.

YOU ARE WONDERING WHY THEY KEPT A LIBRARY.

You're amazing. It's like you can read my mind.

Buruu's amusement echoed in the Kenning like a tiny earthquake, setting her temples throbbing. Approaching the first shelf, Yukiko set her lantern down, picked a scroll at random. The paper was greasy under her fingertips, a thick, heavy vellum that felt almost . . . moist.

Unfurling the scroll, she held it out in the guttering light. Browned with age, edges slightly uneven. She could see kanji inked on the surface, tiny verses she realized were haiku. Flicking her hair aside, eyes scanning the page, budding amazement coming to full bloom.

Gods, Buruu, this is labelled as Tora Tsunedo's work . . .

WHO?

He was a poet in Emperor Hirose's court. Four, maybe five centuries ago. He was put to death by the imperial magistrates, all copies of his work supposedly burned.

POETRY SO AWFUL HE WAS KILLED FOR IT. IMPRESSIVE.

They actually put him to death for 'licentiousness.' Listen:

She brought the scroll closer, squinted at it in the guttering dark.

Between your petals,

Awaits silken paradise,

Your love unfurls oh, Izanagi's BALLS . . .

Yukiko dropped the scroll to the floor, wiping her hand on her trouser leg. Face twisted in revulsion, mouth dry, she looked around the shelves in growing horror.

'YOUR LOVE UNFURLS OH, IZANAGI'S BALLS.' YES. I CAN SEE WHY THEY MURDERED HIM.

Oh my gods . . .

I TRUST IT WAS A PAINFUL DEATH?

Buruu, it's a nipple.

The thunder tiger poked his head through the doorway above and blinked.

YOU MAY NEED TO REPEAT THAT.

On the scroll. The scroll has a godsdamned nipple, Buruu. This isn't paper, it's skin.

She backed away from the shelf, one trembling hand to her mouth.

All of this is human skin.

RAIJIN'S DRUMS . . .

'Hello, young miss.'

Yukiko whirled, hand on Yofun's hilt as thunder crashed again. Buruu roared, hackles rippling down his spine, wings crackling with electricity. Lightning streaked across the sky, brilliant blue-white illuminating the gloom, and in the brief flash, she caught sight of a figure standing in the shadow of the stairs.

'Peace, young miss.' The figure raised its hands. 'You have no need of steel here.'

Yukiko refrained from drawing the blade but kept her grip on the katana's hilt, squinting in the gloom gathered after the lightning flare. The figure stood a little taller than she, wrapped in a simple monk's robe of faded blue. A deep cowl hid its face, but the stature and voice were definitely male.

'Who are you?' she demanded.

'Is this the custom in Shima now, young miss? A stranger breaks into your home, and you are expected to make introductions?'

The voice was calm, somewhat hollow, almost breathless. Her heart was thumping in her chest at the sudden fright, fingertips tingling with adrenaline. Feedback crackled down the Kenning, sudden stress opening pathways to her synapses, Buruu looming louder than the storm. She could feel his senses layered over her own, that old familiar tangle – wings at her back, talons at her fingertips, not knowing where he ended and she began. All of it underscored with a vague fear of the waiting pain. The control slipping through her grip.

'My name is Kitsune Yukiko,' she said, trying to keep her voice even. 'That's my brother Buruu.'

'Well met,' the figure bowed. 'My name is Shun. I am master of this monastery.'

The figure drew back its cowl, revealing a thin and pallid face. Hairless scalp, mouth creased with age, wisdom gleaming in the depths of heavily lidded eyes. His irises were milky, almost white, as if he suffered from cataracts. Yet his gaze was focused, drifting from her feet up to her face. He blinked. Three times. Rapid succession.

I CANNOT SMELL HIM.

Buruu's thoughts crackled across hers with all the fury of the tempest above. She winced, tightened her grip on her sword.

I can't feel him either. No thoughts. Nothing.

'Are you in need?' the pale monk breathed. 'Do you hunger? Thirst?'

'I seek answers, Brother Shun, not comforts.'

'We have those in abundance, Kitsune Yukiko.'

'We?' Looking around the ghastly library, raising an eyebrow. 'The Painted Brethren.'

'Is it true you keep the mysteries of the world here? Secrets forgotten?'

Shun gestured to the shelves and their horrid burden. 'Never forgotten.'

'Do you know the secrets of the Kenning?'

'Hmn . . . I believe Brother Bishamon wore some lore about beast-speaking.'

169

'May I talk to him? Where is he?'

'If memory serves . . .' the old man tapped his lip, eyes scanning the shelves, '. . . there. Third row. Second alcove. Though I fear you may find his conversational skills . . . lacking.'

Yukiko swallowed her disgust, a thick, curdled mouthful, drumming her fingers on Yofun's hilt. 'But I can . . . read him?'

'Hai.' Triple blink. 'But it is traditional for a tithe to be given for access to our athenaeum. A small token of gratitude for the brotherhood's efforts at preserving lore otherwise lost to the hands of time and the flames of fools.'

'I have no money.'

Shun offered a conciliatory smile. 'Then we cannot ask it of you, young miss.'

Yukiko glanced at the clump of oily scrolls the brother had gestured to, saw one with the name BISHAMON carved into its handle. Buruu growled in warning, low and deadly. Lightning licked the windows, and in the shuddering flare, she became aware of other figures in the room. One cloaked in shadows behind Brother Shun, another behind her, two more at the foot of the stairs. All clad in those long bleach-blue robes, frayed hems scraping the floor, hands clasped, heads bowed. Motionless as statues. Silent as ghosts.

She was certain they hadn't been there a moment ago.

GET OUT OF THERE, YUKIKO.

Sweat in her eyes. No spit in her mouth. The Kenning flaring wide, Buruu's fear and aggression filling her, pupils dilating, stomach flooded with butterflies. The pain gripped tight, scalding her arteries, the answers she needed just a hand's breadth away. She reached towards Bishamon's scroll and Brother Shun moved, quick as lizards' tongues, as dancing, fighting flies, grasping her wrist with one pale, ink-stained hand. His grip was cold as fresh snow, almost burning on her skin.

'Let go of me,' she gasped.

'The tithe first, young miss.'

She jerked her arm, unable to break his horrid, glacial hold. The burn scar at her shoulder stretched tight as her muscles strained, arm trembling. Two tons of thunder tiger pounded against a foot of solid granite. Buruu's roar filled the room, rippling on the walls, in her chest, peeling her lips back from her teeth.

'I told you I don't have any money,' she hissed.

'We have no need of iron.' Cataract eyes roamed her body, something akin to hunger swelling in their depths. 'A foot should suffice.'

'What?' Yukiko twisted in his grip. 'You want my feet?'

She jerked her arm again, the sleeve of Brother Shun's robe slipping down, bunching at his elbow. And with a low moan of horror, she saw the entire limb had been peeled like fruit, skin flayed clean off, exposing wet dark muscle and gleaming bone beneath.

'Perhaps fourteen inches . . .' Shun smiled. 'You *did* destroy our door, after all.'

'I said let go of me!' she roared.

Her free hand grasped Yofun's hilt, drawing the blade with the crisp ring of metal against metal, bringing it down on the brother's arm with all her strength. Folded steel sheared through cloth, muscle, bone, the brother flinching away with a shriek. Yukiko pivoted, kicked the monk behind her square in the privates, bringing a knee up into his face as he curled over in agony. The three others stepped forward, cutting her off from the stairs and her escape, hands outstretched. She snatched

Bishamon's scroll off the shelf, backed away from the monks. Away from Buruu. The thunder tiger roared again, pounding the walls.

YUKIKO, COME TO ME!

Head ringing with Buruu's plea, Yukiko glanced at Yofun's blade, noticed it was unstained. Thunder in her veins, the Kenning splitting her skull. Stuffing the ghastly scroll into her obi, she tried again to sense the brothers, seize the life within them as she'd done with Yoritomo, grind it beneath her heel. But there was nothing to grip, no heat or life to hold. Almost as if . . .

As if . . .

Brother Shun looked up at her with empty eyes, a ghastly smile splitting his lips. Reaching down to his severed arm, he plucked it from the floor, thrust it back onto the glistening stump (no blood, none at all) and as Yukiko watched in utter horror, flexed his fingers as if to ease some minor cramp. The brother whose privates she'd brutalized picked himself up off the stone, straightened the pulp she'd made of his nose, tilted his head until his vertebrae popped.

'Secrets in abundance,' Shun whispered. 'As I said.'

They lunged, all five, a rolling, snarling bramble of gibber-grasping hands and milk-white eyes. The constant lessons she'd endured under her father and Kasumi and Sensei Ryusaki, the years of wooden sword drills came back to her in a flood, her body falling into the familiar stance, side-on, knees bent. She moved like liquid, like an angry tide, seething forward and rushing back, Yofun held gently in a double-handed grip, its hilt like a lover's hand in her own. She divested one brother of his outstretched fingers, another of his leg below the knee, a third of his windpipe and jugular, the blade slicing clean through his throat. Through it all, she was backing down the row, feet skipping across the floor, wisps of hair in her eyes, hoping to double back through the shelves and make a desperate dash for the stairs.

No blood flowed from the wounds she inflicted, only mild grunts of surprise accompanied her sword's travels, followed by the wet plopping of whatever extremity she'd removed hitting the stone. She noticed the leg she hacked away was skinless above the ankle. Slicing another monk across his chest, she saw no skin through the rend in his robe – merely grey pectoral muscle and a grin-white rib cage.

Thunder rolled above and she screamed to Buruu, loud as she could, heedless of the blood spilling down her nose. At the sight of the ruby fluid smeared across her lips, Shun and his brethren seemed to lose all semblance of sanity, eyes so wide she could see the whites all around, teeth bared and gleaming. Too many to fight under the best of circumstances, and her circumstances were a god's throw from that. And so, sheathing the five feet of useless katana at her back, Yukiko did exactly what her father had told her to do in the face of overwhelming odds.

She turned and bolted.

Using the alcoves as handholds. Hauling herself up onto one of the shelves, kicking in a brother's face as he seized her ankles. Hopping onto the ledge, she tore Yofun from its scabbard again, taking careful aim at the monk scrambling up after her. With a fierce cry, she sliced clean through his neck, blade cleaving bone as if it were butter. The brother crashed to the floor, head rolling away across the stone. Thunder roared overhead, shaking the walls. And with vomit pressing at trembling lips, Yukiko saw the headless corpse rolling about on the ground, hands groping towards its disembodied head. Lighting strobed, rendering the scene in a lurid, grisly glow. Clawing fingers. Eyes still blinking. Mouth still moving.

Maker's breath . . .

Yukiko turned, leaped over the gap between one shelf and another, back towards the entrance, fighting for balance as the structure shifted underneath her. Shun and another of his brethren had scrambled up behind her, two more cresting the shelves ahead and cutting off her escape route to the stairs. She noticed more figures now, fading out of the gloom, clad in those same bruise-blue robes. Female forms standing in the corners with impassive faces, holding armfuls of their own entrails, lit by strobing lightning strikes. Others hauling themselves up onto different shelves, closing in all about her. Dozens. Upon dozens. Upon *dozens*.

Buruu!

Leaping across to another shelf. Shearing through an outstretched, skinless arm. Sweat in her eyes. Breath pounding in her lungs. Blood on her lips, in her mouth, in her veins. Painted brethren closing in about her. Backing away towards the edge of her last shelf-top and clawing the loose hair from her eyes.

BURUU!

Thunder crashed, shaking the tiles above. Lashing out with her blade. Glancing behind. Grasping hands. Snow-white eyes. Grinning teeth. Ink-stained fingers. Heels at the edge.

Nowhere to run.

Thunder again, closer this time, loud enough to shake the floor. Yukiko gasped as the ceiling above disintegrated, clay tiles smashed to dust and rubble; a tumbling, jagged waterfall crashing onto brother Shun and smashing him to pulp. The shelf collapsed below her and she fell with a shriek, landed hard on the stone. Hands clawing at her, pulling her to her feet. And then a roar, the sound of wind and pistons, a white shape diving through the shattered ceiling and splintering the flagstones beside her. Shelves tumbled like dominos, Buruu roaring again, lashing out and splitting the brother holding her in half. He struck a second time, wings spread wide, clapping together with concussive force, timbers blasted apart, leather scrolls spinning in the crackling air like dead leaves.

SISTER!

Sheathing her sword. Leaping onto his shoulders. A sea of figures all around. Rain swirling through the ceiling, static electricity setting her skin tingling. Talons parting flesh, arms from shoulders, heads from necks. A roar shaking the stones beneath them. But in a rush, the sudden press of a starving gravity, they were airborne, more shelves tumbling in the blast of their wings, soaring up through the sundered tiles and out into the open air. Wind in their faces. Rain in their eyes. Blood on their lips, spilling from their ears. They were flooded (she was flooded), body shaking, nausea rising in a rush, out of her throat and into the void, spraying through their (her) teeth as she clawed and tore and pulled back from the brink, back into herself, into her body, this tiny trembling thing with no wings, clinging to his back, small and sick and afraid.

She slumped on his shoulders, wiping the blood and puke from her lips. The pain in her head was incandescent; a thing of rusted nails and serrated teeth and razor wire, coiled tight at the base of her skull. Panting. Breathless. Aching.

But alive.

Thank you, brother.

Buruu purred, thoughts kept to himself for fear of hurting her. She reached down to her obi, taking hold of Bishamon's scroll, the oily, leathered surface giving birth to another round of nausea. The sight of those shelves lingered in her in memory, the miles of secrets and acres of skin. She wondered about the other truths kept there in the dark amidst that horrid brotherhood. What other secrets lay inked in that library of flesh.

But none of it mattered now. It had cost them precious days, the countdown to Hiro's wedding ticking ever closer. But she'd gotten what she came for. She had what she needed.

She just hoped it had been worth it.

13

Proposal

Blinding light was waiting for Hiro when he opened his eyes.

Squinting against the glare, he tried raising a hand to blot it out and realized he couldn't move a muscle. Not that anything held him down, bound his arms to his side, or his body to the cool flat at his back. He simply felt nothing below his chin. A cold numbness, stained with vertigo, the dull sensation of something tugging at his core. He could hear wet clicking, as if a thousand larvae nested in the air above him, chewing blindly with oily mandibles. He inhaled and smelled blood, the sharp tang of metal.

Chi.

He lifted his head.

A dozen bulbous eyes stared back at him, blood-red, affixed in bone-smooth, mouthless faces, a tiny voice in back of his mind wondering how they breathed. Six figures were gathered around him; vaguely feminine forms with impossibly narrow waists. Clad head to foot in leather-brown membranes, mechabacii chattering upon their chests, buckles and straps running down their bellies and long, blood-spattered skirts. Clusters of eight chromed arms uncurled from their backs, slicked to the first knuckles in blood, clicking as they moved. If he could feel it, he was certain his skin would be crawling.

His eyes traced the long, silver line of the spider limbs down to his own flesh, pupils dilating, every artery running cold. They had peeled his chest open, folded the corners of his flesh back like origami, exposing the ribs beneath. The bone had been pried apart, wet and gleaming. They were planting lengths of glistening cable into his chest cavity, his shoulder laid open like a duck at a wedding feast. And as the horror seized hold and shook him side to side, he saw his right arm was missing entirely. Nothing remained but a ragged stump below his shoulder, punctured by translucent tubes and studded with bloody iron clamps.

Hiro fought to struggle in a body that felt nothing at all.

Drew ragged breath to scream.

And woke.

Woke as he did every morning. Sweat in his eyes. Heart rolling and heaving in his chest. Taste of metal on his tongue. And as he looked down at the mutilated nub of flesh where his sword arm should be, studded with bayonet fixtures and snaking iron cables, he sank his head into his hand – his only hand – and let out a shuddering, bone-deep sigh.

A False-Lifer was waiting outside his chambers, ready with the prosthetic cradled in her arms. He felt its weight as she slipped the limb onto its couplings, jacked hungry inputs with gushing feeds, clicking and snapping and tweaking and twisting, finally slipping a thin robe over his sweat-slick flesh. He flexed the arm back and forth; a slow grind of gears and pistons, a sound like chromed spider limbs. He could feel cable pulling beneath his skin. Smell grease.

Pushing open the balcony doors, he stepped out into the

scorching sun. The city's stink rushed inside, underscored with the sharp, wood-smoke tang of burned buildings and dissent. Garish heat licked his skin, a blast-furnace glare forcing his eyes closed. To the south, Tiger ironclads hung limp about the docking spires, forlorn in the poisoned wind. Faint, choking sparrow calls drifted in the gardens; pitiful wretches flitting about on clipped wings, staring mournfully at the red sky above.

He could feel it moving behind his back; the machine set in motion by the Guild and the ministers intelligent enough to have backed him from the outset. The machine of politics, grinding just beneath the palace's skin. The promises of promotion or coin, the thugs and assassins dispatched to deal with those who could not be bought. Like the clockwork hanging from his right shoulder, smooth and unfeeling. All of this. This estate. This city. This clan.

Soon.

Hiro smiled bitterly. Shook his head. Finding no comfort.

Mine.

'Shateigashira Kensai, exalted Second Bloom of Chapterhouse Kigen!'

Matsu's voice tore Hiro from his brooding. The servant stood behind him, bowing low, shaved head gleaming.

Heavy steps. The hiss of exhaust. Cloying chi-scent. Hiro glanced over his shoulder at the Shateigashira's approach; extravagant polished brass, the beautiful, frozen face of a boy in his prime, black cable flooding from his lips. Kensai joined him on the balcony, floorboards groaning in protest.

'Shōgun Hiro.' The Lotusman covered his fist and nodded.

'Do not call me that,' Hiro said.

'Brethren of Chapterhouse Kawa have sent confirmation.' Kensai inclined his head; a small bow barely worthy of the label.

'The Dragon clanlord has accepted invitation to your wedding, and is en route. You are one step closer to absolute rule of Shima.'

Hiro tried his best to scowl. He forced down the faint thrill that coursed through his veins at Kensai's words, crushing it beneath suspicion's weight.

'You really believe the clanlords will bow to me? I am barely eighteen years old, Kensai-san.'

'Yoritomo was thirteen when he ascended the throne.'

'Yoritomo-no-miya was a blooded firstborn son.'

'As your son will be.'

'This is madness. There is nothing close to Kazumitsu's blood in my veins.'

'It is not your blood that matters. Only that of your bride. It is through *her* you bind yourself to Kazumitsu's line. Through *her* you will restore the dynasty, and bring order to the chaos wrought by those Kagé dogs and that Impure abomination. The war effort against the gaijin has disintegrated without the banner of a Shōgun to rally behind. We have reports of Dragon and Fox forces actually firing upon each other during the retreat . . .'

'Their lords desire the throne for themselves.' Hiro's mouth curled in disgust. 'And is it any wonder? In days past the samurai of this nation believed in honour. In the Way of Bushido. But now?'

'Any nation is only as noble as its ruler.' Kensai's atmos-suit hissed as he shrugged. 'The fish rots from the head down.'

'Have a care.' Hiro glared at the Second Bloom. 'I will brook no insult to the name of my murdered Lord. I am Kazumitsu Elite. My oath to Yoritomo holds even in death.'

'Until it passes to Kazumitsu's heir.'

'Kazumitsu has no heir.'

'Not yet, Lord Hiro.' Kensai's eyes glittered like a viper's. 'Not yet.'

'Why are you here, Kensai?' Hiro turned to the Shateigashira, glare narrowed. 'Any minion could have delivered news of the Dragon clan's acceptance.'

'Lady Aisha is recovering well. Our False-Lifers have deemed she no longer need be kept under constant sedation. She finds herself . . . distressed by her predicament.'

'If I awoke from a near-fatal beating to find myself engaged to a simple samurai's son, I think I would be more than distressed, Kensai-san.'

'The topic of her impending nuptials . . .' Kensai shifted, as if discomfited by the notion, 'has not yet been . . . broached with the Lady.'

Hiro stared at the Second Bloom, incredulous.

'We believe it is traditionally the groom who asks for his bride's hand, after all. And since she has no living father or brother to seek blessing from, the one to vouchsafe the union would be her clanlord.'

A hollow intake of metallic breath.

'You.'

'Godless cowards,' Hiro breathed. 'She is utterly at your mercy, and still you fear her.'

'We simply thought she would take the news better, coming from you.'

Hiro swore he could hear a cruel smile in Kensai's voice.

'I have no desire to play your games, Kensai-san.'

'Oh, I know your desire, young Lord. Why you agree to this trial when tradition demands you take your own life at the death of your master. But know you will never attain it without the aid of the Lotus Guild.' Kensai stepped closer, only the vaguest hint of menace in his voice. 'And so, if I request you do your Lady the honour of informing her of her approaching wedding, you will do so, content that it brings you one step closer to that which you *do* desire – to slay the Impure abomination who murdered your Lord and cast the shadow of insurrection over the shores of this great nation. The daughter of Masaru the Black Fox. Kitsune Yukiko.'

At the mention of her name, Hiro's metal hand snapped shut with a clang. He blinked, forced it open again, to be still at his side.

'The prosthetic is fully functional I see.' Faint amusement in Kensai's voice.

'It will serve.'

'As will we all.' Kensai covered his fist and bowed. 'Shōgun.'

*

She lay on a bed large enough to get lost in, red silk pulled up to her chin, the tune of a hundred ticking clocks hanging in the air. A mountain of pillows was piled at her back, the curtain drawn away from cloudy beach-glass windows, bloody daylight creeping across the floorboards towards her. Machines chattered beside her bed, all dials and bellows, a language of punch cards and clicking beads and stuttering harmonics, cables snaking beneath her sheets. A small black-and-white terrier sat beside her on the bed, worrying a knotted ball of rope with puppy-sharp teeth. Its tail wagged as he entered.

She was not clad in a jûnihitoe as occasion would dictate; just a plain shift of deep red, rivers of long, raven hair spilling about her shoulders. No powder upon her bloodless face, nor kohl around her bloodshot eyes. Her right arm was bound in plaster, her lips pale and bereft of paint, left eye still surrounded by a faint yellow bruise, skin split almost to her chin down the left side of her mouth, stitched with delicate sutures. Yoritomo's beating had been far more brutal than most in the court were allowed to believe.

And still, she was beautiful.

'My Lady Tora Aisha.' Hiro covered his fist and bowed from the waist. 'First Daughter of Shima. Last of the line of Kazumitsu. I am honoured you grant me audience.'

'Lord Tora Hiro.' She smiled faintly, as if afraid to split the sutures on her lip. 'My heart lightens to see a noble samurai of this honourable house. I have not enjoyed such pleasant company for an age, it seems.'

Her eyes flickered to the two False-Lifers flanking her bed, arms crossed over the mechabacii on their breasts. The sound of their breathing was a vacant hiss, muted sunlight glittering on bulbous crimson eyes set in faceless heads.

Hiro knelt by the bed. Spring-driven ceiling fans rocked in the exposed beams overhead, circulating a feeble breeze throughout the room. Sweat beaded on Aisha's brow, but she made no move to brush it away.

'I would speak to the Lady alone.' Hiro looked up at the False-Lifers.

The Guildsmen shared a mute glance, remained motionless.

'Leave us,' Hiro snapped.

'The lotus must bloom.'

The pair bowed, synchronized, walked to the door as if they were two bodies and one mind, their boots clicking across the floorboards in perfect unison. The chromed razors on their backs gleamed as they reached the rice-paper doors, sliding the panels away and stepping out into the hall like dancers taking their place upon the stage. The doors closed with a harsh thud behind them.

'Thank the gods,' Aisha breathed, voice trembling. 'They have been with me every moment since I awoke. You are the first of Yoritomo's men I have seen since . . .' She glanced about with wide eyes, as if the walls themselves had ears. 'They are keeping me like a prisoner, Lord Hiro. They will not permit me to see Michi or any of my maidservants. They let me speak to no one . . .'

She sniffed, swallowed thickly.

'You must get me away from them. The Guild. I cannot believe the court would allow me to be treated so if they knew what was happening here. I have nothing to do, no one to speak to. They drug me. Treat me like a sack of meat. My gods . . .'

She clenched her teeth, fighting the fear, the tears. He could see it took everything she had not to break, to cry like a lost child, alone and afraid in the dark. The puppy stopped playing with his ball, watched her with one ear cocked, tail between his legs. Hiro sat and stared for an age, fists upon knees, face like granite. And then he spoke, his voice hard as a gravestone, as dead and cold as the ashes they'd interred in his Lord's tomb.

'You deserve this.'

Wide eyes clouded with unspent tears, lips trembling like leaves in the autumn wind. A fragile, tiny whisper.

'What?'

'You deserve this, my Lady.' Hiro stared at her, pitiless and unblinking. 'You betrayed your brother and sovereign Lord. The Shōgun of these islands, the man to whom all owed allegiance. You helped that Kitsune whore escape with Yoritomo's prize. And because of you, he is dead, the country in chaos, and this clan in tatters.'

'Not you too?' she breathed. 'Gods . . . have mercy upon me . . .'

'But they have, my Lady. They are far more merciful than I. They have given you the opportunity to atone. To alleviate the shame you have heaped upon yourself with your betrayal.'

'What are—'

'You and I are to be married.'

What little colour remained in Aisha's cheeks faded away, blood draining from her skin as if someone had cut her throat.

'The announcement has already been made,' Hiro said. 'Clanlords of the Phoenix and Dragon have accepted invitation. We will be husband and wife by month's end. And together, we will reforge the Kazumitsu Dynasty, restore the line you helped destroy.'

Hiro took Aisha's hand, iron fingers closing around her own. The movements were clumsy, gears hissing and whirring like a Lotusman's skin.

'So now I see.' Defiance burned in Aisha's stare. Refusal to flinch from his touch. 'Shōgun Hiro, is it?'

'You always were an insightful one, Lady.'

'So the Guild have bought you.' Her voice grew stronger, underscored with anger and faint contempt. She glanced at Hiro's metal arm, lips curling in disgust. 'Paid for and sold.'

'Do not dare pass judgement on me,' he growled. 'Everything I do now, I do to right the wrongs you helped perpetrate.'

'Wrongs?' Half laughing, half sobbing. 'You speak to me of wrongs?'

'He was your brother, Aisha. You were honour-bound to—'

'Do not speak to me of honour,' she snapped. 'Your rhetoric about Bushido and sacrifice. Just look outside the window, Hiro-san. Look what this empire has done to the island we live on. Skies red as blood, earth black as pitch. Our addiction to chi draining the land of every drop of life. We wage war overseas, murdering gaijin by the thousands, and for what? More land. More fuel. Where will it end? When the deadlands split wide and drag us all down into the hells?'

'It will end when she is dead,' he spat.

'Ah.' Aisha looked at him with something akin to sympathy. 'Now I see. It is not my betrayal that cuts you. It is hers. Yukiko.'

Hiro's metal hand snapped into a fist. 'Do not speak that name in my presence again.'

'She loved you, Hiro-san.'

'Shut up!' Iron fingers twitched.

'And still you failed. Even after you tore her heart from her chest, betrayed the girl who loved you true . . . still you failed to save your Lord's life.'

Hiro leapt onto the bed, metal hand closing about Aisha's throat. Her eyes bulged wide, colour blooming in her cheeks as iron bit into her skin. The puppy barked, growling as he sank his fangs into the Daimyo's robe and tugged. Hiro's face was a madman's mask, eyes wild, lips flecked with spittle, teeth gritted. He pressed down with all his weight, watching her face flush with blood.

'Shut your mouth, you honourless whore.'

Aisha's voice was a strangled whisper, tears welling in her eyes.

'I . . . pity you . . .'

Hiro drew his face close to hers, twisted with hatred, staring into her eyes, watching their light fade as the moments ticked by into minutes. But as the end drew near, instead of terror and pain, he saw triumph, gloating and awful as she teetered upon the precipice. She did not struggle. Did not flail or kick or slap at his crushing grip. And with a moan of horror he seized hold of the prosthetic with his other hand and tore it away from her throat.

Aisha collapsed, gasping, her mountain of pillows scattered, thick drifts of hair tangled about her face, like a child's plaything thrown into a corner when it was no longer wanted. The pup licked her fingers, whining. Hiro shrank from the ruin of the bed and staggered to his feet, gasping for breath.

'Very clever, my Lady.' He wiped sweat from his lips on the back of his real hand. 'The men always spoke of how you played us like a shamisen. But not today.' He swallowed, shook his head. 'You do not die today.'

Regaining his breath, he knelt by the bed, rearranged the pillows, straightened the bedclothes. And with trembling iron fingers, he brushed the stray hair away from her face.

'No escape,' he sighed, caressing the new bruises along her jaw. 'For either of us. You will be my bride. The line of Kazumitsu will live on through us. At least long enough to see that bitch buried in an unmarked grave. After that, I don't care what—'

She spit at him, then. A glistening spray, right into his face. He closed his eyes and flinched, lips drawing back from his teeth.

'You bastard coward,' she breathed.

Hiro grabbed a handful of her long, black hair, used it to wipe the spit from his eye and cheek. He coiled it in his fist, pulled her head back as she hissed in pain.

'I will leave you now, love.' He planted a gentle kiss on her brow. 'Think well of me until I return.'

She glared at him, boiling hatred unmasked in her eyes. He stood and straightened his kimono, the swords at his waist, marched to the rice-paper doors. Sliding them apart, he turned to look at her one last time.

'Consider your position carefully, my Lady. Consider the

people you hold dear. The maidservants who even now languish in their cells, awaiting judgement for their complicity in your betrayal.'

'Leave them alone,' she hissed. 'They knew nothing of this.'

'So you say. But consider your life is not the only one at stake here. And consider there are far worse fates than death.'

'To live as you do, you mean?' she said. 'On your knees? A Guildsman's slave?'

'It is honour that bids me kneel, Lady. Honour to my oaths. My fallen Lord.' Contempt curling his lips. 'A concept you would have no understanding of.'

'Honour,' she spat. 'If you had any notion of it, you would have already committed seppuku, Hiro-san. Bad enough you allowed your Lord to perish. But for a member of the Kazumitsu Elite to live on while his Shōgun lies slain . . .'

She glared with narrowed, hate-filled eyes.

'You are a disgrace, boy.'

The ghost of a smile graced Hiro's lips.

As empty as the jade-green eyes that rose to meet her own.

'As I said,' he nodded. 'You always were an insightful one . . .'

14

Intoxication

Nothing.

Not a godsdamned thing.

They sat together at the tip of a black spur, dropping away into a raging sea. Buruu curled up, chin pressed to stone, a barrier of fur and feathers against the howling wind. Yukiko huddled against him, almost drunk on his warmth, the rhythm of his pulse entwined with her own as she pored over her grim prize, line by painstaking line.

Bishamon's scroll was not, as she'd hoped, a work concerned with the Kenning's mysteries. Rather, it was a compilation of mythologies concerning Stormdancers and their mystical bonds to the thunder tigers they rode. Though Yukiko had never really considered it in the past, it made sense that every Stormdancer in Shima's history was possessed of her gift – how else would they bond with the arashitora they rode into battle? The scroll contained accounts of Kitsune no Akira's battle against the Dragon of Forgetting. Kazuhiko the Red's triumph over the One Hundred Ronin. An incomplete account of Tora Takehiko's heroic charge into the Devil Gate (she presumed the rest of the legends were inked on some other part of Brother Bishamon's body). But as to clues about how to control the power, or even accounts of it surging beyond control, there was no mention.

Yukiko hung her head, fighting back bitter tears, pushed knuckles into her eyes. Her hair hung over her face, the rain slicking it to her skin in sodden skeins. Lady Amaterasu was sinking to her rest, the Sun Goddess burning the cloud-choked western skies a scorched and bloody umber. Night was falling, and with it, all her hopes.

Slipping into Buruu's mind, lips pressed tight, trying to focus the Kenning to a tiny point, like sunlight through an aperture of flesh and bone. Her skull ached, warm sickness swelling in her belly, pressing at her gorge. Sharp teeth waiting just beneath her skin.

Can you hear me, brother?

I HEAR YOU.

Wincing. Licking slowly at wind-parched lips. Too tired and disheartened to build her wall, to push bricks into place that would only come crashing down again.

There's nothing in here that will help us. Legends of old heroes, long dead.

A bitter and helpless fury curled her fingers to fists. She looked up at a black sea rolling overhead, searching the skies for answers she knew were not there. The ache in her skull tightened its grip. The frustration made her want to scream.

AT LEAST THE EXERCISE WAS NOT AN UTTER WASTE OF TIME.

Why the hells do you say that?

The arashitora unfurled one clockwork wing, wrapped it around her shivering form. The static electricity made her tingle, wrapping her up in lightning's scent.

NO REASON.

She smiled, closed her eyes and rested her head against him. Holding him tight, she pushed warmth into his mind, the gratitude she felt for him just being near. The promise he'd made her was bright in her memory, etched on the stone she set her back against.

'Beneath and between and beyond anything else I may be, I am yours. I will never leave you. Never forsake you. You may rely upon me as you rely upon sun to rise and moon to fall. For you are the heart of me.'

WE SHOULD HEAD BACK TO THE IISHI. THERE YOU CAN SLEEP. AND I CAN EAT.

I hope the Kagé have been treating Kin decently. I worry about him there alone.

HE IS NOT ALONE. THE GIRL IS WITH HIM.

That worries me even more.

SURELY YOU ARE NOT STILL JEALOUS?

Why on earth would I be jealous of Ayane?

. . . DOES NOT MATTER.

No, say what you mean.

He heaved a sigh, wind curling in the feathers beneath narrowed, amber eyes.

BECAUSE SHE KNOWS A PART OF HIM YOU NEVER WILL. BECAUSE YOU FEAR HE WILL SEE IN HER A KINSHIP HE CANNOT SEE IN YOU.

She pouted amidst her snug kingdom of fur and feathers.

I thought you said you didn't understand human relationships.

DO NOT UNDERSTAND THE WHY. THE WHY NOT IS MUCH EASIER.

I don't know what to do.

NO, YOU ARE SIMPLY FRIGHTENED OF WHAT DOING IT WILL MEAN. HE IS NOT HIRO. HE LOVES YOU.

I know that.

AND YOU HIM?

A part of me must. To feel this way. When I think of him and Ayane alone together, I want to choke something.

AH, YOUNG ROMANCE . . .

As the sun sank towards the world's edge, she surveyed the storm looming on the northern horizon. Lightning arced across the clouds and Buruu turned to watch, melancholy staining his mind a somber blue. She reached out to touch it, still unsure of the Kenning's strength, and as she smoothed it away, she recognized it for what it was.

You're homesick.

THE TEMPEST REMINDS ME. ALWAYS.

Of the Everstorm?

WHERE THE GREAT SEA DRAGONS SLUMBER. WHERE RAIJIN AND SUSANO-Ō SING LULLABIES TO STILL THEIR HUNGER, FROM NOW UNTIL WORLD'S ENDING.

Are there many of you there? Arashitora?

A FEW SCATTERED PACKS. THE LAST OF MY KIND. WE ARE SLOW TO BREED. JEALOUS. PRIMITIVE. LIKE YOU IN MANY WAYS.

The question rose unbidden in her thoughts.

You never really explained why you came to Shima, you know. You said you were curious, but I'm sure there was more to it than that.

. . .

Buruu?

GUILD.

Her senses sharpened at the word, feeling his hackles rise in sharp peaks. Staring towards the horizon, squinting in the growing gloom, ears straining for the sound of engines.

I see nothing . . .

USE MY EYES.

She slipped into the warmth behind his pupils, saw the world as he did, flaring too bright for an agonizing moment as she wrestled for control. She could feel her nose bleeding, slick on her lips, narrowing her eyes as if staring at the sun. The details were picked out in brilliant relief; the shapes of the clouds, of every curling wave and foaming breaker. And to the north, she spotted a shadow, tiny as an infant lotusfly, stark black against iron-grey. The unmistakable snub-nosed silhouette of a Guild sky-ship.

What the hells are they doing all the way out there?

WAR.

Gaijin lands are east, not north. If they're a warship, they're way off course.

WE COULD ASK THEM?

Yukiko looked towards the northernmost tip of Seidai, then back towards the tiny silhouette. She knew they should be flying back to the Kagé. They had to plan the strike on Hiro's wedding, Lady Aisha's rescue. But if they let the Guild ship go, the opportunity might never arise to find out what they were up to again. And she *had* promised to deal harshly with the next ship they sent northward.

She gripped Yofun's hilt, remembering Daichi's words. Remembering the endless miles of deadlands they'd flown over during their visits to the clan capitals, the Guild's stain seeping through every province. The rusted pipelines. The blacklung beggars. The Burning Stones.

Whatever the Guildsmen were doing, she'd bet her life it was no good.

All right.

She nodded.

Let's follow and see what we can see.

*

Mechanical marvels they might be, but in the end, sky-ships suffered most limitations of their sea-bound cousins. The truth is, any dirigible is at the mercy of the Wind God Fūjin, no matter how powerful her engines. Heading directly into a gale consumes enormous amounts of fuel, and as the charred remains of three Guild ironclads and the *Thunder Child* before them could attest, the hydrogen in a sky-ship's gut is highly flammable. Which is why, when Yukiko realized the Guild ship was not only flying directly into the wind, but also headed straight for a lightning storm, she knew the bastards were up to something on the south side of righteous.

They'd been flying for almost a day, and Buruu was showing signs of fatigue. He caught sleep in fits and starts, gliding high on ocean-born thermals, drifting in a kind of sleepwalker state. Yukiko kept watch while he dozed, slowly rebuilding the wall inside her head, but he showed a remarkable ability to remain aloft despite being, for all intents and purposes, fast asleep. Yukiko nibbled on the rice cakes at the bottom of her satchels, sipped water from her last gourd. She watched the horizon, gaze fixed on the ship she could now see with her own eyes.

The Guildsman was headed directly into the storm. Thunder rocked the skies, lightning splitting the horizon in hairline fractures. The distance between them was narrowing; the arashitora cut through headwinds a dirigible couldn't. Yukiko fancied the ship wasn't an ironclad – it looked too small to be a warship, and moved faster than a gunboat should.

Scout, maybe? But what are they scouting for out here?

PERHAPS THE PILOT IS JUST VERY DEPRESSED.

The gale grew stronger as day descended into night, the storm reaching out to them with eager hands, adrenaline coursing through Buruu's veins. The thunder was a rumbling hymn in his ears, and each lightning strike birthed a tiny blue-white thrill of delight in his belly.

Could they be headed to the Everstorm?

WRONG COURSE FOR SUICIDE OF THAT FLAVOUR.

Then where are they going?

THERE ARE ISLANDS NORTH OF HERE. BLACK GLASS. RAZOR ISLES, WE CALL THEM. BUT NO MONKEY-CHILD BOAT COULD SURVIVE THERE.

Well, I'm running out of food. And the wedding is drawing nearer every hour we use up here. It seems a godsdamned waste to turn back now, though. What do you think?

. . .

Buruu?

A long, whining growl rumbled in his chest, adrenaline kicking along his veins, pupils dilating. A feeble mote of scent hung on the air; a half-remembered sliver stirring something primal inside. For a second, Yukiko was overcome; Buruu losing all control and flaring bright inside her splitting head, an impulse travelling down the Kenning and filling their mouths with saliva, making their hearts beat faster, breath come quicker. Butterflies in their stomach, face and neck flushing with heat, thigh muscles quivering. They dug her fingers into his fur, felt every strand across their palms, goosebumps thrilling their skin.

With a gasp of effort, she pulled away, drew back from his mind and slammed hers shut, pawing at the blood dripping from her nose. She realized he'd put on a burst of speed, muscles taut, talons curled into fists. She could feel his heart pounding, taste the lingering rush in her veins. Recognizing the sensation from her nights in Hiro's arms, the anticipation of that moment each evening when their lips would first touch after a day of longing, feeling the warmth spread from her stomach down between her thighs. The way Kin had made her feel in the graveyard, her body pressed against him, breathing him in like oxygen and fire.

It was lust.

No, something worse.

Something further from desire and closer to madness.

Buruu?

She reached into the Kenning, trying to expose only the smallest sliver of her psyche, as if opening a door just the tiniest of cracks. His heat burned brighter than the sun. The headache lurched about her skull, a stumble-drunk thing of avalanches and metal clubs, and she closed her eyes against it, holding her hand before her face as if shielding it from a bonfire.

Buruu? Can you hear me?

His only response was to fly faster. The rivets and bolts in his wing assembly groaned in protest, and he climbed higher, out of the wind snarling at the ocean's face, up into smoother skies. Bearing north like a compass point, blood pounding, thudding, thrumming, focused on the faint fragments of scent now filling his mind, hooks in his skin, drowning out her voice and leaving nothing but the thunderous pulse at his temples.

Buruu, stop. Where are you going?

NORTH.

She reeled upon his back, almost falling, digging fingernails into his neck. So impossibly loud. So awfully bright. The pressure and heat turning her skull to glass and kicking at the insides with iron-shod boots.

She twisted to look behind them. Shabishii Island and the monastery were nowhere to be seen. Nothing but blood-dark ocean now, as the sun's last light guttered and died. Howling wind all around, the break and hiss of vast seas below, and fear raised its cold, smooth head in her belly, spread fingers through her insides. Throwing her arms around Buruu's neck, she pressed her face into his warmth. Tasting the echo of his thoughts, the intoxication filling his veins, like a junksick lotusfiend in a burning valley of smoke. And there, amidst his heartbeat's pounding song, the blood-drunk rush of desire, she caught a hint of it. The thing that spurred him on, robbed him of all reason, reduced him once more to the beast she'd met in the shadows of the Iishi, prowling from the darkness, smeared with oni blood.

Somewhere north, a trace hanging on the wind, knotting itself amongst his feathers and dragging him onward, like lightning towards a spire of copper.

It was a female.

A female in heat.

Tempest

Yet pitiless Death,
*   Claimed Izanagi's pale bride, as night claims frail day.*
*   And in Yomi's depths, pure love turned to darkest hate, her*
thoughts to revenge.
*   The Maker God failed, night swallowing all his hopes, his bride*
left behind.
*   Black kiss on his lips, Izanagi put to law,*
*   The Rites of the Dead.*

The Book of Ten Thousand Days

15

The Hour of the Phoenix

Father was just another word for failure.

Slumped at the table with a bottle in his hand, shrouded in old sweat and liquor. Medals on the wall behind, bright ribbons and tarnished bronze, engraved with kanji like VALOUR *and* SACRIFICE. *Empty eyes in a bloated, sunburned face, a spit-slick sheen on the whiskers at his chin. An ugly stump where his hand used to be, forearm mangled, shining skin. Hair like a scarecrow in a crowless field, shoulders buckled under the weight of regret. Knuckles scabbed from their mother's teeth. The land outside running to ruin while he drank himself stupid and blamed the weather, the blood in his veins, the gods, the war. But never himself.*

Never himself.

'Where've you been, Yoshi?' *he growls.*

The boy is drenched in sweat, pollen fogging his goggles, skin blistered from his day in the sun. He hasn't even had time to wash his face, drink a mouthful of water, and already it's begun.

'Where do you think?' *He holds up his hands, black dirt under broken fingernails.*

'And now you're off to town, eh?' *his father slurs.* 'Prancing about with your pretty little friends? You think I don't know what you do? Who you do it with?'

'Who and what I do is my business.'

'You act like lowborn trash, that's all people are ever going to see.'

'You'd know, right Da?'

'I made something of myself, you little bastard. I was a soldier. A hero. Lowborn or not.' He waves at the medals on the walls. 'I proved to those Kitsune bastards it doesn't matter what blood flows inside a man. It's the heart that beats in his chest.'

'Gods, spare me . . .'

'You're old enough now,' he spits. 'Time to grow up. Be a man. Be a soldier.'

'Tell me more, Da. Tell me all about the man I'm supposed to be.'

'Watch your mouth.' He sways upright, the first unsteady steps of a familiar dance routine. 'You act like a woman, I'll treat you like one.'

Yoshi's mother is in the kitchen, head down, bright blue eyes squeezed shut. Hana comes in from the fields, clad in threadbare cotton and lotus pollen. She pulls her goggles down around her throat and glances back and forth between her father and brother. The boy sees the look on her face. The fear. Her eyes are bright with it, brimming with the terror that darkens her every day. Twelve-year-old girls weren't supposed to have eyes like that.

'Have another drink, war hero,' Yoshi says. 'You look thirsty.'

The man stalks towards him. Hana starts pleading to her father, begging. His flower, his baby girl. The only one he loves. Between all the blood and all the years, the only thing father and son have in common. She won't move him a foot, or sway him an inch. But still she tries. She tries every time.

Yoshi raises his fists.

He won't win. His father is bigger. Seven shades meaner. But the boy is getting stronger every day. Faster. And his father is getting fatter and slower and drunker. Every day.

Yoshi won't win. Not this time.

But soon.

*

Brisk footfalls broke the predawn hush, echoing down the suffocated gloom of Kigen's streets. A pair of long shadows preceded their owners across shattered cobbles, through palls of sweat-stale lotus exhaust; dark slivers wearing the shapes of men. The men themselves wore black kerchiefs, broad hats, shoulders cloaked in dark grey against autumn's chill. They walked empty lanes and broken roads, listening to the Guild criers calling in the Hour of the Phoenix and paying the Daimyo's curfew less notice than Lady Sun pays to Father Moon.

Hida clomped along in front; short, ox-wide, a broad, flat face set with piggy eyes, his ears so deformed from years of fistfighting they resembled an extra set of knuckles on the sides of his head. Seimi followed close behind, taller, leaner, crumbling yellow rubble for teeth, sharp lines of his cheeks and chin betraying a feral, gutter-born cunning. Each man carried a clinking satchel and a wooden tetsubo studded with fat iron rivets. Both clubs were stained at the business end; dark smudges that only a simpleton would confuse with varnish.

A tomcat yowled his lust somewhere in the distance; a solitary cry almost unheard of in Kigen these nights. A pack of corpse-rats perked up their ears, hearing a dinner bell instead. All glinting eyes and crooked fangs, they scampered off through the choking smog.

'Three irons say they get him,' said Seimi.

Hida shrugged, said not a word.

They walked on through Docktown's warehouse district, as sure of their welcome as a groom at a wedding feast. Past rusting shells, empty windows like sightless eyes. As they crossed over the sluggish tar reek of the Shiroi River, Seimi looked south towards the dry-docked sky-ships, hanging around the Docktown spires like flayed rats in a butcher's shop window. The pentagonal flanks of the Guild chapterhouse loomed on their right, yellow stone stained by black rain. Seimi doffed his hat in the building's direction.

When the Kagé rebels dropped their bombshell and kick-started the so called 'Inochi Riots' four weeks back, the Communications Ministry had rebuffed all claims about the fertilizer's manufacture. But that didn't mean the rioters themselves were to go unpunished. Hells, no. Not a drop of chi had been shipped from Kigen's refinery since the uprising. The embargo was a 'reminder to the people' about where their loyalties should lie. And as the engines ground to a halt, as the price of fuel rocketed skywards, they sure as hells remembered quick.

Rationing began almost immediately; sky-ship traffic had slowed since Yoritomo's death, and the trains hadn't run since his corpse hit the cobbles. Commonplace items became luxuries overnight. As the city shivered with tiny ripples of civil unrest, curfews were tightened, martial law extended. Music to the ears of men who made their living in the shadows, who swam in markets from murky grey all the way through to ink-black. Men who made it their business to get people what they wanted. What they needed. Provided the price was right.

Men like the Scorpion Children.

Hida and Seimi turned off the thoroughfare, cutting through

Kigen's network of filthy alleyways. The pair were lieutenants of the 'Children, hard as grave stones, moving through the sprawling labyrinth as easily as a koi fish through still water. The tomcat shrieked nearby, hissing, spitting. Rats screeched, the sound of scuffling bodies rang out in the dark. Seimi grinned through tumbledown teeth.

'Got him.'

The squeezeway was a thin stretch of broken cobbles stinking of beggar piss. It was barely wide enough for the pair to walk down, crawling with sleek, black corpse-rats as long as a wakizashi. But the shortcut would steer them clear of the bushi' patrols on the main drag, not to mention shave a few minutes off their trip. As it was, the Gentleman was going to chew them out for making him wait past dawn, and neither man was really in the mood for a stabbing.

The rats perked up on their mounds of filth, watched the gangsters approach with eyes like black marbles.

'Mei still giving you trouble?' Seimi asked.

His comrade grunted in reply: Hida never used a word when a shapeless noise would do. He could go days at a time without forming a whole sentence.

'If she's such a bother, why keep her at all?' Seimi aimed a kick at a fat corpse-rat running between his feet. 'The little brothers should be dealing with the White Crane gang, not gutting each other over a dancer. Izanagi's balls, we're ninkyō dantai, not—'

Seimi heard soft scratching on the corrugated metal above. He looked up and saw smoke-grey fur, missing ears; a huge tomcat peering at him with bright yellow eyes. The thing stood on the awning overhead, spattered with rat blood. Seimi tilted his hat away from his eyes.

'Well, I'll b—'

'Is that what you call yourselves?' A voice rang out in the smog ahead.

Hida ground to a halt, feet scuffing the gravel, hefting his tetsubo in sausage-thick fingers. Seimi squinted into the rolling pall of exhaust fumes, making out a lone silhouette in a broad straw hat at the alley exit ahead.

'Ninkyō dantai?' The smile behind the figure's kerchief was obvious. '"Chivalrous organization?" Who you fooling, yakuza?'

'Yakuza?' Seimi hefted his tetsubo, he and Hida stalking towards the stranger. 'That's a dangerous accusation to be throwing about, friend.'

'Close enough, *friend*,' the figure warned.

The yakuza kept advancing, knuckles white on the hafts of their war clubs. Seimi could make out the figure a little clearer. His straw hat had a four-inch gouge down the front, as if someone had taken a swipe with a blade and barely missed. Even behind the black kerchief, it was obvious the stranger was young. Pale, dirty skin and big black eyes. Skinny. Unarmed.

Seimi laughed.

'Does your mother know where you are, boy?'

The boy reached into his obi, drew out a snub-nosed shape. The device gave out a small hiss, a stuttering click. Hida and Seimi rumbled to a stop and stared down the barrel.

'Where the hells did—'

'Seems I'm the one who should be singing now, friend.' The smile in the boy's voice was long gone. 'Seems you'd best grab a cushion and listen a spell.'

The men heard soft footsteps behind, saw a figure drop from the rooftop and cut off their retreat. Another boy by the look, straw hat and dark clothes, a club studded with roofing nails.

Seimi was incredulous.

'Do you know who we are?'

'Clueless, me,' the boy replied. 'Now toss the satchels, Scorpion Children.'

Hida spread his stance, rocking back and forth on his heels. The boy at the alley's mouth aimed the iron-thrower at the yakuza's chest, pulling ever so slightly on the trigger.

'Gambler?' The boy tilted his head. 'Partial to a roll myself, matter of fact.'

'Don't be stupid,' the one behind them growled. 'Walk off or be carried. Either way, we get those bags.'

'Hells with it.' The big-eyed boy levelled the weapon at Hida's head. 'I venture we just do them. Two shots is no bother. Boy my age has plenty more in the pipe, after all . . .'

'All right, you little bastards.' Seimi dropped his tetsubo, raised his hands. 'Take it.'

He slipped the satchel off his shoulder, tossed it to the figure behind.

'What about you, Gambler?' The boy wiggled his eyebrows at Hida.

Hida stood perfectly still, face impassive as a brick wall. He stared for a slow minute, down the iron-thrower's barrel, up at the calm black eyes hovering beyond. Sparing a scowl for his partner, he slipped his bag from his shoulder and tossed it to the thief behind.

'Very wise, friend.'

The iron-thrower boy waited until his comrade had slunk off into the fog, yakuza and thief staring each other down. The boy's arm was solid as a statue's, weapon still aimed at Hida's head. The yakuza nodded; a small gesture, barely perceptible. His voice was soft as gravel.

'See you soon. Friend.'

The boy tipped his hat.

'Doubtless.'

He disappeared into the smog like a dorsal fin beneath black water.

*

The Gentleman had killed his first man when he was thirteen years old.

A gang fight in some Kigen back lot, a bloody scrap over a stretch of dirty brick and concrete less than half a city block. He'd dashed into the melee, eager to show his worth to the older gangers. He'd spotted the other boy amongst the crowd, smelled the fear in a heartbeat. So he waded across the mob, blade in hand, and plunged it into the other boy's gut.

He still remembered the warmth and smell as blood gushed over his hands. Viscous, copperish, far darker than he'd expected. He could still see the look on the boy's face as he pulled the knife free, stuck it in again a few inches higher. Punching through ribs, twisting as it went, feeling bone crack. The boy clutched his shoulder as the Gentleman looked into his eyes, pain-bright, pulling out the knife and stabbing again. And again. Not out of any need or lust. Just because he wanted to know what it felt like. To take what could never be given back.

The Oyabun of the Scorpion Children wasn't the most frightening man on the island to look at – truth be told, he appeared entirely unremarkable. Greying hair swept back from sharp brows. Dark eyes, tanned skin. Softly spoken, unfailingly polite. Even his enemies called him 'the Gentleman.' His real name had passed the way of the panda bears of Shima's bamboo forests, the tigers that prowled her in yesterday's dark. Gone. Very nearly forgotten.

Calloused hands around a small cup, he took a sip of red

saké. The bottles came from Danro, the Phoenix capital; quality that was hard to find in Kigen these nights. He savoured the sting, the warmth spreading on his tongue. He thought of the woman waiting at home, soft hands and warm thighs. His son would be long in bed by the time he stepped inside from the smog-filled streets. But she would wait up, even past dawn. She knew by now not to disappoint him.

Where are they . . .

His office was a modest affair; old maple desks, reams of paperwork, a windup ceiling fan clunking away in the creeping autumn chill. Sluggish lotusflies buzzed around a small bonsai tree, suffering silently in the lotus stink. A visitor could be forgiven for mistaking the room as the office of a legitimate businessman; a man who made his living selling furniture or carpets or spring motors.

The Gentleman's accountant, Jimen, sat at the other desk. Head clean shaven, thin and quick, dark, knowing eyes. The little man was arranging coins into stacks, pausing after the construction of each tower to shift a bead across the antique abacus on the desk beside him. His sleeveless uwagi revealed full-sleeve tattoos on both arms. Two scorpions dueled in the negative space on his right shoulder, claws intertwined, stingers raised.

'Books look good.' Jimen flapped a bamboo fan in his face, despite the cool. 'Profit is up seventeen per cent this quarter.'

'Remind me to send a note of thanks to our would-be Daimyo,' the Gentleman murmured. 'On the good stationery.'

He raised the saké bottle with an inquiring eyebrow.

'Never seen the black market this busy.' Jimen nodded, held out his cup. 'The Guild will lift the embargo soon. If this Tiger pup secures the Daimyo's chair, he might even start the trains running to let people attend his bloody wedding. So we'd best make the most of it while it lasts.' Jimen scowled. 'And the White Crane are still a problem.'

'Not for long,' the Gentleman said. 'Downside is ours now. Docktown is next.'

'Scorpion Children.' Jimen raised his glass. 'The last crew standing.'

'Banzai.' The Gentleman nodded, taking another small sip.

As he swallowed the saké, the Gentleman heard floorboards creaking outside his office, soon followed by a soft knock on the door. Heavy breathing. The smell of cheap liquor and sweat. The clink of a tetsubo's studs against iron rings. Hida and Seimi.

'Come,' he said.

His lieutenants entered the room, eyes downcast. He looked up, ready to rebuke them for their tardiness, stopping short when he saw the looks on their faces. The Gentleman took note of the faltering steps. The hands clasped before them.

The *empty* hands clasped before them.

'An interesting morning, brothers?'

*

A single iron kouka in Kigen city could buy you a woman for the night. Not some gutter-trash from Downside, mind. A quality courtesan – the kind of lady who could recite the poetry of Fushicho Hamada, debate matters theological or political, and round out the evening with a finale to make a cloudwalker blush. It could buy you a night in a good inn with a warm meal, a cool bath and a bed with a remarkably low quotient of lice per square foot. It could buy you a bag of decent smoke, a bottle of top-shelf rice wine (local of course, not Danroan) or the promise of discretion from an innkeeper about the nocturnal habits of his guests.

Yoshi was staring at over a hundred of them.

Scattered across the mattress in their bedroom, illuminated by a splinter of sunlight piercing the grubby window. Jurou was crouched beside them with a grin as wide as the Eastborne Sea, dry pipe hanging from the edge of his mouth.

'Izanagi's balls, how much you figure is here?'

'There's enough. That's all we need to know for now, Princess.'

Yoshi's hat was sitting on the mattress beside the kouka piles, and Jurou fingered the four-inch gouge through the brim.

'I'm wondering if it's "enough" for you to splash out on a new shappo.'

'That's my lucky hat. I'd sell you before I sold it.'

Jurou made a face, muttered something unintelligible.

The boys hunkered down by the light of the risen sun, listening to the hymns of the waking streets outside. The sweat from their dash across town was still drying on their skin, smiles still tripping in their eyes. It had been so much easier than he expected. So much cleaner. For all their weight, those yakuza had melted like wax. Like godsdamned *snow*. All thanks to a tiny iron lump in the palm of one little hand—

'Yoshi?' Hana's sleep-drunk voice from outside the bedroom. 'You back?'

'*Shit!*' he hissed, lunging for a pillow as his sister knocked gently and opened the door. He threw himself and his thin, feather-stuffed shield over their haul, a strangled 'oof!' slipping through his lips as Jurou sat on top of him, the pair drawing more attention to the coins than if they'd lit them on fire.

Daken followed Hana into the room, regarding Yoshi with a glittering stare.

. . . smooth, boy . . .

'What the hells?' Hana breathed, sleep-crusted eye growing wide. 'Where did you—?'

Yoshi rolled to his feet, pulled her inside. Glancing across the living space at his sister's bedroom door, he pushed his own shut, quick and quiet. Hana was fully awake now, her frown building up a slow head of steam.

'Where did all this money come from, Yoshi?'

'A friendly kami gave it to me,' he whispered. 'Maybe if you sing louder, it'll flit back with second helpings.'

She fixed him in that paint-flaying, one-eyed glare. 'I'm serious.'

'So am I,' he hissed, glancing at the closed door. 'Volume down. Unless you want your lump of mattress-meat to overhear?'

The pair fell into a silent staring contest, which Yoshi eventually broke from. Hana felt around her eyepatch, touched her forehead, running fingertips across pale, grubby skin. She snatched up the tiny looking glass on Yoshi's dilapidated dresser and made a show of squinting at her reflection, still pawing at her brow.

Jurou frowned up at her. 'What the hells you doing, girl?'

'Oh, I'm sorry.' She glared at Yoshi again. 'I just figured someone had tattooed "idiot" on my forehead while I was sleeping. You take the thrower out for the night and just happen to find a Daimyo's fortune in iron? What are you in, Yoshi?'

'I was all set to ask you the same yesterday before I remembered whose business I'm supposed to mind.'

'Me?' Hana flipped hair from her eye. 'Chamber pots are about the size of my affairs.'

'Must be some scary brown in that palace, if you have to go around shooting at it.' Yoshi folded his arms. 'Or did you think I wouldn't spy the 'thrower was one shot light? And who the hells is that lump of beef in your room? Your whole life, I've never seen you bring anyone back home for a roll, and that cripple has been here two days straight.'

'Don't talk about him that way.'

'You don't tell me how to talk, little sister. I'm the man in this pit.'

'Keep running that mouth, you're gonna wake up a lady, brother-mine.'

Yoshi grinned, despite himself. 'All sweet. You keep your secrets. But this coin is mine. I'll air my skeletons when you decide you've got some. Until then, no questions asked. I'm taking care of us. All of us. Blood is blood. That's about the measure of the knowing you need.'

Hana glowered, looked to Jurou for backup and received only a helpless shrug. With a muttered curse, she turned and stalked from the room. Daken remained behind, wriggling what was left of his ears. The cat sniffed the air, nose wrinkled with contempt.

. . . this room stinks, boy . . .

Yoshi glanced around the grubby little space, into the living room beyond. With all this coin, they could afford something in a nice part of town, far from where the Scorpion Children did their business. A few more rips, they'd have enough to go wherever they wanted. No more scrounging or small-time scams. No more slinging rich man's shit for Hana. No more looking over their shoulder or wondering where the next meal might come from.

He nodded at Daken.

This whole place stinks, little brother. You just keep helping me do what needs to get done, and we'll be scampering from this hole with no looks back.

. . . have Hana help? seven eyes better than six . . .

Hana can't know, you hear? Not about any of this. I'd never hear the godsdamned end of it. I'm the man of this family. I take care of us.

. . . not understand . . .

You don't need to. If she asks, don't say anything at all.

. . . how long will that work . . .

Yoshi peered through the tiny window, out into the swelling shift and roll of the city beyond. He could hear Jurou counting coin, feel the prickle of Hana's glare on his skin. The weight of a fistful of iron in the small of his back. The tingling promise of coin in the palms of his hands.

Freedom.

Long enough, my friend.

He closed the bedroom door.

Long enough.

16

Undertow

Three days.

Three days of screaming gales and blinding rain. Of aching muscle and bitter-sharp cold. Of red water and black fear and snow-white knuckles. Three days long. And in the midst of those endless dark hours, there came a single, awful moment that threatened to break Yukiko entirely.

Not the moment she swallowed her last morsels of food, her final mouthful of water. Not tying her hands around Buruu's neck for fear she might fall asleep and tumble into the void. Not in the wind whipping her across his back like a doll of rags. Not even the complete absence of anything but clouded sky and blood-red ocean, stretching to the brink of every horizon.

It was the moment she realized her best friend in the world was a complete stranger.

She begged him. Pleaded. Screamed into his mind until her nose bled and her head split. He could barely manage monosyllabic replies beneath the rush of blood in his veins, the arousal that spilled into her mind if she lingered more than a moment in his. He was an imposter wearing an all-too-familiar skin, like one of those automated Guild criers, set to a single series of functions.

<seek>

<mate>

<repeat>

Storm clouds mustered to the north, glowering black, and as they'd drawn closer, the need inside him had grown worse. The scent was a drug; a curling heat spreading through his system, rushing towards a terrifying high. Yukiko felt some tiny spark of him behind the thunder in his veins, almost extinguished by the absolute need filling every other part of him. And as hours stretched into days, and she hunched shivering and miserable on his back, she'd realized there was a part of Buruu she didn't know at all.

In days past, she'd only caught glimpses of the animal inside him. Her humanity had leaked through the Kenning from the first time she'd shared his eyes, changing what he was. Even in the darkest hours of their imprisonment, it had tempered the pure, primal edge of him. But now that veil was torn away, ripped to shreds and left drifting in the storm, wings pounding at the air, muscles taut, eyes bright, lungs straining as his heart thrashed against its moorings.

She remembered his promise sailing above the Iishi, the words that warmed her soul.

'I will never leave you. Never forsake you. For you are the heart of me.'

It terrified her, how easily she'd been cast aside. But if the thought made her cry, for its part, the rain did its best to hide her tears.

In the grey, blurry dawn of the third day, she spotted jagged islands in the swell beneath them. Some as big as houses, others no more than slivers. It was as if some great beast lurked beneath the water, mouth open to the sky, baring teeth of dark stone. Towards noon, she spied wreckage; a sky-ship's remains bent and broken over a small island, Guild kanji on the inflatable. Later, as the sun slunk below the horizon like a kicked hound, she could have sworn she saw the ruins of another sky-ship; heavier, armed for war, more Guild markings scrawled across her balloon. She couldn't tell if either were the ship they'd followed into the tempest.

These storms would mean death for any cloudwalker crew, Guild or not. What madness drove them up here over and over again?

The wind was a pack of snarling wolves, howls of thunder and teeth of frost. Sleep came in fitful moments – no sooner would she doze off than it would snatch her like a child's toy, fear flooding her insides as she clung to Buruu for dear life. Lightning intensifying as they flew farther north; dazzling, carpet-bomb barrages that left her comatose, black streaks in her vision, ears ringing in the aftershocks. The rain was a numbing deluge, soaking her lips blue.

On the morning of the fourth day she'd woken from dreams of falling to the sight of islands in the distance. Some were towers, higher than any building, twisting at impossible angles like fingers broken back and forth at every knuckle. Others were flat, squat, as if beheaded by the sword of an angry god. They were made of what seemed to be black glass, glittering like razors as the lightning kissed their edges, veiled in rain and mist.

Buruu, can you hear me? Are these the Razor Isles?

No reply, save the swell of the lust in his mind, the poison of weariness mirroring her own desperate fatigue. The female was close – so close he could taste her. But he could feel her mating time was almost done, scent fading like flowers at the end of spring, and the desperation to find her before she cooled filled every vein, every muscle, every corner of his mind.

Long, cold hours swept by, flying low through the salt spray sting. At first she thought them a mirage; a fever vision brought on by sleep deprivation and the storm's relentless assault. But as Yukiko squinted into the blood-red water beneath them, she realized *things* were pursuing them below the ocean's surface. Serpentine tails slicing the swell, mouths full of needles gnashing at the waves, spines down their backs like the dorsal fins of deep tuna. Eyes as big as her fist, yellow and slitted like a cat's.

She'd seen their pictures painted on drinking-house walls, the backs of playing cards, tattooed down the arms of her countrymen. She'd thought them long dead and gone. But then, she'd thought the same of thunder tigers.

Sea dragons.

The beasts were infants by the look, only twice as long as a man was tall. Bright scales, rolling eyes and serrated grins. And though they couldn't keep pace with Buruu, falling behind and whipping the ocean into angry foam, the very sight of them filled Yukiko with cold terror, enough for her to open up the Kenning and scream into his mind until her nose bled and her whole body shook. And in the end, when he ignored her, when every cry fell on deaf ears, she found herself taking hold of him and squeezing tight, chin and lips slicked with blood at the effort, eyes screwed shut, heart hammering, skull creaking, *forcing* him to pull away from the surface and the monstrosities lurking beneath it.

Shaking with fear and exhaustion. Sick to her stomach, wind clawing her skin. Obsidian hands reached towards them, looming out of the mist like shadows of the hungry dead. Her throat was parched, teeth chattering as she opened her mouth to the rain. Closing her eyes, she saw lightning flash beyond her skin. And beneath the roaring storm, wind howling between jagged black glass, she heard it.

The faint thunder of beating wings.

Buruu whined; a long, grating ululation, like no sound she'd ever heard him make. Yukiko opened her eyes and caught a glimpse of pearlescence between spires of black glass, off through the lightning-flecked gloom. And for a second all the fear and fatigue and sadness melted away, and all she felt was wonder that the world could make something so magnificent.

Arashitora.

She was like Buruu, but not like him at all. Smaller, sleeker, like an edge of folded steel. A hooked beak, black as the stone around them, eyes of molten honey, ringed with charcoal. Her head was the white of Iishi snow, plumage like a fan of knives running down her throat, wings as broad as houses. They cut the air, blade-sharp, feathers spread like vast, white hands, cupping the tempest as if a summer breeze. She was muscle and fur, light and hard, razored talons as black as night, hindquarters and long tail slashed with thick bands of ebony.

My gods, she's beautiful.

Buruu roared, but the female seemed already aware of his presence, spiralling up through a thicket of glass. He followed like an iron filing drawn to starmetal, mind alight with her scent, so overpowering Yukiko broke off the tenuous link between them, thrust herself out into cold air and clean rain, her insides shivering with the strength of his desire.

They twisted through the stone forest, diving and rolling across fangs of gleaming obsidian. She was smaller, faster, and Buruu struggled to keep pace or follow her through the impossible gaps between broken black towers. She led them west,

west towards the muted sunset, and Yukiko reached between the rain with the smallest sliver of herself, narrowing her eyes with the effort, almost blinded by the female's spark.

Hello?

A flash of aggression. Confusion.

Can you hear me?

– WHO? –

Her voice was loud as a thunderclap, honey-warm, edged with a softness like wreaths of blue-black smoke from her father's pipe.

– WHAT ARE YOU? –

I'm the yōkai-kin on the back of the sex-crazed thunder tiger behind you.

The female banked right, swooping up between two fangs of stone. She shot a quick glance over her shoulder, and Yukiko felt curiosity swell inside her. Beneath it, contempt. Anger. Something approaching hatred.

– YOU RIDE THE KINSLAYER? –

Kinslayer?

– FALSE WINGS? –

Yukiko shrieked and pressed herself to Buruu's neck as he banked 90 degrees, streaking between two obsidian knuckles. She felt the stone pass inches from her spine, gravity clutching her, praying the knotted obi around Buruu's neck would hold. She was seconds from slipping off his back when he righted himself, swooped beneath a crooked overhang.

The female was a flash of white through the rain ahead.

Listen, I know it's probably expected of you to make him work for his supper, but if you could skip the foreplay and let him catch you, I'd really appreciate it. We've been flying for four days and he's about to have a heart attack.

– DID NOT COME HERE TO FIND MALE, MONKEY-CHILD. LEAST OF ALL HIM. –

What's so bad about him?

– FOOL. KNOW NOTHING. GO HOME. –

Izanagi's balls, that's what I'm trying to do!

– TRY HARDER. –

They raced amongst the islands, still weaving west. Yukiko could have sworn the female was toying with Buruu, slowing her pace, letting him creep closer before putting on a burst of speed or manoeuvering where he couldn't follow. She could sense grim amusement flickering across the female's mind, screeching as they fell behind yet again, but Yukiko worried about Buruu's metal wings – if Kin's workmanship would hold up under this kind of punishment.

Across miles of red ocean and black glass. Glittering spray and snarling waves. Nature unleashed in all its callous beauty. And there, with Buruu's heart straining to its limits, as Raijin thundered his drums, she saw it – an enormous lopsided structure of metal and stone, rising from the ocean on iron legs, crowned with spires of winding copper. Its roof was covered by an impossible machine, all glass tubes and snarled pipes and thick cable, shuddering and pulsing with a glow that wore the colour of new lightning. A smaller machine resembling a giant dragonfly with three sets of propeller wings was chained on the ceiling. And running about it, swathed in slick yellow oilcloths, Yukiko saw the tiny figures of men.

Of *men.*

They were calling. Pointing at her.

What in the name of the gods?

She heard a sudden roar – nothing like stormsong – the shadow of broad wings falling over them both. Tearing her mind from the female's, Yukiko caught the barest glimpse of burning heat in the Kenning before they were hit; a terrifying impact rattling the teeth in her skull. She felt a flash of pain from Buruu, screamed as she was flung from his neck, clawing the air as she plummeted down through the rain. The water rushed up to meet her, a long-neglected lover with open, bloody arms. She hit the surface like a comet, breath driven from her lungs as a deathly chill reached towards the marrow in her bones.

Akihito had taught her to swim when she was a child; she and her brother Satoru paddling in the stream running by their little bamboo house. But the water there was smooth as crow's eyes, not cresting in waves as tall as a chapterhouse. Foaming white hammers crashed upon her head, clothes dragging her down, katana on her back heavy as lead. The current drove her towards the crooked building's iron legs, but it was all she could do to stay afloat, let alone choose a direction. Finally she couldn't even manage that. The water closed over her head, a suffocating, frozen blanket, driving her below, her last sight the silhouettes of two arashitora clashing in the lightning-bright skies above.

Buruu! Help me!

The current dragged her through an underwater forest as her lungs began to burn; towers of cruel reef snarled with rubbery kelp.

BURUU!

No answer save the roaring surf, the undertow swelling in her ears. She struggled to the last, unwilling to end, clawing dark water in a futile attempt to make the surface. But she didn't even know which way was up. The ocean pushed into her lungs, salt and cold and black, and as the light died and all became nothing, she felt the grip of water kami come to claim her spirit and drag her before the Judge of the Nine Hells.

Would he weigh her fair? With no one to burn offerings and no ashes on her face?

Would Buruu miss her?

Would Kin?

17

The Sweetest Poison

Her lips tasted of strawberries and sweat, warm as spring and soft as Kitsune silk. Wet beneath his fingertips, thighs smooth as glass, a river of glossy black spilling around her face and clinging to dripping breasts. She swayed above him; a long, slow dance in the lamplight, spilling across her contours, down into soft curves and sodden furrows. Soaking all around him, slick and scalding to the touch. She took his hands, pressed them against her, biting her lip and sawing back and forth atop him. Her sighs were the only sound in his world, her heat soaking through to his centre. Her hips moved like a summer haze over lotus fields, climbing the mountain as she moaned his name over and over again.

'Ichizo.' Her lips on his own, breathing into his mouth. 'Ichizo . . .'

He cried out as she finished him, arcs of lightning behind his eyes, every muscle afire. She collapsed atop him and lay there for a blissful forever, sweat mingling with his own, flesh slippery against his. He gasped for breath, the sheets beneath them a soaked and tangled mess.

'You . . .' Ichizo swallowed, '. . . will be the death of me, Michi-chan.'

A shy grin curled her lips as she rolled off him. Dragging a sheet around herself, Michi sat up on the futon's edge, picked up the perspiring bottle of rice wine. He watched her profile in the dim light, throat shifting as she drank, a single droplet running down her chin, pooling in the groove at her clavicle. She tossed long hair back from her face, glanced at him with dark, smoky eyes and offered the bottle. He shook his head, collapsed back onto the pillows.

'Truthfully, are you looking to end me and escape?' His heart thundered behind his ribs. 'I'm helpless after that, you should get it over with . . .'

She laughed, small voice husky with liquor.

'I fear I won't have to lift a finger if you're late for the council meeting, my Lord.' She slipped back into bed, rested her cheek against his chest. 'Your cousin will have you commit seppuku to prove a point.'

'Gods.' Ichizo sat bolt upright. 'What time is it?'

'It must be close to Snake Hour by now.'

'Izanagi's balls!' Rolling from the ruins of the bed, he charged towards the washroom. He cracked a gong, and two serving girls scurried in from the hallway, heads bowed, eyes downturned. 'Why didn't you say something?'

'I did say something.' That same shy, delicate smile. 'Ichizo. Ohhhh, Ichizo . . .'

'Demon woman.' His laughter carried over splashing water. 'Two nights in your bed and you've bewitched me. I should send for a Purifier, have him cleanse me of your taint.'

'What would be the point, my Lord?' She pulled up the sheets to cover herself, curled beneath them. 'When the next night you poison yourself anew?'

Ichizo emerged from the washroom shortly, scrubbed and

smelling of lavender. The servants had slicked his hair into a topknot, arranged a long scarlet kimono upon his shoulders. He sat in front of the looking glass as one of the girls slipped a tall, tasselled hat onto his head, pierced it with long, golden needles. His robe spoke of lavish wealth, the irezumi on his skin was the work of a master inksmith. He stood as the second girl wrapped a silken obi around his waist, and he slipped two ornate chainswords into the folds at his left hip. The daishō had the unmistakable gleam of weapons that had never seen battle, yet he wore them like a man who knew the art of the blade.

At a nod from Ichizo, the servants vanished without a sound.

'Well?' He turned to the girl curled on the bed. 'How do I look?'

Michi pulled the sheet down from her shoulders to expose a few teasing inches of skin, staring up at him through kohl-smeared lashes.

'Still hungry . . .'

'Gods, you *do* want me dead. How would I court you from the underworld?'

'Court me?' A short laugh. 'I believe it's customary to do that *before* you bed me, my Lord Magistrate.'

He leaned close and kissed her, tasted salt on her lips, wine on her tongue.

It had seemed foolish at first, to be spending so much time in Michi's room. But the memory of her kiss on the day they met lingered on his skin, and with all the turmoil at court recently, he supposed a few moments in her company would not be noticed. And so he'd visited each day, watched as she whisked and steeped his tea, eyes drifting up slowly to meet his, gift him with that small, shy smile. Questions about Lady Aisha and the Kitsune girl's assault had given way to queries about her family, her childhood. And two evenings ago, as he bowed to take his leave, he'd straightened to find her standing only a breath away. Lips parted. Cheeks flushed. Shivering. She had breathed his name, just once, like a prayer.

And he had not been able to help himself.

He smoothed the damp hair from her cheek, caressing her skin softly as he may.

'Would it make you happy to be on my arm in public, Michi-chan?'

'Of course.' She sat up straighter, bedclothes clutched about her. 'But I'm not certain that should bring any comfort, considering I'd walk on the arm of the Endsinger herself to escape these rooms.'

Ichizo leaned back, searched her eyes. 'Would you rather still be in prison?'

She lowered her gaze. 'A cage with silken sheets is still a cage, my Lord.'

'I am trying. It will take time.' He touched the old scar fading on her cheek. 'I know how you suffer.'

'But do you?' The small dark line Ichizo had begun to hate appeared between her brows. 'No charge has been brought against me, and still my honour is in question. The Kitsune traitor who slew Yoritomo tried to kill me too. I have the scars to prove it.'

'I know.' He ran a finger across the top of her breast. 'I've seen.'

'You declare affection in the same breath you make jest of my disgrace?'

'These things take time, Michi-chan.' He straightened with a sigh. 'Lord Hiro is about to broker deals with both of his political rivals. Yoritomo's old bodyguard have thrown in with him to a man. The Guild already back him. The Daimyo's chair will be his by weeksend. The plight of Lady Aisha's ladies means very little to him right now, I'm afraid.'

'And how is my Lady?' Michi met his eyes again for just a heartbeat. 'I'm not allowed to see her. Though she betrayed our Shōgun, she was my friend as well as my mistress. I loved her, Ichizo.'

'Precisely why you should *stay away* from her. If you wish to prove your fidelity, consorting with a traitor is the last thing you should do.'

'Lord Hiro is your cousin. Who can convince him of my innocence if not you?'

'My cousin is a complicated man, love . . .'

'Promise me.' The furrow in her brow deepened. 'Promise you'll get me out of here.'

'I will try.'

She sighed, wiped at her eyes. 'Trying is not doing.'

'All right, all right. Izanagi's balls, woman. I promise.'

A smile, bright as sunlight slipping out from behind the clouds. She grabbed his hand, kissing his fingertips, one after another.

'Oh, my Lord,' she sighed. 'Thank you. Thank you for everything you've done. Your kindness . . . I can think of no way to repay it.'

'I am sure we can remedy that when I return.' He straightened again, backed away to the door. 'But now I must go, or Hiro will have my life and all will be for naught.'

She planted a feather-light kiss onto her fingertips and blew it to him. 'I'll miss you.'

'I will return, fear not.'

He slipped from the room with his serving retinue, leaving

her alone amidst the fading footsteps. He did not see the smile fall from her lips like a mask at the end of a kabuki play.

He did not see her wipe his taste from her lips.

He did not hear her whisper.

'I fear nothing.'

*

She was six years old when the Iron Samurai came to Daiyakawa. She remembered the sound their armour made, like a snake pit full of twisting metal, heavy boots drumming on the sun-cracked road. The bushimen came behind, so many that the dust in their wake was as tall as a tsunami. But really, the Iron Samurai would have been enough. The other soldiers were present for show; the feathers of a peacock spread to impress his rivals.

The morale of the Daiyakawa men was worn paper-thin, courage hanging by a thread. It was rage that had given them the strength to defy the government and sow their fields with whatever crops they saw fit, plant the magistrate's head on a spike along the Kigen road. But rage soon gave way to fear; to realization about what they'd done and where it must inevitably lead. Michi was only a child at the time, but in later years she would understand the listless steps and hollow eyes: the look of men who believe they are already dead, and are simply waiting for the world to confirm their suspicion.

But her uncle was a man of courage. He spoke with the voice of a tiger, the voice of a man whom other men would follow. Urging them to resist to the last. That if this was to be their end, then it should be worthy of remembrance. But the Iron Samurai cut through their overturned wagons and pitiful barricades without pause, sheared through leather armour and pitchfork spears like torchlight through shadow. And as they dragged her cousins and aunt into the street and executed them before him, Michi saw her uncle's spirit shatter like glass. In that last moment, in that final breath before they bid him plunge his own knife into his gut, she knew he was broken. And the world knew it too.

She looked at the samurai captain, into cold steel-grey eyes behind his tiger mempō, and vowed she would never share her uncle's fate.

Hard years followed, as Daiyakawa's farmers tried to rebuild their lives, forget their exhilaration as the guardhouse went up in flames; their tiny moment of infinite possibility. The memory was a curse to most, a leaden weight on their backs, doubling the burden of the Guild yoke retied around their necks. And if they spoke of the riot at all, it was with hushed voices in darkened corners, shoulders slumped and tongues bitter with the taste of regret.

Michi's parents had passed when she was five, and now without family to care for her, she felt like a burden and was treated as one. She longed for the day she would be old enough to find her own way. To leave Daiyakawa and the hungry ghosts haunting its streets far, far behind.

And one day a samurai came to the village. Old-fashioned swords were crossed in his obi, gilt cranes taking wing across the lacquer. He wore black cloth, like a man in mourning, a broad, bowl-shaped shappo on his head. A young girl walked beside him, covered in the dust of the road, long fringe and a black kerchief obscuring her features. And as they stood in the village square and the man tilted the hat away from his face, Michi recognized his eyes. The same eyes that had watched from behind an iron tiger mask as his men carved her kin to pieces.

Their captain.

She had screamed then; snatched up a switch of wood and charged, swung it with all the might a nine-year-old could muster. And he caught her up and held her tight against his chest, held her

as she screamed and kicked and thrashed and bit, calling down
the curses of all the gods upon his head. Held her until there was
nothing left inside her, until she sagged, broken-doll limp in his
arms.

And then he spoke. Of regret. Of guilt's burden. Of the falsities
of the Way of Bushido, and the crimes he had committed in the
name of loyalty and honour. Of a group to the north who saw the
truth, who had vowed as she had done, never to kneel again, and
never to break.

He spoke with the voice of a tiger. A voice other men would
follow.

'My name is Kagé Daichi,' he said.

And in that moment, she knew she would follow him too.

18

Contours

Ayane was starting to look like a human being.

Her stubble was a shadow across her scalp, black as the water in Kigen Bay. Even inside her cell, the mountain air had done her good, and the few supervised moments the Kagé allowed her in the dappled sunlight had given her skin just the slightest hint of colour. Fresh fish and wild rice had filled out the flesh on her bones, and when she laughed, her eyes lit up like kindling-wheels on Lord Izanagi's feast day.

Kin was seated outside the bars of her cell, a sheet of rice-paper and some charcoal sticks spread out before him. The girl sat opposite, legs crossed, spider limbs curled at her back.

'You look better with eyebrows,' he smiled.

'They feel strange.' Ayane rubbed her forehead, frowning.

'Well, they suit you. Very distinguished.'

When she stuck out her chin and wiggled an eyebrow in dramatic fashion, they both laughed. Just like real people.

'I had a dream last night,' she said. 'It is the first one I have had aside from my Awakening in as long as I can remember. Has that ever happened to you?'

'No.' A small shake of his head. 'I only have the one. Over and over.'

'Awful is it not?'

'I'm used to it.' A shrug. 'What was your dream about?'

The girl stared down at the fingers entwined in her lap. A faint blush lit her cheeks.

'You,' she said.

Kin was unsure where to look. He cleared his throat, lips twisting into something between a grin and a grimace, feeling his own cheeks flush. Embarrassment stole over Ayane's face and she gave a short, uncomfortable chuckle, eyes searching the room, finally seizing on the paper spread out at his feet.

'So . . . this is your infamous defence perimeter?'

'Ah, it is . . .' He nodded, lunging towards the new topic as fast as his lips would take him. 'A schematic, anyways. The real thing is almost complete. We salvaged seven heavy shuriken-throwers from the ironclad ruins, set them up near the pit traps. I've modified the feeders to work on hand-cranked power, but we're still getting pressure loss in the firing chambers.' A shrug. 'I can't figure it out.'

'I do not know why you are asking me.' Fingers curled beneath her chin, earth-brown eyes scanning the drawings. 'You are Munitions Sect. I am just a False-Lifer, remember?'

'You *were* a False-Lifer.'

Bumblebee lips curled in another small, embarrassed smile. 'I confess I am still getting used to thinking like that.'

'Another set of eyes always helps. Besides, you have a way with machines. I can tell.'

'It would be easier if I could see the modifications firsthand. Instead of just plans.'

'I'm working on it,' Kin shrugged. 'The Kagé have other things on their minds.'

'Arashi . . . I mean, Yukiko?'

'It's been eight days. She should be back by now.'

Ayane looked at him through the bars, head tilted. 'Are you concerned?'

'A little.' A sigh. 'But she's with Buruu. He'll take care of her.'

'Do you miss her?'

'Why do you ask?'

'Well, just . . .' Ayane sucked her bottom lip. 'Just the way you speak about her, is all. I thought perhaps she was special to you.'

'Would you mind if we didn't talk about this?'

'I am sorry.' She reached through the bars and placed a gentle hand upon his knee. 'I am certain she is all right.'

Kin gave her fingers a soft squeeze, turned his eyes to the blueprints.

'Isn't this a pretty picture . . .'

Ayane started at the voice, Kin turning more slowly, cold fear greasing his insides. They were standing in the doorway – three boys around his age; sword-grip hands and battle-hard stares. He felt a surge of adrenaline, the instinctive reaction of a trapped animal, flight and fight tumbling over one another inside his head.

He pulled himself to his feet, jaw clenched, staring at each boy in turn.

'Hello, Guildsman.' Isao ran a hand along the thin stubble on his chin, up through the topknot of long, dark hair. His face was angular, cut rather than molded by the Maker's hand. Short sleeves showed burns where his irezumi used to be, hard muscles and tanned skin.

Two other boys crowded the doorway behind him. Kin knew their names: small and wiry Atsushi, the boy who'd found Ayane in her pit. His big crooked-faced cousin Takeshi, who'd interrupted Yukiko's kiss in the graveyard. Arms folded, jaws set, goggles hiding the flint and steel in their eyes. Both growled salutations ending with the word 'Guildsman.'

'My name is Kin,' he said.

'Your name is shit,' Isao spat.

'What do you want, Isao-san?'

'You gone, whoreson,' Atsushi growled.

'I'm not going anywhere.'

Isao stepped forward, fists clenched. He was a little younger than Kin, but bigger. Weatherworn and battle-tested.

'You're going to the Yomi Underworld for what you've done to these islands. You and this little spider-legged bitch.' He gestured at Ayane, pale and wide-eyed with fright. 'You and all your kind are poison.'

'They're not our kind, Isao.' Kin licked his lips, tried to keep the anger from his voice. 'You have no idea what it cost us to be here. You don't know anything about us.'

'I know you're a traitor.' Isao took another step closer, just a few feet away now. 'A liar who sold out his own kind. And now you're up here spreading your cancer among my family. The little toys you make for the children. Your marvellous machines spitting poison into—'

'They're not chi-driven, you imbecile,' Kin spat. 'The shuriken-throwers are just hydraulics and gas-power. You don't need to burn lotus to—'

'What did you call me?' Isao's lips pulled back from his teeth.

'You heard.'

'Please . . .' Ayane began. 'We want no trouble.'

Isao spit on the decking, glaring at the girl. 'My mother and father both died of blacklung from the poison your machines shit into the sky. Takeshi's mother was executed for sedition when he was six. Atsushi's sister was burned at the godsdamned stake by your bastard Purifiers.' He narrowed his eyes. 'You think we give a shit what you want?'

'We're going to hurt you, Guildsman.' Takeshi scowled at Kin, crooked jaw, cracking knuckles. 'Until you squeal.'

'And we're going to keep hurting you until you see you don't belong here,' Isao said. 'Until you and this bitch crawl back to your five-sided pit and leave us the hell alone.'

'Stay away from us.' Kin kept the tremor from his voice, raising his fists. 'I mean it.'

Isao laughed, looked at the other boys. 'Look out, he means—'

Kin's strike took him on the jaw, rocked his head back on his neck. A bone-hard ball of knuckles, landing heavy enough to split the younger boy's lip. Isao staggered back as Kin grabbed his collar, swinging wildly with his free fist. He got in another solid hit to Isao's temple, knocking his goggles askew before the others tore him off.

The gut punch knocked his breath loose, and his legs were swept out from under him. He fell back, cracked his head on the bars, bright stars bursting in his eyes. Ayane screamed as two kicks thudded against his ribs, curled him into a ball. He lashed out blindly, caught one of the boys on the shins.

'A little fight in you, eh?'

Isao rolled Kin onto his back as Takeshi grabbed his feet, held them in place. The younger boy sat on his chest, pinned Kin's arms with his knees. Blood from his split lip spattered against Kin's cheek. Isao drew a blade from his obi, tore Kin's tunic open, pressed the knife-point into the bayonet socket beneath Kin's collarbone. Kin felt the cable move beneath his skin as Isao twisted his blade. The metals made an awful sound as they kissed.

Skrrrritch. Skrrrritch.

'Stop it!' Ayane screamed. 'Please!'

'You're going to pay for that.' Isao licked his busted lip. 'And maybe when we're done, we'll unlock this cage, play with your little sister here? You think she'd like that, Guildsman?'

A mouthful of spit sprayed into Isao's eye.

'MY NAME IS KIN!'

'You boys!' A woman's shout. 'Leave him alone!'

Kin heard sandals slapping against the floorboards, felt the weight on his chest ease. Isao stood and sheathed his tantō, wiped the spittle from his face. His cheeks were flushed with rage, breath coming in quick, heaving gasps. The blood on his mouth was red as the wounded sky outside, bottom lip already swelling.

Kin rolled to his knees, dry retching and clutching his collarbone. Through the blur of sweat and pain, he saw Old Mari standing in the doorway, brandishing a cane as ancient and gnarled as she was.

'Get away from him.' The old woman's voice was hoarse with indignation. 'Go on, off with you. Three against one? You shame yourselves.'

The boys muttered and shuffled towards the door. Isao straightened his goggles, lips curled into an upside-down grin. He pointed at Kin, spit blood at his feet.

'See you tomorrow, Guildsman.'

Old Mari shoved through the boys as they loped out, smacking Takeshi on the behind with her walking stick. Ayane reached through the bars, clutched at Kin's hand.

'First Bloom, are you all right?'

It took a minute or two for him to catch his breath, crouched with one palm planted on the floor. He touched his ribs and winced, straightened with a groan.

'I'm all right . . .'

'Disgraceful.' Mari clapped her cane upon the boards, scowling after the boys. 'What matter if Isao and Takeshi are oni killers? You'd think before teaching them the sword, Sensei Ryusaki would teach them some damned courtesy.'

Kin looked at the old woman, tried to twist his grimace into a smile. She was a good foot shorter than he, stick-thin, back bent as if she carried the world upon her shoulders. One hand clasped her walking stick, the other a basket laden with fish and rice. Her skin was like leather, grey hair bound in a widow's bun, rheumy eyes pouched in bags so heavy Kin wondered how she could see at all. She was in charge of the Kagé infirmary, had cared for Kin as he recovered from his trek to the Iishi. Her bedside manner was as pleasant as a flying kick to the privates, but she'd patched him up well enough.

'That was damned foolish of you.' She looked him up and down, her scowl undiminished. 'Taking on three at once. Who do you think you are, Kitsune no Akira? The old Stormdancers usually had thunder tigers with them in battle.'

'They cornered us.' He touched the input jack at his collar, wincing. 'I've done all the running I'm going to do. A man faces his enemies.'

'Oh, so you're a man, are you? Ready to take on the world alone?'

'Ready to stand up for myself, at least.'

'The best thing you can do is tell Daichi.'

'No.' Ayane looked at the old woman with pleading eyes. 'I do not wish for there to be any trouble on my account.'

'Daichi won't care, Mari,' Kin sighed.

'Remain a fool, then,' Mari shrugged. 'But if Yukiko were here, she'd—'

'Well, she's not here, is she? And sometimes I wonder why the hells I am.'

Kin ran one hand over the stubble at his scalp, pulled his anger into check. Talking like that in front of Ayane wasn't going to make her feel any more at ease. It wasn't going to make him feel better, either. He glanced sideways at the old woman, sighing.

'What are you doing here, anyway?'

'I heard the False-Lifer cry out.'

'Her name is Ayane.'

Old Mari pursed her lips, utterly ignoring the girl behind the bars. 'Don't you have work to do? Something other than serving as a punching bag, I mean? Ryusaki was looking for you earlier.'

'I know, I know.' He pointed to the crumpled plans strewn across the floor. 'I was just about to head out to the line.'

A scowling sigh. 'Well, I'm on my way to take the boys breakfast now, if you wish to skulk along behind me. Just don't walk too close.'

Kin turned to Ayane. 'Are you going to be all right here?'

The girl offered him a tiny, frightened smile. 'I cannot be anywhere else, can I?'

'I'll come back and check on you tonight, if you like?'

'Hai.' The smile broadened. 'Very much.'

Kin gathered up the scattered plans, nodded good-bye, limped out the door. Old Mari led the way, her cane beating crisp upon swaying footbridges. Nodding and smiling to the other villagers and studiously ignoring Kin, careful not to give the impression they were walking together. The old woman was remarkably spry, even with her arms laden, scaling down one of the winding ladders from the hidden village to the forest floor. As Kin stumbled after her through the undergrowth, autumn's scent wrapped him in soft hands, the warm perfume soothing the ache of footprints on his ribs. Walking miles through beautiful green and rusting hues, Old Mari slowed down enough for Kin to catch up with her. She said nothing, but occasionally the boy caught her watching him out of the corner of her sandbag eyes.

Finally arriving at the first of the emplacements, Kin found a group of Kagé standing beside the bent and scowling lump of a heavy shuriken-thrower. Truth be told, it wasn't the prettiest contraption Kin had ever turned a wrench on; four long, flattened barrels, a twisted knot of hydraulics and feeder belts, planted in the earth on a tripod of hastily welded iron. An operator's seat was affixed to the 'throwers backside, allowing the controller to swivel with the weapon as it moved. Cylinders of pressurized gas were bolted at the base, cable winding up the turret like a cluster of serpents. When fired, the 'throwers sputtered and lurched about like violent drunkards, and were only a little more accurate.

'Ugly as a pack of copper-coin rent boys,' was the descriptor Kaori had chosen when she first laid eyes on them, and Kin had found it hard to disagree. But, unsightly as they might look, the test runs had gone well, pressure fluctuations aside. The forest in front of the 'thrower emplacement was shredded in a neat 180-degree arc – scrubs torn down to miserable stumps, saplings beheaded, bleeding rends torn through ancient trunks.

A half-dozen more of the emplacements were set up along the northwest of the village, the mountains and the pit traps funnelling any potential approach from Black Temple into a relatively defensible zone. Kagé scouts still undertook dangerous patrols out in the wilds, but should it actually come to an attack, at least they wouldn't have to fight hand to hand against a legion of twelve-foot pit demons.

Probably a good thing, since Yukiko isn't here to help them this time . . .

Kin sighed, stomach turning, worry gnawing his insides as the memory of Yukiko's lips set his heart to pounding. He knew Buruu would never let anything happen to her, but still, the fear of having no word, the ache of her absence . . .

The Kagé gathered around the 'thrower were clad in shades of autumn foliage, split-toed boots crunching in dead leaves. Most of the men eyed him with suspicion, the remainder with outright hostility. Sensei Ryusaki was the most senior figure present – a member of the Kagé military council, and a renowned swordmaster who had served under Daichi's old command. The man had deeply tanned skin, a shaved skull and a long black moustache. He was missing his front teeth, compliments of a bar fight in his youth (in one of the few strained conversations they'd had, he'd warned Kin to beware of pretty girls with older brothers) and whistled through the gap almost constantly.

The captain stood, chin buttered with grease, pipe wrench in one hand, smiling at Old Mari. The old woman handed over her basket of food and promptly admonished the captain about eating properly.

Ryusaki glanced at Kin after receiving his dressing-down, narrowed a critical eye.

'Been in the wars, boy?'

'Just a skirmish.' Kin rubbed his input jack again.

'Serious enough to pop your lining.' The man pointed to Kin's arm.

Kin realized the scuffle with Isao and his fellows had opened up the wound he'd earned during the ironclad attack. Blood was seeping through the fabric at his shoulder, staining the grey a deep, somber red.

'You should head to the infirmary,' Ryusaki said. 'Get it looked at.'

'Old Mari has called me a fool twice already this morning.' Kin gestured to the woman. 'That's enough of her ministrations for one day, I think.'

Ryusaki aimed a toothless grin at Mari. 'Been picking on our little Guildsman, mother?'

'Hmph.' The old woman scowled Kin up and down. 'Boy is foolish enough to take on three young bucks at once, he should thank Kitsune some burst stitching was the worst of it.'

'Three?' Ryusaki raised an eyebrow. 'Who did you tangle with, boy?'

'It is no matter, Ryusaki-sama.' A bow. 'My thanks for your concern.'

The captain stared for half a moment, shrugged, and turned his eyes on the 'thrower.

'We took the entire line for a test run early this morning. 'Throwers four through six did surprisingly well. Number one popped a seal and lost power; two, three and seven are still suffering pressure failure. But we're getting there. Kaori was dark as thunder when Daichi approved this madness of yours, but there might be reason to it after all.'

'I think I can fix the pressure issues.' Kin hoisted his schematics. 'I almost have it right in my head.'

'A good thing. That earthquake has the oni riled up worse than a Docktown whorehouse on soldier's payday, no mistake.'

Mari slapped his arm. 'Watch that toothless filthpit of yours before I fetch the soap . . .'

A soft chuckle whistling through missing teeth. 'Forgiveness.'

The captain turned his gaze to the northwest, grin slowly fading, eyes narrowed in the dim light. Kin stood beside him, looking out into the growing gloom. The wind was picking up, howling through the trees, a storm gathering strength among the surrounding peaks. Thunder cracked somewhere to the north, dead leaves falling around the captain like rain.

'I know you weren't there for the battle last summer, boy,' Ryusaki said, voice somber. 'I know you've never seen one of these things up close. And you strike me as the sort who doesn't put stock in what he hasn't seen with his own eyes. But these oni, they're spat direct from the Yomi underworld, make no mistake, and our scouts have seen *packs* of the bastards moving near Black Temple over the last two days. I'm thinking that earthquake tore one of the cracks in the mountain wider, let a few more of the little ones squeeze through. Straight from the Endsinger's belly, full of all her hatred for the world of men.'

'. . . We'd best get to work, then,' Kin said.

Ryusaki nodded. 'I'm heading out tomorrow, by the by. I'll be gone two weeks or thereabouts, so you'll be reporting direct to Kaori.'

Kin groaned inwardly at the thought. 'Where do you go, Ryusaki-sama?'

The captain hid his distrust well, but Kin could still feel it prickling on his skin.

'. . . South,' Ryusaki said.

Kin pursed his lips, nodded slow. No more than he should have expected, truth be told. Turning to the 'thrower, he pried off the firing mechanism housing. Placing it on the ground with a wince, he rubbed at his bloodstained shoulder. The old woman watched him, something a few feet shy of guilt in her eyes.

'Listen . . . if you wish to come back with me, get that wound restitched . . .'

'I am fine,' Kin said. 'Truly.'

Mari clicked her tongue against the roof of her mouth. 'You remind me of my husband, Guildsman. He was stubborn as a mule too. Right up to the day he got killed.'

'I appreciate the concern, Mari-san.' Kin turned his eyes to the machine, tried to keep the anger from his voice. 'But I can take care of myself.'

'Have it your way,' Mari sighed. 'I'll be in the infirmary when the dust settles. But you're a fool if you think you can deal with all your troubles alone.'

The boy plucked a torque wrench from his belt, looked over the 'thrower emplacement with a sigh.

'A man can dream . . .'

*

Hundreds of eyes, red as sunset, staring up at Kin with as much adoration as glass could muster. A sea of brass faces, stretching into dark corners, smooth and featureless. Infinite repetitions of the same iteration; no individuality or personality, no expression or humanity in each razor-sharp contour. His own face, but not his at all. Over and over again.

Walls of stone, yellow and dripping, the songs of engine and piston and gears blurring into a monotone hum, a broken-clock rhythm that seeded at the base of his skull and sent out roots to claw the backs of his eyes. And he stood above them on the gantry, stared down at their upturned faces, felt the comforting weight of metal on his bones and knew that he was home.

They were calling his name.

He held his arms wide, fingertips spread, the lights of their eyes glinting on the edges of his skin. The gunmetal-grey filigree embossed upon his fingertips, the cuffs of his gauntlets, the edges of his spaulders. A new skin for his flesh; the skin of rank, of privilege and authority. Everything they had promised, everything he had feared had come to pass. It was True.

This was Truth.

They called his name, the assembled Shatei, holding their

hands aloft. And even as he drew breath to speak, the words rang in his head like a funeral song, and he felt whatever was left of his soul slipping up and away into the dark.

He knew he was asleep; knew this was only the dream of a thirteen-year-old boy, huddled in the Chamber of Smoke as the poison crept into his lungs. The same vision that had plagued him every single night since he Awakened. But he could still taste the lotus on his tongue, feel the weight of his skin upon his flesh and the gut-wrenching fear as his What Will Be was laid bare before him.

The multitude below fell silent. He looked down at the scarlet pinpricks in the dark, swaying and flickering like fireflies on a winter breeze. His voice was a fierce cry, hollow and metallic behind the brass covering his lips.

'Do not call me Kin. That is not my name.'

In the dream, he felt his lips curl into a smile.

'Call me First Bloom.'

19

Catching the Sky

The pain in her lungs was a living thing; a fire pressing against her ribs as black flowers bloomed before her eyes. The shock of impact, the water's chill clawing at her marrow, rocks as sharp as demon's teeth tearing her flesh – all of it secondary to the burning in her chest, the screaming in her head, the desperation forcing her mouth open to the black and the salt and the death that lay inside a single lungful.

Breathe.

She swam up. Or down. One as good as the other, the swell tumbling her like throwing sticks between forests of cruel stone, slick with grasping weed. Dull roaring in her ears, pressing her down, the blinding desire for oxygen becoming more than just a need; a reflex impulse over which she finally lost all control.

BREATHE.

She opened her lungs to the ocean, and the ocean dived inside.

*

Yukiko woke with a start, sobbing, gasping as sweet, blessed air filled her lungs. Her clothing was drenched, hair plastered to her face in thick, black drifts. She tried to claw it from her eyes, felt restraints around her wrists; leather thongs binding her to the flanks of an iron bed frame, clean sheets entwined about her ankles. She thrashed for a moment, vertigo swelling, staring around the dank, grey room without any idea where she was.

A voice spoke. Tangled words she didn't understand.

She jerked towards the sound, saw a fierce-looking man reaching for her. Perhaps thirty years old, dressed in a long white coat of a strange cut, old bloodstains at the cuffs. Cropped dark hair and a pale, weather-beaten face, framed by a pointed beard.

She shied away, kicked against the ties on her ankles. The man held her shoulders and shook her gently, mouthing nonsensical words as his features coalesced. A long scar ran down his right cheek, another curved along his left, and he was missing his left ear entirely. His right eye was chalk-white; probably blinded by whatever had mangled his face. But beneath salt-encrusted eyebrows, she saw his left eye was a pale, sparkling blue.

White skin.

Blue eyes.

My gods, he's gaijin.

Smoothing the hair from her face, he spoke more of his incomprehensible language. Yukiko pulled back from his touch, but he offered a tin cup, filled with fresh water. The taste of salt was thick on her tongue, throat parched, and she gulped it down without pause. Eyes closed in the mercy of dimming thirst, she was startled by another voice speaking from the doorway.

'Piotr.'

The only round-eyes she'd ever seen were the merchantmen selling leather goods on the Kigen docks, so it was difficult to judge. But as she squinted at the speaker, she guessed this second gaijin was only a little older than she. Damp, shoulder-length blond hair swept behind his ears, a small tuft of beard on his chin, tanned skin. There was a symmetry to his features she might have found handsome if he didn't look so utterly alien. Scruffy red tunic of a bizarre cut, decorated with a shawl of pale-grey fur, thick leather gloves, insignia on his collars, goggles slung around his neck. He stared at her with eyes the colour of tarnished silver, burning with curiosity.

There was something familiar about him . . .

As she watched, he took a small cylinder of white paper from a flat tin box in his coat, put it in his mouth. He drew a small slab of dull steel from a pocket, touched it to the stick. Pale grey smoke drifted from the end of the paper cylinder, filling the room with the scent of cinnamon and honey. His hands were shaking.

The smell dragged a dim memory back up through the sea-drenched fog in her brain: she was curled up on rain-slick metal, coughing lungfuls of brine. A silhouette crouched over her, thick rope lashed around his waist, sodden blond hair plastered to his face.

She remembered her mouth had tasted strange. Something over the salt and bile . . .

Cinnamon and honey.

'You . . .' she said. 'You saved me?'

The blond boy spoke – incomprehensible and guttural. The dark-haired man stood and walked to the doorway, and the pair talked in hushed tones, glancing over occasionally while Yukiko's eyes roamed the room.

Some kind of hospice, lined with metal cots, perhaps a dozen in all. The sharp smell of liquor and burned hair, jars of chemicals stacked beneath a cast-iron sink. Grey walls, glistening with damp, wind howling through ventilation ducts lining the ceiling. Grubby bulbs in rusted, wall-mounted housings, flickering in time with the toneless howl of the wind outside. Beneath it, she could hear the roll and crack of surf, thunder rumbling across sharp rock.

The ocean's song.

She reached out with the Kenning, tentative, the headache cinching at the base of her skull. She could feel the gaijin in the room, just like she'd felt the people of the Kagé village; indistinct smudges of alien warmth. Pushing them aside, she groped around the nearby darkness, felt the impression of something warm; an animal with a familiar shape, far too small to be a thunder tiger.

Gritting her teeth, she stretched into the gloom beyond, trying to wrest the Kenning under some kind of control. It felt like opening herself up to a hurricane, stepping naked into wind and fire, a rolling sea beneath her. She could sense a cluster of warmth; dozens of gaijin crammed together, above, below, around. Pushing out further. Wincing at the pain. Feeling something warm in the distance, the sound of a tempest, a flash of heat.

Buruu?

And then she sensed them. Far below, like nothing she'd touched before. Cold and slippery and bejewelled, staring back at her with eyes of polished yellow glass.

Hissing.

She withdrew, slammed the door shut on her power, folded down on herself and drew a long, shuddering breath. Even with her newfound strength, she hadn't been able to sense Buruu. Was he unconscious? Dead? What had happened to him?

Blinking, ignoring the pounding ache in her head, she tried to remember. The sensation of falling came first; the terrifying split second of inertia as momentum failed and gravity took hold. Choppy red water beneath her, rising fast. Impact knocking the breath from her lungs. Sodden clothes dragging her down, shapes in the sky above as lightning flashed.

Arashitora. Two males.

And they were fighting.

'Shima?'

The familiar word pulled her back into the room, into the half-blind stare of the dark-haired man. The gaijin was looking at her intently, arms folded, a far throw from friendly. The blond boy stared at the floor, sucking on the smoking stick, exhaling clouds of honey-scented grey. The headache was a raw wound drilled behind her ears, chiselled atop her spine.

'You Shima?' Astonishingly, the scarred man was speaking in her own tongue – he had a broken, bowlegged accent, but his words were Shiman nonetheless. Stepping closer, he pointed to her, then waved in a direction she presumed was south. The gaijin walked with a severe limp, and when his right foot hit the stone, she heard the chink of metal.

'Hai,' she nodded. 'Shima.'

The man scowled and turned on the blond boy, raising his hand as if to strike him, spitting angry gibberish. The boy flinched away, smoke stick crushed between gritted teeth.

'Please.' She licked her lips, voice cracking. 'Where am I?'

'Eh?' The scarred man frowned, turned towards her.

'Can you understand me?'

'Little.' He pinched the air between forefinger and thumb. 'Little.'

'Where am I?' She annunciated the words clearly. 'Where?'

He snapped at her – an angry spiel she didn't understand.

'I don't—'

Roaring, face growing red, storming over to the cot. He

raised his hand and she shied away, cringing against the wall. The slap caught her full on the cheek, knocked her near-senseless, kindling the pain lurking behind her eyes. Sinking down onto the mattress, she screwed one eye shut in anticipation of another blow.

'Piotr.' The blond boy spoke a mouthful of tumbling words, concern plain in his voice.

Yukiko looked up at the dark-haired gaijin, blood in her mouth, salt biting at the split in her lip. She thrashed briefly against her restraints.

'You touch me again and I'll *kill* you . . .' she spat.

The man lowered his hand, calloused, broad as a war fan. He stared at his fingers and mumbled, limped back to the blond, spitting out another tangle of nonsense. The boy stalked from the room, wet footprints in his wake. The older man lurked by the doorway, running one finger down the scar beneath his eye, thunderclouds gathered over his head.

With shaking hands, he fished a wooden pipe carved like a fish from his pocket, stuffing it with dry leaves from a leather pouch. Yukiko could see a red jacket with brass buttons beneath his white coat, more insignia pinned to the collar.

Crossed swords.

A soldier?

'Sorry.' He waved to her face. 'He sorry, you.'

Yukiko stared at the man's leg, saying nothing. She could see a metal brace buckled around his shin, a piston-driven actuator at his knee. Flesh, augmented with machinery.

Like the Guild . . .

The man snapped his fingers on another slab of burnished steel lifted from a breast pocket. Fire gleamed in his blind eye, deepened the shadow of the hooked scar along his left cheek as he coaxed his pipe to life. He snapped his fingers again and the flame was snuffed out.

'Who are you people?' she asked.

The man shrugged, muttered words Yukiko didn't understand. She hung her head, breathing deep, suddenly and terribly afraid. The scent drifting from the gaijin's lips reminded her of her father. Of cloying smoke curling up through a greying moustache. Of stained fingers and a bloated body wrapped all in white, waiting for the fire to claim it. And she hadn't even been there. Hadn't even said good-bye . . .

Don't cry.

Don't you dare.

'Gods?'

She looked up at the gaijin's face. He was pointing to the sky, the brow above his blind eye raised in question.

'Have gods?'

'Hai,' she nodded. 'I have gods.'

The man put his pipe to his lips, shook his head, spoke through clenched teeth as he shuffled from the room.

'Pray.'

*

Yukiko sat in the dark for long moments, waiting for the headache to subside. She could hear crashing surf, smell rust and oil hanging in the air. Shivering in her damp clothes, she clenched her fists repeatedly, thongs cutting into her wrists. And finally, when the ache had dimmed to a pale flicker, she pulled her slender defences back together, brick by brick. A bulwark of all the substance she could muster; the rage Daichi had assured her was her greatest strength, mortar made of memories. Yoritomo's blade cleaving through Buruu's feathers. Her father's grave. His blood on her hands. Teeth gritted. Seething. And with her wall in place, she reached out with the Kenning again.

A quick, directionless stab, feeling for any sign of Buruu, like a shout in a darkened room. But there was nothing close to his warmth nearby, and the distant, muddy heat she sensed didn't wear his shape at all. Almost as soon as she opened herself up, the headache flared, the heat of the human bodies around her crackling, flame-bright and brittle. Beneath her feet, she felt those *things* waiting for her, cold and ancient and reptilian. And so she shut it off, locked inside her skull and leaving herself utterly alone.

Her face felt tender where the scarred man had slapped her, tongue probing her split lip. She tasted salt. Blood.

Closing her eyes, she remembered the smaller warmth she'd felt close by. Reaching out with a tiny, narrowed sliver of herself, she found it not far away. Curled up beside a heating duct, just a few doors down. An old blanket beneath him, tail wagging as he worried a strip of rawhide clamped between his front paws.

A dog.

Hello?

Head tilted to one side, tail falling still, one ear standing to attention.

who that!?

I'm Yukiko.

who?

Yukiko.

She could feel the shape of the hound's mind, at once strange and familiar, like an old coat belonging to a stranger, yet fitting like it had been tailored for her. He was warm and soft, all curiosity and energy, tail beginning to wag again as she felt around his mind.

food!?

I don't have any food. I'm sorry. What's your name?

red!

Hello, Red.

where you? can't see!?

I'm in a locked room down the hall.

play!?

Maybe later.

<whine>

Can you tell me what this place is, Red?

. . . is?

What do the men do here?

catching the sky!

Catching the sky?

so silly!

She frowned, trying to puzzle out what he meant, how she could frame the question in terms he'd understand. It had been years since she'd spent time swimming in the thoughts of a real dog; the last she'd Kenned was Aisha's puppy, but she'd known him only briefly. Hounds could be intelligent, but they didn't understand human concepts, focused instead on the immediate, the primary. As if on cue, she could feel the cold, wet nose of his thoughts snooping around the sliver she'd lodged inside his head.

food!?

She seized upon an idea, decided to see where it led.

I think there was food outside.

The dog snapped to his feet, tail a blur.

really!?

I think so.

let's find we share!

I'm going to use your eyes, if you don't mind.

The dog was already scampering away, and Yukiko only

caught a glimpse of his room as she slipped behind his pupils. Grey walls. Metal cot and desk. A strange, crooked machine studded with glass vacuum tubes and buttons beside a stack of too-white paper. A banner on the wall; a black field set with a circle of twelve red stars.

Red nosed a rubber flap open and belted out into a long corridor of grey concrete, wind howling through the ducts overhead. They could smell the sea; the bite of salt, a hint of rust. But there was no rot entwined with it, no refuse like the waters of Kigen Bay. It was fresh and wonderful; a bright, caustic smell clinging to all around them.

They scampered past rows of closed doors, two large gaijin with hedge-thick beards and grubby yellow rainskins chatting beside stairs leading up and down. They could hear engines, a klaxon wailing in the building's bowels, a sharp burst of laughter. Storm rumbling overhead, the structure murmuring in sympathy.

Out of the stairwell, into what looked to be a storage bay, crates stacked to the ceiling, static electricity standing their fur on end. Strange writing, wet bootprints, finally nosing their way through a rubber flap in towering doors. And at last, out into the wind and dark of night.

A gantry of wet, iron-grey stretched out before them, ending at a sturdy railing and a sudden drop into darkness. Forty feet below, black ocean swelled, towering waves crashing into the iron legs holding them aloft, hissing in fury as they were dashed to pieces, again and again. A soup-thick mist hung in the air, lightning whipping the gloom, illuminating long stretches of twin iron cables spilling out from overhead and off into the darkness. Thunder cracked so close they shrunk down against the floor, tail between their legs.

can't smell food you sure!?

Up. Look up.

They turned their eyes to the sky, to the building towering at their back. Square windows watched the sea, lit from within like empty, hollow eyes. Three stories tall, flat walls of grey brick, crawling with piping and cable. Odd, conical structures rose from its roof like the points of a lopsided crown, still more dotting the fangs of rock in the ocean around them; metal rods, twelve feet high, topped with broad, flattened spheres. Each rod had a thinner pipe wound around it, circumference growing wider as it spiralled from tip to base. Orange metal, crusted with bright green oxide, scuffed by the kiss of a thousand scrubbing brushes.

Copper.

A blue-white glow spilled from the roof, shimmering like sunlight through rippling water. Thunder rolled, and they crouched low again as lightning arced down from the sky a hundred feet away, kissing one of the copper spires out on the ocean. Electricity spiralled down the cone in a burst of blinding sparks, crackling across the twin cables back towards the building's roof. The light in the windows pulsed briefly, the glow overhead flickering.

What are they doing?

catching the sky!

The lightning? What do they do with it?

keep in jars!

She peered through the hound's eyes, into the raging storm. Out across the black swell, another burst of lightning struck a copper pylon, cascading along the cables in a tumble of raw electricity, up onto the impossible crown on the building's roof. Darkness and rain and howling wind, thunder shaking their bones and shivering their skin. The dog's terror folded into her, all tuck-tailed and whining, and she finally bid him back inside, away from the elemental fury and bottomless ocean, back into the echoing empty of the building's innards.

The hound shook himself, jowls flapping, spraying rainwater in all directions. The walls around him rocked, mirroring Yukiko's tremors as she closed off the Kenning, pulled back into her own tiny body, her own little self. A frail and shivering girl, cold and wet and alone, a thousand miles of storm and ocean and darkness between her and anything that might resemble home.

And of the brother who had brought her here, the mountain she'd set her back against, the one she'd come to depend on above all else, there was no sign at all.

Gods, Buruu where are you?

20

A Sigh or Two

A match flared in the darkness; a burst of orange and sulphur in the palm of Michi's hand. She cupped the light, gentle as a new made mother, touching it to the candlewick. The wax was glossy, the colour of fresh blood, perfumed with rosehip and honey. A luxury that a girl from a village like Daiyakawa would never have dreamed of.

The wick caught, and she snuffed the match with a single breath, watching the light creep along the walls. Padding across the floorboards, she placed the candle on the windowsill, pressing it against clouded glass; a lighthouse calling her comrade to treason. She stared into the palace courtyard, garden silhouettes shrouded in night, stone ancestor statuary and weeping trees, bent double under the weight of a poisoned sky. Father Moon was a faint pink stain across the haze, a featureless portrait on ashen canvas, face buried in his hands.

Leaving the light burning in the window, she crept back to the bed. She knelt and studied Ichizo's face, the features she knew now almost as well as her own. He wasn't a picture of perfection when he slept, some kami taken human form to lie beside her and steal her breath away. Cheek mashed into the pillow, hair tangled, drool upon his chin. Ichizo was all too real. And that was the problem.

Too good to be true.

She ran one finger across his cheek, smoothed strands of silken black from his eyes. He smiled then, like a little boy on his naming day, murmuring in his sleep.

'I know what you are,' she whispered.

Seducing her jailer had been the most logical route out of her cell, so seducing her jailer was exactly what she'd done. He was mere flesh after all, and she a woman who knew the simple craft of turning a man's head. And if the sour taste of giving over her body bothered her at first, it was soon sweetened by the fact that Hiro's new Lord Magistrate was not an unattractive man, nor entirely unpleasant company if all truths were told. Learned, but not arrogant. A philosopher, a lover of poetry, a noble not inclined to cruelty towards his servants. There were worse men to find keeping the keys to her cell in the palace of the Tora Daimyo.

She was a murderer. A killer who had ended a dozen men and lost not a wink of sleep over it. She'd committed the highest treason, abetted a terrorist, sought to bring down the government of the Imperium itself. What was the thought of giving over her body next to that? If she could take a man's life, destroy everything he was and would ever be with a wave of her hand, she could certainly spread her legs and fake a sigh or two. For the opportunity to escape her cage, to find Aisha and free her from whatever contrivance kept her chained within these walls? She could fake more than a sigh.

The problem being, of course, that Ichizo was almost certainly playing the same game she was.

The first time she'd felt his lips pressed to hers, she'd known.

His kiss was too tender, too hesitant. She'd had to coax his hands onto her skin, throw herself upon him. He played the smitten fool, whispering sweet words, showering her with secret gifts. And it might have been plausible – she might have *almost* believed it, until last night when he'd cupped her cheek in his palm, kissed her on each eyelid and whispered that he thought perhaps he loved her.

Love.

No magistrate, no servant of the Tora could be that obtuse.

This bastard was playing her, as surely as she was playing him. Any night now, she expected him to turn talk to Aisha. To Yukiko. To the Kagé. Only a matter of time. She had to be out of here before he realized she knew exactly what he was.

The nightingale floor began singing; the high-pitched chirp of nails within metal clamps, the creak of dry pine. She heard footsteps, too light to be a bushiman, too cautious to be a servant simply doing her rounds.

No One.

Michi watched Ichizo's face, listened for any catch in his breathing as the footsteps stopped outside her door. But his features were as serene as a sleeping babe's, the rise and fall of his chest smooth as clockwork in a Lotusman's skin. She stood, fluid motion and whispering silk, making less sound than the candlelight shadows flickering on the walls. And in four silent steps, she knelt beside the threshold and waited.

Moments later, a scrap of rice-paper slipped through the crack between door and floorboards. Three inches square, covered in artless kanji.

'*Safe to talk?*'

Flipping the paper over, she marked her reply with a kohl stick.

'Not alone. Must be swift.'

She slipped the paper back under the door, waiting for the reply.

'Who with?'

'Lord Magistrate Ichizo.'

A deathly still pause. A catch in the girl's breath beyond the door. Michi heard her rise, thought for a moment she might be leaving. When she opened the next note, it was hastily scrawled with a trembling hand.

'Are you _mad_?'

'Some would say.'

'Overheard rumour he spoke to Daimyo on your behalf. Wondered why. Makes sense now.'

'Ichizo spoke to Hiro?'

'Asked him to release you. Bushimen said he was mooning over you like lovesick boy.'

Michi glanced back to the bed, eyes narrowed.

'He is a serpent. Nothing more. Hiro's response?'

'Refused. Cares only for power consolidation and Storm-dancer's death.'

'What of Aisha?'

'Saw her yesterday evening on balcony.'

'How was she?'

'Could not ask. Guildsmen with her.'

'How did she _look_?'

'Bruised. Sick. Sad.'

'Wedding?'

'Proceeding. Dragons and Phoenix clanlords both en route.'

'What news from the Iishi?'

'Kuro Street safe house hit in dawn raid. No way to talk to Iishi.'

Cold panic set her jaw to clenching, breath catching in her lungs. She glanced over her shoulder at Ichizo's sleeping form, licked at suddenly dry lips.

'Raid? How? Anyone taken?'

'Akihito safe. Staying with me. Others maybe scattered. Maybe imprisoned. Checking drop box again today with Akihito when shift finishes. No word yet.'

'If we cannot speak to Iishi, must save Aisha ourselves.'

'The three of us?'

'Wedding must be stopped.'

'Cannot even escape room?'

Michi sat for a handful of heartbeats, listening to Ichizo breathing, the wind whispering in the stunted gardens outside. Eyes roaming the bedchamber that was her prison. Mind racing.

'Wait.'

She stood, moving like smoke. Formless. Soundless. Stooping beside Ichizo's clothes tumbled at the foot of the futon, she fished amongst silk and cotton, fingertips finally brushing a cold circlet of iron. And holding it tight in her fist, the *clink* and *tink* muted beneath the fabric, she drew the magistrate's keys out into the flickering light.

With a soft breath, she blew out the candle in her window, its centre melted into a deep scarlet pool about the smoking wick. She poured the wax into a saucer from her tea service, waiting a few moments for it to cool. And holding up Ichizo's keys, she chose the one she'd seen him use on her bedroom door more times than she cared to remember, and pressed it into soft, blood-red warmth.

She watched him, counting his breaths, refusing to remember the feel of him inside her. The way he breathed into her hair afterwards, speaking his lies. Talk of courting and love, promises she would attend Hiro's wedding on his arm, that all whispers of her treachery would soon be put to rest. She'd played the fool of course, pretended she believed him, thanking him in the most obvious way a dishonoured lady in waiting could. But the truth was she was a warrior, this bed just another battleground, her body just another weapon.

The lotus must burn.

Pulling the key free of the candle wax, she squinted at the impression it left behind: good and deep, sharp lines, more than enough to craft a forgery. More than enough to free her from this serpent's nest.

She slunk back across the boards, eyes on Ichizo, not making a sound. Kneeling by the door she slipped the saucer beneath; a soft scrape of porcelain upon polished pine. No One's note swiftly travelled back across the threshold.

'Key to your room? Why not come with me now?'

'Will not leave this palace without Aisha. Can work with this?'

A tremulous pause.

'Can have Akihito carve replica.'

Michi nodded, glanced over her shoulder at the man in her bed.

'Be swift, No One. Sleeping with a snake. Will bite me soon.'

She heard No One rise, quiet as she may, the faint click of her sandals and the scrape of the chamber pot upon the pine. And then she was moving, just another servant on night duty, floorboards singing beneath her. Ichizo frowned and murmured in his sleep, and Michi stood, lotusfly-quick, slipping the kohl stick into her pocket and the keys back into his belt.

She shrugged the kimono from her shoulders. It crumpled about her ankles as she slipped back to bed, crawled naked beneath the sheets. And as the motion across the mattress finally roused him, eyelids fluttering open, she pressed her mouth and body to his, hands descending, whispering his name.

He was awake then, if he hadn't been before. And though his mouth tasted of saké and sugar, she imagined she could taste the venom beneath, the poison of the chi-mongers seeping through his veins and onto his tongue.

But not if I bite you first . . .

*

Daiyakawa was the village where she'd been forged, but the Iishi was the place she was honed.

She'd wanted to be a warrior, to fight in the field with the other Kagé on the day they rose against the Shōgunate. And so she trained hard – perhaps not as strong as the boys, but faster again by half, her blade swift as dappled sunlight through the trees. She practised with Sensei Ryusaki until her fingers bled, until the blade was no longer in her hand, but part of her arm, and more, until there was no blade and no arm at all.

But to fight with steel in hand beneath a burning sky was not to be her fate.

She was perfect, Kaori had insisted. Young enough to unlearn her provincial ways, pretty enough to enjoy the attentions of the duller sex, but not so beautiful she would stand out in a crowd. And so they began training her for a different battleground, just as deadly as those stalked by Iron Samurai and bushimen. A battleground of polished pine and fluttering fans and rippling curtains of blood-red silk.

Kaori had been raised in the Shōgun's court, privy to the upbringing of a 'lady of station.' And so, she became Michi's new sensei. Hour after hour, day after day. Music lessons. Poetry. Philosophy. Dancing. The crushing, mindless tedium of tea ceremonies, intricacies of courtly fashion, poise, diction, face. And then came her weapons training. Innuendo. Rumour mongering. Eavesdropping. Lip-reading. Flirtation. Sex. And if the thought of it all terrified her in the long, empty watches of the night, she needed only think of her cousins lying beheaded in the street, the emptiness in her uncle's eyes as he plunged the blade into his own belly and dragged it right to left, and the fear became less than nothing; the weakness of a girl-child who had perished beside her cousins in the village square.

'Remember,' she would breathe. 'Remember Daiyakawa.'

They smuggled her to Yama, and from there to Kigen. Paid an iron fortune to have her irezumi re-inked by a master artisan, decorating her flesh with the artistry a woman of her 'breeding' deserved. She played the role of a sole-surviving daughter to a noble Tora family, murdered in a fire lit by Kagé insurgents, come to beg the First Daughter for mercy now that the Shadows had taken everything she was. And the Lady Aisha had looked at her with narrowed, puff-adder eyes as Michi told her story, false tears spilling down her cheeks, lower lip trembling just so; an audition for a role in the most dangerous treason afoot in all of Shima.

And then the Lady had smiled.

'You are perfect,' she said.

21

Webs and Spiders

Rebel. Traitor. Servant. Sister. Clanless. Kagé. Nothing. No One.

The line between who Hana was and wanted to be was growing more indistinct by the day. At the turning of dawn and dusk, she would peel away her mask like a snake shedding skin, one identity left crumpled in the corner as she shrugged on the new one, hoping it still fit.

And she had never felt more alive.

Evening hours were spent shuffling through the Daimyo's palace. Watching the wedding preparations unfold, guest rooms being prepared for the clanlords of the Dragon and Phoenix, the huge retinues each would bring in tow. Listening for the *tick-tick-tick* of the spider drones, watching for the palace bushimen, other servants, the house mistress and her powdered scowl. Cautious steps. Downcast gaze. Head bowed. Playing the role of the lowly Shit Girl nobody saw or heard or cared about. Counting down to the day they would have no choice.

By day, she would keep company with Akihito in her room – the big man watching the street from his perch by the windowsill, the girl sitting on her bed as they talked of revolution, of bright

266

futures and distant dreams. He was at least ten years older than she, a decade deeper in the world. But when he laughed, she would feel it in her chest. When he told tales about hunting the arashitora, she found herself squirming on her mattress. She would watch him carve his blocks of clay or pine into works of beauty, the Lady Sun lighting his profile as if the Goddess herself adored him. And Hana would think of the boys she'd known – the clumsy fumbling and promises unkept – and wonder what other tricks Akihito's hands might know.

He slept in the corner, a thin blanket for a pillow, as far from her as he could be. And when she woke in the evening as the sun was failing, he would be gone.

She'd asked Daken to follow him two days ago, more out of curiosity than concern. It turned out Akihito spent his days at the Market Square in the shadow of the Burning Stones. Pillars of blackened rock, the lingering scent of burnt hair, ashes swept into corners by a wailing wind, as if Fūjin himself were ashamed of the sight. The altar where Guild Purifiers burned children in their campaign against 'Impurity.' The place where the Black Fox had been shot, where Hana had seen the Stormdancer kill Shōgun Yoritomo right before her wondering eye.

The square was filled with spirit tablets now, carved from wood, stone, clay. Wreaths of paper flowers rippling in the dirty breeze. Hundreds of names scribed by hundreds of hands. Tributes for the slaughtered gaijin, the Black Fox, sons and fathers killed in the war overseas. Akihito would work on his carvings, occasionally place a new tablet among the others. Daken was unable to read the names he scribed. Hana had a notion she knew who they were for anyway.

When she'd arrived home from her shift this morning, she found a package laid out for her on her mattress – thin black crepe tied with a bow of real silk. Unwrapping it with trembling fingers, she'd found new clothes of soft, dark fabric, a pair of good, split-toed boots. A comb of Kitsune jade and kohl to wipe around the edge of her eye. A bottle of black dye. A handful of coins. Beneath it all, a small note written in a messy hand she'd recognize anywhere.

'Love you, sister-mine.'

She'd stolen into Yoshi's room, but found the bed empty, sheets still warm. She was still smiling as she slipped from her tenement tower a few minutes later, a poisoned autumn wind on her skin, into the bleak and empty dark before the dawn. Daken prowled beside her, his thoughts a soft purr within her own. The streets were near abandoned, smudged with dark fingerprints of exhaust, a few blacklung beggars rocking back and forth before their alms bowls in the muddy gloom. She stepped into the bathhouse on the corner, handed a copper kouka to the old woman yawning behind the counter and sat down to wait.

. . . bath again . . ?

Again? My last one was two weeks ago, Daken.

. . . so . . ?

So I stink like an oni's asshole.

. . . whole city stinks . . . get clean good way to get noticed . . .

Let's hope so.

The old woman nodded that all was ready, and Hana stepped into the bathroom, Daken keeping watch from a rooftop outside. A broad wooden tub was filled with cloudy water, the air hung thick with steam. Hana stripped off her grubby clothes, stared at herself in the fog-blurred looking glass. Insect-thin, long-limbed, ribs showing clearly beneath her skin. A too-flat chest, a narrow neck, hung with a tiny amulet on a leather thong. It gleamed in the candlelight; a golden oval set with a rearing stag, three tiny horns shaped like crescent moons. No matter how hungry, no matter how desperate things got, Yoshi had never let her sell it. It had been a gift from their mother, those brilliant blue eyes shining with love as she'd tied it around Hana's neck on her tenth birthday.

'*Wear it with pride*,' she had said.

All they had left of her.

Sitting on the edge of the tub, rinsing black dye through her hair and watching the stains pool on the tile about her feet, she looked at the pile of new clothes Yoshi had brought her. The cut was good, the thread was fine. The boots alone would have cost two irons. Her thoughts turned to dark places, and she wondered again where her brother's coin had come from. Who was missing it out there in the dark.

She'd asked Daken of course, but the cat had simply set sandpaper tongue to his not-so-privates, pretending like she'd never spoken. Though it had been Hana who raised the tom, though he slept beside her every day, it was Yoshi who'd fished the crying, bedraggled mop of fur from the storm drain all those years ago. The kitten had been near-dead, chewed by vermin, ears missing, tail gnawed; a lucky escapee from one of the last restaurants with coin to run the breathing pens required to keep kittens alive in Kigen's roiling stink. And ever since that moment, there was something between Daken and Yoshi – something beneath the violent jibes and the excrement surprises planted beneath the bedclothes. An affection she supposed brothers would share, hidden behind coarseness and cruel jokes and indifference.

A debt as heavy as a sopping handful of mewling fur.

And so, Hana let it drop, let the cat and her brother keep their secrets. She knew one night she might learn the hard way where the money came from, but for the next few days at least, she had bigger issues to think about . . .

And walking through the predawn streets of the refinery district half an hour later, there he was. Leaning in an empty doorway. Framed by the crumbling shell and boarded windows of an abandoned tannery like some street-side master's portrait.

'Well, well,' Akihito smiled. 'I almost didn't recognize you.'

'Bath day,' she shrugged. 'New clothes.'

'You look nice,' he said, eyes on the street over her shoulder.

Hana smiled, trying to still the thrill of delight inside her. 'I finally spoke to Michi. She has a plan to get herself out of her cell.'

Akihito nodded. 'You can tell me about it when we get back to your flat.'

Daken prowled up to the big man, brushed against his leg, purring. Akihito stooped with a smile, scruffed the tom behind his mangled ears.

'You know he usually hates people,' Hana said. 'Last stranger who tried to pet him got opened up from elbow to wrist. But he's taken to you like a fiend to the pipe.'

'Well, we hunters have to stick together.'

Hana watched Daken push back against Akihito's fingers, purring soft, eyes closed.

Gods, you're a slattern, boy.

. . . nice hands . . .

Don't tease.

. . . my job . . .

'All right then.' She nodded to Akihito. 'Shall we be off?'

'Hai.' He straightened, pulling his hat down over his brow. 'The drop box is secluded, but there might still be bushi' about, so keep your eyes open—' Akihito's gaze snagged on her leather patch, his cheeks flushing.

She smirked to see him stumble, running one hand over his braids, abashed and mumbling and sweet as sugar-rock.

'Gods, I'm sorry,' he said. 'You know what I mean . . .'

'I know what you mean, Akihito-san. And it's fine, really.'

A small smile, hidden by her new kerchief.

I have hundreds, after all.

*

They stole through the gloomy, tangled warren of Downside, Akihito limping in front, Hana close behind. The days were growing colder, night falling heavier. Each afternoon as the Sun Goddess sank to her rest, Kigen's citizens slunk homeward, curfew nipping at their heels like hungry wolves. The distant tread of bushimen ringing across cracked cobbles, the city's once-crowded streets as empty as her throne. And behind closed doors, Kigen's people looked towards the palace crouched upon the hillside, and whispered. Or plotted. Or prayed.

The pair kept to the deepest shadows, the girl taking the lead, quiet as whispers. The smell of Kigen Bay crawled up from the city's nethers, the hiss and stutter-clank of the refinery, strangling the glow of distant stars. Chi lanterns lined the streets; tiny pinpricks of light burning in braziers shaped like lotus blooms. A Guild crier trundled past on rubber treads; looking like a short, faceless fat man of riveted metal, spine dotted with exhaust pipes, bells clutched in each stunted hand.

The smoke in the mechanoid's wake made Akihito's throat burn as they passed by. The scent reminded him of Masaru's pipe, stained fingers, his friend's eyes alight with laughter.

You should never have left them.

He looked down at his leg, the dull pain of his wound flaring every time his right heel struck the ground. He could still see them in his mind's eye; Masaru crouched in the jail cell, hands and lips smeared with red. Kasumi lying against the wall, pool of blood swelling all around her, bubbling on her lips as she spoke her last words to him.

'Fight another day, you big lump.'

The last time he'd ever seen either of them alive.

At least Yukiko had taken Masaru's body with her when she flew north. At least he would've received a decent burial. But would the Shōgun's dogs have burned offerings for Kasumi to Enma-ō? Would they have painted her face with ashes, as the *Book of Ten Thousand Days* commanded? Or did they just throw her body into some dank alleyway to be gnawed by corpse-rats? Would the Judge of the Nine Hells have weighed her fair, with no rites held in her name? Would the spirit stones Akihito left in Market Square be enough to see her soul through?

Curse you for a coward. You should've died with them. And if she was cast into Yomi to languish as a hungry ghost, at least you would've been with her. At least she wouldn't be alone.

Hana grabbed his hand, tearing him from gloomy thoughts and back into the deeper gloom of Kigen's streets. She dragged him into a narrow alley between a grubby textile store and a small temple. Slipping in beside him, she pressed against his arm, breathing low and measured.

'What is it?' he asked.

'Hssst!' A finger on his lips.

Akihito frowned, remained mute. The girl was staring directly at the wall, eye curling up inside its socket, lashes flickering. He heard the sound of heavy boots, peered out into the street, saw two bushimen emerging from an alley half a block away; black iron and blood-red tabards. They were pushing a young woman before them.

Their voices were low, just snatches beneath the refinery's groan and clank, Akihito's heart pounding in his chest. The first bushiman shoved the girl again; a small, pretty thing, clutching a torn servant's kimono at her throat. Tear-streaked face, kohl running down her cheeks, hair tangled across bloodshot eyes.

'Be off.' One bushiman was retying his obi, war club under his arm. 'You'll find no more sport here, girl. Your master should know better than to send you into Downside before dawn.'

The girl ran weeping, back in the direction of the Upside mansions on the hill. The second soldier yelled after her.

'We catch you out again after curfew, we'll send you home with more than a limp!'

Akihito glanced at Hana as the servant passed by, torn clothes, sobbing and wretched. The girl met his stare, shrugging as if it meant nothing – a mask of indifference learned from a life at the bottom of the pile. But he could see the clenched jaw. Trembling fists.

The two bushi' meandered past the narrow alley mouth, chuckling between themselves, passing by without so much as a glance. When their footfalls and rough talk had faded to a whisper, Hana nodded to Akihito, and the pair hurried on through the dark.

'How did you know they were there?' The big man spared a passing glance down the alleyway the serving girl would never forget. Two fat corpse-rats peered at him across shin-high piles of trash. One snuffled the air, baring crooked yellow daggers in black gums.

'I heard them.' Hana didn't look back, kept her voice low.

'Funny that I didn't.'

'Try losing an eye. See how much your hearing improves.'

They flitted on through the haze, stopping several times at Hana's signal, slipping into shadows or squeezeways to avoid bushimen patrols or sky-ships rumbling overhead. The soldiers cut across the streets in random patterns, but Hana never failed to hear them, to hiss a quiet warning and drag him from the light. She moved like a fish through water, falling still as stone when the bushi' drew close, melting away like smoke. It was uncanny. Unnerving.

As they neared the drop box, she pushed him into an alcove beside a baker's shopfront, cracked awnings and cloudy beach glass. Pressing in beside him, she stared off into space. Again, her eyelid fluttered as if in a breeze, iris rolling up in her head. Daken leaped over the space between the rooftops above, his grace belying his bulk.

Akihito thought of Masaru then, stalking the last of Shima's monsters together in long-gone days, Sensei Rikkimaru and Kasumi by their sides. The big man could see his friend clearly, as if the great hunts were only yesterday: yew bow held in stone-steady hands, string taut, arrow nocked, the Black Fox's eyes rolling up in his head as he fired.

Never missing.

And looking now at this slip of a girl beside him, head tilted on a pale, slender neck, eye rolled back in her socket, he knew. Knew why that tomcat clung to her and her brother like iron to a lodestone. Why rats never squeaked at their approach. Why she reminded him so much of Yukiko.

He *knew*.

'We'll have to wait.' Hana pulled her kerchief down to spit. 'More bushi' ahead.'

He nodded. 'As you say, little fox.'

'"Little fox"?' Her smile was crooked. 'I'm not Kitsune.'

'Well, you remind me of a few I've known. You move like them. And gods know you're pale enough to be Fox clan. Even we Phoenix have a little colour about us.' He poked her on the chin, and she smiled again. 'But you're white as Iishi snow.'

'We used to live in Kitsune lands,' she shrugged. 'There's probably some Fox in our blood, way back down the line.'

'You father was lowborn too?'

'Soldier,' she nodded. 'Fought the gaijin in Morcheba.'

Looking out to the street, she scowled and muttered.

'Fought them back here too . . .'

Akihito frowned, unsure what she meant. 'So when did you come to Kigen?'

'When I was ten. We flew on a Kitsune merchant ship. So high we could almost see the whole island.' Her face lit up as if the sun had stolen out from behind the clouds. 'The people below looked like children's toys. I'll never forget it. What I wouldn't give to live up there . . .'

'What happened to your parents?' he asked. 'Where are they?'

'Gone.'

'Don't you have family somewhere?'

'Yoshi and Jurou are my family. The only ones I need. Anyways, why do you care?'

'Well, because this is no way for you children to be living, that's why.'

She turned on him, a scowl darkening her face, eye narrowed near to shutting.

'Children?' Her expression was disbelieving. 'Is that what you think of me?'

'Well—'

'Do you know what it takes to live in Shima's gutters, Akihito-san?' Her voice hardened, became a thing of cold stone. 'Have you ever had to break someone's skull for a scrap of food or a dry corner to sleep in? Ever watched your friends selling their bodies for copper bits? Has your life ever been so awful that a job slinging shit in the royal palace sounds like paradise?' She glanced at the beggars, the bloodstains and rot around them. 'You honestly think children live here anymore?'

'I didn't mean—'

'I know what you meant. Oh, and before you spit on the way I live? In case you didn't notice, you're living right there with me, Akihito.'

'I'm sorry.'

'You don't know me.' Her lips were tight across her teeth. 'You don't know anything about me. The things I've seen. The things I've done. I'm risking my life every day in that palace, and the two people I love most in this world don't even know I'm doing it. *Most* people in this city wouldn't piss on me if I were on fire, and I do it anyway. Because it's right. Because no one else will. Fuck you, calling me a godsdamned child . . .'

He put his hand on her shoulder, squeezing tight as she tried to flinch away. He could feel the too-thin flesh beneath new cloth, the bird-brittle bones beneath that.

'I'm sorry, Hana.'

She stared at him, mute and unblinking, jaw clenched. The breeze blew sweat-damp locks about her eye, bright in the dark, too large in that gaunt and bloodless face. A long minute ticked by in silence, and Akihito saw the truth of her words; the way she stood, fierce and unafraid, fingers curled to fists at her side, muscles overwound, staring him down. There was nothing left of a child inside her. Kigen had stolen every part of it away. And finally, after a breathless span in the chi lamps' flickering light, she relented. Gifted him with a sharp nod. Breathed deep.

'Come on.' She crooked a thumb. 'The bushimen are gone. If we're quick, we can be in and out before they're back.'

She stepped from the shadows, smoke-soft footfalls on hard stone. He limped behind, beneath the cramped archway of a small arcade. The stores were barred, windows boarded up. The cobbles were newly stained; dry blood turned to muddy brown, broken glass glittering in the flagstone seams. They kept to the gloom, Akihito bending with a wince and shifting a loose brick near the storm drain while Hana kept watch, lashes fluttering against her cheek.

He pawed through the dirt, heart lurching in his chest as he felt a small scrap of paper crumpled in one corner. Unravelling it, he quickly scanned the contents. Address. Time. Tomorrow's date. Someone else had made it out from Kuro Street, gotten in touch with the Iishi cell. That meant they still had radio capability. That meant they were still in business.

Thank the gods . . .

Committing the address to memory, he stuffed the paper into his mouth, chewed and swallowed. Replacing the brick, he stood, grimacing, nodded to Hana. He heard the soft whisper of padded feet above, saw Daken flitting back over the rooftops towards the tenement tower. As he and the girl faded into the shadows and followed the tom, Akihito couldn't stifle his grin despite the pain in his leg.

'Good news?' Hana whispered.

'It's news,' he nodded. 'So it's good. I'll tell you all about it somewhere safer.'

As the pair melted into the gloom, a tiny fistful of chrome uncurled from its hiding place in a downspout and stood to watch them go. Eight silvered spider legs clicked softly as it ticked its way across the roof tiles, windup key spinning along its spine. A single glowing eye marked their passing, its light burning softly in the poisoned dark.

Blood-red.

22

Skinned

Sometimes a bowl of puke-warm slop can seem the greatest gift in the world.

The scarred, dark-haired gaijin sat across from Yukiko's cot, feeding her heaped spoonfuls of seafood chowder, wiping her greasy chin with a rag. After four days on Buruu's back with almost nothing to eat, even with her nausea, her icepick headache, the constant fear that every hour she spent trapped here was another hour Hiro's wedding drew closer, the meal tasted more delicious than any Yukiko had eaten in her life.

The man loosened her restraints when he noticed her fingernails were purple, careful to do it one bond at a time. She watched him, eyes flitting over the insignia at his collars, the pistons and brace strapped around his crippled leg. A short knife hung from his belt, flanked by a tube of coiled copper and delicate glass globes that reminded her of Yoritomo's iron-thrower. When he'd entered the room with her meal, his shoulders had been wrapped in an animal skin, but he'd shrugged it off and hung it up as soon as he'd shut the door. She looked at it now; shawl of dark fur, long tail dragging on the floor. Yukiko thought it might be a wolf pelt, but if so, it had belonged to the biggest wolf she'd ever heard of.

The occasional crack of thunder shook the walls, lightning flashing through the small glass window high above her. The room's lights would glow brighter then, buzzing in their sockets as the building vibrated around her.

Catching the sky . . .

'Piotr.' The gaijin pointed to his chest. 'Piotr.'

'Yukiko,' she said, pointing to herself as best she could.

Piotr brushed his fingers across the same cheek he'd slapped. She could feel it bruising. His touch made her skin crawl.

He seemed about to speak again when heavy footfalls rang down the corridor. The gaijin stood with a wince, pistons hissing. He snatched the animal skin off the wall and threw it around his shoulders, just as the blond boy who had saved her life appeared in the doorway.

The boy stumbled forward as if shoved, and a huge gaijin appeared behind him. The man looked in his mid-forties, as tall and broad as Akihito. A thick beard tied in three plaits, short copper hair, hint of grey at the temples, a tanned, windswept face, nicked with scars – chin, eyebrow, cheeks. He held a long cylindrical object wrapped in oilskin. A heavy dark red jacket was smeared with black grease, insignia on his collars trimmed with frayed golden thread. The skin of some enormous animal rested over his coat; bristling fur, front paws as big as Yukiko's head, knotted around his neck. The pelt might have belonged to a panda bear once, save that it was rust-brown all over. A set of heavy welding goggles sat above pale blue eyes, dark lenses glinting the same colour as the disembodied shapes mounted upon his shoulders.

Yukiko's heart lurched as she noticed them. The helmets had

been beaten flat, mounted on his shoulders like spaulders, but the snarling oni faceplates were still recognizable.

Iron Samurai helms. Half a dozen, at least.

The big gaijin was wearing them like trophies.

Behind him stood the first gaijin woman Yukiko had ever seen. Her hair was so blonde it was almost white, tangled into a series of long knotted braids interwoven with insulated wiring, reaching down to her hips. She might have been pretty once, but her face was marred by symmetrical scars; three on each cheek, four running from lip to chin in jagged, lightning patterns. Clad head to foot in dark leather, adorned with wiring and transistors and heat sinks; machine components of all shapes and sizes. Plates of burnished brass covered her torso, shins and forearms. An enormous pair of boots with thick rubber heels lifted her to average height, long fingernails and lips unpainted. Her shoulders were adorned with the remnants of insectoid helmets, severed breather tubes spilling from the mouths, eyes of red glass. Yukiko would recognize them anywhere.

Lotusmen helms.

It was as if she'd flayed the metal skin from their flesh and turned them into skin of her own.

The woman stepped into the room, her movements feline, minimalist. Her adornments swayed and shifted, making a clicking, hollow music. Yukiko would guess she was close to thirty, but it was difficult to tell; beyond the scarification and outlandish clothing, there was something altogether alien about her. She tilted her head and stared, and Yukiko saw her eyes were mismatched; one black as Kigen Bay, the other a strange, luminous rose, aglow like the choking moon. She spoke, her voice low, lilting and completely indecipherable.

The big man wearing the bearskin murmured a reply, nodded. Respectful.

A dog darted into the room, scorched copper fur, eyes to match. He jumped onto the bed and slobbered over Yukiko's face before burying his nose into the chowder bowl. Piotr yelled at the hound, who promptly jumped off the bed and slunk into a corner.

She steeled herself, gathering her wall about her, pushing a tiny fragment into his mind.

Hello, Red.

it's you! girl!

A flare of pain. Brittle-sharp. Bearable.

These are friends of yours?

He blinked at the knot of people in the doorway, speaking in hushed voices.

boy yes men no mean lady no

Mean lady?

she kick me

Oh.

i am gooddog don't need the kicking

I'm sure you're very good.

and men hit my boy don't like it boy is mine my boy i am gooddog yes I am

Can you understand what they're saying?

Red tilted his head to one side, blinking.

Never mind . . .

By the doorway, Piotr's face was flushed, and he stabbed the air with his finger, pointing at Yukiko and making gestures not even a foreigner could mistake for friendly. Yukiko presumed the big man wearing the samurai trophies was an authority figure – when he spoke, Piotr stopped talking, listened intently. The woman in the flayed Lotusman skins simply stared at Yukiko, head cocked, running one fingernail along the helms on her shoulder. The boy who'd rescued her from the sea leaned against the wall and said nothing at all.

'She.' The dark-haired man spoke. 'Pretty girl.'

The gaijin were all looking at her now. Red was eyeing the chowder bowl, wondering how best to steal it without catching someone's boot. Her skull was pounding, stomach lurching, mouth dust-dry and tasting of salt. She felt as though she might vomit.

'Me?' she answered.

'Why here?'

The two gaijin men gathered around the bed, the woman lurking by the door, hands clasped as if in prayer, pale lips curled in a faint smile. The boy quietly shuffled away from her, standing against the opposite wall.

The dark-haired man who'd called himself Piotr pulled up a stool, sat down, wincing as he straightened his crippled leg. The pistons hissed, joints creaking despite the black grease smeared butter-thick on the metal. As he leaned closer, she smelled salt and liquor, chemicals and greasy smoke. His good eye was bloodshot.

'Who are these people?' Yukiko said.

The man blinked, taken aback. 'Me asking in the question.'

'Yukiko.' She pointed to herself as best she could with bound wrists. 'Piotr.' She pointed to him. 'Them?' A nod towards the others.

The man growled, said nothing.

'Ilyitch,' said the blond boy, exhaling smoke. He pointed to the big gaijin with the samurai trophies. 'Danyk.' The woman. 'Katya.'

Piotr snarled something in his own tongue. The big man roared, stepped forward and slapped the boy's face, sending his smoke stick flying in a shower of sparks. The language was coarse to Yukiko's ears, almost frightening. Her temples throbbed. The woman still stared, mute, head tilted, hips swaying as if she heard music.

'Why she here?' The dark-haired man poked her chest to regain her attention.

Yukiko jerked away from his touch, scowling. 'I fell off my thunder tiger, if it's any of your business.'

The man blinked.

'Thunder tiger.' She tried to make a flapping motion with her bound hands. 'Arashitora.'

'Gryfon,' the woman said with a strange, hungry voice.

Piotr made a questioning noise, turned to look at her. The woman spoke again, pointing skywards. Danyk spoke, eyebrows rising to his hairline. The woman nodded and whispered a mouthful of guttural nonsense.

'She snake?' Piotr glared at Yukiko.

'A snake?' she scowled.

'She snake for the pleasing!'

'What the hells are you talking about?'

'Coming here.' Piotr pointed at the ground, growing angrier by the second. 'Taking words away for the Shima, da? Snake.' He clicked his fingers. 'Spy! She spy!'

'I'm not a godsdamned spy.' Yukiko rose up off the pillow, growling, the memory of his slap burning on her cheek. 'I didn't want to come here, you mad round-eye bastard. I flew here on an idiot with his penis where his brain used to be.'

Piotr looked utterly befuddled.

'Penis!' Yukiko pointed at the man's crotch. 'Your other head!

The one you think with for most of your godsdamned lives!'

Piotr covered his groin with both hands, shuffled his stool a few feet away. Katya laughed, clapping her hands as if delighted, and Yukiko saw the woman had filed her teeth into sharp, gleaming points. Even the boy managed a grin, despite the handprint on his cheek. Piotr started yammering, shaking his head. The room devolved into general chaos until Danyk's roar rose above the clamour.

Piotr turned back to her, brow creased in concentration as he searched for the words.

'Beast,' he finally managed. 'Gryfon.'

He made a flapping motion, pointed to the sky.

'Arashitora,' Yukiko said.

Piotr nodded. 'Where is? Where?'

Yukiko frowned. 'I don't know where he is.'

'Die?' Piotr closed his eyes, crossed his hands over his chest. 'Is die?'

'I . . .' Her voice cracked and she cleared her throat. 'I don't know.'

'Call?' Piotr put his fingers to his lips, gave a shrill whistle. 'Calling him?'

'Izanagi's balls, he's not a dog.' She eyed the gaijin one by one, anger swelling her chest. 'And believe me, the last thing you want is him coming here. He'd tear this little tin can of yours to pieces. He'd show you the colour of your insides.'

Piotr shook his head and spoke with an apologetic tone to Danyk. The woman shrugged, addressing the men as if they were children, and with a sigh, the big man nodded. He held up the cylindrical object in his hand, unwrapped the oilskin, and Yukiko caught her breath as she saw her katana gleaming in the half-light.

'Yofun,' she whispered.

She'd thought it'd been lost in the ocean.

'That's mine, bastard,' she hissed.

Piotr offered what she assumed was an abridged translation. Danyk drew the katana, soft music of folded steel ringing against the backdrop of the storm. He tilted the blade, watched the light rippling across the polished face. With a grunt of admiration, he looked down at Yukiko.

'Spy,' he said.

'No.' Yukiko grit her teeth. 'I am not a spy.'

Danyk lowered the blade by inches, until it was level with Yukiko's throat. She swallowed her rising fear, forced away the pain at the base of her skull, the pounding of the world just outside her head. She met the gaijin's stare. Unblinking. Unafraid.

Danyk spoke to Piotr, a sharp mouthful tinged with command.

'What soul you pledge to?' Piotr said.

'Soul?' Yukiko shook her throbbing head, eyes still on Danyk. 'What the *hells* are you talking about?'

'Name.' The man slapped his right shoulder. 'Name!'

'I told you, my name is Yukiko!'

Danyk growled deep in his chest, muttered a word. Piotr reached out and took hold of Yukiko's collar, still damp with seawater.

'Sorry,' he said, meeting her eyes. 'Sorry you.'

'Wha—'

The gaijin jerked her uwagi back and down, exposing her shoulders and breasts. Yukiko's words became a shriek of outrage, bucking on the bed, blood flooding her cheeks as she swore and spit and thrashed in impotent fury, that beautiful, wonderful rage returning with a vengeance. Veins standing out like cable in her neck, restraints cutting into her flesh as she cursed them for cowards, screaming, snarling, vowing if they came near her, she'd kick in their heads, gouge out their eyes, tear their throats apart with her teeth.

Katya caught her breath, mismatched eyes turning deathly cold as she stared at Yukiko's tattoo. Without a sound, she turned and stalked from the room. The boy, Ilyitch, lowered his gaze to the floor, cheeks flushing at her nakedness. Piotr looked to his leader, but his eyes kept drifting back to Yukiko's body.

Danyk lowered the katana until it touched Yukiko's skin. She ceased her struggles, breath hissing through spit-slick teeth, eyes narrowed in defiance. Bringing the razored edge to rest against her throat, he ran it down her naked shoulder, over the beautiful clan tattoo curling around her right arm. The Nine-Tailed Fox she'd not had the heart to ask Daichi to burn away. All she had left of the family she'd lost. The person she'd been. Danyk spoke to Piotr and the man stood, limped from the room. With an apologetic glance, the blond boy followed.

The big gaijin spoke then, ice-blue glare fixed on her ink. Words mangled by his thick accent, cold and hard; an accusation so full of hatred that it fairly dripped upon the floor.

'Keetsoonay,' he growled. 'Sahmoorayee.'

Yukiko found herself terrified, acutely aware of her naked skin, burning under the gaijin's stare. They were the only two in the room now, her wrists and feet still bound, a thousand miles from home, no Buruu, no Kin, no one to help her at all . . .

She narrowed her stare, feeling the Kenning build up inside her, pain crackling across her skull. Remembering Yoritomo collapsing in the Market Square, blood spilling from his eyes. But would she be strong enough without her father helping her? Could she hurt this man before he—

Danyk scowled, muttered something indecipherable, sheathed her katana at his waist. And stalking to the door, he slammed it shut behind him, leaving her utterly alone.

Breathing deep, heart pounding, mouth dry as dust.

Alone . . .

Yukiko closed her eyes, face upturned to the ceiling.

Thank the gods . . .

23

Deluge

The forest-sweet scent of peppermint and cedar, warmth filling him, skin tingling. A wisp-faint breeze slipping through the hole in the floorboards, the cedar bough twisting through the ceiling, as much a part of the furniture as the fire pit. The low rumble of autumn storms outside wooden shutters, fire curling over blackened logs, smoke upon tongue's tip. Kin breathed deep, savoured the taste, understanding why Daichi was spending so much time indoors lately.

It is quiet here. Inside and out.

He pressed his forehead to the matting, waited for the old man to speak.

'Kin-san.' Daichi's voice was dry as the bottom of an alcoholic's bottle. 'Welcome.'

Kin lifted his head, sat on his heels. 'Do you know you're one of the only people in this village who calls me that?'

'Surely no surprise dwells in that house for either of us.'

'No surprise. Disappointment perhaps.'

A sip of tea.

'Kin-san, you do not honestly believe children's toys and a few semi-functional shuriken-throwers will win their favour?'

'Semi-functional?' Kin tried to keep the hurt feelings from his voice. 'The line is fully operational, Daichi-sama. Pressure issues are all resolved, stress-testing is complete. I've arranged for a demonstration tomorrow. In front of the entire village.'

'Even if these trinkets work, will it make people forget who you were? What you were?'

'Everyone here was someone else once. Why not me?'

'Why not indeed.'

Kin sighed, chewed his lip. The old man took another slow sip of tea, eyes never leaving the boy's.

'Do you play?' Daichi asked.

'Play?'

Daichi nodded to the chessboard on the table. It was a marvellous set, obsidian and jade, each figure carved in intricate detail. The dark pieces were Yomi horrors; hungry dead and bone dragons and oni, led by Enma-ō and Lady Izanami upon thrones of skulls. The light pieces were the likenesses of heavenly celestials; Raijin and his drums, Susano-ō and his Grasscutter Sword, Amaterasu the Sun Goddess and Tsukiyomi the Moon Father. The Emperor, of course, was Lord Izanagi, the Maker God. The board was stained oak and pine, tiles inlaid with mother-of-pearl. The seal of a Phoenix artisan was embossed in one corner.

'It's beautiful,' Kin said.

'One of the few pieces of my old life I carried with me.' Daichi's voice was somber. 'That, my swords, my daughter, and my regrets.'

'You were Iron Samurai once.'

'To my everlasting shame,' Daichi sighed. 'Though we may

shed our skins, the stains of our pasts dwell as deep as our bones.'

Kin stared at the board, saying nothing.

'So,' Daichi said. 'Do you play?'

'I play. Although I'm not very good.'

'Much can be learned by defeat.' Daichi knelt by the board, tea in hand, gestured to the other side. 'Sometimes there is no finer sensei under heaven than a boot to the throat.'

Kin stood and took his place opposite the old man. He noticed Daichi had opted to play the dark side, which surprised him more than a little. Jade moved first, and Kin made a standard foray with his pawn. Daichi followed immediately, calloused fingers on black glass. He moved without hesitation or flourish, stone-steady; the hand of a sword-saint. No trace of age or frailty in his motion, even if the same could not be said of his flesh.

They played without speaking, soundless save for the crackling spit of cedar logs, the hymn of fading autumn. Whenever Kin glanced up, Daichi was watching the board, intent solely on the game. Kin considered each step, shifting into gradual attack. Daichi would clear his throat and sip his tea, then move with seemingly little thought, but Kin soon realized the old man was a masterful player. His first attack was repelled, the second ended with a crushing loss, and Daichi's riposte finished with Lord Izanagi threatened on three facings.

Kin laid the Maker God on his side.

'You do not commit.' Daichi poured himself more tea from a charred pot by the fire. 'You defend and attack, at odds even with yourself.'

Kin shrugged. 'My style, I suppose.'

The old man picked up Kin's empress, sitting untouched on the rear line. 'You hold onto her like she will save you.'

'She's the strongest piece on the board.'

'She is worthless unless you *use her*, Kin-san.'

'Losing her means losing the game.'

'Folly. One piece matters, and one only.' He tapped his Emperor upon the head. 'All else is fodder.'

'You can't win the game with only an Emperor.'

'He and a single pawn are enough, if you strip your opponent of all he possesses. It is worth losing almost everything if you leave the enemy with nothing at all.'

'Victory at any cost?'

'The stakes demand conviction. There is no prize for second in this game.'

'You just said defeat could be a great teacher.'

'I did.' Daichi winced as he cleared his throat. 'But there comes a time when the cost of losing is too high. When all must be risked for victory.'

The old man was seized by a coughing fit, a long wracking spasm, stifled with another mouthful of tea. He regained his breath, hawked a mouthful of spit to sizzle in the fire. When he wiped his hand across his lips, Kin's heart lurched about his insides, cold dread stilling his belly.

A black stain glistened on Daichi's knuckles.

'Oh, no . . .' Kin said.

Daichi stared at the smear for a long moment, steady hands, measured breath.

'And there comes a time when there is no time left at all,' he murmured.

'. . . You have blacklung.'

'A fitting end,' Daichi shrugged. 'There are few more deserving.'

'How long have you known?'

'Not long.' The old man sniffed. 'Long enough.'

'I'm so sorry, Daichi . . .'

'Do not be.' He rubbed the burn scars on his arms. 'It is a fate well earned.'

'Does Kaori know?'

'She does not.' The old man glared. 'And she will not learn it from you either.'

'You don't think she's going to find out eventually?'

'In time.' A shrug. 'All things become clear as Iishi rain in time.'

Kin ran his palm through the short hair on his scalp, across the back of his neck. He felt sick, stomach in oily knots, thinking about the fate awaiting Daichi down the road. Not a warrior's end. Not a hero's. He pictured the blacklung beggars in Kigen's gutters; wretches coughing their insides out, trembling hands filled with dark, bloody mouthfuls.

He knew the things Daichi had done, the murder that stained his hands – the Daiyakawa peasants, Yukiko's own pregnant mother. But nobody deserved to die like that.

Daichi took another sip of tea.

'You did not come here to play chess.'

Kin blinked. 'No, I didn't. I want you to release Ayane from her cage.'

'The lotusgirl has done nothing to inspire our faith. Freeing her would be unwise.'

'If you're worried about her, why not release into my care? I guarantee—'

'There are few amongst us who hold faith in you either, Kin-san.'

'But do you?'

The old man wiped blackened knuckles on his hakama. 'A little more each day.'

'Then wouldn't you feel better knowing I was watching her full-time?'

'Why, would you?'

They looked at each other across the ruins of Kin's forces. Brick-heavy silence, firelight flickering in double crescents across Daichi's eyes.

Kin heard soft footsteps on the landing, creaking floorboards. A quiet knock, the door peeling open to admit muted daylight, still painfully bright after so long in the gloom. Kaori stepped into the room with whisper-light feet, fringe swept back under the goggles perched upon her head. Her scar gleamed angry red on teak-stain skin.

'Father, Ryusaki sends word. They are near Jukai prov—'

She stopped short as her eyes adjusted, spied Kin kneeling by the chessboard.

'Jukai province?' Kin blinked. 'You mean the Stain? Is that where Ryusaki was headed? The Guild staging grounds are . . .'

Kaori glared. Mute. Hand on her wakizashi hilt.

'. . . I will take my leave, then.' Kin stood, covered his fist and bowed.

'I enjoyed our game, Kin-san.' Daichi nodded to the board. 'Though when next we play, I will expect more commitment in your attack. Perhaps tomorrow?'

'I'd like that.'

Kin gave Kaori a short bow, but the woman didn't even blink. Her eyes followed him as he left; a bird of prey watching a field mouse in the shadows of long, yellow grass.

Stepping out into the light, he looked around the village; the men dragging venison to the slaughterhouse, women repairing thatched roofs, children gathered at sensei's feet, chalk tablets in hand. The trees around him seemed afire; foliage swaying like flame tongues, curling along dry, brittle branches. Leaves tumbled between the trees as if stars from empty red skies.

So much at stake here. So much to lose.

Kin wondered if Daichi really would risk it all for final victory.

Memories of his Awakening came unbidden to his mind. Hundreds of glowing red eyes, staring up at him with more affection in a single featureless face than lay in all of the Kagé combined. The memory turned his gut slick with dread.

When the time comes, will you?

*

An iron bell in the night. A cry ringing amidst the trees. A word.

Kin opened his eyes, cocked his head, straining to hear.

'Oni!'

A faint cry, almost lost beneath nightsong and the rumble of Iishi storms.

'Oni!'

Rolling from his bed, Kin scrambled to his feet and stumbled from his door, dashing in the direction of the cries. He could see bobbing lanterns in the distance, hear a rising gaggle of voices. Rope bridges swayed beneath him, bare feet pounding unfinished wood, dead leaves falling in a snarling wind. He came upon a group gathered outside Daichi's dwelling – Kaori, Maro, Isao, Takeshi, Atsushi, two dozen others, men and women, warriors all. Daichi stood in the centre of the ring, clad in a banded iron breastplate, a great ōdachi sword in his hands at least as tall as Kin was. The old man's voice was hoarse, tired, but fire burned in his eyes.

'Scouts report an oni war band from Black Temple moving

towards the village.' Daichi's stare roamed from one warrior to the next. 'At least two dozen.'

Uneasy murmurs. An exchange of wary glances.

So many . . .

'Take heart,' he said. 'We have faced such numbers before.'

'With the Stormdancer at our side.' Atsushi echoed Kin's own thoughts. 'But where is she now? How can we face such a force without her?'

'We have another equalizer,' Daichi said. 'Kin's shuriken-throwers will thin the demon's ranks enough for us to deal with the remainder. We will make our stand along the 'thrower line.'

Isao shook his head, raising voice in protest.

'Daichi-sama, we cannot be certain the Guildsman's contraptions will not fall to pieces in battle. And we have no manoeuverability if we chain ourselves to his perimeter.'

'I agree with Isao-san, Father.' Kaori nodded. 'I suggest we ambush. Wait until the oni are moving among the pit traps, then strike from the trees.'

'We did that last time, didn't we?'

All eyes turned on Kin as he spoke. Distrust. Hostility. Anger. The boy ignored the stares, met Kaori's eyes.

'We won't get them the same way a second time,' he said. 'The survivors of the last attack will have told their brethren we struck from the treetops.'

'We?' Isao spat. 'I don't recall seeing you there, Guildsman . . .'

'Because I was locked in your prison,' Kin replied. 'After you threatened to cut my throat. Don't you remember?'

A hateful stare. Clenched jaw. Isao turned back to Daichi.

'This is madness,' the boy said. 'We cannot trust the Guildsman's machines.'

'With all due respect, I agree, Daichi-sama.' Atsushi stood at Isao's back, something close to fear in his stare. Takeshi stood beside him, all nerves and wide eyes, fingernails chewed to the quick.

'Your concern is noted, gentlemen,' the old man said.

'Father—'

Daichi placed a gentle hand on his daughter's arm, eyes still on Kin.

'You truly believe your 'throwers will hold, Kin-san? These are not stones and trees we fire at. These are demons fresh from the pits of Yomi. Twelve feet tall. Claws that rend steel. The strength of the Endsinger herself flows in their veins.'

Kin tore his gaze from Isao's, looked at the old man. Teeth gritted, balled fists, fear in his gut. But the tests had run perfectly, no pressure loss, no chamber failure. He knew it. He would stake his life on it.

'They will hold,' he replied.

Daichi glanced at his captains. Maro was silent, arms folded across his armoured chest, but his eyes spoke no. Kaori met her father's gaze, shook her head. Thunder rocked the skies above, lightning clawing at the clouds, every passing second bringing the demons closer.

Daichi looked at Kin again. Drew one rasping breath.

Closer.

'We will have a small force ambush the demons, and draw them onto the 'thrower line.'

'Daichi-sama—' Isao began.

A cold glare choked the boy's protest. The old man nodded as Isao fell silent, turned to his captain. 'Maro-san, take half a dozen Shadows and bring the oni to us. The rest of you, come with me.'

Maro glanced at Kaori, grim-faced, but still covered his fist and bowed.

'Hai.'

Kin saw dark looks exchanged between Isao, Takeshi and Atsushi. Something else passing between the trio. Desperation? Fear? Takeshi opened his mouth to speak, but Isao shook his head, motioning for silence. A cold dread seeped into Kin's belly. Thunder shook the treetops, shaking his insides.

'Daichi-sama,' he said. 'With your permission, I will come with you. I can operate one of the 'throwers. Free up another blade for those demons who make it through to the line.' He stared at Isao as he spoke, the younger boy's face pale as bleached bones. 'And I'll be there in case anything goes wrong . . .'

The old man nodded, stifled a dry cough with the back of one hand.

'I would have it no other way, Kin-san.'

He looked amongst his warriors, lightning gleaming across steel-grey irises.

'Come. Let us send these abominations back into the hells.'

*

Steady rain falling on the leaves above his head, a thousand drumbeats per minute, shushing all in the world beneath. Sweating still, despite the storm, the boy crouched in the 'throwers-operator's seat, damp palms pressed to targeting controls. He blinked the burn from his eyes, squinting into the dark, blind, deaf and mute.

Kin grit his teeth, tightened his grip on the feeder crank. All around him, Kagé warriors were gathered, hidden in scrub and dead leaf drifts, all eyes on the approach. Daichi was crouched in a thick copse of mountain fern beside Kin's emplacement, so utterly still the boy couldn't tell him from the leaves around him.

The storm was growing worse, thunder jolting him in his seat every time Raijin struck his drums. And there, amidst the fear and tempest and rising doubt, it was all Kin could do to stop himself falling back to the familiar mantras – the words he knew by rote, explaining all about life he had ever needed to know.

Skin is strong.

Flesh is weak.

He felt naked. Tiny. The metal beneath his hands the only comfort, the only certainty. These machines of death he'd assembled, dragged from scorched wreckage and filled with new life – these he knew. But demons? Children of the Endsinger? He'd been raised to scoff at such superstitions. Tales of gods and goddesses were crutches for the skinless. Those who had never breathed warm blue-black in the Chamber of Smoke. Never been shown their Truth.

Call me First Bloom.

A distant cry, a rumbling, croaking roar. Faint sounds through the storm, not unlike music. Bright steel, ringing crisp beneath the cloud's percussion, running feet amidst the hissing deluge. The signal floated down the line – a series of short nightbird whistles. And eyes narrowed, peering into the gloom, Kin saw tiny figures swathed in dark, dappled cloth, dashing back towards the 'throwers fast as swift feet might carry them. And behind them . . .

Behind them . . .

Kin had never seen the like. Not in his bleakest imaginings. Loping and croaking and growling deep, long sinewed arms dragging knuckles on the earth, black, wicked talons at the end of every finger's tip. A dozen shades of blue among their skins, midnight to azure, all muddied and smothered in the cold and the dark, lit only by frantic lightning and the bloody light of their own glowing eyes. Faces wrought of nightmare, adorned with rusted metal rings, tusks curling cruel and sharp from jagged underbites. Their blades and war clubs tall and sharp enough to fell the stoutest tree. A language dark as sin, roared amidst the trees by black maggot tongues.

'They come,' Daichi said.

Oni.

Maro and his scouts were swift, weaving between the Kagé pits with the demons close on their tails. One oni crashed through the scrim of branches and dead leaves covering a trap, tumbled headfirst, twenty feet down into a tomb of sharpened bamboo spikes. Maro's blade was black with blood, the oni enraged, rushing on heedless, another of the demons crashing into a Kagé trap and plummeting to its end. But the monsters numbered in the dozens, twelve feet tall and seething, the death of their fellows seeming only to stoke their fury. Warbling screams and guttural roars, blood-red eyes aglow as pierced lips pulled back from crooked teeth, long loping strides bringing them ever closer to the fleeing scouts.

Kin's fingers tightened on the firing stud. Breath coming fast. Fear rising.

'Come on,' he breathed. 'Faster . . .'

One scout stumbled on a upthrust tree root, slipped in the muck. The oni behind was on him in a moment, tetsubo raised high, bringing it down with a delighted howl and smashing the unfortunate man into mush. The remaining scouts kept running, no time for grief, on through the brambles and ferns and grasping branches.

Kin set his sights on a pit demon, crosshairs centred on its chest.

'Faster . . .'

Lightning struck the skies, splashing all with grisly white. Thunder shook his bones, gut to water, pupils dilated. And as they finally closed within range of the line, Maro gave his signal, and as one, each scout dropped behind stones or fallen trunks, out of sight and out of harm.

'That's it,' Kin hissed.

Daichi rose up from his fern, held his ōdachi aloft.

'Fire!'

Kin squeezed the firing stud, felt his 'thrower lurch, and *chug!chug!chug!chug!chug!* came the song all the way down the line, brilliant and bright and bellowing, filling the air with death. His 'thrower shook like an infant in a tantrum, squealing and shuddering as Kin cranked the feeder belts, short bursts of pressurized gas bursting from its flanks with every shuriken it spat. Spinning, razored death flew from each 'thrower barrel, glittering in the rain as lightning struck again, and as elation surged in his gut, Kin saw the oni begin to fall, one by one, clutching throats and chests and guts, black blood spraying between the raindrops, blood-red eyes wide with shock and surprise as the air about them turned to carnage.

The reverb shook Kin to his core, metal beneath him groaning, shuddering, bucking as his creations tore through the oni lines like a hot blade through fresh snow. A dozen demons fell in the first few seconds, riddled with fresh holes, elation filling him to bursting. He glanced to Daichi, a tiny moment amidst the butchery, a lunatic grin on his face. The old man was looking back at him, gifting him a small nod that for a brief and beautiful moment wrapped Kin up tight, filled him with a sensation he'd almost forgotten.

Pride.

chug!chug!chug!chug!chug!

Chest-swelling, heart-warming pride.

chug!chug!chug!chug!chug!

And then the 'throwers began to fail.

Number three blew first, the seals on the firing chambers bursting like overfilled balloons, gas shrieking in the dark. Kin's 'thrower went next, a bright burst of light and a rush of vapour, the bucking metal beast he rode falling still, sagging like a puppet with broken strings. All down the line, almost simultaneously, the machines coughed and went silent, shivering in their rivets like men dying of blacklung. Murderous percussion replaced with feeble thunder and whispering rain, so dim after the deafening chorus Kin could barely hear them at all.

Dread stole his breath, gripped his heart tight and squeezed. He lurched from his seat, eyes roaming the ruptured seals, fingers pressed to the damage as if with will alone he could mend it. But no time. No time at all . . .

'Oh, no . . .' he breathed.

A roar, black and harrowing, reverberating through the trees. Looking up, Kin saw a tall shape unfold itself from the cover of an ancient maple, its head adorned with the skull of some colossal eagle, armour of bone arrayed on its chest. Taller than its brethren, skin so dark it was almost ebony, all muscle and sinew and fangs. And raising a war club studded with rusted iron rivets, twice as long as Kin was tall, it pointed at the 'thrower line, lips drawing back from broken fangs.

Bellowing hatred.

Daichi tossed his head, wiped the rain from his eyes. His stare was fixed on the demons as the other Kagé emerged from cover, gathered around their leader. Their blades gleamed as the lightning flickered, the scouts dashing across the clearing and rejoining the line. The oni formed up around their dread captain, only half a dozen now, bloodied and grim. But still more than a match for a handful of men and women half their size, armed with tiny, sharpened toothpicks.

Rusted grins gleamed in the light of bloody eyes.

Daichi spared Kin a solemn glance. Cold and empty. And the pride that had swelled his chest a moment before fled on broken wings, shoulders slumping as cold fear seeped in to take its place. Hands shaking. Lips parting as if to speak, and finding no words at all.

Daichi turned to his warriors. Each one in turn. Steel in his gaze. And raising his blade, he pointed to the demon pack.

'Banzai!' he cried.

'Banzaiiii!' came the reply, two dozen Kagé roaring in answer. Thunder crashed, the warriors dashing across the clearing with blades held high. Kin dragged himself from the 'thrower, stumbled down to the soaking earth, watching the foes plunge towards each other through the swirling rain. Tiny figures and giant hellspawn, moving amidst the lightning strobe. His chest thumping, mouth bitter, panic and guilt and rage filling him to blinding, looking up and down the line of useless 'throwers as the Thunder God laughed in the sky above.

How could this be?

The battle was joined out in the dark, Kin stumbling towards it, a heavy wrench dragged from his tool belt to serve as a weapon. He had no warrior's training, but still, he couldn't sit back and do nothing. Figures swayed and danced in the rain, cries of pain and awful roars filling the empty spaces between one peal of thunder and the next. Kaori fighting on the left flank, just a blur in the darkness. Daichi in the thick of it, blade slick with dark blood. Moving as if to music, flowing without pause, step to feint to strike to thrust, cleaving broad swathes of sticky black, swinging his mighty two-handed blade as if an extension of his own arm. A flick of his wrist and an oni's leg toppled to the ground in a spray of dark gore, followed swiftly by its howling owner. A step to the left and a casual wave, cleaving throat to the bone, swaying amidst the blows, a poet writing his masterpiece in warmest, blackest ink.

A rolling seething mob, oni and Kagé falling in equal measure, Kaori scaling one demon's back and plunging her blade into the base of its skull. Maro's arm hanging limp, battling side by side with Isao and Takeshi over a fallen comrade, the three of them slicing their foe's gut open, wading ankle deep in rolling coils of intestine. The tide was turning, the Kagé gaining ground. But the oni lord had cleared a swathe through his foes, eyes set on Daichi, looming through the mob as Kin shouted warning.

The old man turned, steel flashing, stepping to one side as the demon brought his war club crashing down. Mud spattering, dead leaves flying, Daichi's eyes narrowed in contempt as he stepped forward, sliced the oni across its belly. Kin running through the muck, an oni looming out of the gloom in front of him. The boy dodged past its blade, almost slipping on the dead leaf carpet as three Kagé stepped up to meet the demon's challenge. Panic in his chest, knowledge that he had no place here – no business on a battlefield with a wrench in his hand and fear in his heart – but still he turned and fought, bashing at the oni's shins as it whirled to face him, the blow jarring his arms, the stench of funeral pyres assailing his nose, the demon roaring as if all the hells lived inside its mouth. He rolled aside as its blade swept over his head, the Kagé striking from behind, steel and rain and blood and thunder, black spots blooming in his eyes as he lurched to his feet, sparing a glance for Daichi through the now blinding downpour.

The old man's chest heaved, lips pressed thin, blade slicked with gore as the oni lord swung with reckless abandon. The demon was bloodied in a dozen places; arms, legs, gut, face, and had yet to land a single blow on the old Iron Samurai. Rage turned its eyes incandescent, burning with the fury of Lady Sun as it lunged forward and received yet another wound for its troubles. The old man was fighting as if whittling wood, carving off one chunk at a time, dancing back out of striking range and allowing bloodloss and fatigue to do most of his heavy lifting. The power of Yomi versus a lifetime of steel's tutelage. The fury of all the hells versus a tranquility born of the love of the blade, the way of war, the heart of a tiger true.

Until the old man started coughing.

A sputter at first, widening his eyes just a fraction. A wet intake of breath, muscles clenched tight. Stepping aside from another blow, Daichi coughed again, damp and sputtering, pressing one hand to his chest as if pained. Kin yelled warning, roaring to Kaori, turning from the snarling demon facing him and dashing through the rain. Daichi staggered, mouth pressed to sleeve, and as he lifted his blade to ward off a savage blow, Kin swore he could see a dark stain on the old man's lips. A blacklung spasm, gripping him now of all times, the disease slowly reaching into the old man's chest and turning all to ruin.

Daichi fell back, coughing still, Kaori rising from the steaming ruin of a pit demon's corpse and yelling above the storm. Maro answered with a cry – 'To Daichi! Daichi!', the Kagé charging towards their failing captain, blades raised high. And the oni lord lifted its war club, lips split in a jagged grin, spit hissing through its teeth as it swung in a whistling arc, smashing Daichi's sword into glittering fragments. The old man staggered, crying out amidst sodden gasps, the demon lord following up with a savage kick directly into the old man's chest.

Kaori screamed, Kin along with her, Daichi sailing half a dozen feet to land crumpled and bleeding in the muck. The demon lord stepped forward, intent only on the old man's murder, raising its war club high. With a desperate cry, Kin hurled his wrench – just a tiny, gleaming sliver of greasy metal against this towering monstrosity. The throw struck true, cracking into the back of the oni lord's skull, just a flea bite onto hardened leather. But it was enough to give the demon pause, a second to snarl and flinch, and in that moment, Kaori closed in, a black shark through bloodied water, stepping up onto a broken tree stump and leaping through the air, her blade sinking into the oni lord's back. Maro struck a moment later, carving a gouge through the demon's Achilles tendon, the monster roaring in pain, falling to one knee. Others struck now, Isao, Atsushi, Takeshi, blades rising and falling like abattoir knives and beneath the flood, the rain, the flashing steel, the demon lord fell roaring and flailing, silenced at the last by a scything blow from Kaori's blade, ear to pointed ear, bathing the woman in a black, hissing spray.

'Father!' she cried, stumbling to her knees at the old man's side. Daichi lay on his back, hand clutched to chest, drawing bloody breath through bubbling lips. The other Kagé gathered around him, painted in black gore, faces pale and horrified.

Kin caught several dark stares as he approached, muttered curses, glances towards the failed 'throwers. He heard the word 'accursed' and 'Guildsman,' felt angry eyes on him in the dark, and a cool dread seeped into his belly. He tried to push through the mob to Daichi's side, found his way barred by Maro's heavy hand, the Kagé captain looking at him with bitter rage.

'Stay the hells away from him,' he hissed.

'I can help h—'

'Don't you think you've done enough, you godless little bastard?' Maro hissed.

'Maro, forget the Guildsman!' Kaori yelled, tears in her eyes. 'Help me with my father!'

The captain turned from Kin with a snarl, knelt beside Daichi. Four Kagé lifted the old man onto their shoulders and he cried out, clutching his ribs, mouth painted in a bloody O. Kaori bid them run swift, carrying their fallen leader back to Old Mari's infirmary. With a hateful glance at Kin, she selected a few warriors to remain behind and ensure every demon had breathed their last. The remainder were set to task gathering up their wounded brethren.

Thunder roaring overhead. Wind clawing through the trees. Rain hissing like a serpent's nest. Limping and bleeding and dazed, the Kagé headed back to the shelter of the village. Kin stood amidst it all, lost and adrift, knocked aside by one warrior, yet another spitting at his feet. His agonized gaze was fixed on the silent 'throwers, the ruptured seals, wondering again how it was possible. For one to fail, perhaps. Two an outside chance. But for all to malfunction at once? How could it be?

He staggered through the rain towards his emplacement, sickness roiling in his belly.

'Guildsman.'

Isao's voice brought him up short. Grabbed him by the throat and bid him turn to stare.

Three of them stood there in the rain. Isao. Atsushi. Takeshi. Arms folded, fists clenched, anger and contempt unveiled on their faces. Takeshi took a step towards him, but Isao put out a restraining hand, muttered something too low for Kin to hear. With a snarl, the big boy turned to the fallen oni, Atsushi by his side. Walking from body to body, they chopped at the pit demon's throats, sluices of black blood arcing in the rain, ensuring every one of them was dead.

Isao remained. Eyes narrowed. Sword sheathed at his back. And lifting one slow hand, he pointed at Kin, then made a sawing motion at his throat.

Dread lined Kin's guts with a sickly chill. The other Kagé had already moved off, his knowledge that he was alone out here burning with sudden clarity in his mind. And so he slunk into the scrub, into the shadows, finally bolting for the Kagé prison. It was the only place he could think to go. He knew now the boys would stop at nothing. If they were willing to do this, they were willing to do anything.

He recalled Isao's appeal for Daichi not to fight at the 'thrower line. The boy had been pleading. Almost desperate. And now, Kin finally understood why. The image lingering in his mind's eye as he ran – Isao sawing away at his throat, the telltale black stain in the flickering stormlight.

Grease stains on his hands.

24

Mercies

Ichizo watched the Daimyo of the Tora Clan raise his sword, blood-red sunlight gleaming on the blade, level with his opponent's throat. Hiro's foe drew breath through clenched teeth, weapon hanging from his grip as if it were an armful of bricks. Hiro glared at the samurai facing him across polished boards, amidst the lifeless stares of hollow men, muscles gleaming, iron arm spitting a thin plume of exhaust into the stifling air.

Then he lunged.

Ichizo could barely track his cousin's movement, Hiro's prosthetic a blur, his blade smashing aside his foe's guard, the Daimyo spinning on the spot and bringing his katana in a sweeping arc across the man's ribs. The wooden blade cracked against the samurai's breastplate, denting the metal, a spattered, damp exhalation leaving his lips as the man fell to his knees, clutching his side, face twisted in pain. Hiro stood above him, sword raised above his head for the would-be deathblow.

The samurai raised his hand in surrender.

'Yield, great Lord,' he rasped. 'I yield.'

Ichizo's applause mingled with that of the servants, Hiro's

four other sparring partners, bent and bruised and hovering at the training dojo's edge. Their Daimyo had been beating on the men for the best part of an hour, Ichizo hovering outside, listening to the sharp cries, the grunts of pain, until he had finally lost patience, entering to seek words with his clanlord.

Hiro helped his opponent to his feet, and noticing Ichizo amidst the retinue, raised an eyebrow in question. The Daimyo was fighting unarmoured, all muscle and sweat, flesh gleaming in the fading light. Long black hair was drawn back in a tail, a sodden river trailing down his chest, clinging to his skin. A short puncture scar marred the taut pectoral muscle above his heart, just a few inches shy of a killing blow. The flesh at his right shoulder was inked with a mangled tiger tattoo, an iron collar affixed around his bicep, hiding the union between his flesh and the prosthetic the Guild had gifted him. Ichizo was unnerved by the sight – the union of meat and machine far too akin to a Lotusman for his tastes.

Shōgun Yoritomo had always kept his distance from the chi-mongers – always kept the delineation between throne and Guild clear. But it seemed Hiro had thrown in with them without so much as a backwards glance. He knew the power the Lotusmen offered his cousin, knew how much rode upon this union between Hiro and Lady Aisha, what would become of the nation if the clans fell to civil war. And yet, unease at this overt alliance with the Guild grew in him daily – more than the threat of Kagé insurgents hiding in the shadows, the Stormdancer fermenting discontent from the north. And he wondered what price the Daimyo would truly pay for his throne.

And yet Hiro was his cousin. His blood. His Lord. To think such things—

'You wish to speak with me, Ichizo-san?'

Hiro dropped his bokken to the floor, the wooden sword striking the boards with a sharp clatter. A servant scuttled from the periphery with a cup of almost clear water, hovering by his Lord's side.

'It is no matter, great Lord.' Ichizo bowed. 'I should not have interrupted your training. It can wait.'

'Well, you have interrupted now. We might as well kill two birds with one stone.'

The Daimyo motioned to the row of wooden katana, the training dummies clad in practice armour. A small smile on his lips.

'I fear I would prove little contest for you, great Lord,' Ichizo said.

Hiro grinned. 'Since when did that stop you in the past?'

'Oh ho.' Ichizo grinned in return. 'I recall besting you once or twice, at least.'

'Make it three times, then. Or are those magistrate's robes I put you in sending you soft?'

Ichizo bowed with a wry smile, walking to one of the wooden figures and slipping on the training armour, a servant buckling it in place. Hiro sipped his water as Ichizo suited up – heavy gauntlets, breastplate, a cowled helm – watching his cousin test a half-dozen practice blades before he found one with balance to his liking. The Lord Magistrate finally stepped into the sparring circle, raised his sword in salute. The Daimyo tossed his cup to another servant, swept his ponytail back over his shoulder and flourished a new bokken with his iron sword arm.

'Defend yourself,' Hiro hissed.

The Daimyo charged across the room, footsteps echoing floor to high ceiling, bringing his sword down towards his Lord Magistrate's head. Ichizo parried, impact jarring his wrists, knocked aside amidst the hiss and whirr of Hiro's prosthetic. A foot to his chest sent him stumbling back, hissing and coughing, opening his eyes just in time to fend off another flurry of blows from Hiro's blade – face, chest, gut.

He backed away, astonished at the ferocity of the attack. Hiro smiled, watching him over the edge of his blade, waiting for his counter.

'So,' he said. 'Speak.'

Ichizo lunged, once, twice, Hiro fending off both strikes with practised ease, the sharp notes of wood cracking against wood ringing in his ears.

'It is of little import, great Lord.'

Strike. Parry. Lunge.

'Come now,' Hiro said, dancing away. 'It seems I speak of nothing these days save wedding plans.' Strike. 'Of ministers who cannot be allowed to sit with magistrates at the reception because of slights three decades old.' Feint. 'Of whether to offer insult to the attending Guildsmen by serving food and drink they consider impure, or insult by serving nothing at all.'

'My sympathies, cousin.' Ichizo ducked a scything blow aimed at his head, fell back for breathing room. 'I suppose dominion over an entire nation comes with its drawbacks. But the wedding at least will be over soon.'

Feint. Dodge. Lunge.

'Hai,' Hiro nodded. 'All the oni in the hells could not stop it now.'

'. . . Would you wish them to?'

Hiro struck, clipped Ichizo's shoulder, kicked him again in the chest. The Lord Magistrate staggered away, blade at half-guard, but the Daimyo did not press.

'Come,' Hiro said, breathing easy, flexing his iron arm. 'Speak your piece. Your intrigues offer welcome diversion if nothing else.'

Ichizo waved the request away with one hand, sweat burning his eyes.

'I fear it is a trifling thing, great Lord.'

'Trifling. This would be about your prisoner, then . . .'

Ichizo felt his stomach turn. He risked a glance at the servants. The other samurai. A humourless smile creased Hiro's lips, and he dismissed the retinue with a wave of his blade. The group shuffled from the room with low bows, the sparring partners looking particularly grateful. Silence descended on the dojo, broken only by the sparrows choking in the gardens outside, the creak of the boards beneath their feet, Ichizo's sodden gasps dragged into burning lungs.

The Lord Magistrate cleared his throat. Swallowed hard.

'You have heard.'

'You would be surprised what the Guild knows about the happenings in this palace.'

Ichizo glanced at the spider-drone perched on the railing of the mezzanine above. That cursed blood-red eye, seeing and telling all. 'It displeases you?'

Hiro's eyes were as hard as the prosthetic at his side. Just as cold. Just as lifeless. Ichizo searched his cousin's face for some remnant of the boy he had played soldiers with around his father's estates; toy bokken in their hands, swiping the wooden swords at imaginary legions of Shima's enemies. Always smiling, always laughing.

Centuries ago.

'It displeases me,' Hiro said.

'She is beautiful, cousin. Like the first flower after winter's end.'

'She is dangerous. I asked you to question these girls, Ichizo, not bed them. You have lost your clarity. Her mistress is purest poison. Who is to say how far her taint spread?'

'Yoritomo's assassin tried to murder this girl. Cut her to pieces and nearly caved her head in. That hardly seems in keeping if they were allies. I am not a fool, Hiro.'

'No? And what does your beauty say when she lies in your arms at night? That she loves you?' Hiro flourished his blade in his iron hand, hissing fingers drumming across the hilt. 'A woman's betrayal cuts bone-deep, cousin.'

'Not all of them are liars, Hiro. Not all of them are false.'

'What would you have of me?'

'To set Michi-chan free. Under my recognizance. She wishes to see her mistr—'

'We have spoken of this before.'

His breath returned, Ichizo struck without warning, the blow narrowly missing Hiro's face. The Daimyo struck back, ferocious, no smile on his lips, pressing hard with blow after blow until Ichizo again backed away.

'Tenacity is one of my strengths, great Lord,' he grinned, gasping.

'You ask the impossible, Lord Magistrate.'

'I would consider it a personal favour, Daimyo.' Ichizo looked at his cousin, eyes pleading. 'To a kinsman who ran with you when the deadlands in Blackstone province were still lotus fields, and who always let you beat him with the bokken.'

'Let me beat you?'

Hiro laughed despite himself, his smile bright. For a brief moment, the facade of the Daimyo, the Iron Samurai, fell away, and all that remained was the boy Ichizo had always known. The boy he'd grown up with. The boy he trusted.

'Lord Izanagi strike you down for a bastard and a liar, cousin,' Hiro grinned.

'Please, cousin.' Ichizo stepped closer, smile slowly fading. 'There is much to be said for a merciful rule.'

Hiro stroked his goatee, breathed deep. He stood for a silent minute, motionless as the training dummies surrounding them. Blue-black smoke hung about his brow, turned his eyes the deep green of lotus leaves. When he finally spoke, his voice rang across the dojo, cold and hard as a knife sinking into Ichizo's back.

'Those boys you spoke of are men now, Ichizo-san. Those days you spoke of are gone. Best to forget they ever were, and remember what you *are*.'

'I am a man in love, cousin.'

Ichizo looked at Hiro with pleading eyes.

'Surely, you remember what that was like?'

Without a sound, Hiro raised his blade and struck, faster than Ichizo would have believed possible. The blade cracked across his shoulder, another strike smashing his sword from nerveless fingers. Hiro circled behind, struck him across his back so hard the blade simply shattered, a hail of splinters filling the air along with a damp spray of spittle, a strangled cry as Ichizo stumbled forward, collapsed to his knees.

The Lord Magistrate rolled onto his back, wincing, gasping, empty palm upheld in surrender. His Daimyo stood above him, shattered blade clutched in his iron hand. His voice was cold as tombs.

'I remember what it was to be a man in love, cousin.'

Hiro cast the broken sword onto the floor with a clatter, held up iron fingers, curling them into a solid, hissing fist.

'Every single night.'

*

'I wonder what you would say, if I asked you to marry me.'

They lay entwined amidst the bed's ruins, sweat drying on their skin. Michi's hair adrift across her cheeks, her head upon his chest, lulled almost to sleeping by the song of his heart. But his words dragged her back into full waking, incredulity creeping into her voice as she raised herself up on one elbow and stared at the viper in her arms.

'. . . What?'

Ichizo was watching the ceiling, one arm behind his head, the other wrapped around her shoulder. Her body was pressed tight against him, the swell of her hips and breasts, the leg thrown over his thigh, like puzzle pieces made to interlock perfectly with his own.

Like all men and women interlock, foolish girl . . .

'I said I wonder what you would say, if I asked you to marry me.'

A slow blink.

'You are asking me to marry you?'

'No,' he smiled. 'I simply wonder what you would say.'

'I would say you were crazed, my Lord,' she scoffed, resting her head back against his chest. 'I would say you have only known me for a handful of heartbeats. I would say the lotus you were smoking must be of a rare breed indeed, and wonder if you might lend me your pipe when you were done.'

A soft chuckle. 'That is what I thought you might say.'

'A good thing, then, you did not ask.'

Ichizo was silent a moment, a frown slowly creeping into his voice.

'What do you mean I do not know you? I have known you since last spring festival.'

'You knew me after a glance across a crowded room and a three-minute conversation about poetry?'

'I knew you were beautiful. Intelligent. Possessed of a keen wit and a romantic soul.'

'Oh, indeed? A romantic, am I?'

'Poetry calls not to a heart of stone, Michi-chan.'

She was silent, one finger tracing the lines of muscle down his stomach, a landscape of hard foothills and deep valleys, traversed by a thousand goosebumps.

'And why should we not be married?' Ichizo was truly frowning now, rolling her off his chest, raising himself up to stare into her eyes. 'I know you better than Hiro knows Lady Aisha, and *they* are to be wed.'

'To prevent the entire nation falling into chaos,' Michi replied. 'To reforge a dynasty two centuries deep. I hardly think the Imperium will come crashing to an end or spring miraculously back to life if we make our little fling official, my Lord. Not to mention the difficulties we might face squeezing our guests inside this pleasant little prison cell of mine.'

'A fling?' He blinked. 'Is that what you think of me?'

'Better that than the alternative.'

'What, that I love you true?'

She stared deep into his eyes, watching his pupils for fight or flight response.

'That you still believe me part of the Kagé rebellion,' she said. 'That all this is simply a magistrate interrogating a suspect.' A small smile, just the right mix of hopeful and afraid. 'That at the end of all this, you will break my heart.'

Warning in his eyes. Pupils dilating. Fear? Suspicion? She had struck true, surely . . .

'I might say the same about you.'

Too much, silly girl. Too far. Pull away. Swiftly.

She pushed him back with a long kiss, straddling him,

pinning his wrists above his head, long dark hair draped about her face. Leaning in close, swathed in perfume and fresh sweat, feeling him stir as she breathed the words, lips brushing as if feathers against his own.

'Say it then, my Lord. Say you do not trust me. Say all this is a lie.'

'But that would be the greatest lie of all,' he whispered, leaning in for a kiss, denied as she drew back out of reach. 'I am yours, my Lady. At your mercy. Ask anything. Give voice to any question and I will answer.'

His smile seemed true. No veiled intent behind his eyes. He was so good at this.

So good it frightens you.

'Do you love me, then?' She moved her hips, the simplest gesture, shifting the entire world. He sighed with her, muscles flexed as she pressed at his wrists, leaned in close again, breathing into his ear. 'Love me true?'

Her mouth upon his, gifting him the kiss he'd sought as he shuddered beneath her.

'I love you,' he breathed. 'Gods help me, I do.'

This is not real.

A voice in her head. The voice of a girl who watched her family butchered in Daiyakawa square. Who had grown hard and cold and fierce in the shadow of the Iishi. Who lived only to see Aisha freed, the wedding stopped, the Guild's plans turned to ash and ruin. Who hated this man, his masters, the entire Imperium with everything she had inside her.

This is not real.

But as they rolled amidst the silk, his hands on her skin and his breath in her lungs, she almost forgot who she was, where she was from, why she was here. The little girl from Daiyakawa evaporating, scorched away beneath the fire of his touch, the heat of his skin, the flame of his tongue, leaving only her; a woman, loved and beloved, pure and unscarred and unafraid beneath a choking sky.

This is not real.

She almost forgot.

This is not . . .

Almost.

This

is

. . .

25

Impetus

Blood.

On his talons. On his tongue.

Buruu awoke on black glass, howling wind pushing sea spray into his eyes, his wounds, bringing a bitter, antiseptic sting. The gash on his belly ached, and he licked the matted, bloody fur, grateful that the gouge wasn't gut-deep. His metal wings had borne the worst of it.

The very worst.

A dead weight on his shoulders, snapped pivots and shredded canvas, groaning as he moved. The harness and frame had protected him from the blindside, at least – if he'd been mere flesh and bone, he would never have had the opportunity to fight back, to give as hard as he'd received, rending and tearing, knuckle-deep, locked together with his foe and plummeting from the sky. But in the aftermath, the wreckage of his false wings was a handicap, a twisted snarl hampering movement, bereft of any former synthetic grace.

He was weak. Hungry. The island around him was barren stone, jet-black and cruel, as if Susano-ō had seized a fistful of obsidian and squeezed. A strange spire of coiled metal rose at the promontory, twelve feet high, twin lengths of thick iron cable connected to its core and trailing out over thrashing water.

And off in the distance, Buruu could smell him: The other male, crashed onto the same outcropping as he, torn from rib cage to haunches by his hind claws. Dying? Vengeful? Or yet overcome with lust for the prize?

The female's scent still clouded Buruu's senses, now tempered by pain and the stink of his own blood. And amidst the rolling dark and howling rain and copper tang in his mouth, one thought swam above the mud of pheromones and endorphins. One thought to make his chest ache more fiercely than any wound from beak or claw.

The thought that he had lost himself again.

The thought that he had failed her.

Just like he had failed them.

YUKIKO?

*

'Buruu!'

Yukiko shouted his name, lurching upright in the cot, pulled up short by the leather bindings at her wrists. For a second she thought she was back in the Iishi; wondered at the salt in the air, the absence of wisteria and mountain wind. And then she recalled where she was, the shape of him in her dream, feeling a flood of relief so deep she almost burst into tears.

He's still alive.

She stretched out the Kenning, straining to her limits, heedless of the pain and growing nausea in her belly. She felt Red's small warm glow, dimmed near to nothing in slumber. The gaijin around her, like a storm of fireflies. Far in the distance, she felt the heat and shape of the female arashitora wheeling amongst the thunderclaps, glowing in her mind like fireworks. She could feel cold flickering beneath her, the sheen of scales under the water, eons deep. But out on the edges, she found a newly awakened heat, so distant it was simply a blur, almost too soft to see. And yet she knew it all the same.

Yukiko pushed her voice out into the black, screaming as loud as she could.

Buruu!

No answer. No flicker of acknowledgement. She whispered a prayer to Kitsune, begging for the Nine-Tailed Fox's fortune. Screwing her eyes shut, she reached down inside herself, heart straining, tearing away her wall to expose herself utterly, pain arcing at the base of her skull and crackling towards her temples. Something warm and sticky dripped from her nostrils, painted her lips in salt.

Hello?

Nothing save the rolling black, the empty, howling wind.

Hello?

– YŌKAI-KIN. YOU YET LIVE. –

The female's voice was small, fragmented, as if she were shouting over some great distance into barking, snapping wind. Yukiko sighed, felt relief threatening to spill over once more into grateful tears.

I'm alive, yes.

– STRONG SWIMMER. –

I need your help.

– WITH? –

My friend. The arashitora I came here with. He's hurt. Can you help him?

– WOULD HELP HIM WHY? –

He's *arashitora* like you. One of the last ones left. You can't just let him die!

– WRONG. –

Please!

– CAME HERE TO AVOID MOTHERHOOD. NOT CODDLE A FULL-GROWN LIKE A NEWBORN CUB. –

You came out here so no one could mate with you?

– NEVER AGAIN, MONKEY-CHILD. –

The female's mind burned with impossible heat.

– NEVER AGAIN. –

Well, you didn't come far enough. Buruu could smell you days' away.

– WIND BLOWS SOUTH HERE. TRUE ARASHITORA DO NOT FLY SOUTH. –

What about the other male? He must have smelled you too?

– SO? –

So why did he attack us?

Laughter in her mind.

– HE IS MALE, MONKEY-CHILD. –

Well, my friend is hurt now. He can't fly and can't hunt.

– AND? –

And I'm asking you to help him. Please.

– NO. –

Why not?

– WILL NOT AID THE KINSLAYER. –

His name is Buruu.

– HE HAS FORSAKEN ANY RIGHT TO A NAME, YŌKAI-KIN. –

. . . You know him?

– BETTER THAN YOU. –

The contact broke; a bullwhip crack that left a searing trail of pain across her brow. Yukiko winced, wiping her nose on her shoulder, smearing blood across her lips and chin. Her skull ached as if it had been stomped underfoot, ears ringing with a steel-toe tune. She felt absolutely awful— 'Like an oni had shit in her head,' her father would've said. And the thought of him washed over her in the dark, five days' worth of fatigue crashing down with the weight of anvils, threatening to tip her over the precipice.

Don't you dare cry.

She thought of him on his slab. Ashes caked on his swollen face. She thought of his last words, bleeding out into her arms in the skies above Kigen. She searched for the rage but could find none, tears welling instead, clotting her lashes, and she screwed her eyes shut as if she could stop them spilling over.

She reached out on instinct for Buruu; a reflex action, like she'd reach for a handhold if she felt herself falling. But there was almost nothing waiting for her; just a tiny blob of muddy heat in the cold, vast dark where he used to be, laced with the hunger of reptiles. And that was the last push that sent her sailing over the edge.

She curled up in the dark, like a child in womb's black.

And she wept.

*

The smell of warm porridge and hot tea roused her from dreams of growling wind, and she woke to find the noise was the hunger in her own belly. Dim daylight shone beyond the tiny window, smeared storm-grey. Piotr was sitting beside the bed, metal tray on his lap, watching her intently with his one good eye.

As she blinked the grit from her lashes, he said something in his rolling, guttural language and reached over, pulling her uwagi up around her shoulders, covering her naked chest. She flinched away, cheeks burning, remembering the blinding outrage she'd felt as he pulled the tunic open, exposing her tattoo and all else besides.

What the hells was so important about the ink on my skin?

Piotr smoothed the tangle of hair from her face, offered a spoonful of porridge. As much as the way he looked at her was unsettling, the memory of her indignities still smouldering in her mind, the food smelled delicious. Her empty stomach murmured, and she swallowed her pride along with the first mouthful, wolfing down everything he gave her.

When she was finished, she tugged the bindings on her wrists and ankles, looked at them pointedly.

'Can you untie me?'

'He cannot.' Piotr scowled and shook his head. 'Pretty girl.'

'Where am I going to go?'

Piotr touched her cheek, tucking stray hairs behind her ears. He gathered up the utensils and bowls, set them aside, leaned back in his chair. Reaching into his white coat, he retrieved his fish-shaped pipe, stuffing it with that same dried, brown herb.

'Better she not here.' He shook his head. 'Better all.'

'You could let me go?' Yukiko pulled at the restraints again.

'Too late.' He lit the pipe with his flame-box, exhaled a cloud of ignition fumes into the air. 'Is now coming she, they.'

'What?'

'Zryachniye,' he sighed. 'Zryachniye.'

'How do you speak Shiman?' Yukiko titled her head. 'Were you a merchant?'

Sadness and anger thickened his voice. 'Prisoner.'

Realization arrived with a wave of nausea, and at last she understood the man's animosity. The slap to her cheek. Scarred face, blinded eye, crippled leg.

Samurai believed it was better to commit seppuku than fall into enemy hands. A gaijin soldier who allowed himself to be captured would have been viewed as beneath contempt; a wretch without honor or worth. If Piotr had been a soldier captured by Shōgunate troops during the invasion, she could only imagine what he'd been through at her countrymen's hands.

The man seemed an utter bastard. But nobody deserved to be tortured.

'I'm sorry,' she murmured.

'Sorry?' The gaijin sucked his pipe, breathed pale grey. 'Save sorry for herself.'

He stood, limped out the door and closed it behind him. The wind howled like a lonely dog, a solitary voice in dark wilderness, dawn a lifetime away.

As the hallway light was shut out, she realized at last that she was alone out here. On an impossible metal island in the middle of vast oceans, surrounded by people who saw her as a spy, an invader, an enemy. She had no idea which way land might lay. Nobody knew she was in trouble, and even if they did, nobody knew where to find her.

No one could help her. No Buruu to fly her to safety. No Kin to build mechanical wings that could see them freed. No Kagé, no father, no friends. She realized if anyone was going to get her out of this, it was her. But if she didn't do it soon, Buruu was going to starve out there in the storm. Hiro's wedding would go ahead unopposed, Aisha would be slaved for the sake of his legitimacy, and the nation would simply have traded one Shōgun for another. Everything they worked for, her father died for, all of it would be for nothing.

So enough with sitting here in the dark and crying herself to sleep. Enough with waiting for lightning to strike. Time to stand instead of crawling. Time to start digging out of this hole with whatever tools she could scrounge.

If she found none, there was always her fingernails.

Buruu's warmth had emanated somewhere north, dulled with the distance between them. Somehow she had to get out to those islands, fix his wings. She considered the flying machine on the roof of the complex, but realized she had no idea how to operate it. The female arashitora was going to be no help at all; that much was clear. As for the gaijin, Danyk and Katya clearly saw her as an enemy, and the memory of Piotr slapping her, ignoring her struggles as he tore off her uwagi, still filled her with bitter, helpless outrage.

But she needed someone. By herself, she had no chance of getting out of this room, let alone rescuing Buruu.

Ilyitch was her best bet. He was young, didn't get along with Danyk or Piotr, seemed to be an underling afforded little respect. And of course, he'd saved her from the ocean, risked his life for hers. Surely that spoke of a good heart? A kind soul? Guilt swelled at the thought of what might happen to him if his fellows caught him helping her, but she quickly quashed it under the weight of the stakes in play: Not just her life. Buruu's. Aisha's too. All of Shima.

She had to get back. There was still hope. If they left soon, she might still reach Kigen in time to stop Hiro's wedding. And besides, if she couldn't trust the boy who'd dived into a freezing ocean full of sea dragons to save her life, who the hells could she trust?

But he doesn't speak Shiman. How do I even talk to him?

She sighed, shutting her eyes. She opened up the Kenning again – just a fraction – feeling about as gently as she could beyond the wall of herself. Again, she could sense the gaijin around her, muddy and indistinct. The headache reared up like a snake behind her eyes and she whimpered in pain.

She remembered touching Yoritomo's mind at the Burning Stones, crushing it to pulp with her thoughts. Her father had been there to help her that day, augmenting her strength with his own. But whatever was happening to the Kenning inside her, it had grown so strong she was certain she'd be able to hurt someone by herself now. Maybe not kill them outright. But definitely make them bleed.

But could she talk to them?

Not hurt them – just do something as simple as speaking?

She wouldn't even know where to begin. The Kenning had been with her since she was six years old, seeming totally natural to her as a child. She was able to use it because nobody ever told her she *couldn't*. And she'd grown up taking the gift for granted, as reflexive as walking or breathing. But this was something new. Something utterly untested, more like turning a cartwheel than placing one foot in front of another. Would she hurt him? Kill him? If she put words into the boy's head, would he simply think himself mad?

Only one way to find out.

She reached into the Kenning, felt for the boy's mind amidst the rolling, seething storm of gaijin around her. But almost immediately, she realized she had no way of telling one blinding tangle from another. It wasn't as if she could read their thoughts to tell them apart – the mental reflection of every round-eye felt nearly identical. And even if she *could* tell one from another, she was uncertain if she could project herself into their minds without line of sight.

Line of sight . . .

Red.

The dog lifted his head, rawhide strip in his mouth, curled up on his blanket in His Boy's room. His tail began wagging.

girl!

Red, will you do something for me?

will try i am gooddog!

Find your Boy.

food?

I'll get you some food, yes.

Red jumped up from his blanket, and she slipped into the glass-smooth space behind his eyes. It was like being in the bamboo forest of her childhood again; she and her brother Satoru wrapped inside their old hound's head – the original Buruu who died defending them from a starving wolf.

She felt the faint disconnect between the dog's motion and her own stationary body, the influx of scent, the clarity of sound. Machines rumbled in the building's belly, the storm wailed with enough fury to shake the foundations. The relentless sea pounded the iron supports as if it wished the building scrubbed from its surface, nothing left behind save rusting metal and clean, feather-white bones, sunk too deep for sunlight to ever touch again.

Red scampered through the corridors, past a large room set with tables and dozens of chairs, food-scent hanging in the air. He trotted through what Yukiko presumed were barracks; bunk beds and a strong, musty scent that was distinctly male. He tried to make it up to the roof, but the door was shut with no dog flap to slip through. Red turned and padded back down three floors, slipped into a broad corridor and finally came to a halt outside a pair of heavy doors, slightly ajar. The dog whined and paced back and forth, ears pressed flat to his head.

What's wrong?

not allowed here . . .
Why?
loud place bad place!
Is your Boy inside?
Red sniffed the air, the concrete floor.
yes . . .
Come on, let's look. You're too clever for them to catch you.

Uncertain but overjoyed with her flattery, the hound nosed his way into what looked like a vast boiler room. Dozens of men in dirty red coveralls were at work on a great system of cables and valves cast in greasy iron. Enormous, glittering spirals of glass descended from metal intakes in the ceiling, down to a series of strange, lopsided machines encrusted with incomprehensible controls, tight bundles of coiled copper and glass cylinders filled with a thick solution the colour of urine. Thunder shook the walls around them, shivering the apparatus in their brackets. As she watched, the ceiling pulsed with a lightning strobe, and the glass spirals filled with a blinding blue-white illumination that danced across the mirrored lenses of the gaijin's goggles. Every globe in every wall socket grew momentarily brighter, and she felt Red's fur bristle in the crackling air.

A hollow, sucking hiss filled the room, and Red cringed as raw current arced and twisted down the copper coils and into the cylinders of yellow liquid. Yukiko felt ashamed at having tricked the dog into a situation he was so obviously frightened of, but the thought of Buruu pushed her misgivings aside. The men shouted to each other, throwing switches and clamping cables. As the light faded, squat metal trolleys were rushed in, and the gaijin shuffled the glass tanks along squeaking iron rails. The solution inside had changed colour to a luminescent blue-white, a frosting of condensation forming on the glass. The smell of ozone was hung fog-thick in the air alongside a fading, high-pitched squeal.

Catching the sky . . .

keep in jars so silly can't eat sky!

Let's find your Boy.

not allowed here . . .

Please, Red.

they yell at me they hit

Please?

He whined.

shouldn't be baddog

Red . . .

going now i am gooddog

The hound turned to leave. Yukiko thought of Buruu again, bleeding and starving out in the storm. Her best friend in the world. Her brother. More to her than life itself. And though the guilt made her wince, the breath catch in her lungs, she reached inside the Kenning, and found herself making it hard. Iron. Not the soft voice of suggestion, or even the subtle press of manipulation. It was crude and heavy-handed; a subtraction of will, the strings of a puppeteer upon a flinching marionette. Head pounding as if it might burst, warmth trickling over her lips.

Red. Do as I say.

Not asking. Commanding.

And with another soft whine, the dog tucked his tail and obeyed.

He stole across the generator room, several gaijin shouting at him, trying to shoo him away. Yukiko noticed none of the workers had insignia on their collars or animal skins on their shoulders. They looked messier than Danyk and his fellows, more unkempt. Several sported what looked to be burn scars on their exposed skin.

The hound nosed his way up onto a gantry of steel mesh, into a thicket of pipes and bright red valve handles. A large picture hung on the wall, covered in gaijin writing. It resembled a spider's web; a central hub connected to smaller nodes by thin, fluorescent wires. Each node was set with a small globe and scribed with a symbol. One bulb in the topmost corner was glowing faint blue-white, a trail of fluorescence leading back to the web's centre, light slowly fading as the static electricity in the room died. Yukiko noticed a stylized sea dragon curled around what looked like a compass in the bottom corner and realized what she was seeing.

A map.

A map of the lightning farm and the surrounding pylons.

Gaijin men were gathered around a cluster of controls nearby, and one of them soon spotted Red standing before the glowing diagram. A hulking uniform-clad shape Yukiko recognized as Danyk appeared, bellowing at the top of his voice. Red cowered low, belly to the floor. Blue-white light glinted across the flattened samurai helms on the big man's shoulders.

told you baddog now . . .

I'm sorry, Red. I really am.

Danyk picked up a wrench and made to throw it at the dog, roaring again. Ilyitch appeared from behind a cluster of pipes, a dripping mop in his hands, faint hand-shaped bruise on his cheek. The big man cuffed the boy across the back of his head, sending his goggles flying. Scooping them back up off the grille, Ilyitch grabbed Red by his collar and dragged him down the stairs, berating the hound in his strange language. She sensed Red's shame, vague resentment mixed with confusion about why he'd done something so thoroughly *baddog*. She felt awful guilt; a pity-sick disquiet that she'd turned the Kenning into something so overt. So cruel.

She eased away from the contact with the hound, blinking hard, licking at the blood drying on her upper lip. And tentatively, she projected herself through Red's eyes, reaching out to touch the boy's thoughts. The migraine grew awful; like a metal vise grinding the base of her skull. She had to fight to maintain her grip, to stay inside the noise and light of a human mind, so utterly different from the beasts she'd swam in for most of her life.

The boy dragged Red across the catchment room floor, through the double doors, and up the spiral stairwell. Yukiko tried to speak into his head, to frame words Ilyitch might understand, but they slipped away from her, all a-tumble, white and empty noise, like hollow pipes falling upon a sodden floor.

The boy stopped, looked around him with a frown. Red whined, hackles rising. She could feel the dog's trepidation, his instinctive sense that something was very wrong.

She tried again, to form a greeting and project it through the dog, but it collapsed like a castle of sand between her fingers; just a muddled jumble of consonants and vowels and hissing static. Ilyitch tilted his head to one side, eyes screwed shut, holding his nose and trying to pop his eardrums. Yukiko backed off, lingering on the edge of his warmth, and he grabbed Red's collar again, hauled him up the stairs.

This isn't working. I can't form the words.

It was as if the constructs in the boy's head were too different from her own: square pegs into round holes. Language was never an issue with animals, but perhaps that was because animals didn't really speak? Perhaps the Kenning was never meant for this?

What could she do? How could she leap the barrier between them? She needed a way of communicating that they both understood . . .

She recalled Danyk looming over her, the katana blade slipping down over her tattoo. His eyes fixed upon the picture inked into her skin, the symbol he understood without her needing to speak a word.

'Keetsoonay. Sahmoorayee.'

. . . That was it.

The answer.

Not words. Pictures.

Yukiko formed an image and pushed it into Ilyitch's mind; herself, sinking beneath the waves as he dove into the thrashing waters to save her. The boy reeled back against the railing, hand to his brow. She gave him another image; of her and Buruu flying through clear skies, her arms around his neck. She tried to inject emotional content into the picture, the simple warmth of friendship and trust.

Ilyitch steadied himself, blinking as if he'd been struck in the face. Sure enough, the boy loosened his grip on Red's collar and looked to the stairwell above. He ascended at a scuffing, cautious pace, Red on his heels, heavy footfalls ringing on metal as he reached the landing and started down the corridor towards her room.

The sensation was disorientating, almost nauseating; watching the boy walking down the hallway, Red beside him, hearing their footfalls through Ilyitch's ears, the same footsteps coming closer in her own. So she broke full contact and opened her eyes, wiped her nose as best she could on her shoulder and leaned back against the wall. As she did so, she pushed one last picture out to the gaijin boy; an image of herself, helpless, frightened and wretched. Bound wrists and pleading eyes, desperate and alone, looking to him, her only hope.

When Ilyitch opened the door a few moments later, that was exactly what he saw.

26

Footprints in the Snow

The Gentleman knelt on a satin cushion at the head of a long oaken table. The reflections of the overheads on its surface were tiny stars on lacquered midnight, twinkling with more vibrancy than the real stars overhead could ever dream. A pretty duet of koto and shamisen music drifted through the drinking house walls, competing with the growl of the generator downstairs.

The table was dressed for eight, each place set with fine porcelain, a saké cup, a thousand-thread linen napkin; all as white as Iishi snow. Jimen the accountant sat at the Gentleman's right hand. Each other cushion was occupied by a yakuza lieutenant; a collection of muscle and scars, narrowed eyes and gleaming, tattooed flesh. Five men and one woman, each stripped to the waist, every inch of flesh below their necks and above their wrists sporting beautiful, intricate ink work. Canvases of flesh, painted by the greatest artisans in Kigen.

Seimi knelt with fists upon knees, Hida beside him, pawing at one cauliflower ear. The room was cool as autumn's kiss, the heady scent of liquor veiling the stink of sweat and exhaust from nearby sky-docks. Seimi could see the horizon through the bay windows, the shades of night studded with the silhouettes of docked sky-ships, forlorn as abandoned lovers.

And not a breath of wind.

'Brothers.' Jimen looked around the room. 'The Gentleman thanks you all for coming.'

As one, the lieutenants covered their fists and bowed. The Gentleman nodded in return, saying nothing.

'Why are you here?' Jimen asked.

Uncertain glances flickering amongst the yakuza. No one made a sound.

The Gentleman waited a long, silent moment, breathing slow, the mournful notes of the duet drifting in the air like the scent of old chi.

He clapped his hands.

Half a dozen serving girls slipped into the room, charcoal eyes downcast, painted faces pale as the hungry dead. Pink kimonos, drum bows the colour of rain clouds at their waists, tiny steps as quiet as smoke. Delicate hands laid two rice-paper bundles before each lieutenant. The packages were long and cylindrical, arranged on the place settings with all the precision of a tea ceremony. When they were done, the girls bowed as one to the Gentleman, then scuttled from the room with eyes still on the floor.

'Open them,' Jimen said.

The room was filled with the whisper of tearing paper, translucent strips fluttering to the ground. When he was done, Seimi stared down at the gifts before him. The thicker package contained a tantō in a short, lacquered sheath, mother-of-pearl inlays gleaming on the hilt. The second gift was a six-inch iron file: sawtoothed and thoroughly ordinary.

'Each of you has failed our oyabun.' Jimen stared around the room, not a hint of anger in his voice. 'Each of you has been robbed by these gutter-thieves who plague us. Each of you will now be given the opportunity to atone.'

The Gentleman said nothing. Simply folded his arms and waited, patient as a glacier.

Seimi and Hida glanced at each other, then picked up their napkins. The other lieutenants followed suit, using the snow-white cloth to tie a tight knot around the top knuckle of their left-most fingers. Several were already missing the tips of their smallest digits and were forced to tie the knot at the second knuckle. Seimi unsheathed the tantō, watched his fingernail turning purple. The lieutenants filled the room with the ring of drawn blades.

All save one.

'Nakai-san.' Jimen aimed a cold stare in one man's direction. 'You falter?'

The other yakuza looked at Nakai. He was a few years older than the rest, greying hair swept into a thin topknot. His ink was faded with the slow press of time, blacks running to blue. A knot of lean muscle, bloodshot eyes and a slightly grey hue to his skin telling his fellows that he'd been hitting the smoke a little too hard recently. He stared at his left hand, at the empty knuckle where his little finger should have been, the ring finger already missing its first joint. He held it up to the Gentleman, blinking over severed digits.

'Oyabun,' he said. 'My sword grip will be ruined.'

'Why do you need a sword?' Jimen raised an eyebrow. 'In a room full of your kin?'

'Not here.' He nodded towards the window. 'Out there.'

'On the street?'

'Hai.'

'The streets where children play in shadows they once feared? Where two guttersnipes are enough to see a lieutenant of the Scorpion Children hand over his iron, then tuck tail and run? Those streets, Nakai-san?'

'You do not speak to me that way,' Nakai spat. 'You're a godsdamned accountant. A book-monger. You know less than nothing about life in this city.'

'I know you shame yourself now.' The little man's voice was soft. Dangerous. 'Just as you shamed yourself when you handed over our coin to children.'

'They had an iron-thrower. What was I supposed to—'

The Gentleman hardly seemed to move at all. Nakai paused midsentence, staring like a half-wit at the tantō handle protruding from his chest, the thin line of blood running down his belly. He sucked in a shuddering breath, coughed scarlet. Clutching the hilt, he gurgled and slumped forwards onto the table. Blood leaked across polished wood. The smell of urine mingled with sweat and smoke.

'You were supposed to do that, Nakai-san.' The Gentleman wiped already-spotless hands on his napkin. 'Something like that would have served you well indeed.'

Nakai twitched once and was still.

'Know that I am not ashamed of any of you.' The Gentleman glanced around the room. 'But I tell you truly that I have never been less proud.'

Seimi slapped his hand onto his dinner plate, fingers spread. With a single fluid motion, he sliced his little finger clean through at the top knuckle. The others around him followed suit, each removing a segment from their smallest digit. The blood upon their plates was bright, almost gaudy. Pale chunks of bloodless meat remained behind as each yakuza elevated their wounded hand, wrapped the napkin over their severed digit, curled their fingers into fists. Seimi looked down at the plate, noted his fingernail wasn't purple anymore.

The Gentleman nodded once, lifted a saké bottle from the warming tray and poured himself a shot. He raised his cup, waited until each lieutenant had done the same. He looked each one in the eye.

'Scorpion Children!' he barked.

'Scorpion Children!' Six shouts in return.

The Gentleman and his crew threw back the liquor, returned their cups to their proper place. Several shared uneasy glances, but none seemed eager to speak. Finally, Hida growled, picked up the iron file and held it out to his oyabun.

The Gentleman smiled at him. 'Hida?'

The Gentleman *never* smiled.

'Why?' Hida looked from his oyabun to the iron file and back again.

'A hound. A hound to set upon thieves, brother.'

'How do they know where we're moving coin?' Seimi kept the pain of his wounded hand from his voice, gritting the yellow ruin he called teeth. 'We follow no set route, yet they've hit us four nights running.'

'They don't strike the stash houses.' A pock-faced lump called Bao spoke. 'They hit us when we move. They ambush, like the jade adder. Like the pit spider.'

'Someone inside?' The female lieutenant, Geisu, voiced the ugly thought every man was afraid to speak. 'A traitor?'

'Impossible,' came the muttered replies. 'Unthinkable.'

'Then how are they doing it?' Seimi slapped his good hand onto the wood.

The room descended into brief clamour, each man offering

his own theory. The Gentleman's voice cut through the noise like a tantō through knuckle.

'We can ask them when we catch them.'

'How?' Hida still held the file in his fist, still stared at his oyabun.

'Footprints in the snow, my brother.'

The Gentleman smiled again.

'Footprints in the snow.'

27

A Mountain of Bones

The blood on Daichi's lips was a bubbling lather, pink as the hyacinths on the western rises. Shuddering groans running the length of him, froth bubbling from his nostrils as his pulse grew dim and the light in his eyes dimmer still.

Old Mari cut the straps of his crumpled breastplate, peeled the iron away and sliced his uwagi open, the flesh beneath already bruised, collarbone to belly. Her hands were flecked with blood, hair a bedraggled mess about her face, yelling at the Kagé onlookers with a shrill, shaking voice.

'If you're not in here helping, get out of the bloody room!' She whirled on a younger girl. 'Suki, fetch more lanterns from next door. Eiko, we need boiling water, I don't care how, but get it fast. And somebody get me some lotus, for Amaterasu's sake!'

Daichi drew his legs up as the pain overtook him. He coughed, bloody foam spattering the air. The wound was lung-deep, and Mari knew there was little they could do. Several men held Daichi down as she leaned in close, pressing at his ribs, feeling bone shift and pop, cursing again for more light.

'Is he going to die?'

Kaori stood nearby, wretched and trembling. Sodden fringe draped down over her scar, steel-grey eyes bloodshot with rage and grief. To see him go like this . . .

'He's not going to die,' Mari said. 'Not if I can help it.'

But she couldn't. And she knew it. Daichi was halfway to the Mountain of Bones already. Blood trickled from his lips with each bubbling gasp, pooling beside his head. Every breath was a labour, thinning by the moment, his blood pressure steadily dropping with each struggling beat of his heart.

The best anyone could pray for was that he passed without pain.

'Where is that lotus?' she shrieked.

She heard a clamour on the veranda outside, angry voices swelling. Kaori looked up, jaw clenched, scowling like Enma-ō himself as Kin walked into the room, drenched to the bone. Following the boy was a tall, slender girl with earth-brown eyes and dark, cropped hair. Her lips were the colour of bruised roses, so full it looked as if someone had cuffed her across the mouth. Dressed in a threadbare hakama, bare feet, a dirty uwagi with a hole torn in its back to accommodate the swell of a silver orb, a cluster of chromed, insectoid limbs curled at her back.

A gaggle of onlookers gathered in the doorway, dark stares and darker mutterings.

'Mari, you've met Ayane,' said Kin.

'Gods above . . .' the old woman breathed.

'What is the meaning of this?' Kaori hissed. 'How did you get out of your cell?'

'She's here to help, Kaori,' Kin replied.

The False-Lifer stepped up to the bloody table, eyes sweeping Daichi's body. She peeled back one of his eyelids with her thumb, pressed two fingers against his throat and leaned close to hear the breath rattling in his lungs. The old man coughed, spattering her face with blood. She stood, turned to Kin and blinked once. Twice.

'His lung has collapsed. He will be dead soon.'

'By all the gods in the heavens, Guildsman, are you insane?' Kaori still glared at Kin, outrage in her eyes. 'You seriously believe I would let this accursed freak treat my father?'

'Would you rather he died?' Kin asked.

'This is madness. Are you going to run cables beneath his flesh? Plug him into one of those cursed mechabacii? I'd rather bury you both alongside him.'

'What's wrong with you?' Kin slammed his hands on the table. 'She's offering to save his life, and you repay her with threats?' Kin glared at the faces peering through the windows. 'Aren't you supposed to be the ones who'll free this island? You should be better than this!'

Kaori stepped close to Kin, her face inches from his. 'If it weren't for your damnable machines, none of this would have happened!'

'Your people are the reason this happened! The shuriken-throwers were *sabotaged*, Kaori!'

'You are wasting time.' Ayane's voice cut through the clamour, soft as silk, sharp as the limbs on her back. 'With respect, this man has precious little left. If we do nothing, he is as good as dead. I do not see how allowing me to try can make matters worse.'

Kin ran his hand over his scalp, met Kaori's stare with defiance.

'What say you, Kaori? Will you trust Ayane, or watch your father die?'

Kaori's eyes drifted to her father. His struggles had grown

feeble, shallow breath sucked ragged through bloody teeth. Fear carved long furrows across her brow, into the corners of her mouth. Clenched fists, clenched jaw, trembling breath. She looked at Ayane, moments ticking by like minutes, like hours, like *days* until at last Daichi started coughing, *coughing*, his whole body shaking and shuddering, lips painted with blood. Kaori knelt by her father's side, clutching his hand. Tears welled in her eyes.

'Can you really save him, girl?'

The chromed arms uncurled from Ayane's back one pair at a time, like peacock feathers, gleaming in the lantern light. She touched the blood spattered on her face, smearing it between her fingers as if savouring the sensation.

'I can save him.'

Kaori sighed.

Nodded once.

'. . . Then do it.'

28

Moving Pictures

There is power in words.

There are words that bid us laugh and make us weep. Words to begin with and words to end by. Words that seize the hearts in our chests and squeeze them tight, that set the skin on our bones to tingling. Words so beautiful they shape us, forever change us, live inside us for as long as we have breath to speak them. There are forgotten words. Killing words. Great and frightening and terrible words. There are True words.

And then there are pictures.

It was a slow process at first. Sitting opposite one another on the metal cot, Yukiko pushing images into Ilyitch's mind, waiting for him to form his clumsy replies. His eyes were wide, mouth slack. And though he had no idea how it was all happening, the boy seemed enthralled enough by the process that he didn't waste time seeking explanations.

Ilyitch's images were blurry impressions; finger paintings in the rain, running and bleeding at the edges. By comparison, Yukiko's thoughts were intricate, full of light and colour. But they found an equilibrium between them, and she soon found enough meaning in the gaijin's mental shorthand to understand his intentions. She tried to inject emotion into her thoughts, to make him feel like she was a friend, but had no idea if she was succeeding.

Her nose started bleeding almost as soon as they began, and it took a long time to explain that the blood was nothing to be concerned about, that there were more important things at stake. Her skull was close to splitting, the wall she'd once again built herself trembling with the strain, barely keeping the Kenning's fire at bay. But something held it in place, stopped it collapsing utterly; something fierce and bright and desperate inside her. Born perhaps of fear for Buruu, lost out there in the dark, or perhaps rage at her own helplessness to save him.

She started by showing Ilyitch an image of Shima's armies in retreat, packing up and flying home after Yoritomo's death. She tried to show him the war was over. That she was not an enemy, or at least, not his.

In turn, the young man showed her burned crops and gutted buildings. Gaijin soldiers cut down under white flags, prison camps, wailing children dragged into sky-ships and flown away, never to be seen again.

She showed him Yoritomo, murdered in the Market Square. An empty throne.

Ilyitch replied with the image of a tall woman in a stone chair, grim and terrible. She had blonde hair, the same mismatched eyes as Katya – one black, the other glittering rose-quartz. She wore a suit of iron, black feathers adorned her shoulders, a huge bird's skull with a cruel, hooked beak on her head. Twelve stars lay at her feet, and she gathered them in her lap, one by one.

He showed her legions of stern-faced gaijin, skins of great wolves and bears upon their shoulders, naked swords in their hands. A fleet of ships, iron fortresses floating on a storm sea, powered by the lightning they hauled from the sky.

And then Ilyitch showed her an hourglass, its sand almost run out.

So Yukiko turned away from the war and focused on Buruu. She formed pictures of the great hunt on the *Thunder Child,* their time trapped alone in the Iishi, their captivity in Kigen and the battle with Yoritomo's samurai in the arena. Ilyitch watched her with something like awe during this passage, jaw slack, running his fingers over the fur at his shoulders.

The boy projected a stylized picture of Yukiko, katana held aloft, sunlight in her hair, thousands of samurai kneeling at her feet. The picture was tinged with uncertainty.

His eyebrows raised in question.

She smiled and shook her head. Showed the Kagé village in the mountains; a peaceful place, herself and Buruu laying in dappled sunlight. A quiet life.

He frowned at her then, as if he didn't quite understand.

Yukiko projected an image of Buruu, bleeding and twisted on the rocks. A compass needle pointing north, and the pylon she'd seen near Buruu in her dream.

Ilyitch shook his head, pushed her a childish version of the map she'd seen on the wall downstairs. Dozens of pylons, studded all over the islands around the lightning farm. Not all of them were connected directly; most of the cables threaded amongst multiple towers back to the central hub, like strands of a crooked spider's web. If the picture she'd shown him was correct, Buruu was trapped at the very end of the lines.

Miles away.

Yukiko used one of his own images; the hourglass running out of sand. A picture of food. An arashitora skeleton on black rocks.

She reached out, leather thong tight around her wrist, fingers stretching towards his own in vain. He frowned, put his hand in hers. She squeezed tight.

'Please,' she said, tears welling. 'Please.'

Ilyitch sighed, glanced at the doorway behind him. Avoiding her eyes, the boy stood, pointed at Red and spoke a stern command. Red lay flat and wagged his tail.

'W-wait.' Yukiko sat up straighter, frowning. 'Where are you going?'

The gaijin spoke a handful of words, held up both hands as if urging her to be still. Then he turned and clomped out of the room, shutting the door behind him.

Where is he going, Red?

don't know i stay here am gooddog

Yukiko listened to Ilyitch's footprints receding down the hall. She had no idea if she'd convinced him, no clue as to whether he was headed to get supplies to help her, or to turn her in to Danyk. But for the first time since she'd arrived here, she found herself alone with Red.

So either way, she wasn't going to wait to find out.

*

The dog had gnawed through one of the tethers binding her wrists and was halfway through the second when she heard stealthy footfalls in the corridor. She looked at Red, paused with his teeth upon the leather, one ear pointing to the sky as his tail started wagging.

Is that Ilyitch?

The dog blinked.

Your Boy? Is that your Boy coming?

. . . no

Yukiko strained against the weakened strap, finally tearing

it loose, tugging at the bindings on her ankles as the footsteps arrived in the hallway outside. She was up and coiled in the shadows as the handle turned and the door opened wide.

A figure limped into the gloom, and she struck, wrapping the bedsheet over its head and kicking the back of its knee. The figure dropped to the ground with the whine of pistons and a muffled cry of pain. She grabbed the contraption on his belt and tore it from its holster. The figure pulled the tangled sheet away from his face and turned to face her, and she recognized Piotr, pale as the sheet she'd wrapped him in, hands reaching for the ceiling.

'Stop!' His one good eye locked upon the device in her hand. 'Don't!'

Yukiko realized the man was drunk; the reek of liquor on his breath and skin so strong he might have bathed in it. She pointed the contraption at his head, finger poised over what she hoped was the trigger.

'What are you doing here?' she growled.

'Please.' He motioned to the hallway. 'Please. I am wanting for you.'

'Why? What do you want with me?'

'Using you.' He licked his lips, gaze roaming from head to toe. 'The body. Using for the body.'

'My body?'

He reached up, put his hands on her shoulders, ran them down over her breasts. Yukiko took a step back, lip curling in disgust.

'Please.' Piotr looked her up and down, put his finger to his lips. 'Wanting you. Come for me. We must come.'

'You sick bastard,' she growled.

'Sick?' The man frowned. 'No get sick, is—'

Her knee collided with his crotch midsentence, her elbow with his jaw. His head twisted across his shoulders, spittle and blood spraying between split lips, eyes rolling up in their sockets as he hit the concrete with a wet thud. Red hopped off the bed and snuffled at the man's face, licking his nose with a hopeful wag of his tail.

killed!?

No, I didn't.

She massaged the pain in her knuckles, stared at the gaijin with utter contempt.

Although I should. Godsdamned pervert. He's old enough to be my father.

A quick search of the man's clothing revealed his carved fish pipe, a satchel of the strange leaf that gaijin all seemed to smoke, and a ring of iron keys. She was eyeing off the strange weapon in her hand when Red heard Ilyitch's footprints in the corridor. She stood and pointed the device at the doorway, not knowing how her benefactor might react upon seeing his unconscious comrade.

Ilyitch stopped at the threshold, frowning. As his eyes adjusted to the gloom, he saw Yukiko and the contraption coiled in her hands. He raised one eyebrow, letting the three satchels he was carrying fall to the ground. Catching sight of Piotr collapsed beside her, he shuffled forward with hands raised, crouching and searching for the man's pulse. A stream of nonsensical words followed, hissed through clenched teeth, accompanied by furious hand gestures.

Yukiko pushed the picture of Piotr's attempted assault into his mind, the image of his hands pawing her chest. The boy fell silent, looked at his fallen comrade with an uneasy expression. He put a comforting hand on her shoulder but she shied away, and Ilyitch let his arm drop. Turning to the satchels he'd brought with him, he knelt and rummaged inside the largest. He tossed Yukiko a dirty red coverall, heavy boots, and a yellow rubber rainskin. Not needing to be told, Yukiko slipped into the coverall and rainskin (too big), sat on the bed and buckled up the boots (also too big). She pulled the hood over her head, tugged the hem-ties as tight as she could.

Ilyitch had two coils of thick rope looped over his shoulders. He peeled one off and hung it around her neck, hefted one of the satchels, handed her another. The bag was heavy, stinking of raw fish. She guessed it was Buruu's dinner, and she was momentarily overcome with gratitude for this strange boy with tarnished silver eyes.

She stepped up and kissed his cheek, careful of the swollen, purple bruise. His skin was salty smooth against her lips.

'Thank you, Ilyitch,' she said.

The gaijin shot her a pretty smile, scratching at the base of his skull and blushing. She stooped to pat Red, let him lick her nose.

You stay here, all right?

can't come with you?

Not unless you can fly.

flew here

You did?

from houses on the water

Houses?

so many so loud!

'Yukiko.'

Hearing Ilyitch say her name pulled her from the dog's mind. The boy nodded towards the door, motioned for her to follow.

Good-bye, Red. I'm sorry about before. For making you be bad.

She gave him an affectionate scratch behind his ears.

You're a gooddog. Always.
you goodgirl too
A faint, grim smile.
Not that good.

Hood pulled low over her eyes, she followed the gaijin from her cell.

*

'You can't be serious!'

Shrieking gales snatched the words from her mouth, dragging them off to drown in the sideways rain. Cautious feet had brought them up an auxiliary stairwell near the catchment room and from there onto the roof. The storm was so heavy it seemed night had fallen, and the glow of grubby tungsten was all that stood between them and almost pitch blackness.

Black clouds rolled overhead, thunderous, flashes of lightning catching the world in freeze-frame. All around them, copper spires stretched into the sky, twin cables as thick as her wrist leading off into the dark. She could hear the ocean below, waves crashing against the structure and shivering it in its moorings. The cables hummed in the wind; a lonely, metallic dirge over the percussion of Raijin's drums.

Ilyitch laughed and handed her the contraption, took another from the storage locker at the base of the lightning spire. Yukiko stared at the device he'd given her, stomach sinking towards her toes.

It was solid iron, slippery with rain and grease. Four grooved rubber wheels lined up along a cross-shaped bar, fixed at either side with what looked like crank handles. A leather harness was affixed to a clip at the bottom of the crossbar, and Ilyitch was already strapping himself in. Yukiko had a dreadful feeling she knew where this was going, buckling herself into her own harness as the storm raged about them. She leaned against the railing as the wind buffeted her like a plaything. Lightning struck a spire out on the ocean to the south, raced along the cables up to the building's roof. Yukiko flinched, shielding her eyes against the blue-white burn seething through the vast machine behind them. Goosebumps trawled her skin.

Ilyitch looked to the sky, then scampered up the lightning spire, using the copper coils like a ladder. He slung the contraption onto the double lengths of cable, grooved rubber wheels fitting snugly around the circumference of each. In one smooth motion he kicked off the tower, the device whizzing along the cables, sending him thirty feet out into the gloom. He dangled from the harness beneath the crossbar, reached up to the hand cranks and began turning them. The contraption wheeled slowly back towards the tower. Ilyitch spun the cranks the other way as if to demonstrate, the contraption travelling in the opposite direction. He looked at her and smiled.

It's a flying fox.

Yukiko yelled over the wind.

'What happens if lightning hits our cables?'

A raised eyebrow.

'Lightning!' She pointed at the sky, then along the iron, gave her best impression of an explosion.

Ilyitch held his finger aloft, then hooked it through a metal pin at the front of his harness. Without a sound, he yanked the pin free and fell down into darkness.

Yukiko screamed, reached out for the falling gaijin, knowing he was too far away to save. But five feet into the fall, a rubber thong in the harness snapped taut, and Ilyitch jerked to a sudden halt. He held out both hands and grinned, twisting in the storm like a wind chime.

'You bastard,' Yukiko muttered.

Ilyitch climbed the tether hand over fist, swung up and hooked his legs over the cables to give himself enough slack to reinsert the pin.

He beckoned with one hand, yelling over the wind.

Yukiko licked her lips, tasted fresh salt, clean rain. Her knuckles were white on the railing, heart pounding against her ribs, fear-born nausea slicking her insides. Lightning arced across the clouds above, and she made the mistake of looking down. The ocean was a black, thrashing snarl, roaring and crashing in towers twenty feet high. But in the split second before the lightning faded and the blanket of gloom fell again, she saw the glint of a long, serpentine tail cutting through the waves.

Sea dragons.

Reaching out with the Kenning, she felt them below. Smooth as polished steel, cold and sharp and hungry. Their shape was ancient, stirring a primal fear inside her, much deeper than the thought of lightning striking the cables or the journey to come. Her mind shied away instinctively; a child fleeing into the safety of a parent's bed.

Her hands were shaking.

But then she pictured Buruu, alone and bleeding, somewhere out there in the dark. And she grit her teeth and snatched up the flying fox, climbed the lightning spire and slung the device over the cables without another thought.

Holding her breath, eyes wide, she kicked out into the windswept dark.

29

A Trembling Earth

Sometimes Hiro could still feel his hand.

He would wake in the deep of night, troubled by some itch or spasm, reaching towards it and finding only an empty mattress, the slippery kiss of silken sheets. In the dark, he would search the place where his arm should have been, groping about until he found the nub of flesh they had left him with: the puckered suture scars, the gristle-twisted knot of meat studded with bayonet fixtures, not even half a bicep remaining below the swell of his shoulder. And in the quiet and the still, he would picture her face and dream of all the ways he could break it.

'Yukiko.'

He breathed her name as if it were a toxic fume. And every time he woke to that nub of flesh, every time his hand itched and he couldn't scratch it, he was poisoned anew. She was inside him. A cell-deep sepsis. A wound refusing to heal. Like the scars of blackened ash drifting away below his feet, the thrum of motors settling like cancer in his bones.

The ironclad *Blessed Light* was a thumbprint on the waking dawn, smoking black against bloody red as Lady Amaterasu crested the horizon and set fire to the sky. Hiro stood at her prow, half a dozen Iron Samurai looming around him, the sunrise tinting their bone-white armour immolation-red. The Daimyo of the Tora clan clasped his hands behind his back, sea-green eyes upon the tortured soil of Jukai province below.

The snowcapped spires of the Tōnan Mountains lay to the west, and Hiro knew somewhere amidst those peaks crouched the impregnable perch of First House – the heart of the Lotus Guild in Shima. It was there the Guild had begun, two centuries ago, just after Kazumitsu I took his throne. When the Tiger, Dragon, Phoenix and Fox zaibatsu began consuming the lesser clans; the blood of Falcon, Panda, Serpent and their fellows just a feast for the Four.

The first production-grade crops of blood lotus had been cultivated here, centuries ago. Once this had been the most fertile region in all of the Imperium, but now all was ashen earth and black smoke curling from the cracks – as if a master painter had spent his last on a landscape of rarest beauty, and some jealous lover had smudged inch-thick handfuls of charcoal onto the canvas, drying and splitting in the noonday sun. On maps, the ruined land was still named Jukai province – a name meaning 'Evergreen.' But Shima's citizens knew it by another name.

The Stain.

'It's getting worse.' Hiro glanced at the Guildsman beside him. 'So much worse.'

Second Bloom Kensai refused to look down, bloody eyes fixed on the proving grounds ahead. The rising sun kissed his perfect, metal cheek, the smooth features of a gilded youth retching up breather cables, his hulking atmos-suit spitting fumes and hissing with every breath. A child's head atop a monster's body.

'All will be well once inochi supplies are restored.' Kensai's voice rumbled in Hiro's gut. 'But now you see why the war must be renewed. We need more prisoners, Shōgun. More gaijin to feed the lotus. And more land to plant it.'

Hiro frowned, his mind turning to dark places. 'Is there no other way? Some other—'

'No.' Kensai folded his arms. 'Sacrifices must be made. The lotus *must* bloom.'

'It troubles me to think—'

'Nature knows not of mercy. The blood of the meek slakes the conqueror's thirst. This is not a law unique to the Guild. This is the way of all things, Shōgun.'

'Do not call me that.'

'And why not?'

'Because I am *not* Shōgun. Just because two clanlords have deigned to attend my wedding, does not guarantee they will swear allegiance.'

'They will kneel before you, young Lord. All of them.'

'And if not? How will the clans fight the Kagé or the gaijin if we spend our strength fighting each other? You wish to craft me a throne of my countrymen's bones?'

'You need not fight the other clans, Shōgun. All they require is a rallying point. A banner grand and terrifying enough to stand behind.'

Kensai pointed into the distance.

'And so we give it to you.'

Hiro looked at the proving grounds, coalescing out of the ashen haze ahead. Forges and smelting plants rising like blood blisters behind a barbed-wire forest, wreathed in smoke. Trains rolling on rusted tracks, hauling iron and coal from the Midland mines, broad roads of black gravel, dotted by watchtowers. The grounds swarmed with activity; atmos-suits moving to and fro, a hundred cutting torches twinkling like stars in the long-lost sky. Row upon row of armoured machines, like soldiers at muster, fifteen feet high even in repose, scythe arms ending in sawtoothed chainblades. Four legs a piece, each one thick as tree trunks, skin gleaming yellow in the light of the scorching sun. Hundreds of them.

Hiro raised his eyebrows.

'Shreddermen suits?'

'The Kagé feather their nests in the Iishi forest,' Kensai said. 'So we will leave no forest standing in our wake.'

Hiro squinted through the pall to the far end of the grounds; gantries and walkways built around a towering shadow. Cutting torches arced and spat, Lotusmen trailed bright blue flames around the hulking figure, rocket packs blazing. The Guildsmen were insects beside it – some vast sleeping giant, nodding off in a sea of mosquitoes, too enormous to feel their sting. Three hundred feet high, eight legs curled up beneath its bloated metal belly like a waiting spider. Saw-blade arms with teeth big as men, pistons tall as houses, great chimney stacks running down its spine and piercing the sky like blades. The sound of its engines was a choir of earthquakes.

A machine. A colossus. A behemoth of black iron and blacker smoke.

Hiro stared in wonder. 'What in the name of the gods . . .'

'Look now upon the doom of the Kagé.'

Hiro wiped the ash from his goggles, stared at the metal giant. It was beyond anything he'd dreamed. A looming, rumbling, cast-iron impossibility.

'The Shadows have their standard bearer,' Kensai continued. 'Now we have ours. Our creation will be the rallying cry to unite the zaibatsu. Dragon, Phoenix, Fox: none are foolish enough to field an army against such a machine. They will fall into line, one after another, with you at their head. And you will lead them into the Iishi, and level every tree, crush every stone, until there are no more holes for the rebels to hide inside. You will avenge your Lord and restore your honour. You will kill the Impure one and the fools who follow her.'

Hiro licked his lips, tasted chi smoke. Adrenaline sour in the back of his throat. He struggled to swallow.

'It's incredible.'

'It will be ready to march within weeks. All of Shima will tremble at its approach. You will march in the vanguard, that the other Daimyo will have no illusions about where the Guild's allegiance lies. We will end this petty civil war and set the clan armies to task. The Kagé must be eliminated. And that Impure abomination must burn.'

Behind that perfect mask, Hiro could hear the smile in Kensai's voice.

'And you said you did not enjoy surprises.' He bowed, hand over fist. 'Shōgun.'

Hiro looked at the towering colossus of iron and smoke. He closed his eyes, inhaled the fumes, savoured the taste on his teeth and tongue. He could feel the fingers on his missing hand itching, the iron arm they'd given him trembling in sympathy. A phantom reminder of all she'd taken from him. The promise of everything he would take from her.

'Does it have a name?' he asked.

'Of course.'

Kensai spread his arms wide.

'Behold the Earthcrusher.'

*

360

The ground was a sea of ashes wreathed in blackened fumes. Every step raised a cloud of vapour, swirling about their ankles and hanging from their shoulders like shrouds. Dawn struggled to pierce the haze; sickly, vomit-grey, the air cold as winter snow. They were somewhere east of the Guild bastion of First House, miles deep into the plains where the first production-grade lotus crops had been grown, centuries ago, the earth ruined beyond repair.

Ryusaki knew now why this place was called 'the Stain.'

The Kagé captain's breather was choked and useless, the device like a stone about his face. The internal mechanism had failed yesterday, and only the filter scrims kept the deadly fumes at bay now. He felt dirtier than he could ever remember; like he'd taken a bath in fresh sewage and dried off by rolling in rotting corpses. Every breath was a black ache, eyes scummed with charcoal tears behind his goggles, throat parched, lips cracking. But he dared not remove the breather to drink, not even for a second. Not even for a mouthful.

He knew the Guild had built their factory here in the Stain for that very reason – an aerial approach would be intercepted by ironclads, the roads and rail lines were a bottleneck, always watched, and an approach overland through the deadlands was virtual suicide. The soldier in him had to admire the bastards.

'How you faring, boys?'

Ryusaki looked back at his fellow Kagé and saw Shintaro and Jun both looked like hell. Faces hidden beneath breathers and goggles, swathed head to foot, heavy gloves and boots, tied off at the hemlines. But their postures showed both were feeling the effects of the deadlands just as much as Ryusaki was. Jun in particular was doing it hard – he'd puked into his breather last night and had to take the mask off to clean it, sucking down a few lungfuls of fumes. His eyes were so bloodshot, Ryusaki could almost see them glowing behind his goggles.

A weary thumbs-up from Shintaro was all he got, so he turned and slogged on, earth crumbling beneath his weight as if the surface was a rotten, hollowed shell. Deep footprints marked their trail from the northern rail lines; the trio had stowed away on a freight train loaded with iron, hitching as close to the staging grounds as they dared before leaping off into the deadlands the night before last.

One day and two nights in the hells . . .

Daichi had asked for volunteers, and Ryusaki had known the risks when he stepped forward. But the message from the Kigen cell was clear: the Guild was building something in the Stain, and at this stage of the game, the Kagé couldn't afford to be blind. If the Stormdancer had returned, the council could have used her eyes. As it was, they had to do it the hard way. The way they'd been doing it for years before the girl arrived on her thunder tiger.

Suited Ryusaki just fine.

The three Kagé trudged through the wasteland, following sky-ship exhaust trails. Chill winds howled across the desolate plains but utterly failed to stir the vapour: the fumes clung to the soil like a toddler to its mother's kimono. The rents in the earth were worse than he'd ever seen; some stretching ten feet deep, and the trio was forced to climb down into the fissures if they proved too wide to leap across. The vapour hung heavy within these cracks; a tar-thick, sticky smog, deathly cold, choking daylight utterly. In the deepest of them, he swore he could hear a voice, lilting and sweet, whispering just beyond the edge of understanding.

A woman's voice . . .

They marched on, one shuffling step at a time, until his feet bled and his legs trembled. At last Jun could walk no more, sinking to his knees. He retched again into his breather, black and vile, filling the eyeholes. And Ryusaki was forced to watch, helpless, as the young man tore his mask away and puked again; a gurgling fountain of grey and scarlet, slumping face-first into the corrupted earth.

His eyes had turned black.

Twenty-two years old.

They whispered a prayer to Enma-ō, begging the Great Judge to weigh the boy fair. They had no offerings, no wooden coin or incense to burn for him. Looking at the deadland ashes already caked on the boy's face, Ryusaki hoped they would be enough to grant his soul a hearing at the Court of Hells. The entire countryside had been burned to produce them, after all. That should be offering enough for any judge.

Miles. Hours. Fumes so thick his vision swam, head buzzing, the taste of death chalked on his tongue. Shintaro stumbled behind him, fell under the weight of his pack, and Ryusaki dragged him upright and slapped his back, promising a decent cup of Danroan saké when they returned to civilization. The boy was nearly delirious, but he nodded and kept walking, shoulders slumped, like a man on his way to the executioner's scaffold.

They crested a small hill near dusk. And across the sea of fumes, they saw it.

The Guild staging grounds.

Ironclads hanging in the air like bloated lotusflies. Walls of razor wire, halogen lamps and cutting torches burning as Lady Amaterasu slipped towards her rest. Ryusaki fumbled with the spyglass at his belt, thumbed the ash from the lenses, cursing beneath his breath as he held it to his eye. Squinting into the

Guild compound, blinking black tears, he caught sight of hulking machines lined up in formation, close to a hundred in all. Four legged, brittle-yellow, chainsaw blades for hands. It took a few moments to realize they were shreddermen suits.

Why would the Guild need a legion of those?

He hissed through gritted teeth as realization dawned.

To cut a forest down . . .

He shook his head, started to turn away when he spotted it. Just a glimpse; a shadow within shadows, something vast and black lurking amidst the smog. But then Lady Sun hit the horizon, flaring bright as she laid down to sleep, and he saw it; a kettle-bellied, sawtoothed colossus with smokestack spines and the legs of some vast, iron spider. A machine the likes of which he had never seen.

'Raijin's drums, what is that?' he breathed.

Shintaro slumped down in the ash, staring at his hand as if amazed he owned a set of fingers. Ryusaki coughed, tasting black on his tongue. Unbuckling Shintaro's pack, he pulled aside its oilskin, revealing the graceless bulk of a wireless transmitter. He cranked the handle, but the machine made a sound like a meat grinder, refusing to register power.

'Shit.' Ryusaki thumped the radio as Shintaro keeled over beside him, gasping like a landed fish. 'Come on, you bastard, work . . .'

If it heard him, the transmitter made no effort to obey.

He could feel a sickness in his belly that had nothing to do with fear. An ashen, blackened nausea, creeping into his bones, up towards his heart. He could feel it inside him. Death taken root. Fear beside it. But not here. Not yet.

Ryusaki lurched to his feet, cut loose his own gear and slung the transmitter's weight across his back. Shintaro was spasming, black foam filling his breather, and Ryusaki knelt long enough to give him a blade to the heart. Better to die quick. Better not to suffer.

Not like he was going to.

The Kagé captain drew a ragged breath, adjusted the transmitter on his back and turned north, towards the rail lines. He had to get far enough from the smog that the device might work, send a message to the closest listening post, on again, until it reached the Iishi. Because Ryusaki knew now he never would.

Never see those mountains again, hear the wind song in the trees, watch flowers bloom in a blessed spring. Never see his brother again. Never again be scolded by his mother for not eating right or cursing too much. Never to see this war end.

He closed his eyes, willed away the grief, the fear, the despair. Not a second to waste on any of it. Because he refused to die for nothing. To allow Shintaro and Jun to have died for nothing. This news would reach the Iishi, even if it killed him.

Head bowed, fighting for every breath, Ryusaki began trekking north.

Even if it killed him.

30

A Moment of Empty

Even though he'd broken the lock on her cell, Ayane had insisted she return to her prison after seeing to Daichi's wounds. Quietly closing the door behind her and sitting in the dark to wait, despite all of Kin's protests. She said she wanted permission before she would leave her cage again. Validation. Vindication. Finally given by an old man with bruised and ragged breath, awakening yestereve from a sleep that would have become death, if not for the accursed lotusgirl and her gleaming spider limbs.

Freedom at last.

Ayane stepped from the cell and threw her arms around his neck, her smile as wide as the sky. She smelled of sweat, damp cotton, dried blood. Kin gave a weak hug in return, waiting for her to release him. Her arms slipped away from his shoulders reluctantly, and she stepped back to look him over with those dark, liquid eyes, skin as pale as moonlight.

'Kin-san, what's wrong?'

'. . . Nothing.'

'First Bloom, you could not lie a little harder, could you?' A wry smile. 'That way I could at least *try* to believe you.'

'Why do you still do that?'

'Do what?'

'Swear by the First Bloom. You're not Guild anymore.'

'Old habit?' The girl shrugged, silver limbs rippling on her back.

'It makes you stand out. Reminds people who you used to be. Daichi agreed to release you because you saved his life. But the less they think of you as Guild, the better.'

'Then who should I swear by? Thunder Gods and their drums? Maybe the Maker and his testicles?' She adopted a gruff voice, slapped a mock frown onto her face. 'Izanagi's *bawwwwls*.'

Kin smiled despite himself. 'You do that very well.'

'My thanks, my Lord.' The girl bowed from the knees, like a lady of court. 'Now, will you tell me what troubles you, or should we pretend you are a halfway decent liar and have you show me the bathhouse instead?'

'Just . . . all of it,' he shrugged. 'The 'thrower malfunction. Daichi nearly dying. They think it's my fault. Everything has gone to hell since Yukiko and Buruu left.' A sigh. 'And they should be back by now.'

The words sounded as though someone else were speaking them. Someone in a distant room, indulging in idle gossip, too foolish to even contemplate.

Yukiko missing? Nonsense. The last time he'd seen her, they'd had a screaming fight. Fate would never be so cruel as to take her away without giving him a chance to—

'You are worried about her,' Ayane said.

He stared at the floor. Nodded.

'I am certain she is all right, Kin. Wherever she is. She is the Stormdancer. She destroyed three ironclads without so much as a scratch. Killed a Shōgun simply by *looking* at him.'

Kin shook his head.

'That's not her. The way you all see her . . .' He sighed, rubbed the crease between his brow. 'You don't know her at all.'

Ayane touched his hand, fingertips as gentle as cobwebs across his skin. A frail smile bloomed on her lips.

'You are very sweet, you know, Kin-san. You always think the best of everyone.'

He glanced down as her fingers touched his, raising un-expected goosebumps on his skin. Looking up into her eyes, he realized how close she stood. And before he knew what was happening, her lips were touching his, full and soft and warm, her body pressed against him, gently, as if he might break. He lingered for a second, and two, and three, breath caught in his lungs, white noise in his ears, until at last he broke away, stepping back and raising his hands. Ayane stood still as stone, eyes closed, silver limbs unfurling and rippling about her, bruised-pink lips curled in a delicate, tiny smile.

'So that is what it feels like,' she breathed.

'Why did you do that?'

Ayane opened her eyes, blinking rapidly. The silver limbs shivered.

'Just to feel,' she said. 'Just to know.'

'You shouldn't do something like that. Not without asking first.'

'You did not like it?'

'No, I didn't.'

Didn't you?

'I am sorry. I just thought . . .' She clasped her hands together. 'I thought if you did not want me to, you would have stopped me . . .'

'Don't do it again, please.'

'Do not be angry at me.'

'I'm not angry . . .'

'You are.' Tears welled in the girl's eyes. 'I am sorry. It is just . . . everything, all this . . .' She shook her head, groping blindly for the words. 'Now I have the chance to feel something, I just want to feel it *all* . . .'

The tears spilled over her new eyelashes, down those moon-pale cheeks.

'I am so sorry, Kin-san.'

'It's all right.' He opened his arms, offered an awkward hug. She pressed against him and shivered, chest heaving softly, and he ran his hand over the stubble on her head and whispered, 'It'll be all right, don't cry, hush now,' feeling altogether wretched.

Not long ago, he was just like her, spreading his wings for the first time in a world he'd never known. He remembered what it was to feel that way; to be the unwanted one, the one outside looking in, and for one brief, impossible moment, he forgot about a girl with long dark hair and skin like smooth cream and eyes so deep he could drown, flying away on her thunder tiger and taking his heart with her. Forgot that she was missing, that she could be dead, that the last time he spoke to her could be the last time they ever spoke at all.

Forgot about her entirely.

But only for a moment.

A single, empty moment.

*

Angry stares prickled on the back of his neck.

Ayane walked beside him, seemingly lost in the flood of sights and smells, a small smile on her face as she squinted at the treetops and breathed deep, as if every lungful were her first and last. But Kin could feel it. See it in the Kagé's grim expressions, shoulders set, pausing in their labours as the pair walked by and making the warding sign against evil when they thought he could not see.

Some looked upon Ayane with vague approval; it seemed rumour about her saving Daichi's life had spread. But for him, there was only mistrust. Anger and contempt.

They stepped onto a footbridge, Ayane chattering about the way the wind made the hairs on her arms stand up in tiny rows, how it felt like static current, and how strange it was to have hair on her arms at all. Kin prickled under the angry stares, teeth gritted, rankling at the injustice of it all. If not for his 'throwers, that oni war band would have been unstoppable – the Kagé could never have met them in battle, let alone *bested* them. If not for his perimeter, even now those hellspawn would be roaming the forest with abandon, and the Kagé would be holed up in their trees and praying for Yukiko to return. Before they failed, the emplacements had taken out more than a dozen of the monsters. But did that matter to anyone? Did anyone take even a second to think what might have happened if Kin had not been here at all? And did no one else think it suspicious that every single 'thrower failed within seconds of each other?

How the hells did they get those seals to rupture?

'Guildsman.'

The voice was a fist in his gut, hard and freezing, the memory of the knife twisting his input jack setting his teeth on edge.

Skritch.

Skriiiitch.

'Go away, Isao,' Kin said.

The boys were standing at the end of the footbridge, cutting off their passage to the bathhouse; Isao in front, Atsushi lurking like a shadow behind. Kin stopped, pulled Ayane to a halt. The girl blinked and looked around, doe-eyed and confused.

'What is it, Kin-san?'

'Go back to the prison.' He kept his voice low. 'Wait for me there.'

'I told you what would happen if you didn't leave.' Isao hefted a pair of tonfa; wooden clubs with a short handle perpendicular to the shaft. 'You should have listened.'

Kin noticed movement behind him; Takeshi standing at the other end of the bridge, smile stretched across that crooked face. He looked around to the villagers on the other platforms, but none would meet his gaze. They picked up their bundles, or simply abandoned their tasks and walked away. The boys were all oni killers – if they had issue with the Guildsmen, it seemed not many Kagé considered it their business after the disaster at the 'thrower line.

Kin squeezed Ayane's hand, pulled her behind him.

'Stay out of the way, Ayane.'

'Your accursed shuriken-throwers nearly got Daichi-sama killed,' Isao spat. 'I warned you.'

Ten feet away.

'My 'throwers?' Kin hissed through gritted teeth. 'You're the bastards who sabotaged them. That's why you begged Daichi not to fight at the line. You set them to fail, but you wanted them to blow in the test run with the whole village watching, not in the middle of—'

'How the hells would I know how to sabotage your machines, Guildsman?'

'I saw your hands after the battle, Isao. They were covered in grease.'

'Grease, you fool?' Isao scoffed. 'Was it black? Sticky? Like oni blood?'

Five feet.

371

'When Daichi hears about this—'

'And how is he going to hear about it?' Isao smiled. 'Dead men don't talk.'

Two feet. Close enough to see the sweat beaded upon the boy's skin. The hatred unveiled in his eyes.

'Isao, don't—'

The tonfa whistled past his jaw, Kin jerking away and cracking the back of his head into Ayane's nose. The girl squealed and put her hands to her face, staggered back, grasping at the rope railing for balance. The bridge swayed beneath them.

Kin stepped forward and grabbed the second tonfa, wood smacking sharply against his palms. He tried to wrestle the weapon from Isao's grip, but the boy lashed out with the other club, once, twice, cracking into his solar plexus and ribs, bringing the wind up from his lungs with a mouthful of vomit. Kin aimed a clumsy elbow as he fell, clipping Isao's chin. A foot to his gut curled him up on the deck as he heard Ayane cry out, a sharp snatch of laughter from Takeshi as he seized the girl's arms.

Isao hauled Kin to his feet, punched him in the stomach again, and again, and again, until the pain burned white and his breath turned red and the world lurched side to side as if a giant were shaking it in clumsy, fat fists. He felt himself being pushed against the railing, bridge rocking beneath them, Isao's hand wrapped in his collar, the other clutching his obi and dragging him upwards, dangling him out over the sixty-foot drop to the forest below.

'Do you have a machine to help you fly, Guildsman?'

Kin wheezed, tasted blood, clutching the hand at his throat. He could feel the forest breeze, cool and crisp, leaves the colour of fire tumbling from the canopy and falling into the space below. Would he flutter as they did? Spinning end over end, down to sudden rest, closing his eyes and dreaming no more? Was this how he ended?

Was the Chamber of Smoke all a lie?

Hundreds of eyes, red as sunset, aglow and unblinking and staring up at him with as much adoration as glass could muster.

His own face, but not his at all.

'Do not call me Kin. That is not my name.'

Stray sunlight glinted through the canopy, a lance of bloody red, dazzling his eyes.

Yukiko, where are you?

He felt a wet spray across his face, heard a scream over whistling, silver music. Isao released his grip, lurched away, Kin crumpling to his knees as sharp cries of fear and pain filled the air. He blinked into the shifting light, saw Ayane standing over him, bloody face, hands outstretched, trembling fingers splayed as if feeling the air. The spider limbs were arched at her back, each one glazed with a thin film of scarlet.

Isao was backing away, clutching his face, fingers painted red, eyes fixed on the swaying silver at Ayane's back. Atsushi was behind him, howling like a hungry baby, fingers shredded, forearms and biceps punctured as if he'd tangled with a needle-thrower. Takeshi lay curled on the bridge, clutching his arm, thin ribbons of scarlet trailing up towards his shoulder, spattered on the wood beneath him.

Ayane's lower lip trembled, dark eyes wide with fear.

'Stay away from him.' Her voice small, shaking. 'Do not touch him.'

'Monster,' Isao spat. 'Abomination.'

The girl glanced at the boy behind her, back to Isao, cheeks wet with tears and blood.

'Just leave us alone,' she whispered.

Takeshi pulled himself to his feet, dragging himself away, scarlet footprints left behind. Isao and Atsushi also retreated, eyes fixed on the trembling girl, brimming with hatred. Leaves fell from the branches above, filling the gulf between them with patterns of orange and yellow and soaking blood-red, a slow and beautiful dance spiralling down, down towards the place they all knew it would end.

They were gone.

Ayane took hold of Kin, helped him to his feet. She was shaking so badly she could barely manage his weight. His stomach felt like it had been put through a meat grinder, every breath a battle, copper marching on his tongue. She slung his arm around her shoulder and led him away. Her voice was small and fragile as snowflakes.

'You told me the Kagé were good people, Kin-san. That they believed in what was right.'

Kin wiped his mouth with the back of his hand, brought it away bloody. It hurt to speak the words. More than he could imagine. And yet he spoke them all the same.

'Maybe I was wrong.'

31

Precipice

Blistered palms and aching muscles and sweat burning her eyes. The scarred flesh where Yukiko's tattoo used to be a knot of constant pain, arms shaking with fatigue as she turned the hand cranks and propelled herself over the thirty-foot drop to the raging ocean below.

They were twelve hours and twenty-seven cables deep into the network now, the lightning farm a distant smear of light, blinking behind the rise and fall of the waves. The first half of each run was an effortless journey; the natural sag in the lines would propel them as if they were rolling downhill, the flying foxes giving off a high-pitched whine. But halfway, inertia would pull them to a halt, and they would have to turn the hand cranks along the rest of the line, up the steepening incline to the next tower. The few final feet were always the worst, and the ascent to the last tower had almost beaten her.

The wind pushed her back, rain trickling down her oilskin's sleeves, the rope coiled over her shoulder a soaking, leaden weight. Headache swelling in her skull, a thing of knives and rust and broken glass. And all the while, she sensed long, sleek shapes coiling through the water below, staring up with hungry, slitted eyes.

A hush fell; a split second of stillness as if the storm itself was drawing breath. An arc of brilliant blue-white hit a tower not two hundred feet east of theirs. Yukiko watched raw current crackling across the neighbouring cables, off towards the lightning farm. She wondered if she'd be fast enough to pull the pin on her harness if their line actually got struck.

Ilyitch had made the next tower, jumping down onto the small island it sprouted from. He turned back to her, shouted words she couldn't understand. She gritted her teeth and kicked her legs as if she were running, hands shaking, gaining inch by agonizing inch.

In the last few feet, her arms were trembling so violently she could barely turn the cranks. Ilyitch climbed the tower and held out his hand. She snatched at it, fingers slipping on his own, wind buffeting her as if she were a dandelion seed. Lunging, he caught her sleeve, dragged her towards him, wrapping strong arms around her chest and pulling her in tight. She could smell him; cinnamon and honey, mixed with the faint scent of grease and rubber. They struggled to unhitch her flying fox from the cables, Ilyitch's boots slipping on the tower as the contraption finally came loose. The pair tumbled onto the stone in a tangle of limbs and curse words, Yukiko landing atop the gaijin, her hair draped over his face. The flying fox landed beside them with a clang.

She rolled off him and they lay together on rain-drenched rock, breathless, too tired to move. Reaching out with the Kenning, pushing the bricks of her wall far enough apart to reach through, fumbling in the dark as her head throbbed. She could feel the female arashitora circling above, revelling in each peal of thunder. She could feel the cold shapes of the sea dragons circling the island, filling her with dread. She could feel Ilyitch beside her. And in the distance, she felt a surge of bright warmth that wore a familiar shape.

'Gods, Buruu . . .' she breathed.

Ilyitch was busy rubbing a bruised shin. Yukiko grabbed his arm and screamed over the storm.

'We're close!'

She pointed north, dragged herself to her feet, pain and fatigue forgotten. Closing her eyes, reaching out beyond her barricade, she threw her thoughts into the void.

Buruu, can you hear me?

A long silence, empty and awful.

YUKIKO.

Gods, yes, it's me! Are you all right?

FALSE WINGS BROKEN. BUT MY MIND IS MY OWN AGAIN. I AM SO SORRY . . .

It's all right.

HER SCENT. I COULD NOT—

I'm on my way, just stay where you are.

NOT MUCH CHOICE.

We'll be there soon. Just hold on.

BE WARY.

I know, I feel the dragons.

NOT DRAGONS. THE OTHER ARASHITORA. HE IS HERE WITH ME.

Is he hurt?

YES. AND HE IS HUNGRY.

*

Buruu had curled up in the shelter of an obsidian splinter, curved against his back, shielding him from the wind. His belly had long ago ceased grumbling, his hunger reduced to a gnawing, hollow ache, clutching fistfuls of his insides. His thoughts still swam with the female's scent, driving him near to madness, the stone around him gouged with frustrated desire. But even though he could smell her lingering in the storm above, the impulse had weakened over the last day: her mating time must be very close to its end.

Yet still, her musk made his blood sing when the wind blew the right way, breath coming quicker, shuddering need filling his mind. He fought it down, clung to the knowledge that he'd failed Yukiko, endangered her by giving himself over to it. He'd lost too much to the beast inside him, in darker days beyond the desire for recollection.

He'd almost lost her too.

The minutes ticked by like hours; rain and thunder and snarling ocean the only sounds, until a long, low growl shook him from his melancholy. Lifting his head from beneath his wing, blinking in the downpour. He caught the scent of old blood, a breath-brief snatch of ozone amongst snarling winds. He heard talons ring upon razored stone, shale crumbling beneath titanic weight. And then, piercing the dark, a long roar of challenge.

LICKED YOUR WOUNDS ENOUGH, I SEE.

Buruu rose from his shelter, padded out into the open. The island they'd crashed on was perhaps three hundred feet across, crooked sheets of black glass slanting up towards the north. The copper lightning catcher rose on the southernmost tip, seven or eight feet from the ocean's surface. The northern shore stood perhaps forty feet above sea level, a bluff dropping into the teeth of the sea. It was from here the male approached.

Buruu answered the roar, all thunder and spittle, the stones beneath him quavering. He saw a shadow slink across the tumbledown stone on the bluff, saw the play of faint lightning across his wings. He didn't recognize the scent, doubted any of his former pack would have flown this far south anyway.

A NOMAD, THEN.

He roared again, asking who it was that challenged.

The nomad shrieked its name.

The arashitora prowled closer, and a flash of lightning overhead gave Buruu a good look at his foe. Smaller. Younger. Barely past his blooding by the looks, the stripes on his haunches indistinct, claws still smoke-grey. The feathers at his neck were matted with gore, and he favoured his right side. Buruu could see the nomad's wings were intact, but long gashes trailed from his shoulder into the muscle across his spine. The nomad had avoided flight with the wound still fresh, but territoriality and the female's failing scent had forced him to challenge as soon as he felt strong enough to win.

Buruu remembered what it was like to be a slave to that instinct, the monster within. He'd thought himself beyond it, that his bond with Yukiko had laid that demon to rest and washed the taste of his own from his tongue. But how easily he'd fallen back inside. How quickly he'd taken up the mantle of who he used to be.

He deserved what they'd done to him. What they'd taken from him.

Buruu roared warning that he would give no quarter. That this was not a ritual fight for mate or pride of place in a pack. That there was no Khan's law here. That this would end in death.

Yours, came the reply.

Yours.

*

Yukiko had taken the lead, energized by the knowledge that Buruu was close. The agony in her muscles, sweat burning the raw blisters on her hands, all of it faded beneath an electrifying rush of adrenaline. She pushed herself across three more cables, barely stopping to rest between them. Ilyitch was lagging behind, and she would stop occasionally to look back and scream over the storm, begging him to hurry in words she knew he couldn't comprehend.

Nothing mattered. Not the pain. Not the sorrow. Not thoughts of her father, or of Hiro or Kin or the Guild. She was an engine, a machine, cranking along iron cables one desperate foot at a time. Wind in her face, pushing her back, howling she was too small, too weak. Her flesh trembled and her fingers bled, weak and human and threatening to break at every hard-won foot.

But something inside wouldn't let her stop; a fire burning within her chest that made her grit her teeth, suck down one more desperate lungful, force her arms to move one more foot when everything inside her screamed to stop, to rest, to buckle. And she saw it for what it was, saw that within it lay a strength far deeper than the watered promise found in hatred or fear or even anger. Saw in it a light that left no substance to the shadows she'd filled herself with after her father died. Saw it as the strength behind the wall she'd built in her mind, the bulwark to keep the Kenning's fury at bay. And she saw it was all that mattered.

Love.

Inch by inch. Foot by foot. The flailing, grasping hands of the wind, the rain pounding like a nail-thrower upon her skin. Lightning struck a tower to the west, cascaded down the cables back the way they'd come. Too far away to remember now. Too much effort to think what lay behind. Worse backwards than forwards. Standing still meant lying down.

And then she saw it through the spray and hissing downpour. A hulking fang of obsidian shale, rising like an upraised fist out of the ocean ahead. She reached out with the Kenning, flinching away from the serpents beneath her feet, sensing three bright sources of heat to the north. The dimly remembered shape of the arashitora who had struck them, rippling with challenge. The blade-smooth lines of the female overhead, tinged with curiosity, drawn to the conflict despite herself. And the shape of her friend. Her brother. Her one constant in a world that had shifted and spun so violently over the last few months, she'd lost any and all sense of direction. She'd lost *herself* – in anger, in liquor and guilt. She had lost her way completely.

Forward, she realized.

The way is forward.

Buruu, I'm here.

*

The pair touched the way black powder touches naked flame.

A charge across broken stone, sparks curling on their wings and the glass at their feet. The nomad pounced into the air, talons spread like a fan of knives, roaring challenge. Buruu rose to meet him, sheared feathers and narrowed eyes, colliding with the force of a hurricane. The nomad seized a talonful of harness and kicked out with his hind legs as Buruu raked at his throat, blood purchased on both sides, crashing earthwards amidst broken shards of obsidian.

Raijin pounded his drums as they rolled apart, Buruu lashing out with his claws and sending the nomad springing back with a growl. Fresh blood at his throat, repainting old gore, eyes alight with fury. Buruu's own neck and gut were torn, water-thinned scarlet dripping from his fur.

He was bigger. Stronger. But weak from starvation. Still

exhausted from his flight. And the nomad was faster. Younger. Hungrier.

Buruu, I'm here.

He glanced over his shoulder, saw Yukiko working her way along the cables, perhaps fifty feet away. He glimpsed someone behind her, fell backwards as the nomad sprang to attack, aiming a flurry of talons at his face. Buruu thrashed his wings, the broken mechanism along his spine groaning in protest, canvas feathers torn loose, gaining a few precious feet. Landing on a broken outcropping, retreating as the nomad lashed out again, sparks flying. Clapping his wings together, giving birth to a thunderous peal of Raijin Song; a sonic boom blasting the younger arashitora back across the stone. He clapped his wings again, raindrops shearing sideways in the shock wave, spraying into the nomad's face.

The attacker circled away, roared in defiance.

Buruu retreated, put the lightning tower to his back, getting between Yukiko and two tons of furious thunder tiger.

She was drawing closer. Thirty feet now.

STAY AWAY.

Are you mad?

HE WILL KILL YOU.

The nomad took to the sky, bloody wings launching him high into the air, swooping down into a razored dive. Buruu stepped aside, ground shattering on impact, lunging at the nomad's wing and tearing away a mouthful of feathers. They fell into a snarling tangle again, talons locked as they reared up on their hind legs, flashing feathers and snapping beaks, low rumbling snarls of fury.

He felt Yukiko at his back. Stubborn as a mountain runs deep. Pain of her aching muscles in his head. Blisters on their hands. Desperate need.

Twenty feet away.

STAY BACK.

I can help you!

Buruu thrust the smaller arashitora away with a thundering roar, sending him twisting over onto his back. Pressing the advantage, he tore the nomad's ribs, trying to seize a mouthful of throat as the young one rolled away. Wings thrashing, snarling as he scrambled to his feet, bright red droplets flying between the raindrops and painting snow-white fur the colour of slaughter. It was the nomad's turn to use the Raijin Song now, blasting Buruu back as the thunder from his wings threw puddles high into the shivering air. The downpour bent like a bowstring, droplets as fat as lotusflies splitting into blinding steam-thin spray.

The thunder tigers circled each other, both blooded and wary. The nomad crouched low, gathered for a spring. He looked beyond the crest of Buruu's wings, caught sight of Yukiko on the cables, the gaijin struggling behind her. Eyes flashing. Pupils dilating. A guttural snarl of outrage.

Interlopers. Monkey-children. Meat.

He spread his wings, springing skywards, eyes on the girl.

NO.

Buruu leaped into the air, beating broken wings with all his fury, rivets and ball joints shrieking. He collided with the younger buck and held him close, bore them both down into the stone. The nomad landed on his back, breath spraying from his lungs, snarling, screeching, all flashing claws and thrashing wings. The thunder tigers rolled across the shale in a tumble of twisted metal and orphaned feathers.

Buruu felt Yukiko crank across the last few feet of cable, hook her legs around the tower and pull herself in. She turned to help the gaijin, elbow crooked around the copper spiral, fingers outstretched. They grasped hands and she pulled him closer, one leg hooked in the spire as they struggled to uncouple him from the contraption connected to the cables above.

The nomad's roar was an ear-splitting bellow of rage. But beneath that, Buruu heard Raijin suck in a breath, felt faint electricity tingling down his spine.

YUKIKO, GET OFF THE TOWER.

I'm trying, the harness is—

YUKIKO, GET OFF NOW!

An arc of impossible blue crackled across the clouds above, reached down with a single, crooked finger. Yukiko had time to scream a warning and push the boy away before she jumped backwards, hair streaming in a long, sodden ribbon. The world stilled in the split second before impact, frozen and silent and perfect. The bolt struck copper with a metallic *whump* and the hiss of superheated vapour. She threw her arms up over her face to blot out the light, brighter than the sun. Crashing onto black stone, head cracking against broken glass.

The aftershock sucked the air from Buruu's chest, scorching his fur, crackling across his own wings and his foe's as they broke apart in a spray of rain and blood.

The world after the strike seemed muted, as if the storm sat within an old, rusty soundbox on the other side of a darkened room. Yukiko blinked at the black stains upon her eyes, rolling about on her back, head still ringing with one constant, high-pitched note. Buruu backed off, stood between her and the nomad, wings spread, feet planted like the roots of mountains.

ARE YOU ALL RIGHT?

I think so . . .

LUCKY.

Kitsune looks after his own.

THE BOY?

Yukiko sat up, squinted into the blurred gloom.

'Ilyitch?'

'Yukiko!'

A faint cry, almost inaudible over the crashing waves, the roaring storm. And with dread rising in her gut, Yukiko realized the gaijin had been knocked away by the lightning strike, plummeting over the precipice and into the raging ocean below.

'Ilyitch!'

Yukiko scrambled to her feet, ran to the tower. The rain was hissing where it touched the copper, sizzling like oil on a skillet. She stepped back, too frightened to touch it. Screaming the gaijin's name again, she saw him thrashing for a brief moment between towering breakers, reaching towards her. The ocean rushed into his rainskin, and the flying fox he was still buckled to dragged him down, fingers clawing at the surface as if it were solid enough to hold onto.

But it wasn't.

32

Tremors

They'd stepped out into chilled autumn air, tall and proud as lords.

Jurou in charcoal silk, a splash of Tora red at his obi, neck adorned with new jade. Yoshi in black, balloon hakama about his legs and a thigh-length uwagi of tailored silk, hair bound in tight braids, streaming down his back like snakes. The pair had sauntered down the boulevard, Yoshi tipping the split brim of his hat to anyone who looked their way.

A fine day to be alive.

Upside seemed busier than usual, people running to and fro, more bushimen than Jurou could ever remember seeing. Palace Way was awash with grimy flesh, motor-rickshaws running on fumes. They'd caught a foot 'shaw to Docktown, Yoshi tipping the finger-thin driver handsomely, stepping into the tattoo parlour's confines. And there they lay, shirtless in the mild chill, as an ancient little Fushicho man and his pock-faced son drew forth bamboo needles and bottles of Danroan ink and set about inflicting an enormous amount of pain in the name of vanity.

Yoshi had commissioned a new piece; a beautiful portrait

of Lord Izanagi stirring the formless ocean of creation with his spear tip, running from the mouthwatering curve of his right pectoral muscle down to his hip. Jurou was having some flourish added to his clan irezumi; great and beautiful Tiger prowling around his bicep, looking as if he were about to leap off the boy's flesh and tear the world to rags.

Jurou's pipe dangled from his lips, and he ran a gentle tongue upon the tip, sucking down lungfuls of beautiful blue-black. He knew he shouldn't be on the lotus, knew the price paid for his little high was waist-deep blood. But the itching need had been hitting him hard the last few days, and it wasn't as if he couldn't stop if he wanted. He listened to the buzz in the streets outside, the lotusflies in the rafters, swelling velvet and soporific between his ears. Sensation faded beneath the familiar lotus kiss, tongue too thick for his mouth, staring at the boy he loved, flinching and flexing as the old man's needles danced upon his skin.

'You should get Lady Izanami done on the other side,' he said, pointing to Yoshi's chest.

The old man looked up sharply, gave the warding sign against evil.

'Smoke is going to your brain, Princess.' Yoshi winced as the old man's needles began dancing again. 'Never let the dragon steer the ship.'

'Why not?' Jurou exhaled a plume of sweetness in Yoshi's direction.

'Why the hells would I have the Endsinger inked on my skin?'

'Life and death. Light and dark.' A hand waving, vaguely. 'You know, symmetry.'

'Crazier than a Docktown whore, you.'

'Lady Izanami wasn't always a death goddess.' The pock-faced artiste seemed to be digging his needles extra hard, but Jurou couldn't bring himself to care. 'She was the Earth Mother once. Gave birth to this entire island and seven more besides. It's not her fault Lord Izanagi couldn't get her back from Yomi. It's not her fault he left her there in the dark.'

'Why don't you get her inked on you, then?'

'Maybe I will.'

'And maybe I'll find myself a boy who doesn't paint himself for life while smoke-drunk.'

'Mmm.' Jurou smiled, heavy lids over dark, knowing eyes. 'Somehow I doubt that.'

Yoshi looked him up and down, smiled in return, crooked and beautiful.

'Me too.'

*

'I love you, you know.'

They were crouched atop a three-storey tenement, waiting for the game to begin again. The moon was entirely hidden behind a veil of exhaust, shadows tumbling thick upon the cobbles below. It was the kind of dark that left you feeling alone, even if you were skin to skin. The kind of dark that turned your eyes inwards, since there was nothing to see without.

'Hmm?' Yoshi was perched upon the gutter's edge, eyelashes fluttering, like some carrion bird awaiting supper. 'D'you say?'

If it was brighter, Jurou could have seen it from up here, even all the way from Downside. The estates clustered on the hills east of the Daimyo's palace, trying desperately to keep their nose above the stink-line, the noble-born inside averting their eyes from the squalor below, all their pretty gardens turning grey. His father's house amongst them, high ceilings and gardens of smooth stone where he and his brother Kazuya played as children. His father watching, potbelly swelling his Kitsune-silk kimono (only the finest), bald pate gleaming with sweat as he fretted for his money and honour and name.

'*Family*,' he would say. '*There is nothing more important in this world. Show me a man's friends, I will show you the man. But show me a man's sons, I will show you his future.*'

They were trained, he and Kazuya, from the day they could walk. To stand amongst Kigen's nobility, to inherit the family estates; the vast farmlands their father had bought from struggling farmers at firesale prices, now worked by gaijin slaves. Jurou had been betrothed when he was thirteen, a daughter of a family ally, a pact to seal friendship in blood. And to his lasting surprise, Jurou found himself utterly smitten, struck to the core by dark beautiful eyes and full lips and smooth, sweet curves. Not his betrothed, of course, poor thing.

Her brother.

It had been brief, and blinding, and beautiful. But it ended as it was always going to – with discovery. Not by a servant or his bride to be, but by his brother; little Kazuya stumbling across them in the sweat-soaked shadows of the garden pavilion. And the boy had run quick as silver, singing like a nightingale, clever enough at ten years old to know a sole heir would be wealthier than a second-born son. And his father had grown pale, rent his kimono in anguish, and cursed Jurou as a bastard, a wretch, a disgrace.

'*What did I do,*' he'd cried, '*to deserve the shame of a son such as you?*'

Jurou pictured him now; the image that superseded all others, overshadowing the smiling hugs on naming days, the pride at family dinners. Spittle on his lips, katana held high as he chased Jurou from his house, vowing to kill him if his shadow ever darkened the doorstep again.

'*No blood of mine,*' he'd screamed.

'*No son of mine.*'

And there on the rooftop, waiting for the game to begin again, Jurou brushed at his eyes, stared in the direction of the house he'd grown up in. Now so distant, so empty, a hollow ache that clung to the inside of his ribs and pulled the breath from his lungs.

Dark night. Darker thoughts.

'I said I love you,' he whispered, to no one in particular.

A strong arm around his shoulders.

Lips on his cheek.

A crooked smile, close enough for him to see every perfect detail, no matter how dark it got. Here. Now. All that mattered.

Yoshi.

'I love you too, Princess.'

*

There were four of them, broad as doorways, moving quick despite their bulk. Shappo pulled low over their features, creeping down alleys and dashing across streets, hearts all a-flutter. Yoshi watched them through glittering black eyes, yellow teeth in his gums, hide crawling with blood-fat fleas. He ran with them down the narrow cracks between buildings, the labyrinth of Downside streets, the tangled knot of crushed brick and bloody gravel and graffiti scrawled in letters ten feet high.

ARASHI-NO-ODORIKO COMES.

'Should send that bitch flowers.' He smiled, eyelids near to closing. 'These boys wouldn't be half as rich without Little Miss Thunder Tiger.'

He watched the yakuza darting closer, shadows within

shadows, fat satchels and war clubs in dirty hands. Moving across the rooftops to intercept. Rats to the cat. Flies to the spider.

'How do, gentlemen?'

The iron-thrower hissed as Yoshi engaged the pressure, finger kissing trigger, arm extended and pointing death at the lead yakuza's head. The men skidded to a halt, fourth bumping into third, narrowed eyes and kerchiefed faces. They looked up at Yoshi, crouched on the gutter at the alley's end, tipping his split-brimmed hat in their general direction.

'You,' the second one hissed.

'Looks like.' Yoshi smiled crooked, aimed the iron-thrower between the talkative one's eyes. 'If you'd do me the honour of tossing those satchels, my little sponge cakes, you can all be on your way back home to mother. Kiss her on the mouth for me, hear?'

Jurou stepped around the corner, same alley's mouth the yakuza had entered by. He upended a sack with a flourish, contents ringing brightly upon broken concrete. They were 'crow's-feet'; two lengths of sharpened wire, braided together and bent so that one of the four points always faced upwards. A hundred of them now covered the deck between the yakuza and retreat. Yoshi and his iron-thrower hovered above their advance.

Jurou stepped back with his roofing-nail war club, watching the gangsters close. He didn't bother minding the street: Yoshi had other eyes in play.

What you seeing, Daken?

. . . no guards down. moving riverside to look up . . .

'Don't be mistaking me for the type who asks twice, Scorpion Children.' Yoshi waved the iron-thrower. 'The iron. Count of five.'

'You know who we are then?'

The lead yakuza pulled his kerchief down, tipped back his bowl-shaped hat. He was a wide, red-faced fellow, freshly shaved and sweaty, his ugly smile missing four front teeth.

Yoshi's hands were stone. 'Four . . .'

'We're gonna get you, you know.'

'Three . . .'

'A little shit with big coin isn't hard to find in streets this narrow.'

'Two . . .'

The yakuza relented, aimed his gap-toothed grin in Yoshi's direction, hefted his satchel with fat, stubby fingers. And then a frown crossed his face, one eyebrow creeping skywards as he looked around in alarm.

The roof beneath Yoshi began to vibrate, a subtle tremor at first, increasing in intensity. He thought for a moment the house might be collapsing, brickwork giving way beneath his weight. But then he realized the yakuza were feeling it too; a shivering rumble reaching up through the earth, as if the whole island were moving beneath their feet.

'What the hells?' Jurou called out in alarm.

. . . what is that? . . .

Yoshi crouched low, one hand on the eave to steady himself. He watched mortar dust drifting from the walls, listened to the fragile tune of splintering glass.

Another earthquake.

Just as suddenly as it had begun, the tremor subsided. Stillness fell over Kigen, angry voices and wailing babies splitting the still of the predawn dark. Yoshi collected his wits, turned back to the yakuza. Still, it happened so quickly, he almost didn't catch it.

A glimpse of movement. Just a flash of pale light on steel,

speeding from the gangster's hand towards Yoshi's heart. Jurou cried out as Yoshi rolled, quake forgotten, just fast enough, knife slipping past and opening him up rib-deep. Yoshi twisted sideways, hissing in the spray of heat and wet. And without thinking, he bit down and pulled the trigger.

The iron-thrower roared.

The shot caught the yakuza in the chest, just above his heart, blooming at his back like lotus blossoms in the first light of spring. The fat man clutched the eyeball-sized hole, dark red spilling down his uwagi, coughing once as he dropped like bricks onto the alley floor. The three other gangsters bolted, sprinting away from Jurou's crow's-feet towards the other end of the alley. Yoshi fired again as they ran beneath, another gangster falling, gasping, big body skidding to a damp halt on the gravel. The remaining two were ghosts, already gone, feet pounding the street as confused residents spilled from their tenements, pale and shaken in the quake's aftermath.

Yoshi lay against the tiles, hand pressed to gashed ribs, sticky and red. His ears still rang with the iron-thrower's roar. He hissed, rolled off the roof and landed in a crouch, stuffing the still-warm 'thrower back into his obi. The red-faced fellow was laid out, motionless, eyes like clouded glass. The other gangster was moaning, flopping onto his belly and drawing his legs up underneath him, ground painted scarlet.

'Yoshi!' Jurou shuffled carefully through the crow's-feet and ran to his side. 'Izanagi's balls, are you all right?'

Jurou cradled his head, pale with fear, pulling Yoshi's uwagi off to inspect the wound. His eyes widened at the blood, so much of it, soaking into the bandage over the new tattoo, spattered on the bare flesh of Yoshi's right arm.

The gangster groaned again, pink froth on his lips.

'Yoshi, is it?' he bubbled, grinning like a drunkard, teeth slicked and gleaming dark. His eyes were fixed on the place where Yoshi's clan tattoo should have been. 'You're fucking dead, Burakumin Yoshi . . .'

. . . coming . . .

Daken's voice rang out clear in Yoshi's mind.

. . . heard shots. iron men coming . . .

The gangster rolled over onto his back, his uwagi soaked through, a hole in his chest the size of a fist, coughing thick and red. Yoshi climbed to his feet, wincing, one hand pressed against his bleeding side, the other scrabbling for purchase on a chunk of broken cobblestone.

Bushimen were on their way.

The yakuza might be dead before they arrived.

But he might not.

And he knows my name.

'Yoshi, don't,' said Jurou.

The gangster pulled himself up into sitting position, blood streaming down his chin. Yoshi stumbled forward, blinking sweat from his eyes, white-knuckle grip on the stone. He was fourteen years old again, his father rising from the table, lashing out with the saké bottle, glass meeting bone and painting the walls blood-red.

. . . they are coming. run, boy . . .

'Yoshi, don't.' Jurou tried to drag him away. 'Don't, please.'

'Don't, please.' The gangster affected Jurou's voice, high-pitched and mocking. 'You two married or something? Who wears the dress?'

Yoshi raised the stone above his head.

Fourteen years old.

His sister screaming.

394

Mother bleeding.

Hands curled into fists.

'You don't have the balls, you little bitch,' the gangster spat.

He was wrong.

33

Between Bending and Breaking

The bruises spread like an oil slick; a swirling pattern of blacks and greys and dark, fermenting reds, traceries of broken blood vessels spun out like embroidery across his belly.

It hurt to move.

It hurt to breathe.

They were holed up in Yukiko's room, empty saké bottles on the floor, reminders of her everywhere he looked. Kin didn't think it was safe to stay at the infirmary. Truth be told, with Daichi laid up, he didn't know anywhere in the village that would be safe anymore.

Ayane's eyes never left the doorway, as if she expected the Kagé to kick it down at any moment, drag her out and hurl her over the balcony for attacking one of their own. Silver limbs curled around her in a thin, razored cocoon, knees drawn up to her chin, arms wrapped about her ankles like a bow. A perfect little package of fear.

The balm Mari had given him dulled the pain to a deep ache.

The old woman had obligingly clucked over him for the few moments he was in her care, but he noted bitterly how relieved she'd seemed when he'd hobbled from the infirmary. The old woman seemed glad to be rid of him. Distracted. Worried.

They all seemed so very worried.

Fear about Daichi's near-death and Yukiko and Buruu's absence had spread amongst the treetops, settling in like rot in a blacklung victim. No children running across the bridges, arms spread in flight, roaring challenges to imaginary enemies. No songs in the dark, no easy talk around burning firesides. Just hushed voices on the wind, running footsteps, a tension settling like fog. And beneath it, he and Ayane stayed low, the question hanging in the air between them like wisteria perfume. Invisible. Omnipresent.

Why are we still here?

By evening, Kin felt well enough to walk. He struggled to his feet, holding his stomach as if it might burst and wash the floor with his innards. He leaned against the wall, wincing, Ayane watching him with big, frightened eyes.

There was a knock at the door.

'. . . Who is it?' Kin called.

'Kaori.' The woman's voice was muffled by wood and rice-paper.

'What do you want, Kaori-san?'

'My father wishes to speak with you, Guildsman.'

Ayane stared, shook her head. Kin sighed, ran a hand over his scalp. His hair was getting longer, smooth against his palm, the sensation still so alien it barely registered as his own.

'I'll meet you there,' he called.

Kaori hovered a few moments longer, a shadow on the landing. Finally padding away without a sound.

'Do not go, Kin-san.' Ayane's voice was small and frightened.

'I need to speak to Daichi.'

'Do not tell him what they did. It will only be more trouble for us.' The girl hugged her knees. 'For me.'

'Do you want to come with me?' Kin asked.

Ayane looked at the doorway, and her silver arms trembled like a child in winter's chill. She shook her head. Her voice sounded as if it came from someplace dark and empty.

'I was a fool to come here.'

'Don't talk like that. It's going to be all right, Ayane.'

She looked at him, lips pressed into her knees. Feeble moonlight seeped through the open window, gleaming on wet cheeks. He shuffled over, knelt with a wince, brushing the tears away as gently as he could. Her words were muffled against her skin, but he could hear every one, clear as mountain rain.

'I knew I would never truly be one of them, but I hoped . . . I thought . . .' She shook her head. 'But there is no place for me here. Nothing here for someone like me.'

Someone like me . . .

'It will be all right.' His voice was weak. Weary. 'I promise.'

He bent down and kissed her eyes, one after the other. Warmth on his lips, tasting of salt and nothingness. She found his hand, squeezed it tight, her words a frail and breathless plea, sharp as silver needles.

'I do not belong here, Kin-san.'

She turned her eyes to the floor.

'*We* don't belong here.'

*

They were waiting for him in Daichi's house, three figures around the fire pit, warm glow and cold stares. Kin hadn't knocked, simply shuffled up amidst hushed and angry voices, slid the door aside and stepped into the Kagé council meeting.

Kaori knelt to the left, eyes downturned to the flames. Maro on the right, bloodshot eye, cheeks damp, his left arm in a sling. He was dressed in mourning black, head bowed, shoulders slumped. Daichi sat in the centre, tea in one hand, bound in bandages, belly to throat. A small bloodstain seeping through from his ribs, cuts scabbing on his face and knuckles, breathing hard. His eyes found Kin's as the boy stepped through the door, his voice the sound of crumbling shale and weathered hinges.

'Kin-san.' He cleared his throat, wincing.

'Should you not be in the infirmary, Daichi-sama?'

The old man brushed the question away with a wave.

'I am more comfortable here. Old Mari has . . . other matters to attend to.' He gestured to the other side of the fire. 'Please, sit.'

'I'll stand.' He tried to keep the ache of his stomach and ribs from his voice, much as the old man did. 'If it is all the same to you.'

'Are you well?'

He thought about answering truthfully. Telling Daichi all of it; the beatings, the threats, the murder attempt. He wanted to place his faith in this man, as Yukiko did. He wanted to believe. The words were on the tip of his tongue when Kaori spoke, her voice flat and cold.

'We have more pressing concerns than the Guildsman's well-being, Father.'

'Godsdamned right,' Maro nodded, glowing embers reflected in his tears.

And the desire in Kin died then, snuffed out like a candle. Despite his own pain, his own troubles, Daichi might care; might honestly see him as more than what he'd been. But Kaori and

Maro? They cared about their own, their revolution. They cared only about his mistakes, about the blood spilled because *he* had somehow *failed*. And though they might deny it, Kin knew the simple truth. Had known it for as long as he'd lived here.

In their eyes, he was still the enemy.

'You summoned me, Daichi-sama?' he said. 'If this is about the 'thrower failures, I've not yet—'

'Hells with your accursed 'throwers.' Maro's voice was taut. Controlled. 'We have word from the south. Word my brother and two other Shadows died to bring us.'

Kin blinked. 'Sensei Ryusaki is dead?'

A slow nod. Narrowed stare. 'Hai.'

'I am sorry, Maro-san. Please give my condolences to—'

'Enough,' Kaori snapped. 'This is no time for false sympathies, Guildsman.'

Kin met the woman's cold stare, as tired as he could ever remember being.

'Speak then.'

'The Guild are building an army northwest of Kigen,' Kaori said. 'Hundreds of shreddermen suits, no doubt intended to rout us from this forest.'

'But more concerning is the machine they are building to lead the vanguard.' Daichi spoke carefully, hand pressed to ribs. 'A colossus, Kin-san.'

A flicker of dread in Kin's stomach alongside the ache.

'Three hundred feet high,' Kaori said. 'Black iron and chain-saw blades as broad as sky-ships. Chimney stacks that pierce the sky. Engines that shake the very ground.'

'Earthcrusher,' Kin whispered.

'You know it?' Maro's eyes narrowed. 'You knew this thing existed?'

'Existed? No.' Kin licked at dry lips, tasting Ayane's tears. 'But I knew the concept. It was a pet project of the Tora Shateigashira. A man named Kensai.'

'Second Bloom of Kigen,' Daichi muttered.

'The same,' Kin nodded. 'He'd talked about it for years. A machine to end the war in Morcheba and bring the gaijin to their knees. A weapon that could reduce entire cities to rubble. Like nothing the round-eyes had ever seen. But he never had support to build it. Something must have happened, to get the First Bloom onside.'

Father and daughter looked at each other, each reading the other's thoughts.

'Yukiko,' said Kaori.

'Ayane said Chapterhouse Kigen requisitioned most of Yama's Munitions Sect,' Kin breathed. 'It must have been to work on the Earthcrusher. Gods, they're actually building it . . .'

He could scarcely believe it. Kin had seen a copy of the plans years ago – Kensai had enlisted Kin's father to help on the fuel intakes and engine designs, and their work was held up to initiates as an example of rare genius. But the Guild would have to expend enormous resources in the Earthcrusher's construction. The chi alone required to run it was unthinkable; enough to operate twenty ironclads and a full complement of Guild crew simultaneously.

They must want her dead so badly . . .

He stared at the flames, holding his breath.

Yukiko, where are you?

'So why are you telling me this?'

'We must destroy this machine,' Maro growled. 'The question is how.'

'You can't,' Kin said.

Maro's spit hissed upon the embers. 'You lie.'

'I'm not lying.' Anger flared in Kin's chest, bright and hot. 'I saw the plans years ago. I could destroy it from the inside, but attacking this thing frontally is suicide.' He turned to Daichi. 'They're building it at the proving grounds in Jukai province, right? The Stain?'

Daichi nodded, shifting with a wince. 'Hai.'

'The place is a fortress, surrounded by deadlands.' Kin shook his head. 'It's probably the most tightly guarded Guild facility on the islands next to First House. They have more firepower than any chapterhouse in Shima. We'll never get in there.'

Kaori glared at him across the blaze. 'Who is "we," Guildsman?'

'There is still Aisha,' Daichi said. 'Hiro's wedding.'

'Aisha be damned,' Maro spat. 'There's more at stake now that the virtue of—'

'She sacrificed everything for us, Maro-san.' Kaori's eyes flashed. 'Do not dare dishonour her name.'

'I mean no disrespect, but this army will spell the death of the Kagé!'

'We can't leave her to be raped for a throne!'

'We cannot risk all for one! Not with this Earthcrusher threatening everything. What can we do against an army of shreddermen, let alone a machine like this?'

'This is not just about one! What do you think will happen if the dynasty is reforged? If Hiro is given legitimacy? Everything we've done will be in vain!'

Kin watched them go back and forth, saying nothing. His head swam with the noise, the smoke, the ache in his stomach and chest. And as wretched as he felt, he was glad he hadn't brought up Isao and the others to Daichi. If he'd done so, he would have felt pitiful now. A child crying over a skinned knee.

Instead he felt utterly alone. Detached and swimming in lightless black. The outsider. The other.

'Who is "we," Guildsman?'

Stepping to the doorway, he slipped outside.

The others were too engrossed in their rage to mark his passing.

*

He walked quietly, hands in his sleeves, shadow to shadow on bare feet. Father Moon's light was weak and choked, piercing the canopy with thin spears of muted grey. The night sang around him, a thousand lives calling and hunting and fleeing out in the dark. He moved through the forest, no more than a murmur amidst the whispering trees and falling leaves, until at last he stood before the towering silhouette of one of his shuriken-throwers.

The machine looked mournful, slumped and listing to one side, as if ashamed it had failed in their hour of need. Kin climbed up the ladder into the controller's seat, the pain in his ribs and gut like someone had replaced his intestines with bundles of razor wire.

A bird screeched somewhere out in the dark.

The wind whispered to the trees.

Secrets.

Warnings.

Kin peered around in the dark, and seeing no one, struck a match against the pump's flank. Orange light and sulphur heat, flaring bright. He lit the paper lantern he'd brought with him, too frightened for a moment to breathe. He imagined Isao and his cohort stumbling upon him here in the dark, the easy accusations that would spill from clenched teeth. The bloodshed that would follow, easier still.

The 'thrower groaned beneath him.

He leaned close, uncoupled a hatch and peeled it back from the machine's skin. Taking a wrench from his belt, he lost himself in the work, minutes slipping past like thieves. Remembering countless days in the chapterhouse belly, the patient voice of his sensei, his father's gentle hands, the warming praise as he excelled. He was gifted, and he'd known it; even before the Chamber of Smoke, even before he was promised a destiny greater than most Guildsmen could ever dream.

He remembered Second Bloom Kensai, his father's close friend; a man he might have called uncle if they were normal people with normal lives. He remembered the grief in Kensai's voice as he told Kin his father was dead, clumsy metal hands on his shoulders. He remembered crying inside his skin, tears flowing down cheeks he couldn't touch, watching as they consigned his father's corpse to the Inochi vats, words of the Purifiers ringing in his ears.

> 'The prelude was Void,
> And unto Void we return.
> Black as mother's womb.'

But even in grief, there had been the warm sunlight of burning solder, the shelter of housings and transistors and gears, the scripture of interlocking iron teeth. A language he knew as well as his own. It whispered to him, all those long and lonely nights. Telling him he belonged. That he was home.

Had being in the Guild really been so bad?

He shook his head at the thought. It had been worse than bad. It had been slavery, and he a prisoner within a cage of brass. Captive of predetermination, of the Inquisition and their What

Will Be and their black metal smiles in the Chamber of Smoke, their whispers of a future so terrifying it woke him sweating every night of his life.

'Call me First Bloom.'

Witness to the wholesale slaughter of innocents for the sake of more chi, more power, more fuel to drive the war machine. Never to feel the touch of another's hand. Never to know true friendship. Never to know love.

But what friendship do you know now? In this hole you call freedom?

The voice in his head was his own, a metallic rasp within a mask of burnished brass, the hiss and swoosh of breather bellows, reeking of chi.

Whose love do you know now?

He blinked hard, elbow deep in the 'thrower's innards.

. . . Yukiko.

Laughter in his mind, like the chatter of the mechabacus. Like the wings of a thousand lotusflies.

Love you? She doesn't even know *you.*

His hands fell still, fingers resting upon smooth piping and greasy metal. The machine knew him. Knew everything. Its place. Its purpose. Its function. All it was, and all it would ever be. A simple matter of placing the right component in the correct sequence, engaging the proper force at the precise time. No unsolvable mysteries, no problems that simple intellect and experience couldn't unravel.

If only it were that easy with people.

If only it were that easy with her.

Isao's words surfaced unbidden in his mind; the memory of a knife twisting the input jack in his flesh, the metal that would always be a part of him, that he would never, ever be rid of.

'*You and all your kind are poison.*'

And there in the flickering lantern light, in the shadowed guts of that machine, he saw it. The answer that had been in front of him the entire time, coming upon him so suddenly it stole his breath away. A shuddering intake of cold air into bruised lungs, a picture so clear he could almost reach out and touch it. The awful truth, as hard and real as the metal in his hands.

Inescapable.

Undeniable.

They will never let me know a moment's peace here.

The wrench fell from nerveless fingers, clattering upon iron a thousand miles away, the noise as distant as Father Moon and his feeble light.

They will never let me be.

And without a sound, he descended and shuffled back into the darkness.

*

He'd closed the door when he left her. And now it stood ajar.

A cold lump of fear in his throat, squeezing his windpipe shut as he hobbled onto the landing outside Yukiko's room, close enough now to hear quiet sobbing. He pushed through the door and saw her curled up in the far corner, and the first thing he noticed wasn't that her clothes were torn, how she flinched at his footsteps like some beaten dog, how she kicked at the floor with her heels in some vain attempt to push herself farther back into the corner. It was the way the blood on her skin, on her face, between her legs, looked so dark it was almost black.

'First Bloom . . .' he whispered. 'What have they done?'

She wailed in fear as he stepped closer. Bruises on her face, those bee-stung lips swollen further still, ugly purple around her wrists, across her thighs. And blood.

So little, and yet so very much blood.

'Ayane.' One hand stretching into the space between them. 'Ayane, it's me.'

He knelt beside her, ignoring the pain in his gut and ribs. And at the sound of his voice she latched onto him like a child, like a broken porcelain doll, and the sobs that shook her whole body travelled down through the floor, into the earth at the roots of ancient trees, and sent the whole structure shaking.

Another wail of terror spilled over bloody lips, her fingers digging into his skin as the room shuddered, empty bottles rattling upon the sill. Kin realized this was actually happening; the room *was* shaking, the island trembling in the grip of yet another earthquake. Dust drifted from the ceiling, dead leaves falling outside like a flurry of dry and curling snow.

He held her tight, palms pressed to bare and bloodied flesh. The sobbing wracked her, shook her; a cutting, bone-deep sound he prayed he would never hear again. As suddenly as it had begun to tremble, the world fell still. Still and quiet as the space between seconds, the empty brink between one torment and the next.

'Who was it?' A hard whisper. 'Who did this to you, Ayane?'

It was a long while before she caught her breath, faced pressed into his chest as her spider limbs closed around him like a flytrap plant, needle points dipped in blood.

'Isao . . .' A whispered curse. 'Isao and . . . the others.'

He exhaled, vile and hateful. Her whole body shaking in silent sobs. Gasping through clenched teeth. Kin hung his head, closed his eyes.

How did it come to this?

'Let's just go, Kin.' Her voice was cracked and broken, raw with tears, slurred behind swollen lips. 'Let's just leave, please.

We don't belong here. We should never have come here, oh, *please* Kin . . .'

'Where would we go?' he asked, already knowing what she would say.

'Home.' She squeezed so hard he couldn't breathe, pushed her face into his neck, skin slick and warm with tears. 'We have to go *home*, Kin.'

He held her tight and listened to her weep, staring at the black beyond the window glass. This place he thought he could belong. This place he had sought peace, and failed to find a single, solitary moment of it. His voice was an echo in the darkness, darker still.

'We'll go home.'

He squeezed her tight as she sobbed in relief.

'But not without saying good-bye.'

34

The Jagged Shore

The iron pulled him beneath the waves with half a breath in his lungs, dragging him down like an addict to the bottle's lip. Ilyitch clawed at the harness, fumbling in his gloves, wasting precious seconds to slough them off. He kicked at freezing water with leaden boots, the call of the waves above an all-too-distant roar. His fingers found purchase, iron buckles finally snapping loose. Twisting underwater, he shrugged the harness off his shoulders, watching it spiral away into the dark beneath his feet.

And then he saw them. Long ribbons of silver, snaking up through the depths below. Mouthfuls of needles, the kind of eyes that stared from children's closets in the dead of night. A stab of terror in his chest so sharp he actually screamed, wasting what was left of his breath, rushing over his lips in a bubbling flurry. Hundreds of perfect spheres, glass-smooth, tumbling up, up, up towards the surface. With all the speed his panic could muster, he followed.

The silver shapes did the same.

*

Yukiko saw Ilyitch break the surface, sucking in a desperate lungful and spending it immediately in a terrified wail. He was fifteen feet from the ledge, struggling to keep his head above water and suck down breath enough to scream again.

Buruu's eyes were locked on the snarling nomad, circling to attack again, but he risked a quick, desperate glance as she kicked aside her oversized boots, sloughed off the rainskin. The rope was wrapped around her waist, the knot looped through copper coils as tight as she could make it.

YOU CANNOT DO THIS.

He did the same for me!

I WILL NOT LET—

He saved my life, Buruu! When you couldn't even hear me screaming for help. I'd have drowned if not for him.

Without looking over her shoulder, Yukiko dove arrow-straight into the seething black. She could feel them in the water around her, spiralling upwards in broad, lazy circles, nowhere for their prey to run. Gleaming and slick, eyes of slitted gold, ribbon fins along their flanks and spines undulating in the water at the whim of the thrashing swell.

Forked tongues and razors.

She struggled through the waves, barely able to swim herself. But her dive had taken her most of the way, and a crashing wave got her close enough to throw her arms about Ilyitch's neck before he sank again. Buruu glanced over his shoulder, roared a warning as a long, serpentine head broke the surface, slowly rising from the water just five feet away. It moved like a cobra, rearing back and spreading the fins at its throat in a broad, shivering fan, dripping salt water and venom. A long, chattering hiss spilled from its needle-lined maw.

BEHIND!

A second dragon rose from the depths, echoing its cousin's rasp, cutting off retreat. A third dorsal fin sliced in a broad arc around them, all spines and scales and long, smooth lines. Buruu gathered himself on the jagged shore, ready to dive into the waves and stain the ocean a deeper red. But the nomad crashed onto him from behind, the pair falling into a snarling, screaming heap, clumsy as children fighting over a new toy. Buruu bellowed with rage, lashing out with all his strength, tearing and biting in a desperate attempt to break loose from the nomad's grasp. Knowing he was too far away to help. That it was already too late.

NO! YUKIKO!

Six cold reptilian eyes peered down at Yukiko and Ilyitch, angry hisses spilling through bared fangs. Thunder rocked the heavens, wind shrieking like a wounded oni. Ilyitch closed his eyes, muttering what sounded like a prayer, struggling to remain above the rolling, crashing swell. A blinding arc of lightning reached out across the sky. The largest dragon snarled and swayed, spines at its throat rattling, drawing back and opening its jaws for the death strike.

And Yukiko held up her hand.

Water sparkled on her skin; tiny droplets pooling along the underside of each fingertip before falling back into the ocean around them. The storm held its breath. The rain became a hushed whisper between loving cloud and gentle earth, Raijin stilling his drums with broad, flat hands, time crawling upon its belly for the sheer wonder of it all.

And the sea dragons fell still.

Breath hissing in the caverns of their lungs, venom dripping between translucent katana teeth. They narrowed their eyes, heads tilted, leaning so close she could smell the poison and salt upon their breath, see tiny silver shards amongst the smooth gold in their eyes. They watched her watching them. And they wondered.

Ilyitch clutched the rope connecting Yukiko to the lightning tower. Wrapping his legs around the girl's waist, he hauled them both towards the shore, desperate, half-mad with fear. The dragons watched them go, snakes before the charmer, swaying to the ocean's pulse and the music of her mind. Ilyitch reached the island, bellowed at Yukiko. The girl slung her arm about his neck, one hand still extended towards the dragons, staring at them through half-closed eyes. Towering waves crashed against them, battering them on the stone, threatening to drag them down into cold and empty black. And with her holding tight, Ilyitch climbed the sodden rope, teeth gritted, muscle and tendon stretched to tearing, dragging them both from the sea.

The arashitora were still locked together in a screaming, tumbling frenzy. Buruu managed to finally break loose, kicking the younger thunder tiger away with his hind legs. The nomad rolled backwards, landing skull first upon shattered stone. Buruu was on his feet in an instant, pounding back towards the island's rim, eyes alight with panic. He saw Yukiko's rope taut with weight, sawing across razored shale, coming apart strand by strand.

Two tons of blindside crashed against his ribs, spinning him up onto a sharp outcropping. Shards splintered in the impact, iridescent metal screeching beneath his furious roar. The nomad was on him in a blink, foot planted on his wing. Beak descending towards his exposed throat, shrieking like an oni fresh from the gates of the Nine Hells.

'Stop!'

Yukiko's roar was louder than the storm above, echoing like thunder. The nomad froze, turned to the girl with a snarl. She lowered her chin, eyes narrowed, dripping floods of seawater onto the stone.

'*Don't you touch him.*'

She spoke with lips and teeth and tongue, but her words echoed down the Kenning, swimming in their thoughts as burning, living things. Her hair was a smooth sheet of black draped over one half of her face, single eye glaring between closing curtains. The rain fell upon her skin as if she were stone, trickling down her cheek and beading in her lashes. Stepping forward, the boy splayed and coughing on the rocks behind her, she held up one bloody hand, the other curled into a fist. Trembling, pale and rigid, teeth clenched, a spray of rain from bloodless lips accompanying every word.

'*Do you know what I am?*'

The force of her bore down on the nomad like deep summer and a noonday sun. Raijin bent double and pounded his drums as if the world itself were ending. The Kenning fairly rippled with the heat of her, voice resounding in the umbra as she took another step forward. The nomad took one step back, cringing low to shattered stone, her words burning in his mind.

'*I am a daughter of foxes. Slayer of Shōguns. Ender of empires. The greatest tempest Shima has ever known waits in the wings for me to call its name, and its coming will shake her foundations like the drums of the Thunder God.*'

The clouds crashed above her, a halo of lightning playing in the sky over her head.

'*I am a Stormdancer. And you will hear me now.*'

35

Children of the Grave

The door to the apartment burst open, Hana almost screaming in fright. Akihito loomed to his feet as Jurou dragged Yoshi inside, kicked the door shut behind. Both boys were painted bloody, her brother leaning on Jurou's shoulder, his face agony-pale.

'Gods, Yoshi!' Hana was on her feet, rushing to his side, helping him to his pile of cushions. 'What happened?'

'Bar fight.' Wincing, Yoshi peeled back his bloody tunic and emptied a bottle of seppuku onto a vicious cut across his ribs. Hana tore off her kerchief, pressed it to the inch-deep slice, warm and sticky-slick beneath her fingers.

'A bar fight?'

Yoshi nodded, tipping the last of the rice wine into his mouth. 'Drunken beggar monk came at me with his prayer beads. Those things are bloody sharp . . .'

Hana pulled back, hands on her hips. 'Yoshi, can you be serious for once in your godsdamned life?'

'Now where's the sense in that?' He took a moment to catch his breath, looked her new outfit up and down, smiled crookedly. 'You scrub up prettier than springtime, sister-mine.'

Hana scowled at the flattery, fingers slick with Yoshi's blood. She looked to Jurou, the boy obviously panicked, fresh scarlet on his hands, dark, dew-moist eyes wide with new fear. Akihito stood in the corner, silent as tombs, looking back and forth between the siblings. Finally, she turned to glare at Daken, curled atop his customary throne over the windowsill, unblinking.

'Someone tell me what the hells is going on . . .'

With no answers forthcoming, she reached out into the Kenning. Feeling amidst the local corpse-rats; a quick flight through a dozen sets of eyes within shouting distance of the tenement tower. And there in the distance . . .

. . . the distance . . .

. . . a brood of six, gathered on the body of a dead beggar. Her siblings scattering like lotusflies at the sound of approaching boots. She looked up from her meat, glittering black eyes, fur and whiskers slick with blood. Squealing in anger.

Soldiers. Polarized goggles. Naked steel. And her belly wasn't even full.

A split-toed boot descended towards her head . . .

'The rats,' Hana breathed. 'Oh shit . . .'

She looked to Yoshi, his eyes losing focus, growing wide as they met hers.

'Shit's about the size of it.'

'There's at least a dozen . . .'

'Out back maybe. Look in front.'

'What is it?' Jurou asked, glancing between the pair.

'Bushimen.' Yoshi pulled himself to his feet, wincing in pain. 'Lots of them.'

'Who says they're after us?'

'You fixing to wait and find out?'

Daken slipped out through the tiny window, darting across

the eaves below and crawling up a downspout onto the roof. Jurou disappeared into their bedroom, returning with four bulging satchels of what could only be coin slung over his shoulders. No time for questions – Hana grabbed Akihito by the hand, and the four were slipping out the door without a backwards glance.

Yoshi took the lead, bloody hand pressed to his side, the other on the iron-thrower at the small of his back. Jurou brought up the rear, Akihito second, Hana stumbling between them, eyelid fluttering as she rode Daken's sight. They avoided the stairwell, padding to the broad rice-paper window at the end of the hall. Yoshi tugged at the swollen wood, and the window gave way with a rust-red groan, opening out onto the three-storey drop between the ramshackle tenements. The sun's scarlet glare was sharp on the cobbles and gutter below, shockingly bright.

Hana crawled out first, clinging to a corroded downspout. She scrambled down spider-quick, Yoshi close behind. Slinging one leg over the sill, Akihito hauled himself out of the window, grasping the pipe with hands as broad as dinner plates. He descended using only his upper body strength, his good leg scrabbling against the brick. Jurou had more trouble, slipping and cursing his way down the spout, doubled over like a monkey and shimmying down the last twelve feet.

Yoshi gave a soft wolf whistle, whispered up at the other boy.

'Fine view down here. But you might want to up with the hurry.'

'Shut up, you'll make me fall.'

'I'll catch you, Princess.'

Jurou managed to scramble low enough to drop to the ground, hitting the concrete and rolling to his feet with something approaching flair. Yoshi gave a small round of applause, pulled his kerchief up over his grin. Upstairs, they heard heavy boots in the stairwell, followed by splintering wood and angry shouts.

'Time to go.' Hana pulled on her goggles.

'Doubtless.'

Yoshi slipped down the exhaust-choked alley on the tips of his toes, the others following close behind. Hana reached out to the nearby corpse-rats again, mind awash with rich gutter-scent and maddening flea-itch. She could still sense a few rogues in the drains out front, but the pack at the building's flank had scattered when the guards approached. Too few eyes. Too few breaths. Fright drawing her stomach tight, her gums chalk-dry, lips sticking to her teeth.

The quartet stole eastwards along one crud-ridden alley, Akihito's hand wrapped in hers. She glanced at the big man. His face was cold and hard, his kusarigama clutched in one fist, blade glinting in the scorching light.

Her voice was a whisper. 'Do you think they're—'

'Daken seeing anything, Hana?' Yoshi glanced over his shoulder.

'He's up top.' Hana scanned the rooftops, voice cracking. 'The way out front is no good, we'll have to—'

Yoshi and the bushiman rounded the corner simultaneously, ran straight into each other at almost full-tilt. Yoshi's face bounced off the soldier's breastplate and he staggered back, hand to nose, cursing up a storm. The bushiman fumbled for his naginata – a long spear with a three-foot blade – bringing the weapon to bear and adopting a front-foot battle stance.

'Halt in the Daimyo's name!'

Yoshi blinked away tears, the red knuckles he wiped across his nose coming away bloodier. The bushiman was clad in scarlet and black iron, tigers embroidered on his tabard in gold thread. His jaw was set, stance fierce, naginata's blade glittering and death-sharp.

'Against the wall!' A bark of command. 'Now!'

'Corpsefucker, I think you broke my nose . . .'

'I have him!' the bushiman yelled over his shoulder. 'He's here!'

Hana heard the heavy drum of approaching boots. Metal on metal. Shrill whistles. More soldiers on the way, corpse-rats fleeing into the drains as the bushi' thundered across the cracking concrete, beggars and lotusfiends scattering.

The bushi' fixed his glare on Akihito, blade levelled at the big man's chest.

'I said against the wall, Kagé scum!'

Yoshi blinked. Looked back and forth between the bushi' and Akihito as Hana's stomach dropped into her toes.

'Kagé?' A darkening frown. 'Wait . . . you're here for *him*?'

Akihito released her hand, stepped forward, a blur of move-ment, wrapping his kusarigama chain around the bushiman's spear and dragging the boy off balance. Teeth bared in a silent snarl, he swung his sickle blade upwards, burying it beneath the soldier's chin, punching straight out through the top of his head. More soldiers were rounding the corner as Akihito tore his blade loose, the bushi's lower jaw with it, and with a howl, the big man waded into the mob.

He slung his chain across one soldier's face, cleaved a naginata off at the haft. Hana whirled as she heard soldiers behind, three more charging down the alleyway at their backs. The roar of flame above, the girl shielding her eye against the blast-furnace sun as she looked up and saw two Lotusmen alight on the eaves overhead, red eyes aglow, pointing with brass-clad fingers.

'Alive!' one cried with a cicada voice. 'Take him alive!'

The shot rang out, shattering the air, bouncing off the narrow walls and making her wince. A bushiman fell with half his face missing, screaming, bloody gauntlets clutching the gaping wound. His comrades ducked for cover back around the corner, cursing as Yoshi fired again, blasting a star-shaped hole through the back of a fleeing soldier and dropping him like a stone amidst a spray of fine red mist.

'He's got an iron-thrower!'

The acrid stink of burning chemicals filled her nose. Yoshi whirled on the spot and levelled the weapon at the bushi' behind them, the Lotusmen above them, figures scattering like autumn leaves in a storm wind. Jurou was yelling something, screaming, but the echo of the shots was filling Hana's head, the sight of the blood, boys no older than she lying dead on the ground, puddles of bright and sticky red, water-thin yellow, howling voices, Yoshi's face, bloodless and snarling. She was thirteen years old again, the weight on her chest, broken glass pressed to her cheek as she screamed and screamed and screamed.

'I can get them out . . .'

'Hana, move!' Yoshi roared, pushing her towards Jurou. The boy had peeled back the storm drain cover in the alley's gutter, was already disappearing down into the dark. She blinked, pulled herself together, Daken's voice a whisper in her mind – *gogogo* – as she fell to her knees and crawled into the drain, down into a stinking rush of dark, ankle-deep slush, a pipe of black stone, ten feet wide. She heard her brother snarl a warning to the other soldiers as Akihito dropped down beside her, Yoshi tumbling on top of them a second later. A burst of high-pressure flame rushed in through the drain, Jurou dragging her down into the filth as the fire scorched the air above their heads, Lotusmen shouting, faint and distorted.

Heavy tread.

Ringing steel.

Blurred sunlight spilled down the grubby stone walls, the reek of smoke and shit and old death filling her nose. Jurou had her by the hand and was up and running, splashing, stumbling in the dark, the echoes of their footprints amplified tenfold in the bottomless gloom. A pain-hoarse cry behind, the whistling song of Akihito's kusarigama chain in the black. She reached out to the rats above and below, pulling Jurou left through a junction, straight at the next, footfalls and gasping and sweat in her eye, slick on her hands, stink making her gag. Running, running until her breath was fire and her legs shook, until her heart pumped oil and acid and her stomach rolled, cold and churning. Corpse-rats streaming about her, dark and sharp, shit-slicked, dead doll's eyes piercing the murk ahead.

Footsteps behind them, dozens splashing through the filth, lantern light setting their shadows dancing on the moist black walls. Akihito's heavy breath, limping tread, grunts of pain. Yoshi stumbling, hand pressed to his bloody ribs. The Lotusmen would have been too big in their suits to follow, but it sounded like half the Kigen army was still back there, metal-clad hounds running swift, fangs bared, tight tight tight on the rabbits' trail.

She reached out into the Kenning, the tiny minds and tiny eyes and long yellow grins. Turning fear to anger, flooding them with it, the sleek broods and hulking rogues gathered in the quiet, lovely dark – *their* dark – now filled and fouled with the noise and the reek and the steel of these accursed men. Calling them to her, one by one, looking over her shoulder to her brother, his face pale and blood-spattered, eyes wide, loose tendrils of black hair scrawled like cracks upon his skin.

'Help me, Yoshi,' she gasped.

He swallowed, winced, nodded. Together, entwined, reaching out and calling, pulling, pleading. The flood began with one black droplet, streaking past them with dirty fangs bared. A handful more followed, then a dozen, heeding the call scritch-scratching at the backs of their minds, ringing in the empty behind their eyes, swelling, rising, all mangy fur and tails like lengths of old knotted rope, filth-encrusted claws and mouths bathed in death. Hana heard a soldier cry out, the clang of steel striking stone, more of the mongrel, gutter-born flood flowing past them as they ran on and on and on.

More shouts behind. Screams of pain. No time to stop and listen, to press or to fight. Just to run, to run when every new step seemed an impossibility, when the vomit rose scalding and boiling in the back of her throat to the edge of her teeth, when every muscle wept and screamed, drawn taut and tight and stretched to snapping. Turning blind at every junction, straight, left, left, right, the black stabbed through by occasional blinding light from the drain grilles overhead. Akihito finally gasped, fell against the wall and collapsed into the filth, hands pressed to the weeping wound at his thigh. Yoshi skidded to his knees, blood spilling thick and red and hot from his side down his fingers. Hana on all fours, retching, gasping, weeping, tears on her cheeks as the reek scored her throat.

And as her heartbeat pounded in her temples, as her breath seethed in her chest, she stretched out to the children of the grave around her – the scabrous, worm-ridden hoarde – and found no other men in their eyes. No soldiers in their fears. Only them. Only her. Licking scabby jowls with flat grey tongues, and wondering if she fell face down into the murk right now, spent her last throes inhaling that soup into her lungs, what her pretty, pretty eye might taste like.

'They're gone . . .' she gasped, coughing. '. . . we . . . lost them . . .'

Jurou leaned against the concave wall, chest rising and falling like sparrows' wings. 'Izanagi's balls . . .'

Akihito reached out, groping for her hand in the dark. 'Are you . . . all right?'

'Worry about yourself, whoreson!' Yoshi snarled, jamming the iron-thrower up under Akihito's chin and forcing him back against the wall.

'Yoshi, stop it!' Hana cried.

Though he outweighed the boy by eighty pounds and stood half a foot taller, Akihito allowed himself to be pressed against the slimy brick, the 'thrower's barrel jammed against his larynx. He raised his hands slowly, scarlet-slicked, eyes fixed on Yoshi's.

'Calm down, son . . .'

'You fixing to be my da, old man? Because I promise that'll end less than pretty.' Yoshi leaned closer, pressing harder on the 'thrower, his tone a boiling cocktail of incredulity and rage. 'You're a godsdamned rebel hiding out in my home? Dragging my sister into your shit? The bushi' through our front door? I should *end* you!' Spittle flying. 'I should feed you to the fucking rats!'

'He didn't drag me into anything, Yoshi!' Hana shouted. 'Stop it!'

'Izanagi's balls, Hana, he's in the fucking Kagé!'

'*I'm* in the Kagé!'

A hollow silence, lined with teeth, Yoshi turning and peering at her in the dark with bewildered eyes. 'Tell me you're joking . . .'

'I joined weeks ago. After the Stormdancer came back to—'

'Have you lost your godsdamned mind?' Eyes narrowed to knife cuts. Voice rising to a roar. 'I said have you lost—'

'I heard you the first time!' Hana shouted.

'What the hells were you thinking?'

'I told you! They stand for something, Yoshi! They stand and they fight. The Guild, the lotus, inochi, all of this shit. I swim up to my eyeballs in it every single day and it makes me want to puke. There are people out there fighting and dying for this! For us! And you want me to sit back and do nothing? Hope someone else fixes it for me?'

'You know what we are.' Yoshi turned on her, pointing to the streets above their heads. 'You know those bastards up there wouldn't give one *speck of lotusfly shit* for you or me if they really knew. We don't owe them a thing. Not a godsdamned drop!'

'Yoshi,' Jurou pleaded, touching his arm. 'Calm down.'

Akihito's voice was soft. 'Listen to your—'

Yoshi whirled, aimed the 'thrower between Akihito's eyes.

'You wanna stay handsome, best stay quiet,' he spat. 'This is family talk now.'

He turned back to Hana, voice growing cold and hard as ice.

'This little dance is over, sister-mine. You ran with heroes and had your fun and now it's done. We're ghosting, right now, and leaving this fellow to his tricks. We don't see or speak to him again. We're walking away. And we're not looking back.'

Hana shook her head, scowled. 'You don't tell me what to do, brother-mine.'

'Not telling you what you're doing.' Yoshi stood slowly, took Jurou's hand and hauled himself out of the muck. 'Telling you what *we're* doing.'

Hana glanced at Jurou, the boy's face pale and pained. But he stood beside Yoshi, smeared in rot, squeezing his hand tight. 'Please, Hana . . .'

'I'm not dying for folks who'd gladly light me on fire,' Yoshi said. 'I'm not waiting for the bushi' to kick down my door again, drag me to die blind and starved in the belly of Kigen jail. Not for people who wouldn't spare a drop of piss for me if I was dying of thirst. Not now. Not ever. Now you think about that, and you decide if they're worth dying for.'

'Your brother's right, Hana.' The siblings glanced over as Akihito got slowly to his feet, clutching his bleeding thigh. 'You should go with your family.'

Yoshi blinked, confused.

'Doubtless,' he finally nodded.

'This is my fault,' the big man said. 'I should never have brought it into your home. Never placed your family in danger. I'm sorry.'

'Akihito . . .' Stupid, girlish tears welled inside her and she clenched her teeth, stamping them down into her boots. 'I can't turn my back now . . .'

'You should go. I've seen enough of my friends die over this. Over what I could have done and failed to do.' He stared down at those broad, clever hands, smeared in blood and filth. Shrugging helplessly. 'I don't want to be carving spirit stones for you too.'

'*Mreowwwwl.*'

The four of them looked up, Daken's silhouette peering down at them from the storm drain above, etched in black against the scalding, garish daylight.

'I'll keep moving,' Akihito said. 'Exit a few blocks down, nowhere near you three.'

'You do that,' Yoshi growled, sparing him a toxic glance. He held out his hand to Hana, eyes locked on hers. 'Come with?'

The tears were flowing now, spilling and burning down her cheek. Hateful, horrid things, making her feel a weak and frightened girl, the child she'd tried to kill long ago. She was thirteen years old again, small and afraid, shaking so hard she couldn't stand. Yoshi rising from the ruins, fists clenched, drenched in scarlet . . .

She couldn't leave him now. Not after all he'd done. All for her.

All for me.

Hana hung her head. Took one step towards her brother, a few inches and a thousand miles, reaching out to clutch his hand. She looked back at the big man, blurry through her tears.

'I'm sorry . . .' she sobbed. 'Akihito, I'm so sorry . . .'

'It's all right,' he said, forcing a smile. 'You've done enough. More than most.'

The big man spared an apologetic glance for Yoshi and Jurou, met by a pitiless scowl and uncertain, doleful eyes. And then he turned, hand pressed to thigh, foot dragging through the muck as he limped into the dark. The sound of his tread echoed off the sweating walls, bounced down into the tunnel depths, in the cavern of her chest and the empty in her heart.

Thump-slush.

Thump-slush.

'Don't fret now, Hana.' Yoshi took her hand, looked her in the eye. 'I take care of us. Always. Blood is blood, remember?'

Lips trembling. Cheeks burning. Throat squeezed tight. But still she managed it. To force them out. The words. The vow. All she had left.

'. . . Blood is blood.'

36

Take

The rain sang a hymn of white noise on the ocean's skin in the space between one thunderclap and the next. The nomad was pressed low to the ground, blood-drunk and snarling. Buruu hauled himself to his feet, shook himself like a sodden dog, glaring at the younger thunder tiger as hackles rippled down his spine. Yukiko held out a gentle hand, took one step closer to Buruu's foe. Her voice rang in the Kenning, loud enough for them both to hear.

'It's all right, don't be afraid.'

FEAR NOTHING. NO ONE.

The nomad's thoughts were a shout in her skull, bright as a shot from an iron-thrower, loud enough to be felt as physical pain. She winced, shuddering with effort, pushing her wall between them in the Kenning, as if she were damming a river and allowing only a trickle of him through. His trepidation was obvious; his fear in the face of this strange girl who spoke to his thoughts, whose will beat upon him heavy as the storm itself.

'I'm not going to hurt you.'

CAN TRY.

'I want to talk to you.'

HOW YOU TALK IN MY MIND?

'I am Yōkai-kin.'

The nomad blinked, looked at her with narrowed, amber eyes. The intensity of his thoughts was making her head ache, even behind her mental barricade. She realized her nose was bleeding again.

'You're a wanderer? You have no pack?'

WILL MAKE MY OWN.

Yukiko glanced up at the female she could still feel wheeling about their heads.

'She doesn't seem interested, friend.'

FEMALE STRONG. NEEDS STRONGER MATE. ONE WHO HAS WON GLORY. SUCH IS OUR WAY.

'I have a better way.'

BETTER?

'A way to win glory untold.'

. . . HOW?

'Join our pack.'

The nomad looked at Buruu, made a snorting sound that sounded like laughter.

SKRAAI JOIN KINSLAYER? NEVER.

Yukiko blinked the rain from her eyes, frowning.

'Why do you call him that?'

WHAT HE IS.

'But you call yourself Skraai?'

MY NAME.

'Before I met him, Buruu didn't have a name. I didn't think . . .'

Buruu stepped forward, eyes downcast.

YUKIKO . . .

The nomad tossed his head, snorting again.

KINSLAYER HAD NAME. THEY TAKE FROM HIM, MONKEY-CHILD.

The sound of retching drew Yukiko's attention away. Ilyitch was curled on wet stone, hair tangled about his face, coughing up seawater. Her concern swelled, the conversation with Skraai momentarily forgotten. She walked to her fallen satchel, hauled out two deep tuna, each as long as her leg. Sliding one across the ground to Buruu, she tossed the other to the nomad with a grunt.

'You two think you can enjoy a meal without tearing each other to pieces?'

The arashitora regarded each other with wary stares. Yukiko knelt beside the gaijin, smoothed the hair from his face. The tempest had lessened, wind slowing to a gale, rain falling in sheets rather than blankets. Ilyitch looked up at her and gave a weak smile, leaned back against broken rock and pulled his wolf skin tight about himself. Running one hand over the pelt, fingers in sodden fur, he murmured beneath his breath. Eyes closed. Head bowed. He seemed to be giving thanks. Yukiko wondered what gods he prayed to.

After a sentence or two, Ilyitch pulled a tin box from inside his coveralls, produced one of his smoke sticks and put it to his lips with trembling hands. Realizing it was soaked with seawater, he spit it out again in disgust.

Yukiko stood and walked over to Buruu, running her fingertips along the misshapen lines of his clockwork wings. Some of the canvas quills had been ripped loose in the struggle with Skraai and the harness was badly torn, but the skeleton seemed reasonably intact. Bent and crumpled, certainly; it'd be impossible to fly with them in their current state. But with the right tools, she might be able to beat them back into shape.

Problem was, they hadn't brought any tools with them.

She turned back to Ilyitch, still slumped on the stone, catching his breath. She pushed a picture into his mind; the shape of tools, of hands working on the mechanical wings. The boy wiped his mouth with the back of his hand, gave a weary nod.

'So how do we get the tools out here?' Yukiko pointed to the cable network again, made a pedalling motion with her hands. 'We have to go back and get them.'

The thought made her entire body ache.

The gaijin held up a finger as if to say 'watch and learn.' He reached into his own satchel, produced a bundle wrapped in brown oilskin. Unfolding a few layers, he revealed a cylinder of black metal, perhaps a foot long. Yukiko helped him to his feet, and he smiled and muttered what she presumed was thanks. Walking to the island's edge with the oilskin beneath his arm, he twisted the cylinder, held it above his head, pointed to the clouds. A puff of smoke spat from the haft, the tube hissing. Magnesium-bright light flared, and an object shot into the sky, fifty feet into the tempest. A tiny second sun, hissing and popping in the rain, trailing a long cloud of pale-grey smoke. Buruu and Skraai looked up from their meals, watched the white fire glowing above. Buruu growled. Yukiko stepped forward, confused and frowning.

'What are you doing?' She raised her voice, as if it would help him understand her better. 'Ilyitch? Won't they see that from the farm?'

The gaijin turned to her with a smile. Reaching into his oilskin he drew out a tube of coiled brass and delicate glass globes. He raised it towards Buruu.

'Oh gods, n—'

A crackling arc of white light burst from the tube, reaching across the space between Ilyitch and Buruu and filling it with thunder. The arashitora reared back and took the bolt to his chest, knocking the breath from his lungs and sending him crashing into the rocks behind. Yukiko screamed and lunged towards the weapon, and a backhand from Ilyitch landed on her jaw, sent her tumbling. Skraai roared, spread his wings and charged headlong into another burst of deafening white light. It hit him like a wrecking ball, rolling his eyes back in his skull as he collapsed, skidding to a halt three feet from the gaijin's toes, steam rising from his fur.

Yukiko blinked black light from her eyes, reaching towards Ilyitch's mind with the intention of crushing it to pulp. He aimed a savage kick at her ribs and the wind left her lungs, accompanied by a spray of spittle and the clap of iron-capped boots on bone. He kicked her again in the back of the head and she curled into a ball, stars bursting and falling behind her eyes.

Ilyitch fished around in his satchel, weapon pointed lazily at the stunned arashitora. Yukiko struggled to roll onto her belly, get her wind back, ignore the broken-glass pain in her skull. Ilyitch growled a warning, weapon aimed at her face, shaking his head. Thunder rumbled above, lightning crackled across roiling black. The boy produced another flare and fired it shrieking into the sky. Yukiko rested her cheek against the obsidian beneath her, wonderfully cool, slick with rain. It called out to her with a voice as old as the earth.

Sleep.

Sleep now, child.

She clenched her jaw, voice strangled. 'Why are you doing this?'

Ilyitch snarled incomprehensible words, waved the brass tube, finger to his lips.

Ignoring the pain blooming bloody across her thoughts, she reached out to Buruu through the Kenning. She could feel his warmth, run through with vertigo; the sparkling numbness of a newly landed fish, cracked across the stern to render it senseless. Skraai was in a similar state, clawing back towards waking from a darkness lined with coils of brass and tiny glass globes.

But they were alive.

'Godsdamn you . . .' Yukiko clawed sodden hair from her mouth, tried to pull herself up. 'I saved your life. *Why are you doing this?*'

Ilyitch's shout was as good as fingers around her throat, squeezing tight. Yukiko pressed her hands to her bruised ribs, arms wrapped around herself. Moments passed – minutes or hours, her concussion fading all to grey. But finally, beneath the storm's howl, she realized she could hear a rhythmic pulse, a dull *whumphwhumphwhumph,* swelling at her back, drawing ever closer. She didn't even need to turn to see what it was – the flying machine from the lightning farm's roof. The metal dragonfly.

She reached out through her wall and touched the boy's thoughts again, resisting the impulse to squeeze. But what would it cost her to kill him? How much would she spend of herself? How much would be left to fight the gaijin headed towards her in the belly of that metal insect?

He used me. Used me to catch them both. But why?

She watched Ilyitch rummaging in his bag again, stare falling on the pale wolf pelt across his shoulders. Yukiko thought back to the brown bearskin on Danyk's back, the samurai helms bolted on his broad shoulders, the flayed Lotusman skin over Katya's leathers. Every gaijin soldier she'd seen wore the skin of an enemy or an animal.

But nothing so fantastic as an arashitora.

Oh gods, no . . .

The thought turned her stomach, filled her with a fear that dwarfed anything felt in Yoritomo's clutches.

He couldn't . . .

The boy found what he was looking for, dragged it from the satchel with his right hand. It gleamed as a flash of lighting lit the sky, at least a foot long, hooked and cruel.

A knife.

'No, you can't . . .'

She tried to claw her way to her feet, her skull ready to split open, seizing hold of his thoughts and squeezing tight. His eyes widening in pain and flooding bloodshot, Ilyitch stepped up and kicked her in the head, the world falling away as she briefly flew, shoulders crashing upon broken black glass. She blinked at the storm above, only dimly aware of the boy grabbing her hands, binding them tight. He punched her in the face again and again, consciousness threatening to flee on dark wings.

Buruu . . .

She could hear the gaijin flying machine drawing closer, its engines like the pulse throbbing at her temples, the beating of distant drums.

Whumpwhumpwhump.

She flopped over onto her stomach, vision blurred, watching Ilyitch crouch beside Buruu. The twitching tail was the only sign of life, but she could feel him, struggling towards the surface, the rippling light of a distant sun above. She tried to reach into the Kenning, but her thoughts slipped away between the cracks in her skull, bleeding from her ears.

Buruu, WAKE UP!

Ilyitch scowled as he inspected the metal wings, running his fingers over iridescent metal, ball joints, pistons and false quills. Lifting the canvas covering, he pawed at the blunt, severed feathers that were Yoritomo's legacy, hacked off in Kigen arena ten thousand lifetimes ago. And with a muttered curse, the gaijin boy stood, spat on the ground and stalked over to Skraai.

Boots crunching on shattered obsidian.

Howling wind.

Thunder.

Whumpwhumpwhump.

The nomad was stirring, talons that could rend an ironclad like cloth curling into fists, leaving gouges in the black glass beneath. Ilyitch ran his fingers through the feathers at the arashitora's neck, over the mighty wings, breathing deep, a slow smile alighting on his face. The quills glowed with a faint luster; the charge of static electricity, lighting his eyes with hunger.

He nodded.

Whumpwhumpwhump.

'No,' she moaned. 'Don't . . .'

Ilyitch straddled the arashitora's head, one boot on either side, face turned to the sky.

'Imperatritsa, butye svidetilem!' he cried. 'Moya dobicha! Moya slava!'

Whumpwhumpwhump.

The boy raised the knife.

'Ilyitch, *don't!*'

Lightning in the skies, reflected in the blade.

Descending.

'NO!'

And with a flash of steel, an impossible gush of red, the boy opened up the thunder tiger's throat.

Ashes

Prayers first for the Judge,
  Offerings for Enma-ō, burned in blessed flame.
  Coin and holy words, invocations unto him, that he judge them fair.
  And from fire's belly, when all heat and light shall fade, a handful of ash,
  Spread upon cold skin, bloodless faces and dead lips,
  That we shall know them.

The Book of Ten Thousand Days

37

Offerings

He always knocked on her door. As if she had some say whether he entered or not.

Michi plastered on her smile as Ichizo nodded to his retinue of bushimen, sealing them outside in the bustling, servant-strewn hallway. She stepped across the room, joy on her face if not in her eyes, pressing her lips to his and wondering how long it would be before the serpent in her arms reared back to strike.

'My love,' he said. 'I missed you.'

'And I you,' she lied. 'I get so lonely without you.'

Her hands slipped to his waist, over the hilts of his chainkatana, steel calling to shivering fingertips. How easy would it be, to close her fist about that plaited cord and draw it forth, thumb the ignition, listen to the engine sing . . .

She began untying his obi.

'Wait, love.' He caught up her hands and kissed each fingertip; eight feather-light touches, eyes sparkling. 'I thought we might go for a walk.'

She allowed her eyebrow to rise slightly. 'Around the room, my Lord?'

'I thought we might take some fresh air by the sky-docks,' he smiled. 'Such as it is.'

A blink.

'You mean I'm—'

'Lord Hiro has assented to you leaving your rooms for a stroll in my company.' He put a finger over her lips, cutting off her cry of delight. 'The Daimyo of the Phoenix and Dragon clan are due to arrive this afternoon. Lord Hiro wishes his court present to greet them.'

'Oh, gods!' She threw her arms around his neck. 'You did it!'

'Not quite. Once we are done, you must return to your room. But it is a beginning. I said you would be on my arm at the wedding, love. Tora Ichizo keeps his promises.' He kissed her lips. 'Now, go change into something that will dazzle them. I will be waiting.'

She turned and ran to the dressing room, still smiling even after she turned away. And if there was some kernel of true feeling behind it, it was only because she hadn't stepped outside her room in nearly a month. Or perhaps because she might catch a glimpse of Aisha at the reception. Not because he'd lived up to his promise. Not because even in the midst of all this, he'd somehow made her happy.

No, not at all.

The sun was drowning at the edge of Kigen Bay.

Even through her breather, Michi could smell the reek slinking in off the water, the shambling sea breeze carrying rot in its arms. The docking towers along Spire Row loomed over the sun-bleached boardwalk, a lone seagull above drawing aimless circles in tar-spattered skies. Greasy water slurped and burbled at the rotting pier, the blood-red air vibrating with the murmur and hum of thousands upon thousands of people – half the populace of Kigen, surely – gathered at their Daimyo's command to greet the masters of the Phoenix and Dragon clans.

Countless faces swathed in grubby kerchiefs and ash-fogged goggles. Silks of every shade of red imaginable, Tiger banners snapping and rippling in the poison breeze. She fancied she could hear the dissent, building like a tide against a crumbling dam. Looking around the thousand faces, the rotting shell of this diseased city, she found herself smiling.

One day, all this will be gone.

The court was gathered in all its finery – magistrates and scribes, courtiers and officials, soldiers and courtesans. The Lotus Guild had also turned out in force, no doubt to impress their support of the Tiger clan upon their Dragon and Phoenix visitors. Dozens of brass-clad insectoid figures stood amidst the crowd, rank and file Lotusmen along with the fanatical Purifiers in their white tabards and soot-stained gauntlets. A dozen more surrounded the glacial menace of Shateigashira Kensai, Kigen's Second Bloom, his boyish facemask reflecting the blinding glint of the setting sun. Banners bearing the Guild's sigil loomed at his back, green as lotus leaves.

But of the Lord of Tigers or his fiancée, there was no sign.

Bells rang out across the water, the song of iron entwined with the hiss of black salt, and Michi turned her eyes to the armada closing in on the bay. A half-dozen ships – real, old-fashioned sailing ships – were cutting across the foam-scummed waves. The vessels were heavy, triple-masted fortresses with towering sterns and snarling dragons at their prows, wonderfully crafted but still, practically antiques. Michi found herself smiling behind her breather.

Tall ships were rarely seen since the advent of sky-ship

technology, and they would certainly not be considered 'proper' to transport a Daimyo and his retinue under normal circumstances. But the Dragon zaibatsu had been a clan of raiders in the uncivilized days before the Imperium. Terrors of the seas, not beholden to any law. The Dragon clanlord, Ryu Haruka, was no fool. Arriving in such a fashion was certainly intended to send a message to his would-be Shōgun – a reminder of what the Ryu clan had been, and could easily become again. A display; hackles raised, teeth bared. But if the Dragon Daimyo wished his display to make an impression, he would no doubt be cursing fate that he had to share his entrance with a Phoenix.

A shadow fell across Michi's face, ash and dust whipped in a growing prop-blast wind, the drone of massive propellers drowning out the songs of the bay. She looked into the sky and her heart skipped a beat despite herself, awed and outraged at the sheer majesty of it. A goliath loomed in the skies above, growing larger by the moment.

The '*Floating Palace*' they called it. The largest sky-ship ever built. Three hundred feet of polished wood and towering walls and pyramid rooftops stacked one upon another. Sunflower-yellow flags rippled from its flanks, its inflatables daubed in the same hue, like some vast golden sun burning overhead, spewing a breathtaking plume of exhaust into the already suffocating sky. It was said the Daimyo of the Fushicho clan never set foot on the tortured earth of their homelands anymore. That any pleasure within the Seven Isles could be found in those opulent halls. The fuel it must have taken to keep it afloat – let alone fly it all the way to Kigen – made Michi sick to her stomach. Extravagance and arrogance in equal, nauseating measure.

She looked at the beggar children in the crowd around her, the women and children who didn't know where their next meal might come from. Fingernails biting her palms.

'Incredible, is it not?' Ichizo said beside her.

'It is, my Lord,' she breathed.

The air about the *Floating Palace* was swarming with swift corvettes – three-man sky-ships with balloons shaped like arrowheads, a blazing phoenix painted on each. Swooping and rising like long-lost hummingbirds, they danced in the air to the delight of the crowd. As the grand old ships of the Dragon clan docked at Spire Row, and a small contingent of corvettes flew down from the palace above, the sun finally slipped below the edge of the world. The sky exploded with a blinding fireworks display – pinwheels and dragon cannon lighting the dusk, the citizens below applauding the arrival of the Daimyo's noble guests. Michi's eyes roamed the retinues, fixing on each clanlord in turn as they alighted from their respective craft.

The Dragon clanlord, Ryu Haruka, was an elderly man, short and wiry, a long goatee and thinning grey locks swept away in a topknot. He was clad in a sapphire-blue kimono and an embossed cuirass. A silver dragon-maw breather was affixed below jet-black eyes, deep as the bloody sea in which dragons once roamed. An elegant woman (Michi assumed a wife) stood beside him, face hidden by an elaborate breather fan. The pair were surrounded by Iron Samurai in ō-yoroi of silver, blue tabards reaching to the filthy ground. Dour stares and iron eyes.

By contrast, the Phoenix retinue was all motion and colour. Their two Daimyo walked side by side – tall, beautiful men, painted faces, clad in identical kimono of burnt yellow and gold. Shin and Shou were an oddity amongst Shima's clanlords – twin brothers choosing to rule jointly rather than squabble over who had been plucked from their mother's womb first. The pair moved with an eerie synchronicity, neither straying from the other's side. Their retinue was made up of swaying dancers with eyes shadowed the colour of flame, slender men shifting balls of flaming glass between their fingers. Even the armour of their Iron Samurai seemed crafted for beauty first, function second – helms sculpted like phoenix heads, tabards of flame-coloured feathers upon their shoulders.

The Herald of the Tiger court, grand old Tanaka, stood amidst the crowd, paunchy and scarlet-clad. His warm welcome spilled from the speakers clustered beneath his tiger-maw breather, announcing each Daimyo in turn. Michi covered her fist and bowed with the rest of the court, eyes to the floor. Obedient. Deferential. Playing the good woman. The loyal subject. Her stare drifted to the chainswords at Ichizo's waist.

Soon.

Her whisper was meant for her jailer's ears only.

'Pardon, Lord, but where are Clan Kitsune? Will they be arriving later?'

'Daimyo Kitsune Isamu refused our Lord's invitation,' Ichizo whispered in reply. 'The Fox zaibatsu will not attend the wedding, nor swear allegiance to Shima's new Shōgun.'

'May I ask why not?'

Ichizo shrugged. 'Perhaps Isamu-sama tires of living . . .'

Drums rang out in the dusk as the luminance of the fireworks died. Michi turned with the rest of the throng, watching as a long convoy of motor-rickshaws trundled down the Palace Way. The vehicles were squat, beetle-shaped, chi lanterns at their snouts setting the smog around them aglow. A dozen Iron Samurai marched in the vanguard, arrayed in golden tabards of the Kazumitsu Elite, bone-white armour spitting plumes of blue-black. A stomping, clomping legion of bushimen followed, naginata at rest on their shoulders, Tiger banners streaming from the hafts.

Looking around the crowd, Michi saw sheer adoration – genuine or contrived, she couldn't tell. Applause and cheers, the tune of flute and drum and string spilling through the rust-clad speakers of the public address system. As Lord Hiro's motorcade approached, she saw movement on a rooftop at the corner of her eye, glancing across to see a small clockwork spider crawling from a downspout on silver, needle legs, red eye aglow. Her stare grew wide and she flinched, grasping Ichizo's arm.

'What in the name of the gods is that?'

Ichizo glanced at the contraption, muttered beneath his breath.

'I beg pardon, my Lord?' Michi said, leaning closer to hear him over the clamour.

'A Guild device.' Ichizo spoke a little clearer, turned his eyes back to Hiro's approach. 'The palace teems with them.'

'What do they do?'

'What they see, the Guild knows.'

'My honorable Daimyo Hiro is content to let the Guild into his bedchambers?'

'Apparently so.'

She watched the device ticking across the rooftop of a crumbling store shed, a windup key spinning upon its back. Glancing around, she saw several others, tiny red lights hiding in the shadows of lean-to warehouses or storm drains, silver limbs rippling.

'The Guild has done much for my cousin,' Ichizo murmured. 'Returned the arm that the Impure assassin took away. Given him the power to seize the Four Thrones. But Yoritomo-no-miya's old guard warned against tying ourselves too closely to the Guild. As time wears on, I wonder if there was wisdom in old men's voices.' He ran one hand over his neck. 'At least the Guild keep their spies in the open, I suppose. Not hidden in shadows.'

She glanced at him, trying to read his features. His voice was low and measured, tinged with metal within his breather, but she swore she caught a hint of emphasis on the word 'shadows.'

'Do you think my cousin will make a good Shōgun, Michi-chan?'

Michi blinked, attention sharpening at the question. She looked around – the jubilant crowd, the soldiers just a shouted order away. Maybe this was where it happened: here in public, right on this boardwalk. Where the viper bared its fangs to strike.

'My Lord?'

'Hiro-sama.' Ichizo nodded towards the approaching procession. 'Do you think he will make a good ruler?'

'It does not matter what I think.' She turned her eyes to the floor, trying to appear embarrassed. 'I am not worthy to judge.'

'But you have made a judgement nevertheless. That is only human. You knew him briefly, when he courted the Kitsune girl. How did he strike you? As a fair man? Balanced?'

'He was Kazumitsu Elite. His honour was impeccable, his conduct above reproach.'

They stood in silence for a long time, listening to the crackling music, the fireworks popping anew, the percussion of the approaching legion. Ichizo was staring at her, but she refused to meet his eyes, to show any kind of strength. If this was a play, she didn't quite know what to make of it. He spoke again, his voice so low she could barely hear.

'When we were children, Hiro and I would play soldiers. Fighting side by side against the gaijin hoardes or demons from the Yomi underworld. It was all either of us wanted to do: Defend the throne. Preserve the might of the Shōgunate.' He glanced at the Daimyo of the Dragon and Phoenix clans, their gathered entourages. 'But never once, not in all the times we played, did we imagine our enemies would be our own people.'

She kept her face still. Breathing steady. Wondering what shape her end would take. How far she would get before they cut her down . . .

'Do you have something to tell me, Michi-chan?'

She licked her lips. Just once. Finally met his stare.

'My Lord?'

'I want you to trust me.' He put his hand on her arm as the noise of the crowd swelled. 'I want you to know you can tell me anything.'

Of course you do.

'If you hide things from me, I can't protect you.'

'Protect me from what?'

'Yourself.'

So here it is. He must suspect something. Perhaps he'd heard her as she stole his keys. Perhaps one of those accursed Guild machines had been spying in her bedroom ceiling or through her window. She was in danger. No One was in danger. *Aisha* was in danger . . .

Thoughts of personal peril vanished as Hiro's motorcade pulled to a creaking stop at the boardwalk's edge. The final vehicle in the row of motor-rickshaws was a large palanquin on rolling tank tracks, its hull fashioned to resemble a snarling hoarde of golden tigers. Atop their backs in a massive, ornate love seat were propped the couple of the hour. Lord Tora Hiro was resplendent in his bone-white ō-yoroi armour, face covered by a snarling tiger helm, his clockwork arm held up to the cheering crowd. But it was not the would-be Shōgun of the nation who caught Michi's attention, held her transfixed, sent a fierce pride swelling in her breast.

445

Yoritomo-no-miya had discovered his sister's treachery in the hours before his assassination, and in his rage, had beaten the First Daughter near to death. And yet, here she was. Looking out over her people. Still breathing while her brother's ashes filled a tomb beneath the palace. Such strength. The strength to defy every impulse within her, to rise up from a place of luxury and privilege and recognize the suffering of the people beyond the palace walls. To strive for something better. The strength to say no.

'Aisha,' Michi whispered.

The First Daughter was a beauty from the pages of poets, a woman wrought of alabaster and fine black silk. Her face powdered pearl-white, deep smears of kohl accentuating knowing eyes. A tiger-maw breather covered the lower half of her face, her hair bound into elaborate braids, pierced with gold. Her gown was scarlet, embroidered with a rippling pattern of lotus blooms and prowling tigers, rising into a high throat and an elaborate choker of gold and jewels. Hiro held her hand, fingers entwined, lifting it to the cheering crowd. Though the boy Daimyo might be a pretender, Kazumitsu's blood flowed in Aisha's veins. She was the last remnant of a mighty dynasty, a living link to Shima's glorious past. The people loved her for it.

She sat poised, immaculate, still as midnight, her eyes roaming her adoring public and twinkling with firecracker light. Her seat was surrounded by Guildsmen of a breed Michi had seldom seen before – wasp-waisted women with long, insectoid limbs made of chrome at their backs. Their eyes glowed red, mechabacii chittering on their chests.

Hiro released his fiancée's hand, stepped down off the palanquin, surrounded by a sea of his white-clad Iron Samurai. As one, the crowd sank to their knees. The Daimyo of the Phoenix and Dragon stepped forward, bowed low, first to Lady Aisha, then to her betrothed. Hiro covered his fist, returned the bow.

'Noble Daimyo Haruka-san, Shin-san, Shou-san,' Hiro said. 'My fiancée, the First Daughter of Kazumitsu and I bid you welcome to Kigen, and extend our humble thanks for your attendance at our wedding celebrations.'

Haruka gave a gruff nod. Shin spoke then, his voice soft and sweet as fresh plums.

'Daimyo Hiro. Ours hearts are gladdened. We had heard rumour you had gained the support of the Kazumitsu Elite . . .'

Shou glanced at the Iron Samurai, picking up his brother's trailing sentence. '. . . but we could scarce believe it.'

'And why is that, honourable Shou-san?'

'In truth, noble Hiro-san,' Shin replied, 'we expected every one of them would have committed seppuku to restore their honour after their Shōgun was slaughtered by a common-born girlchild.'

A sudden hush fell over the crowd, heavy as stone, uneasy murmurs rippling at the periphery. Bushimen glanced at each other in the ringing silence, the *click-clack* of dozens of mechabacii filling the void. Shateigashira Kensai stepped forward, arms folded, his voice that of a hundred dying lotusflies.

'Shin-san,' the Second Bloom said. 'You shame our host. And his bride to be.'

'No disrespect is intended, Second Bloom.' Shou bowed. 'Especially to First Daughter.'

'Perhaps we simply do things differently in the west,' Shin said. 'If our Elite guard had stood idle as a teenager snuffed us out like candles, there is not a man among them who would not willingly suffer the cross-shaped cut to their bellies . . .'

Daimyo Haruka drummed his fingers on his chainkatana hilt. 'Shin-san . . .'

'Noble Daimyo Shin is quite correct,' Hiro said, his voice flat and cold.

The twin Daimyo of the Phoenix clan blinked slowly.

'You agree?' Shou asked.

Hiro nodded. 'Each of these men, every man who wore the golden jin-haori as Yoritomo was murdered suffers the stain of unendurable disgrace. As do I. But to restore the honour of the Kazumitsu line, we have chosen to endure the unendurable.'

Hiro reached up and unbuckled the mempō covering his face. As he pulled the mask away, the crowd gasped, stared in open-mouthed horror at their Lord. Michi's hand sought Ichizo's, clasped it tight.

The Daimyo had painted his face with ashes.

A thick white pall covered his features, clung to his eyelashes, like the face of a corpse before it was assigned to the pyre. He glared at the assembled Daimyo as his Elite removed their helms, revealing faces as white and ash-streaked as their Lord's. Michi felt a cold fear in her gut at the sacrilege – an instinctive revulsion at the perversion of traditional funeral rites.

'Honourable Daimyo,' Haruka growled. 'What is the meaning of this?'

'Of what do you speak, Haruka-san?'

'To paint the faces of living men with ashes is to invite the deepest misfortune,' the Dragon clanlord replied. 'This is a practise reserved for corpses. It will bring death's touch to the ones so marked.'

'But we *are* dead.'

'. . . Daimyo?'

'Every samurai in the Kazumitsu Elite has disgraced himself for allowing his Shōgun to perish. As our noble Phoenix cousins have said, we should already have committed seppuku. But first we must turn our blades to the execution of she who laid noble Yoritomo low.'

He stared at the other clanlords, toxic wind whipping hair about his ashen face.

'Therefore, we have consigned our souls to Enma-ō. Burned our offerings of wooden coin and incense to the Judge of all the Hells, begged him to weigh us fairly, and painted our faces with the ashes left behind. As is the way with any dead man.

'We are the Shikabane.' He eyes were dark jade against ashen white. 'We are the Corpses.'

Michi watched the clanlords glance at each other, uncertain. Perhaps even fearful. All the pretense of their grand entrances stripped away, left naked before those burning green eyes.

'I wish to be clear upon this.' Hiro's gaze flickered from one Daimyo to the next. 'I will honour our fallen Shōgun. I will marry Lady Aisha, sire a new heir to the Kazumitsu line, see this nation's future assured. But once this duty is served, I will set about hunting and executing Yoritomo's assassin and all who abet her. I will serve this nation as Shōgun until the Impure whore, Kitsune Yukiko, is dead.'

Hiro blinked like a man who had forgotten how.

'Your oaths bind you to the Kazumitsu house. Once my beloved and I are wed, I will be as a son of that noble line. And *my* sons shall carry the name into this nation's future. So know this . . .'

Hiro replaced his mempō, covering his ashen features. The iron face of a bone-white tiger snarled at the nobles, and the voice within was the ringing of footfalls in an empty tomb.

'If you choose to dishonour your vows and stand against me, I will kill your families. Your wives. Your sons. I will kill your neighbours, your servants, your childhood friends. I will burn your cities to the ground, sow your fields with salt, make a desolation of everything you know and care for. And at the last, when all you love is ashes, I will kill you.'

Silence. Soft as baby's breath.

'Now.' Hiro gestured with his clockwork arm to the palace glowering on the hill. 'I believe welcome drinks are being served in the dining hall.'

Ichizo's hand was back on Michi's arm. She tried not to stiffen at his touch.

'I should return you to your room.'

'If that is your wish, my Lord.'

There was no anger in his voice as he spoke. 'Do you think me a fool, Michi-chan?'

She looked into his eyes then, gleaming above coiled breather pipes. Were they the eyes of a serpent, toying with its prey? Or the eyes of a loyal man, torn by duty to Lord and heart?

Who are you?

'No,' she said. 'I do not think you are a fool, my Lord.'

Ichizo looked at the Tiger Daimyo, climbing back into the palanquin, taking his fiancée by the hand. The faces of the shocked crowd, pale and drawn and stricken with fear. The faces of the Dragon and Phoenix entourages, all bluster and pomp evaporated, taking their seats in the motorcade, silent as berated children. The faces of the Iron Samurai, caked thick with funeral ashes. And the face of Lord Hiro, a walking dead man, only a heartbeat away from dominion over the entire Imperium. His cousin. His blood. His Shōgun.

Ichizo's face was as pale as his Lord's.

'I think perhaps we both are.'

*

She had hated Aisha at first. From the very core of her soul. Here was a woman who had everything. Born to privilege and power. Spoiled by her parents, indulged by her brutish pig of a brother, never lifting a finger all the days of her life.

Months had passed after Michi arrived from the Iishi. There was no hint of the Kagé fighter supposedly dwelling behind the First Daughter's facade, and the pair were never alone long enough to speak. She would occasionally catch Aisha's eyes, stare with unspoken questions, but there was nothing in the woman's face that might betray her. If she was playing a part, Aisha would have put the greatest actors in the Shōgunate to shame.

Michi kept her head down, worked hard, fortunate enough to avoid Shōgun Yoritomo's advances in the shadow of prettier, more cultured ladies in Aisha's company. Yoritomo-no-miya seemed to take pleasure in deflowering the First Daughter's retinue, and for her part, Aisha seemed perfectly content to whore her ladies out to her brother whenever the mood struck him. She was a harsh mistress, temper flaring over the slightest foible – especially in front of her brother, who relished her cruelty. And Michi found the hatred inside her turning to poison.

Why had the Kagé sent her here? There was no more rebellion in this woman's breast than there was humanity in her brother's. This was no battlefield. This was no war.

And one night as Michi ran a brush through her mistress's hair, the other girl assigned to her bedchamber – a sweet and clever Ryu girl called Kiki – knocked over a bottle of perfume, glass smashing on the floorboards. Aisha had risen from her cushion, lightning in her eyes. She raised her hand, and Michi moved before she had a chance to think. Reaching out with that terrible speed that had served her so well in swordplay, catching the older woman's wrist as it descended, knuckles white upon her arm.

'Don't,' she'd said.

And Aisha had smiled then; the first time Michi had actually seen her smile in all the months she'd served. Beautiful and bright, like the first rays of dawn after winter's longest night.

'There it is,' she said.

Aisha had dismissed Kiki with a wave, the terrified girl scuttling from the room with an apologetic glance to Michi, sliding the door closed behind her.

'I had wondered how long it might take,' Aisha had said.

'Take?'

A nod. 'For you to risk all.'

Michi had blinked, remained mute.

'That girl is nothing to you.' Aisha motioned to the doorway Kiki had left by. 'Yet you dared lay hands upon the First Daughter of the Kazumitsu Dynasty in her defence. Jeopardizing your mission. Showing defiance that could spell your death.'

'Let it come,' Michi had said.

Aisha stepped closer, placed both hands on Michi's shoulders.

'I know who you are, daughter of Daiyakawa. And I admire your conviction. Truly, I do. But this is no place for an inferno. Daichi-sama sent you to be my hand, my eyes, and you can be neither if you are blinded by the fire inside you.

'Let it burn slow. Be as I am. Keep it all inside, hidden until the day it will truly matter, when standing up and risking all will be worth the blood you wager. The day we can win.'

'You would have me sit by and let innocents suffer?'

'I would,' Aisha said. 'And I know how much I ask in that. One day I may ask even more. I may ask everything of you. But not for the sake of one person. For the sake of this nation. For the lives of every man and woman and child upon these islands.

'These are the stakes we play with now, Michi-chan. There is *no prize for second in this game. This is no sortie for a hill amongst boys in iron suits. This is a war for the very future of Shima. And you must understand that if you are to serve the Kagé here. You must witness atrocity and remain mute. Watch others suffer, even die, and lift not a finger to help. You must be as patient as stone until the time comes to strike, and harder than stone when you finally draw your blade.'*

Michi stared, as if seeing her for the first time. The conviction in Aisha's eyes, the breathless passion in her voice. And she did not see the spoiled princess she'd learned to hate. She saw fire, every bit as bright as the one in her own chest; a fire that gave birth to Shadows.

Aisha took up her hands, held them tight, stared hard.

'Do you understand me, Michi-chan?'

Michi looked down to the hands that held her own. Back up into Aisha's eyes.

'I do.'

'Can you let it burn slow?'

'I can.'

'And when I ask it of you, will you give all?'

She licked her lips.

Nodded.

'I will.'

38

Terminus

The metal dragonfly flew with less grace than the real thing. It spun its wings rather than flapped them; three propellers pinned around the craft like points on a triangle, angled at 45 degrees. Its skin was dark metal, crusted with oxidization, gleaming with rain. The craft seemed lopsided somehow, held together by excess solder and sheer bloody-mindedness rather than engineering prowess. Two glass domes shielding the cockpit gave the impression of eyes. Its engines spat a clanking growl, like a wolf with a mouthful of iron bolts.

The propellers *whumphwhumphwhumphed* as the vessel descended, more like a fat, wobbling bumblebee than a dragonfly. The pilots hammered at their consoles, struggling to hold the craft steady in the gale. Rain sluiced off the windshields as it touched down, shearing sideways across the glass as the wind tore at its hide.

Yukiko was slumped against an outcropping, barely conscious, her face black and blue. She'd watched Ilyitch cut the young arashitora from throat to belly, begin peeling the skin back from his flesh, so much blood she could taste metal as she breathed. She'd pushed feebly into Buruu's mind the entire time, but Ilyitch's lightning-thrower had knocked him into a slumber deeper than blacksleep could ever manage. Smooth, reptilian shapes pulsed in the water around them, but unless they could grow legs, the dragons wouldn't be of any help. She could sense the female thunder tiger circling overhead, like a carrion bird above a battlefield.

Head splitting, blood pouring from her nose, she reached out to the arashitora above.

They're going to skin him.

A mental blink.

– *YŌKAI-KIN.* –

Yukiko closed her eyes, maintained the link despite the volume and pain.

The gaijin killed Skraai. They're going to do the same to Buruu.

– *AND?* –

Doesn't that mean anything to you? These monkey-children are going to cut the skins from your kin's backs and wear them as godsdamned trophies!

– *WEAKLINGS TO BE CAPTURED AT ALL. SPENT THEIR STRENGTH FIGHTING EACH OTHER. AND FOR WHAT? I, WHO WANT NEITHER.* –

They were captured because of me! Because I trusted—

– *FAILING YOURS. NOT MINE.* –

You can't just let Buruu die!

– *ONE LESS BUTCHER. ONE LESS FOOL.* –

With a bitter curse, Yukiko broke contact, pushed the female away with all her strength. She flexed her fists, trying to slip her hands free of her bonds. Her eye was swollen shut, bloody drool slicked on her chin. But the Kenning still roared inside her amidst the agony of her beating, so far beyond hurt it ceased to have meaning at all.

She could kill Ilyitch. She knew that now. She could feel it surging in her, stronger than it had been when she and her father lay Yoritomo low. But what about the rest of them? Could she kill them all?

If they touched Buruu, she'd sure as hells try . . .

The metal dragonfly's belly split open, a hatchway disgorging half a dozen gaijin in red jackets, dark furs and bronze insignia. Danyk walked in the lead, still wearing her katana at his belt. A furious-looking Piotr stepped out behind him, a bloodstained bandage around his head. He scowled as soon as he spotted Yukiko, limping across the island towards her.

Danyk and the other gaijin gathered around Ilyitch, amazement on their faces. The boy flourished his knife, covered head to foot in blood, motioned to the butchered arashitora at his feet. Several younger gaijin clapped him on the back, all grins and laughter, as if he'd done something extraordinary rather than commit an atrocity. Even Danyk managed a grudging smile, extending a hand which Ilyitch shook with great enthusiasm.

They treat him like a hero . . .

Piotr knelt beside her, looked her over. Yukiko's head was splitting; she could see three of the dark-haired gaijin swimming in the air before her. The ache grew blinding, the song of sledge-hammers ringing in her skull.

'Not move.' His voice came from underwater. 'Head. Head.'

Something thick and soft was being wrapped around her brow. She tried to reach up with bound hands, wrists rubbed raw, blisters on her palms torn and bleeding. She forced her eyes open, stared at the gaijin as the storm howled all around them.

'Stupid girl.' He shook his head. 'Stupid.'

'Go to the hells,' Yukiko spat.

He reached towards her face and she flinched away, lashed out with her feet.

'You touch me I'll turn your brain to soup, round-eye.'

'Eh?' A raised eyebrow. 'Help. I help.'

'Help? You wanted to rape me, you bastard! Get the hells away from me!'

Piotr stared at her, aghast. 'Rape? Trying to *help you,* girl.'

He glanced over his shoulder to the gaijin near Ilyitch's prize, lowered his voice to a furious whisper.

'Stupid! I warn! I say! Tell for you to come with me. Using for the body!' The gaijin pointed to the arashitora laid out upon the stone, ran his hands down his shoulders, over his chest. 'Using you. Gryfon body! Gryfon!'

'Arashitora . . .'

'Da! Arashitora body.'

'You . . .' Yukiko's voice caught in her throat. 'You were trying to warn me . . .'

'Now too late.' He shook his head. 'Too late. Wear for the body. Great strength. Much prize for Ilyitch. Much prize.'

'Why would you warn me?' She narrowed her eyes. 'Why help me?'

'Promise friend.'

'What friend?'

'Piotr!'

Danyk's voice startled the scarred gaijin. He looked over his shoulder, made a questioning sound. The round-eye leader barked an order, beckoned with one broad hand.

Piotr helped Yukiko to her feet, the world slipping away underneath her, Ilyitch's kicking still ringing like a thousand iron bells in her skull. He guided her over to the others, standing in a pool of watery blood around Buruu, speaking in a babble of gruff voices. The smell from Skraai's corpse was nauseating; a rancid mix of blood and guts and excrement, bile and copper on her tongue. She looked at these men with hatred swelling in her chest, a bitter loathing threatening to steal the very breath from her lungs. Eight of them.

How many of them can I kill before they take me?

She looked down at her friend's body on the stone, groped for him in the darkness.

Buruu, please wake up. Please.

The gaijin seemed to be debating about Buruu's wings. Two of the younger ones were prodding the crumpled machinery running down his spine, the torn harness affixing the contraption to his pinions. Danyk spoke to Piotr in his rumbling baritone, waving at the arashitora. Lightning arced across black skies, the downpour growing heavy again; so thick it was almost blinding. The sound of the rain upon the ocean was a constant, rolling hiss.

'Danyk ask what wrong with this one.' Piotr's voice was harsh, but there was pity in that single blue eye. 'Is cripple?' He pointed to his leg, the metal brace around it. 'Cripple?'

'What if he is?' she said.

'Will not wear for the cripple body.' The gaijin shook his head. 'No strength. No prize.'

Her heart skipped a beat. A glimmer of hope. She nodded to Danyk.

'He's a cripple.'

Danyk gritted his teeth, spat what sounded like a vicious curse. He waved the younger gaijin aside, commanded a pale black-haired fellow to step forward. The man was broad, jaw like a brick house dusted with black stubble, eyes of blue glass. He drew a long, double-bladed axe from his belt.

'What are you doing?'

Yukiko's eyes were wide with disbelief. Piotr dragging her away.

'No, why would you kill him? Stop! Stop it!'

BURUU, WAKE UP!

'Kak zal,' Danyk said, watching the soldier raise the blade above his head.

'NO! *NO!*'

Yukiko reached towards Piotr, slammed into his mind with everything she was. The round-eye released his grip on her arms, fell to the ground, senseless and mute, nose and ears gushing. Turning on the axeman, she seized hold of his mind and squeezed as hard as she could, two bloody handfuls, tearing side to side like a wolf worrying a piece of meat. The gaijin made an odd, strangled sound and staggered as if she'd struck him, dropping the axe and clutching his temples. She screamed, lips peeling back from her teeth as she felt it rise up inside her, the heat of a collapsing star, the roar of a thousand hurricanes. And with blood pouring from his ears, nose and eyes, the gaijin crumpled to the stone.

She whirled on a third, smashing into his skull with everything inside her own, his head flopping about as if she'd broken his neck. And with a roar, Danyk seized her by a handful of sodden hair, pulled her back as she screamed and cursed and kicked and spat, nails and teeth and fists, mouth agape, eyes rolling in her head. Madness had taken her, a rage so deep it was suffocating, stealing away everything she was and leaving a shell behind; a burning, shrieking thing wearing her skin. She bucked in his hands, tore loose from his grip, a handful of hair clutched in his fist as she reached out to crush his mind like eggshells.

He punched her; a hook to her jaw that rocked her sideways,

lit a fire at the base of her skull. And then, with almost casual brutality, he hauled back and buried his fist deep in her belly.

Pain.

Awful. Wet and tearing.

PAIN.

A scream, somewhere in the back of her mind, a voice that sounded like her own. A burst of light in her head, flaring bright as the world fell perfectly still.

She could feel it. All of it. The men gathered around her, each a tangled thread, a thousand knots thick – so intricate it hurt just to look at them. Buruu at her feet, a shape she knew as well as her own, a distant pulse still struggling towards consciousness, flickering with the taste of stolen lightning. Skraai's shell, just a shadow of lingering heat in his bones as all he was escaped into the ether. The dragons in the snarling ocean around them, swaying with the current, cold as the lightless depths of the sea. High above, the female, circling in the blood-scent, the knowledge she should protect her kin burning bright in her mind, overshadowed with a rage born of heart-deep grief; a severing so terrible it hurt her to even begin remembering.

What she had lost.

What he had taken from her.

And in Yukiko's belly, where the knuckles had been buried in her flesh, nothing but pain.

She slumped to her knees, gasping, screams growing louder in her ears, feeling the pulse of the world and knowing something was terribly, terribly wrong.

What's happening to me?

Danyk placed his boot on her chest and shoved. She fell backward, curled up, fetal and tiny beneath the storm. Blood spilled from her ears, her nose, filmed her eyes with scarlet.

She reached for Buruu with bound hands, groping along the gleaming black glass to find his claws, fingertips barely touching. Danyk drew Yofun from his belt with a gleaming, silver sound, folded-steel glittering with sea spray, rain skirting the katana's razored edge.

It can't end like this.

The gaijin raised the blade above his head, took aim at her throat.

Buruu, I love you.

The sword began to fall.

Buruu . . .

A white shape, plummeting from the sky.

A scream of outrage, the sound of thunder and lightning and a tempest unleashed.

Danyk looked up towards the sound, jaw slackening. And then he simply wasn't there anymore. A pale blur, a moment of impact, shattering bone. The katana spun end over end as it descended, ringing bright as it hit the stone beside Yukiko's head.

Tearing sounds from above.

Red rain.

The gaijin cursed, fumbling weapons from their belts, swords and lightning-throwers, eyes upon the sky. She fell on them like a shadow, swooping from behind, silent beneath the roar of the storm. Wet crunching sounds, screams of pain, one man's torso falling away from his legs, another clutching the bloody stump where his head used to be as his body toppled backwards and spilled on the stone. Flashing blades touched snow-white fur and the female screamed in pain, bounding into the air as the space between her and prey became blue-white, bright arcs spitting from the mouths of their lightning-throwers.

But the little monkey-children and their silly toys didn't

know her for what she was; a daughter of thunder, Everstorm-born, swimming in bolts of brilliant blue-white since first she took to the wing. Without earth beneath her feet to ground her, the current spilling from their trinkets was a cooling shower, a delightful prickle over feathers stained blood-red. They screamed as she swooped low, running for the cover of their crooked metal dragonfly. And she in her rage, drunk with the taste of them, alighted atop the flimsy tin can and peeled it open like ripe fruit, disassembling them as they screamed, one by one by one.

Except the one she'd missed.

Ilyitch had ducked low as she swooped for the kill, pressed against the butchered nomad, drenched in his blood. And she, so intoxicated with her fury, had failed to see him, his scent lost in the male's ruins. Now he rose from the cover of bloody wings, reaching out with his stolen lightning and blasting her from the flying machine with a shriek of superheated vapour.

She crashed earthwards, steam rising from her feathers, dazed and senseless.

Ilyitch lowered the lightning-thrower, its charge spent, dropped it on the ground with the brittle sound of smashing glass. With a hissed curse, he drew the butcher's knife from his belt, still wet with arashitora blood, and knelt behind Yukiko's head.

She blinked, eyes rolling, the ache in her belly receding to a dull ebb.

He grabbed a handful of hair, pressed the knife to her throat, spitting a curse.

The katana slipped out through his chest with barely a sound. Just a hollow clip of breath and a tiny metallic rasp as it disappeared back through the hole it had made. Ilyitch's eyes grew wide as the pain registered inside his skull. The blade punched out through his chest again, blood bubbling on his lips, oxygen slurping through the hole between his ribs, emerging from his mouth as a sodden cough. And with a gurgling whimper, the boy slumped onto the stone, as dead as the thunder tiger beside him.

Piotr stood over him, blind eye gleaming white, wiping his bloody nose on his sleeve, katana clutched in both hands.

'Promise,' he wheezed. 'Promised.'

39

Fragile

Each raindrop was a whisper.

.Not the gentle whisper of a lover in Kin's ear, she in his arms, he entwined with her hair's perfume. He didn't know what that whisper might sound like. And not the whisper of father to son, looking upon a world of metal and rivets and iron teeth as he leaned down and said, 'All this, I give to you.' That lay too far back in his life to even remember now. Not the whisper of the earth, the breath of this great thing beneath our feet that holds us close from cradle to grave, opening at the last to keep us in her arms as we forever sleep.

No, it was the whisper of the machine.

He could hear Kaori's voice as he raised his hand outside Daichi's door, low and urgent, no pause for breath. He could smell peppermint and cedar, the faint scent of wisteria. And his hand fell still, hovering just a breath away from the knock that would change it all forever.

He looked around the Kagé village; this tiny knot of life carved in the deepest wild, this cluster of insurgency threatening to bring down a nation. He saw the will it had taken, to shape it from raw wood and empty boughs, to walk out here alone, away from everything and everyone, to be the first to cry 'enough.' But most of all, he saw the people, with their little lives and their fragile dreams, their hopes for a better future, for their children and children yet unborn.

It is not too late to stop. You don't have to do this.

He thought of the girl waiting in Yukiko's room, huddled in a corner, breathing fear like a fume. He thought of her lips on his, gentle hands and a sad smile. Blood on her skin. Weeping. And he gritted his teeth and made his heart a flint-black thing inside his chest, curled his fingers into a fist and smacked it sharply against the door frame.

Yes, I do.

'Come,' Daichi said, his voice like sandpaper.

He pulled the door aside, stepped through, blinking in the gloom. The old man sat by the fire, looking thinner and paler than Kin could remember. Chest still bound in bandages, bruises upon his skin and smudged beneath his eyes. Kaori knelt beside him, face hidden behind a curtain of hair. Her father's hand sat in hers, smeared with black fluid. When she spoke, he could hear tears in her voice, anger so terrible it threatened to choke the life from her.

'What do you want, Guildsman?'

'Kin-san.' Daichi swallowed with a wince. 'This is not the best time—'

'Yukiko isn't coming back.'

Even as he said the words, he couldn't believe them. They were heavy in his mouth, falling from his lips rather than spoken, clumsy and cold.

'What makes you—?'

'She's gone, Daichi.'

He shook his head. 'She'd never leave us like this, something has happened to her. We can't rely on her to save us, we don't have time. Hiro will wed Aisha and cement his claim, the Earthcrusher will march upon the Iishi, and these islands will fall into a darkness no sunlight will end. But I can see a way through. A way to end it all.'

The earth shuddered beneath their feet; a faint tremor deep within her bones, underscoring Kin's words.

'Do you remember our chess game?' Kin stared at the old man across the embers, the fire burning in tired, steel-grey. 'What you told me?'

Daichi stared, unblinking, cold and reptilian. Wheels within wheels, weather-beaten and aged, weighed down by guilt and responsibility and the lives of those who needed him. Now more than ever. Now, when he was at his weakest.

A slow nod, black stains on his lips. 'I do.'

'Then we need to talk.'

He nodded to the old man's daughter.

'Alone.'

40

Fodder for the Judge

Her dreams were of broad, strong hands.

Drenched in blood.

Fingers broken.

Tears.

Yoshi was waiting for her when she dragged herself from her bedroom. He was slumped at the table, bandage across his bare chest, the dazzling new mural of Izanagi and his spear running over hard muscle, shoulder to hip. The iron-thrower was laid out in front of him, a few inches from outstretched fingers. His hair was a knotted curtain framing sunken cheeks and too-pale skin.

Fistfuls of coin covered the tabletop; dull iron amongst the bloodstains. The air stank of sweat and lotus burn, sunset light cutting scarlet through the ash. Their room was practically palatial; a slick suite in an Upside bedhouse, all polished boards and white walls. The overweight steward who ran it had scowled down a flat, spotty nose as they'd walked in from the street, covered in shit and tears and blood. Yoshi had slapped ten iron kouka onto the countertop, demanded the best room in the house. The fat man's disdain had dissipated like lotus exhaust on a sea breeze; less palpable, but its scent still hanging in the air. He'd handed over the key with a reluctant bow.

Daken lurked above the windowsill, watching as Hana emerged from her bedroom, tail switching back and forth.

. . . he is in a mood . . .

What else is new?

'Sleep good?' Yoshi's voice was hoarse from liquor and secondhand smoke.

'I have to go, Yoshi. I have to leave, now.'

Yoshi stared at the tabletop, eyes losing focus, a faraway place reflected in flint-black irises. A dozen voices skittered in his head, scratching claws and scabbed feet, the taste of waste in his mouth. After a minute, he returned to the here, to the now, frowning at his sister.

'There's no bushimen coming, what's the—'

'I have to go back to the palace.'

Yoshi rolled his eyes. 'Are you smoking? Don't let Jurou fool you, that shit will roll you faster than a Docktown manwhore, girl.'

'Listen to me, Yoshi.' Hana's eye was wide, liquid. 'There's a room in the Shōgun's palace. Inside it is a Kagé infiltrator named Michi, who's planning on rescuing the Lady Aisha before her wedding to Daimyo Hiro. I was supposed to get Akihito to carve an impression of the key so she could escape her room.'

'So?'

'So when the bushi' kicked in our door, I left the mold behind. But without that key, the whole plan goes to the hells. I have to get back in there. Get another mold somehow. Find someone who can make a cast of it. Or find Akihito and get him to carve one for me.'

Yoshi gave her a sour look, rubbing the pale dusting of whiskers on his cheeks. 'We've run our mouths about this as far as we're going to, sister-mine.'

'Yoshi—'

'No!' His fist slammed down on the tabletop, setting the bottles and iron-thrower jumping. 'Can you hear yourself? You're talking about ghosting back into that palace? They know your face, Hana! Figuring you'll just stroll past the gate dogs with that shy little smile? Dragon and Phoenix and Tiger Lords up there and all?'

He kicked back his chair, sent it spinning across the room, adopting a lilting voice.

'Pardon me, noble Lords, I'll just flip this rebel bitch her room key and help her steal the First Daughter right under your noses. Oh no, don't get up, I can see myself away . . .'

'I can't just leave her in there, Yoshi.'

'Fuck her!' Yoshi shouted. 'Fuck all these people. It's our business like black is white's. If this city had half an inkling of what we are, they'd chain us to the Burning Stones and set us on fire. If they had the full reckoning, they'd give us an ending the *gods* would get queasy on. We don't owe them shit.'

'Where's Jurou?' Hana stormed towards the bedroom. 'Maybe he can talk some godsdamn sense into you.'

'He's not in there . . .' Yoshi said.

'He's not in here.' Hana's voice trailed out from the bedroom. 'Mm-hmm.'

Hana walked out into the living area, Daken prowling around her legs. 'Where is he?'

'Out.' A shrug. 'Getting supplies.'

'You just let him go without telling you where?'

'Girl, you seem a good deal confused about the control I have over that boy.'

... hungry ...

Hana hefted Daken onto her shoulder. She petted the tom as he purred like a sky-ship engine, sucking her bottom lip.

... he speaks true. no way for you to return to palace ...

I have to try.

... so tired of living ... ?

I can't just leave her in there, Daken.

... bored now ...

You're not really being helpful, you know.

... bored and hungry ...

Hana sighed, pressed at the ache building in the bridge of her nose. Yoshi was impossible, just stubborn and pigheaded and stupid and she wanted to grab him and shake him and scream—

'Even if you had some way of getting back into the palace, you're not gonna find Akihito anyways.' Yoshi touched his bandaged ribs and winced. 'Not unless you're looking in Kigen jail. He's fodder for the Judge.'

'You don't know that.'

'Think he danced away from the bushi' on that leg of his? Fooling yourself.'

'Shut up, godsdammit!'

Hana slumped amongst the cushions, rocked back and forth, refusing to let it get on top of her. Refusing to think about what might have happened after they left him alone, what might be happening to him right now. To think of the people she was letting down. To cry. Yoshi took a deep breath, ran one hand over his braids. Crossing the room, he knelt beside her, took her hand in his. Daken leapt into her lap, staring back and forth between them, half-tail twitching side to side.

. . . ear itches . . .

'Listen, I know you think you're helping.' Yoshi scratched the tom's ear nubs without thinking. 'You're doing something important. But these people . . . they're not worth risking your skin over. You think they'd do the same for you?'

'You don't get it . . .' Her face crumpled and she squeezed her eye shut, holding her breath as her shoulders shook. 'You just don't understand . . .'

'Life's bad all over.' He wiped her tears away with gentle hands. 'But the sun's gonna shine and the shadows'll fall, with or without us. Just the way it rides. We need to look out for ourselves. Nobody else is going to. Let the clans fight their wars. Let the Kagé and the Guild scrap in the streets. It's none of our business, Hana.'

She said nothing for the longest time, just concentrated on holding back the tears until the urge to shed them died. She reached beneath her tunic, took hold of the little golden amulet hanging around her neck, running her thumb over the stag embossed on its surface. A gift from a mother long gone, a memento of a life long over. And then she ran her nose along her sleeve, sighing as she looked him up and down.

'Your roots are showing.' She nodded to his hair. 'You need to dye it again.'

'I know. I asked Jurou to get some ink.'

She stared into space, five years gone. Saw the glint of candlelight on broken glass. Felt warm and red spattered on her face.

'I can get them out . . .'

'You know when you drink like this . . . when you yell like

this . . .' Hana felt her voice go soft and fragile. 'You remind me of Da.'

Yoshi tensed, eyes roaming the ceiling as he breathed deep.

'Don't do that,' he said. 'Don't say that. I take care of you. I'll never leave you. Never hurt you. No matter what. Blood is blood.'

'That's what scares me, brother-mine.'

She hung her head, stared at nothing at all.

'That's what scares me.'

*

'Don't let in the flies.'

Miho's growl rose above the chimes over the door. Slamming it behind him, her new customer stepped inside amidst the tinkle of hollow brass. She didn't look up from her newssheet, flicked a stray lock of hair from her eyes.

She was close to thirty, pretty in a hard, Docktown kind of way. Her sleeveless uwagi was open at the throat, showing the scrolling tapestry of phoenixes burning above her breasts and down each bicep. Her forearms were painted with old myths: Enma-ō on his bone mountain wrapped around her left, the Stormdancer Tora Takehiko and his thunder tiger charging into the Devil Gate on her right.

The shelves of her little general store were almost bare, rationing and the sky-ship lockdown having cleared out most of her stock. Bags of rice, cheap liquor, a few odds and ends, the prices punching holes clean through the roof. If not for her friends in the black market, she'd have shut down weeks ago. Foot traffic scuttled past outside, blurred shadows beyond glass-brick windows: Kigen residents hurrying to finish their errands in a city poised on the brink.

Her customer returned to the counter, dropped an armful

of items, cleared his throat. Miho continued scanning the newssheet. The headline sang about Daimyo Hiro and Lady Aisha's wedding, only a day away. The ink was fresh, sticky on her fingertips. A distant crier rang ten bells for the Hour of the Crane.

'I'd like to buy these, please.' Young voice, lotus rasp.

Miho glanced up. Brown rice. Red saké. Black ink.

'You can't afford those, boy.' She turned a page, wiped her brow with her forearm. A sheen of sweat made the thunder tiger and its rider gleam.

'You haven't even looked at me.'

'I can smell you. Anyone who smokes as much as you do can't afford those.'

A fistful of kouka rained down upon the old oak counter-top, a clattering, metallic tumble, knocking tiny dents into the varnish. She glanced up briefly at the coins. Each one was a full plait of iron-grey, stamped with the date of its minting. The bottom edge of each braid was sawtooth rough, gleaming like it was fresh clipped from the mold. It was as if someone had taken to the end of each coin with an iron file, rasping away a thin sliver of tarnished skin to expose the new metal beneath.

'Certainly, young master.' Miho straightened with a smile. 'That much coin will even warrant some change.'

She reached beneath the counter, into her strongbox. And as she handed over a half-dozen coppers, she brought up her other fist, fast as blinking, brass knuckles gleaming, smashing them hard across the boy's jaw and dropping him like a brick to the floor.

Miho stepped around the counter, locked the front door and flipped over the CLOSED sign. She looked the unconscious boy over with a critical eye. He was just a teenager by his look. Nice cheekbones. Expensive tiger ink on his upper arm. Dark bangs hanging around darker eyes, sweet as sugar-rock, a dusting of whiskers on his cheeks and upper lip, now split and bleeding.

He was pretty, and that was a real shame.

Seimi-san liked to hurt the pretty ones.

41

A Thousand Diamonds

Consciousness was hard-won, harder still to hold, swimming up to the light of waking and struggling to tread water, body and head one throbbing knot of pain.

Yukiko blinked up into roiling black and found Piotr looking down at her, just a silhouette, lighting snared in the white of his blind eye. He crouched beside her on the cold glass, smoothed the hair from her face and murmured in his own tongue. Her hands and brow had been rebandaged, a bundled satchel placed behind her head, Piotr's big wolf skin draped over her to shield her from the storm. She had no idea how long she'd been out for.

'Care,' he said. 'Head.'

Yukiko sat up slowly, clutching her gut. Every part of her ached, the rain fell like iron-thrower shot against her skin. She couldn't remember hurting so badly in all her life.

'Thank . . .'

Her throat seized closed on the words. Wincing, breathing deep, she tried speaking again.

'Thank you for helping us, Piotr.'

'Tell you.' He nodded proudly. 'Promise.'

Yukiko crawled across the blood-slick rock and leaned against Buruu, running her fingers through the feathers at the base of his skull. He stirred, eyelids flickering, the pupils beyond so dilated that his irises almost drowned in the black.

She turned back to Piotr slowly, lest her head fall completely off her shoulders. The Thunder God pounded his drums, the tremor beginning in her temples and rumbling all the way down her spine.

'Promised who?'

'Prisoner,' he said.

She blinked away the rain, frowning. 'The ones who kept you prisoner? Kitsune? Samurai?'

'No, no.' The man sighed, exasperated. 'Not *me* for the prisoner. Us *keeping* for the prisoner. There.' He pointed towards the lightning farm, his good eye lighting up as he remembered a word. 'Guild!' He snapped his fingers. 'Guild!'

'A Guildsman?' Yukiko recalled the ruined Guild ships on the rocks at the edge of the Razor Isles, the beaten brass on Katya's armour. 'A Guildsman who crashed here?'

'Da, da,' Piotr nodded. 'Fix me. Fix leg. Walk me.' He pointed at the mechanical brace on his leg, the blind eye in its ravaged socket. 'He prisoner for us. My accident is falling. Leg crush. Face, da? He fix me. Saving for the life. Teach for me the Shiman. Piotr friend too, da? Is friend.' A sigh. 'I make for the promise if Zryachniye take him.'

'A promise?'

The gaijin pulled a worn leather wallet from his coat, hunched over to shield it from the rain, unfolded a scrap of paper inside.

'Taking back.' Piotr touched his chest, touched the paper. 'Taking back for the Shima. He for the saving my life. Good man. Was good.'

The paper was worn, slightly mildewed, covered in fine black kanji. It was a letter, she realized. A letter from Piotr's Guildsman. Yukiko scanned the text, struggling to focus, a lead-grey sorrow welling in her chest.

*

Beloved,

I know I will never see your face again. The skin upon it, nor flesh beneath it. But the memory of it keeps me warm, when all else turns to winter and all hope is gone.

I am prisoner to the gaijin. Our ship crashed in the tempest, only five of us rescued from the waters. And now they keep us here as prisoners, waiting for spring to ease the storms enough to transport us to Morcheba, and from there, to a fate only the gods can know. But the gaijin who delivers this note is a friend; greater than any I deserve for the life I have led. If you are reading this, Piotr has fulfilled his vow against all odds. Treat him well, love.

I wish I could hold you one last time. I wish more than anything to feel your body against mine. I wish our daughter could know her father's face. I wish I could see her in all her perfection, before the False-Lifers run her flesh through with cables and encase her beauty in cold metal. I wish I could see the day when the machines are torn from Shima's skin, when the mechabacus falls silent for the last time, when the rebellion smashes First House to flaming splinters. When a love like ours can bloom in the sun, not endure silently within prisons of brass.

But I will not do any of these things. This is my fate. And for my part in the world we created, I deserve no better. I think myself blessed to have known you for the brief moments I did. And I go to my end with a gentle smile, at

*peace with the knowledge that, for all my crimes, fate saw
fit to grant me you. Such a gift would not be wasted on one
who is damned. Perhaps what little I did to aid the rebellion
is enough to see Enma-ō judge me fair.*

*Pray for me, love. Pray that the Judge of the Nine Hells
weighs me true. That when I stand before him, he will not
only consider what I did, but what I made possible. And
I will pray for you, for all the rebels that remain, that you
may finish what we have started: Death to the Serpents. An
end to the Guild. Freedom for Shima.*

*I love you. With all I have in me. Tell our daughter I
love her also. Know that in my final moments, I will think
of your face. With my last breath, I will whisper your name,
Misaki.*

Always yours,
Takeo.

*

Yukiko stared at the page long after she'd finished reading,
letting the words sink into her skin. So it was all true. Ayane's
story about a hidden faction within the Guild. An army of
insurgents, just as devoted as the Kagé, working to bring the
Guild to its knees.

And she had thought the girl a liar. A spy.

Just like the gaijin thought about me.

'Death to the Serpents?' she whispered.

What in the name of the gods did that mean?

'I have to get out of here.' She folded the letter carefully, put
one hand to her throbbing brow. 'I have to get back.'

'Back Shima?' Piotr took the letter, returned it to the leather
wallet with a strange reverence. 'Find Takeo love? Find Misaki-
san?'

'Hai,' she nodded. 'I will find her.'

The gaijin placed the leather wallet in her hands.

'You hold,' he said. 'You take.'

'I will.'

'You promise.'

Yukiko smiled.

'I promise.'

*

Buruu awoke beneath sweet, cool rain, and for a single, brilliant moment, he had no idea where he was. Just listening to the storm, feeling electricity dance on his skin, remembering the days when there had been nothing but this; the freedom of black cloud and rolling thunder and roaring wind beneath his wings.

His wings.

The metal creaked as he hauled himself to his feet, the stench of murder in his nostrils, the pain of talon and beak carved into his flesh. And then he felt warmth in his mind, a thunderous, gushing heat, and her arms were around his neck and her face pressed into his cheek, and she squeezed him so tightly it made her arms shake.

Gods, Buruu. You're all right.

APPARENTLY SO.

I love you so much.

He blinked, nuzzled close.

AND I YOU.

I thought I was going to lose you.

I THOUGHT YOU WERE ALREADY LOST.

Nothing is going to keep us apart again, you hear me? Not oceans, not storms, not armies. I'm by your side, always. I'll die with you, Buruu.

SUCH MELODRAMA, GIRL.

Don't be mean.

He smiled into her mind.

LET US HOPE IT DOES NOT COME TO THAT, THEN.

She held him for the longest time, saying nothing at all. And then she let him go, hand drifting to the hessian still bound to his back, shredded and bloodstained. Most of the satchels had been lost somewhere in the chaos of the past few days – in the attack or the crash or the bloody brawl here on broken black glass. Only one remained. He could feel the fear in her, the tremors in her fingers as she reached inside, hoping beyond hope. And then her fingers closed about it, drawing it forth, a miracle in lacquered wood. A shape as familiar to Yukiko as her own face. Her ninth birthday present.

'My tantō,' she breathed.

She had almost lost it. Just as she'd almost lost herself. In the hate. In the rage.

Walking to the island's edge, she stood there in the wind, him beside her, watching the ocean sway. In her right hand, she held the blade her father had given her when her brother died. A gift from the man who had given everything of himself to keep her safe. A man she hadn't truly mourned, whose loss had cut her too deep for tears. In her left, she held the sword Daichi had given her, naked and gleaming, the old man's call to cherish her anger, to fill the empty of her father's loss with fury. The storm howled about her as she stood as still as stone, and beyond the razored shore, Buruu could feel the sea dragons curling beneath black water, looking at her with glittering eyes, rolling with the breath of the waves.

He could feel it inside her. The weight of it all. The reality of what lay before her, the awareness of what she'd become, what she'd been. The grief she'd never given voice, allowing it to blacken and fester, like the cancer eating Shima's heart. The hate she'd clung to, thinking it would make her strong. That it would be enough. That it was all she needed.

She lifted the katana, made to hurl it towards the water, rid herself of the anger Daichi had named a gift. Blue-white lightning kissed the skies above, thunder giving her pause, a frozen silhouette with the blade hoisted above her head. She breathed deep for a lifelong moment, filled with the howl of lonely winds, finally lowering her arm and looking again at the blades in her hands. Strapping the scabbard to her obi, she sheathed the sword at her waist, the tantō beside it. Not one or another. Light and dark. Water and fire. Love and hate.

Together.

And then she turned and slipped her arms around his neck and cried until no voice remained of her grief. Until her body shook and her chest burned and there were no tears left inside her. Nothing but an old wound finally beginning to scab, and the memory of a man lifting her into his arms amidst a forest of swaying bamboo. Of lips pressed to her cheek. Of whiskers tickling her chin.

'*I will be with you,*' he'd said. '*I promise.*'

A memory that at last made her smile.

*

Buruu watched Yukiko and the gaijin fish around the metal dragonfly's belly until they found a heavy box the colour of dying leaves. The man made a triumphant sound, grinned like a fool. Yukiko pried it open, found it brimming with greasy wrenches and spanners and cutting torches; anything and everything required to repair the strange lopsided craft in the event of a crash.

And so Buruu sat and licked his wounds as Yukiko and the

gaijin beat his metal wings into shape as best they could, riveting the torn harness back together, bending and pounding the iridescent frame, straightening crumpled feathers and pinning them down with iron bolts. And though there was precious little grace left in Kin's contraption when they were done, Buruu flapped his wings and felt creaking, squealing lift beneath them, enough perhaps to return them to Shima.

To the war that awaited.

He dove off the promontory and soared out over the waves, the roaring storm beneath his wings, lover-sweet whispers in his ears. Lady Sun was reaching towards a new dawn, and Yukiko stood on the shore and screamed in triumph, hands in the air, a smile on her face that seemed to him as wide and as bright as summer skies.

Yukiko's howls finally roused the female from her coma, and she clawed her way to her feet, shaking side to side to rid herself of the rain's weight, wings spread in a broad fan, eyes still half-clouded with shock. Snow-white fur ran to scarlet in the breaking light, and she turned towards the pale warmth, wind caressing the feathers at her throat, the fur on her flanks, her stripes like black clouds across a sunset sky.

Just as magnificent as he remembered.

Yukiko reached towards Buruu, hand outstretched, eyes narrowed in concentration as she wrapped both him and the female up in the Kenning, drawing the pair of them into her thoughts. He could feel the wall of self Yukiko had built in her mind, pain crackling along its surface, seeping inside and making her wince. But still, despite the lingering ache, he felt a warmth and peace more comforting than any home he had ever known.

Yukiko spoke to the female, thoughts as gentle as mother's hands.

You're awake. Are you all right?

– I WILL LIVE, YŌKAI-KIN. –

The female looked at him across the gulf between then and now, tail switching, eyes narrowed, talons shredding the shale beneath her paws. He could feel her in the space Yukiko had created within the Kenning, a bitter, jagged heat in the corner of a blood-warm room, and as he spoke, she turned towards him, the sound of his thoughts echoing upon the walls.

HELLO, KAIAH.

She blinked, said nothing. Yukiko looked back and forth between them, wind blowing her hair about her face in sodden drifts, amazement in her eyes.

Wait, you two know each other?

The female snorted.

– KINSLAYER KNOWS NOTHING OF ME. I, TOO MUCH OF HIM. –

He could feel Yukiko's curiosity burning like fire. But brighter still was the need to get back to Shima, to see if there was any chance of stopping Hiro's wedding, to return to the people she knew were relying on her – the storm waiting for her to call its name.

Buruu should be able to fly now. We have to get back home.

– THEN GO. –

Will you come with us?

– WOULD DO THAT WHY? –

Because there's a war waiting for us. Because two thunder tigers are better than one.

– YOUR WAR MEANS NOTHING TO ME. SHIMA IS A WASTELAND. NOTHING WORTH FIGHTING FOR. –

Then why did you help me?

– DID NOT HELP YOU. HELPED THEM. –

Yukiko blinked, tilted her head.

Buruu and Skraai? You said they were—

– NOT THE MALES, MONKEY-CHILD. RAIJIN TAKE ME SHOULD I HELP THE KINSLAYER. –

Then who do you mean? Who is 'they'?

– YOU REALLY NOT KNOW? –

Kaiah looked at Buruu, disdain in her gaze, fur gleaming like fresh winter snow.

– CANNOT FEEL THEM, KINSLAYER? NOT HEAR THEM SCREAM WHEN THE MONKEY-MAN STRUCK HER BELLY? –

Realization dawned, a cold slap to his face, an understanding so bright he wondered how he didn't see it before. All of it . . .

All of it made sense now . . .

Yukiko's illness at the rising of the sun. Her moods, constantly shifting, like sand upon a windswept beach. The heat and light of the world growing along with her strength, her inability to shut it out. The amplification of the Kenning, her power doubling over the course of the last few months.

Yukiko looked at him, eyes bright with uncertainty.

No, not doubling.

Tripling.

YUKIKO . . .

What is she talking about?

– TELL HER. –

Tell me what? Who is they?

Buruu sighed, storm howling overhead, lighting reflected in the bottomless black of her eyes. The girl he loved more than anything in this world. The girl he would do anything to protect, to spare her even one more second of pain.

But he could not spare her this.

YUKIKO . . .

Oh, gods, no . . .

The sigh came from the heart of him.

YUKIKO, YOU ARE WITH CHILD.

She stared at him, mouth agape, hands moving slowly to her belly.

'Them'?

YES.

He nodded.

TWINS . . .

Yukiko sank to her knees, clutching her abdomen and staring at nothing at all. The gaijin knelt beside her, asking if she was well. She was pale as death, wide-eyed, fingers splayed on black glass as if the whole world were shifting beneath her.

Which he supposed, in a very real way, it was.

HELP ME WITH HER, KAIAH.

– SPEAK NOT TO ME. –

He looked at the islands around them, the spire of rusted copper, the nomad's corpse, skinned and bloody, the gaijin torn to ragged meat and food for worms. This place that lay days from the Everstorm. Riddled with monkey-children like fleas on a cur. Miles from the islands the arashitora called home. Why was she here at all? Why was she not . . .

WHY ARE YOU HERE INSTEAD OF WITH KOUU?

She stepped forward with a snarl, hackles raised.

– SPEAK HIS NAME AGAIN AND DIE. –

He looked down at Yukiko, shell-shocked on the stone, fingers pressed to her belly, mouth agape as she sucked in breath after heaving breath.

YOU RISKED YOUR LIFE TO SAVE THESE CHILDREN, NOT YET BORN.

Kaiah growled as he padded towards her.

WHY? MONKEY-CHILDREN MEAN NOTHING TO ARASHITORA.

– . . . –

WHY, KAIAH?

– *NO MORE YOUNGLINGS DIE. MONKEY-CHILD OR OTHER. NO NEWBORNS. NO UNBORNS. NEVER AGAIN.* –

WHERE ARE YOUR CUBS, KAIAH? WHERE IS YOUR MATE?

– *MUCH CHANGE AFTER YOU LEFT, KINSLAYER.* –

He sensed a terrible sorrow within the Kenning, a river running too deep for Kaiah to hide it all.

– *MUCH LOST.* –

TORR?

– *YES.* –

FATHER, SAVE US . . .

– *NOTHING TO SAVE US NOW.* –

COME WITH US. FLY WITH US.

– *WHY?* –

He nodded to Yukiko.

FOR THE TWO WITHIN HER. THE TWO YOU RISKED ALL TO SAVE. I CANNOT PROTECT THEM BY MYSELF.

– *IF CANNOT PROTECT, DO NOT FIGHT.* –

I GO WHERE SHE GOES. AND SHE WILL FIGHT UNTIL HER DYING BREATH.

Kaiah looked at the girl, something close to pity in her eyes. Waves crashed against the rocks, the roar and hiss of surf interwoven with the song of their father's drums. She looked up at the storm-torn fray, breathed the scent of salt and rust and blood.

I CANNOT DO THIS ALONE, KAIAH.

- TOLD YOU NO, KINSLAYER. -

She tossed her head, rain spraying from her feathers, ghosts in her eyes. They stared at each other as Lady Sun crept higher in the sky, just a smudge of light behind the rolling clouds in eastern skies. The dawn was almost as dark as the night had been. Almost as if Amaterasu had never bothered to rise from her slumber.

Yet she *had* risen, as she'd done every day before this, and would do every day until the ending of the world. And every now and then, as the clouds shifted across the eastern heavens, a ray of light would pierce the grey horizon; just a tiny moment of illumination, a heartbeat long. And in that brief second, the sunlight would catch the falling rain and turn it to a thousand diamonds, sparkling like the long-lost stars as they tumbled from the sky. It would catch the edges of the islands around them, slick with red ocean's kiss, dancing like flame on the edges of razors as Fūjin sang the song of the wind. Even here. Even now.

Even on the darkest day, the world could be beautiful. If only for a moment.

He could feel the little ones inside Yukiko – two tiny sparks of life, shapeless and bright, intertwined with her own heat. They pulsed, too formless to know true fear, but real enough to feel their mother's terror, shock, sorrow through the Kenning. The fear spilled into him, fear for them, for the one who carried them, for the beating, bleeding heart of his world.

He knew Kaiah could feel them too.

PLEASE.

Kaiah growled, deep in her throat, tail whipping side to side.

- NO. WILL NOT FIGHT FOR YOU. -

Buruu bowed his head, breathed deep, tasted defeat on his tongue. Nothing he could do. Nothing he could say. He could feel the ache in Kaiah's heart. The ache that drove her to this razored shore. A sorrow too vast to see the edges. Little ones. Precious ones. Loved ones.

Gone.

Taken.

Kaiah padded over to Yukiko, knelt on the stone before her. The girl looked up, swollen, trembling lips and frightened, blackened eyes. An age passed, there in the howling storm, the clawing wind, the driving rain, until at last, the thunder tiger leaned in close, pressed her head against Yukiko's belly, and listened.

The sun slipped out from behind the clouds.

Just for a moment.

– *BUT I WILL FIGHT FOR THEM.* –

And the rain about them turned to falling diamonds.

42

Pulse

Ka-chunk. Ka-chunk.

The rhythm of the tracks matched the one in his chest, the spectral pulse of the mechabacus inside his head. Kin watched the countryside spin by beyond the beach glass windows, miles upon miles of lotus fields, the towering six-legged figures of harvestermen cutting through the plants like they were made of smoke, drifting up into a scarlet sky.

The train was filled to bursting, mostly sararīmen and their families; mothers, fathers, children, all crammed together in their little metal shells and speeding down the lines towards the great capital of the Shima Shōgunate. The news that Kigen had reopened her rail yards to admit well-wishers for the Daimyo's wedding was received with buzzing excitement, and people from all over the country were descending on the Tiger capital to celebrate the holiday and catch a glimpse of the man who would be their new Shōgun.

Ka-chunk. Ka-chunk.

So handsome, were the whispers. So brave. A man who gave his sword arm in defence of Yoritomo-no-miya, who crushed the Inochi Riots almost single-handedly. A man who stepped forward at the hour his people needed him most and wrought order from chaos. A man worthy to marry the last daughter of Kazumitsu and usher in a new, golden age for this mighty nation.

Or so the wireless said.

Kin scowled, stared at the countryside beyond the glass, tried to block out the tinny voice piping in through the speakers. He wondered how many of the people around him actually believed the Guild broadcast. Packed in so tight they could hardly move, the smell and sweat and noise enough to make a person sick. And yet, still they came. To witness history. To be part of something. To escape the drudgery of their little lives for a heartbeat, pressing their faces against the glass, looking in at perfection they would never have.

At least there was one benefit to the cabins being so full – Kin didn't have to talk to the other Kagé. They were spread out along the train's length so as not to draw attention. Daichi and Kaori and two dozen others; as many fighters as they could spare without stripping the village of its defences. Kin knew Isao was amongst them, Takeshi and Atsushi too. But the boys kept their distance, and their stares and insults to themselves.

Ayane had spoken to him as they trekked through the forest to Yama city, his arm about her shoulders. Her voice had been no more than a whisper.

'*You did not tell Daichi-sama what happened, did you?*' *Anguish in her eyes.*

'*He won't care. But don't worry, Ayane. It's going to be good.*'

Ka-chunk. Ka-chunk.

'*It's going to be perfect.*'

He looked at the girl now as she stared out of the window beside him, wide, dark eyes reflecting the rolling green beyond, the grey wash of storm clouds above. She was pressed into the groove between seat and wall. A heavy cloak and a large straw hat strapped around her shoulders covered the swell of the silver arms at her back.

He recalled his meeting with Daichi, the hushed voices over the chessboard as he outlined the plan that would spell an end to everything. Kin almost felt pity when he looked into the old man's eyes, when he considered what was coming. He almost felt afraid of what it would mean. Where it would lead.

Almost.

Ka-chunk. Ka-chunk.

But he pictured Ayane curled bloody and beaten in the corner, the way she'd trembled for hours after the earthquake ended. The way she woke screaming in the night and stared at nothing at all until dawn lit the sky. And he realized that he'd known all along how this would end. The Inquisitors had shown him after all.

Thirteen years old. Breathing in sweet blue-black, the What Will Be laid out before him. A future that, try as he might, he now knew he could never escape. No matter how fast he ran. No matter how deep he dug. No matter how hard he prayed.

Ka-chunk. Ka-chunk.
Ka-chunk. Ka-chunk.
Ka-chunk. Ka-chunk.

*

Ayane refused to let go of his hand.

The Shadows stepped off the train at Kigen station, Kin among them, fading amidst the crowd and wreaths of fumes. The rail yard was a series of broad concrete platforms, stained beneath black rain, encircled by razor-wire fences and corroding boxcar skeletons. The majestic figure of the Phoenix's *Floating*

Palace loomed over Kigen like a second sun, the Dragon tall ships swaying in the blackened bay. The refinery could be heard in the distance; steam whistles and hissing smoke, boiling into the sunset sky.

Kin and the Kagé fighters moved swift through the streets, shadows within the throng. Kigen's citizens were already caught up in the festivities, the sounds of drunken revelry spilling from every saké bar, bedhouse and brothel in Downside. A royal wedding – even a hastily arranged one – would last several days. Tradition held that bride and groom would gather with family and friends to bid a ceremonial good-bye the eve before the ritual. Vows would be exchanged the following morning, just as the Sun Goddess crested the horizon.

Presuming, of course, nothing interrupted the occasion.

'You are well, Kin-san?' Daichi asked over his shoulder, his new walking stick clicking upon the cobbles.

'We're fine, Daichi-sama.'

'Stay close,' he rasped. 'The local Kagé may not look on you kindly.'

Kin glanced into Ayane's wide and frightened eyes.

'That will be a switch,' he muttered.

They doubled back several times to ensure nobody followed them, Kaori and the other Kagé splitting off on different routes. But eventually, they came to a grubby house in Downside's western slums, close to the pipeline. Daichi knocked four times, coughing, lifting his kerchief and spitting black on the cobbles, rubbing at his ribs. Kin watched the street around them, every beggar, every corner courtesan, every drunkard stumbling from a tavern or bar. Iron butterflies in his belly. Sweat on his palms, fingers entwined with Ayane's, her hand trembling.

The door opened, and a small, wiry woman motioned them

inside. She was dressed in dark cloth, hair tied in a single braid. She had no eyebrows, and the skin on her face was pink and shiny, as if she'd been recently scalded.

'Daichi-sama.' A low bow. 'You honour this house with your presence.'

'Grey Wolf.' Daichi covered his fist and bowed. 'This is Kin-san and Ayane-san.'

Kin felt like the old woman looked right through him.

'The Guildsmen . . .'

'I vouch for them,' Daichi said. 'They have risked more than most to be here tonight.'

The woman chewed at the inside of her cheek, turned and walked down a narrow hallway. The trio followed, Daichi limping hard, past a cluttered kitchen, corpse-rats strung up and bleeding over a cast-iron sink, descending twisting wooden stairs into the cellar. A broad oaken table dominated the space, spread with a map of Kigen city, the pieces from three or four different chess sets arranged across the labyrinthine streets. Kaori stood near the stairwell, speaking with a man the size of a small house. They were surrounded by dozens more people; young and old, men and women and children. As Daichi entered the room, everyone stopped and stared, placed palms over fists, eyes filled with unveiled adoration and relief.

'My friends,' the old man smiled. 'My brothers and sisters.'

'Father.' Kaori motioned to the big man beside her. 'This is Yukiko's friend, Akihito-san.'

'Daichi-sama.' The big man limped forward and bowed low. 'We heard you were wounded. It gladdens us all to have you with us.'

'Akihito-san.' Daichi clapped him on the shoulder, a fragile tremor in his voice. 'Yukiko-chan spoke of you often.'

'How is she? I'm surprised she's not here.'

Murmurs around the room. Nods of agreement.

'The Stormdancer is entangled in business to the north.' Kin noted Daichi phrased the statement so it wouldn't be an outright lie. 'I am certain we are in her thoughts. But it is not for her alone to pull this country back from the brink.

'When you place too much faith in one person, in me, in the Stormdancer, whomever, you lose sight of the power within yourself, my friends. Each of us must risk all. For each of us has as much to lose if we fail.' He coughed, wiped his knuckles across his lips. 'Everything.'

Daichi looked around the room, caught the eye of each man, woman and child. Kin saw uncertainty in them to match his own. Desperation. Even fear. They saw the old man's weakness. The new frailty. The walking stick. The hand pressed to battered ribs.

'Take heart, brothers and sisters,' Daichi said. 'You will tell your children you were here. Tonight, as we take one step closer to throwing off the chi-monger's yoke and freeing this nation once and for all. We bring the dawn after blackest night. We bring fire to all the dark places of the world. They say the lotus must bloom. We say it must burn.'

'Burn,' came the scattered reply, a soft murmur from a few uncertain voices.

Daichi licked his lips. Eyes like cold stone roaming the Kagé members.

'Say it again,' he said, his voice growing louder. 'The lotus must burn.'

More voices now. Stronger.

'Burn.'

Daichi shook his head, his voice harder still, steel ringing in his tone. 'Speak it as if your lives depended on it.'

Every voice in the room now, raised in unison. All save Kin and Ayane.

'Burn.'

Daichi was shouting now, drawing strength from them, they from him, a perfect circle of flame and will and rage. 'Say it as if you and you alone stood between this nation and utter ruin!'

'Burn!'

'The slavery of your children!'

'*Burn!*'

'The end of *everything* you know and love!'

'*BURN!*' they cried, roaring from the bottom of their bellies, fists clenched, teeth bared, spit flying. '*BURN!*'

'And that is *exactly* what we will do.' The old man nodded, surveyed the chess pieces on the map. Picking up a black empress, he placed it in the chi refinery. 'Burn it all. Right into the ground.'

Kin watched silently as the old man split the Kagé into groups; street ambushers, palace assault, bridge gangs. He watched the locals issue weapons; kusarigama sickles, iron tetsubo, staves, crude knives, even an old katana in a battered sheath for Daichi. Kerchiefs tied over faces, hats pulled low over narrowed eyes. Embraces and kisses of farewell, hands clasped, hollow bravado ringing in their laughter. He looked at the people around him, folk from every walk of life, united in their hatred of the thing he used to be.

The thing he could still try to run from.

Ayane pressed against him, hand still clasped in his.

Too late for that. Too late for all of it. The pieces were in place, moving towards confrontation, homemade chi-bombs clutched in their hands. To think they believed they had a chance. To think anyone here believed there could be a way out of this. To stand against the colossus of iron and smoke that even now would be stretching its limbs, gunning its motors, chainblades blotting out the moon.

There was no fighting it. Not this way. Against the Earth-crusher, this rabble had no chance at all . . .

'You're Yukiko's Guildsman.'

Kin blinked his way free of his reverie, focusing on the big man now standing in front of him. Akihito looked him up and down; a mountain carved in flesh, impassive face, massive arms folded across a barrel-broad chest.

'You were on the *Thunder Child*,' he said.

'I was,' Kin replied.

'They say you helped her escape. Built metal wings so the arashitora could fly her free.'

'I did.'

The big man stared hard, eyes as cold and black as flint. Kin felt other stares upon him, sweat tickling the back of his neck. Slowly, deliberately, Akihito extended one massive paw.

'Then you have my thanks. And I would call you friend.'

Kin glanced around the room, at the sharp stares and pursed lips, distrust hanging so thick in the air he could scrape it away with his fingernails. He looked back at the giant, down at the extended hand, tongue cleaving to his teeth.

'I'm not so sure you want a friend like me, Akihito-san.'

Daichi was standing near the map table, caught Kin's eye and motioned him closer, asking him to outline the refinery layout to the strike team one last time. Kin stepped away from the giant with an apologetic bow and looked at the assembled Kagé – the Shadow crew that would slip between the cracks and light a conflagration in the Guild's innards. Kaori would lead them, taking a dozen men into the refinery core and reducing it to cinders. The rest of the Kagé would disperse in the city, drawing out forces from chapterhouse and palace, making the Shōgun and Guild denude their stronghold defences to protect their streets.

Daichi would oversee the Shadow strike into the Tiger palace – just a swift handful, light as knives, stealing through the chaos and wresting the Lady Aisha from her wedding bed. Kin stared at the Kagé who would guard their general on the back lines, young and fierce as tigers. The faces of the boys who had tried to kill him. Who had hurt Ayane.

Isao. Atsushi. Takeshi.

Their distrust was palpable, stares drifting to the input jacks at his wrists, the pale slip of a girl behind. The legacy of her assault was still carved on their arms. Their vengeance written in her hollow, haunted eyes.

Daichi patted Kin's back; a show of endorsement, of faith despite it all. The way his father used to do in the workshop, in days before he dreamed of dissent or betrayal or revolution. Before he even knew what those words meant.

Kin unrolled a hand-drawn map of the refinery sewage system, took a dozen chess pieces and began to speak. He outlined approach. Breach. Security. Contingencies. Every nuance, every possible outcome. He took Kaori over the homemade chi explosives again and again, explaining in minute detail how to arm the devices and where they should be placed for optimum results.

'The explosion will be large enough to damage the refinery core and draw out their troops,' he said. 'But you need to place the charges in the catalyst tanks on level two. Anywhere further along the line, you risk setting off a reaction that could ignite the chi stores.'

'So?' Kaori said. 'The more damage we do, the better.'

'There are close to fifty thousand gallons of chi in those tanks. If they ignite, they take most of Kigen with them. You *must* hit the tanks on level two. Nowhere else.'

Kaori scowled. 'You should be coming with us. You know this pit better than anyone. This city is a bleeding scab, but I've no mind to blow it all to the hells.'

'I'm no warrior.' Kin shook his head. 'The battle with the oni should be proof enough of that. And believe me, you're going to need warriors inside. Even drawing out their forces, the refinery will still be crawling with Lotusmen. You're going to have to fight your way out.'

'Nevertheless, we could use you, Guildsman.'

Kin felt Ayane slide up behind him, press against his spine, slip her hand back into his. He remembered her sobbing in the dark.

The taste of her tears.

The echo of her voice.

'We don't belong here.'

'Just stick to the plan,' he said. 'I'll be of more use elsewhere.'

43

Not Falling

Michi sat alone in the dark, red candle burning in the window. Waiting for the *tickticktick* of the Guild drones, or the bushimen come to arrest her, or No One to arrive against all hope and deliver the forged key beneath her door.

But none of them came.

Night fell with no sign of her fellow conspirator, and her hopes began to fade. Unless she'd been discovered, No One would have found some way to get word to her. If she was compromised, she was probably in a torture cell right now, trying to keep Michi's name from spilling into the air along with her screams.

All around her, she could hear wedding preparations underway; servants running past her doorway, raised voices, distant music. She peered through her barred window, saw great amulets of red silk strung from the garden balconies, cooking smoke billowing from the kitchen doors, the children of some Fushicho noble playing with wooden swords in the garden. Would the Kagé let this happen? Would Yukiko? Surely they were on their way? In Kigen already? And she knew nothing of their plans.

Blind. Deaf. Dumb.

Gods, I feel so helpless.

She was trying to unscrew the bolts in the ceiling with her bare hands when she heard the *tickticktick* of a drone above her head, traversing the narrow spaces that had once been just another hallway to her and her fellows. She tried picking the lock on her door to no avail. And finally she punched the door frame, bloodying her knuckles, pacing her room like the tigers imprisoned in the palace grounds. Breath heaving. Heart pounding.

'Burn slow,' she whispered. 'Burn slow.'

But she couldn't. This was the moment everything hung in the balance. Not just the fate of the First Daughter, the Tora clan, Kigen city. This was the future of the entire country. The wedding would give new life to the dynasty that had enslaved Shima to the chi-mongers. Another monster on the throne. Another century of slavery, death and suffocating smoke.

She crouched in a corner, banging the back of her head against the wall, her hopes breathing their last. No One wasn't coming. She'd been discovered. They were undone, here, at the eleventh hour. Fists clenched. Mouth dry. So far away.

And then came a knocking at her door.

She looked up at the sound of a key in the lock, smoothing the hair from her face, wiping frustrated tears from her eyes. She stood, gritted her teeth, ready to go down fighting as the bushimen seized her. As good a place as any to die, she supposed. But they'd never take her alive. On her feet. Not crawling. Not falling. Never.

Never.

A figure stepped into the room, nodded to the bushimen outside, closed the door behind him. Smile upon his face. A large package in his arms.

'. . . Ichizo?'

'Hello, love.' He held up the package; a long box of scarlet card, set with a white, silken bow. 'I brought you a gift.'

She blinked. Standing motionless. He was dressed in a beautiful blood-red kimono embossed with roaring tigers. His hair was swept up in coils, pinned at his crown with four long golden needles, chainsaw katana and wakizashi crossed at the small of his back – a new luminary of his clan, arrayed in his finest. A golden breather was strapped across his mouth and jaw, fashioned like the maw of a snarling tiger. But the eyes above it were soft with concern.

'Have you been crying, Michi?'

'No, my Lord.'

'You look upset.'

'What are you doing here?'

He proffered the box, and she took it into her arms as if it might burst into flames.

'Open it.'

She looked at him for a long moment, mouth dry as grave soil. She was conscious of the iron keys at his obi. The chaindaishō at his waist. The bushimen outside the door. Placing the package on the bed, she untied the bow. Inside was a radiant jûnihitoe gown; twelve layers of beautiful scarlet and cream, embroidered with small tigers and tiny jewels, a broad obi of golden silk to match his own.

'I was hoping you would attend the feast tonight,' Ichizo said. 'As my lady.'

Her gaze drifted from the dress to his eyes. 'Why?'

'Because I love you, Michi-chan. With everything inside me. Every part of me.'

She simply stared, mute and unblinking.

'I brought you something else,' he said. 'Just in case.'

He proffered a smaller box, no bigger than the palm of his hand. As she took it, she heard something rattle inside. Even before she opened it, she knew what it was; pulling back the lid and tipping it into her own hand. A saucer, filled with blood-red wax, set with the impression of her room key.

No One had failed.

'We found this in your accomplice's home, along with a palace servant's uniform.' There was no anger in Ichizo's voice, just a wounded, wilting sadness. 'I need only say the word and the bushimen outside will step in here and drag you back to Kigen jail.'

'So do it.'

'I do not want that, Michi-chan.'

He stepped forward, put his hands on her shoulders, looked into her eyes. 'Your plot is undone. But I can protect you.'

'Why would you do that?'

'Because I love you. Godsdamn me for a fool, but I do. And I look into your eyes and know some part of you loves me too.'

'I . . .'

'I am a good man, am I not? Have I ever treated you ill? Done anything but care for you? Even now I betray my oaths, my very blood to keep you safe. I love you, Michi.'

Too good to be true . . .

'I don't believe you,' she said.

'What do I gain from doing this? And what do I lose?'

'You're lying.' Michi shook her head. 'You want me to betray the others. Give away the location of the stronghold. Identities of the city cell—'

'I don't care about your rebellion!' His voice was a fierce whisper, and he glanced at the doorway, the bushimen just beyond. 'I don't *care* about the throne or the dead man who would sit on it. I don't care about *any of that*. We can run away once the wedding is done. You and I. As far as we want. I have money, I have favours. We can leave all this behind us.'

Michi said nothing, lips parted, struggling to breathe.

'Tell me you do not love me,' Ichizo said. 'Tell me you do not feel *something*.'

'I . . .'

He tore the breather from his face, seized her wrists.

'Look me in the eyes and tell me you do not feel what I do. When you feel my lips on yours. When you whisper my name in the dark. Tell me there is *nothing* between us.'

She felt tears spilling down her cheeks. Lower lip trembling. Hands shaking as he searched desperately within her eyes. She opened her mouth to speak, but no words would come, and her face crumpled like someone had kicked it in.

'Don't cry . . .'

He kissed her eyelids, one after another, the same way he'd done when first he said 'I love you.' Hands pressed to her cheeks, gentle as feathers.

'I know you,' he whispered. 'Who you really are. You're not a traitor. You're not a Shadow. You are my lady. You are my love.'

She fell into his arms, mouth seeking his, hot with the flush of her tears.

'You are my love . . .'

She tasted salt as their lips touched, his body against hers. And in that brief pin-bright moment, she saw everything she thought she'd never have. A life spent in peace, far from blackened shores. A good man to share it with; a man who'd risked everything to be with her, who loved her more truly than Daichi or Kaori or Aisha ever would. A glimpse of happiness she'd long ago given up any hope of holding, here, now, in her arms, if only she could find the words to speak it.

She pressed her hands to his cheeks, running her fingers through his hair, breathing the words into his mouth.

'I'm sorry, Ichizo . . .'

Fingers around the golden needle holding his hair in place.

Slipping it free, quick as flies.

'I truly am . . .'

Sliding it up under his ear, behind the curve of his skull and into his brain. Her mouth over his to smother the gasp, the feeble, choking cry as his eyes opened to the sight of hers looking back at him, filled with tears. And his legs gave way and she caught his weight, lowering him twitching onto the bed. The mattress creaked beneath him as she pulled the needle free, leaving a tiny spot of blood on his skin.

'But I am not your lady,' she whispered. 'And I am not your love.'

She slipped the needle into his heart, just to be sure. A fool's heart, to love a girl who'd abandoned the very idea of it, too long ago now to remember.

'I am Kagé Michi.'

*

The key turned and the door opened wide.

The girl was dressed in a beautiful jûnihitoe, all scarlet and cream and smooth, smooth skin. Her face was powdered white, thick kohl rimmed about her eyes, a vertical stripe of cherry-red paint on her lips. She was facing to the left of the door, smiling, bowing from the knees.

'Thank you, my Lord,' she said.

The four bushimen straightened, waiting for Magistrate Ichizo to appear behind her. The girl stepped into the hallway, tiny steps hobbled by the gown's hem, and her feet caught upon the threshold. With a small cry she lost her balance, pitched forward. Two bushimen stepped up to catch her and she straightened, arms extended, driving hair needles up under their chins before either could blink.

Quiet gurgles. Stupefied expressions. Men dropping like stones.

The other two guards cried out, hefted their nagamaki; four-foot blades of polished steel with hafts of equal length, far too long to wield in the narrow corridors of the servant's quarters. And Michi drew two more of the long, glittering needles from her hair and stepped between them, whirling as if she danced, burying one into each man's eye.

This is what I am.

The bushimen hit the boards like lead, limp and breathless, armour ringing on polished pine like iron bells tolling the changing of the hours. The air was stained with the stink of blood and urine. She lifted her chin, closed her eyes and breathed deep.

This is where I belong.

Scanning the corridor, she grabbed each corpse and dragged it into her bedroom, struggling with the weight. Blood wiped from the floorboards with a scarlet tabard, staining golden tigers red. Hefting one of the nagamaki, she rucked up the outer layer of her jûnihitoe and slit the eleven layers underneath, all the way up to her thighs. She wiped the needles clean, reinserted them into her hair, staring at her reflection in the looking glass. Finally the face of the girl she knew – the vacuous, servile mask torn away and left bleeding on the floor.

In the distance she heard a low roar, a rumbling that shook the earth. Looking through her tiny window, she saw flames lighting the sky, daubed upon the clouds in clumsy, orange strokes. She heard faint cries. Iron bells. Running feet. Looking around the room at the bodies, slowly cooling, these men who had thought her a mouse. A fool. A whore.

She smiled.

And picking up the box Ichizo had brought her, now lighter than it had been before, she stepped into the corridor and locked the door behind her.

44

The Hammer Falls

There comes a point where the bite of cracked ribs amidst every breath, the searing kiss of salt in fresh wounds, or the throb of bamboo shards beneath your fingernails makes you want to sing. Where any absence of new pain feels for one delirious moment like the greatest gift you've ever received, and it seems you should blubber thanks through swollen lips at the men who've stopped hurting you, if only for that wonderful, shining moment. Where the thought of one more blow, one more second of fresh agony becomes so terrifying you'll say anything, do *anything* to avoid it.

But the boy wasn't there yet.

'Whoresons.' Bloody drool spilled over his lips, gathering below his chin to drip onto the floor. 'Whoresons, the both of you.'

Seimi stepped into the dim light, licking the yellowed rubble lodged in his gums. The yakuza's face was calm, spotted with stray flecks of blood.

'How did you know where the money was being taken?' His tone was that of a man asking for the daily specials, or directions to the sky-docks. 'How did you know where we were moving it?'

'You father told me.' A ragged, bubbling gasp. 'When he was done swallowing.'

Seimi grinned, sipped a cup of red saké with rock-steady hands. Hida stood by the doorway, arms folded, scratching at one cauliflower ear. A lukewarm bottle of liquor sat on a table beside a collection of tools; a hammer, pliers, tin snips, blades of varying lengths. A stained rag. A handful of bamboo slivers. Five bloody toenails.

The boy was naked save for his trousers, wrists bound with thick rope, suspended from a hook in the ceiling just long enough for his toes to touch concrete. His ankles were chained to the floor, a lonely globe casting a circle of pale light on bloodstained ground.

Seimi hefted the hammer. Its claw-head was dull, rusted iron, the wooden handle grubby and unfinished. He patted his palm with the business end and sat crossed-legged in front of the boy, smiling up into swollen eyes.

'Where's your friend? The one with the iron-thrower?'

'Your mother's house.'

'What's his name?'

'She's never asked. She doesn't talk with her mouth full.'

Seimi looked over his shoulder and smiled at Hida, shook his head. He grasped the boy's ankle with his left hand, lifted the hammer with his right. The boy curled his toes up instinctively, breath coming quicker. Teeth gritted. Muscles taut. Sweat rolling through the bloodstains and glazing his lips a watery red.

Seimi slammed the hammer down on his smallest toe.

The sharp crack of metal on flesh, the wet scrunch of splintering bone. Seimi felt the impact through the floor, heard the boy scream through clenched teeth. He closed his eyes, listened to the wail trail off into silence as the boy's breath ran out, the sharp intake of oxygen into empty lungs, the whimper bubbling over split lips.

'How did you know where the money was being taken?' He lifted the hammer again, stared up into glistening tears. 'How did you know where we were moving it?'

'You cowards. Miserable, gutless—'

The hammer fell again. The scream became a roar, the open-mouthed howl of a wounded animal. The boy thrashed against the ropes, sawing skin raw, head flailing, muscles stretched, tendons standing out sharp in his throat. His face was red, tears streaming down his cheeks.

'I'm g-gonna kill you.' Teeth clenched. Spittle flying. '*Fuck* you!'

Seimi's voice was heavy as a brick in a wriggling burlap bag, cold as the river water it was tossed into.

'No, little boy. Those nights are done. It's us fucking you now.'

He brought the hammer down.

Again.

And again.

When Seimi stood and picked up the pliers, he saw Hida turn and leave the room without a sound. He had to stop halfway through his routine to get more saké. There were threats and pleas, showers of bloody spit, brief periods of unconsciousness ended with handfuls of salt. The smell of burning hair. The sound of snipping. And clipping. And screams. Big and bright and beautiful.

But finally, the boy arrived.

That blessed place, where the absence of new pain is the greatest of all gifts. And the man who stays his hand, even for a heartbeat, becomes the god at the heart of your world.

And at last, in that wonderful, shining moment, he sang.

45

Ten Thousand Years

Lord Hiro stood at the head of the table, staring down the length of polished oak to his legion of guests. The feasting hall was decked in scarlet silk, paper blooms, bright lanterns hanging from the rafters, talismans of joy and fortune on the walls. A small army of serving girls moved among the celebrants, soft pink kimonos, arms decked with platters of steaming saké and real fruit juices, filling every glass. The Phoenix retinue knelt at Hiro's right, a swathe of sunburnt yellow and flameburst orange, Daimyo Shin and Shou sitting so close they touched. The Dragons were arrayed at his left, decked in bright azure and silvered iron, Daimyo Haruka looking dour and out of sorts.

'Your fiancée will not be joining us for the feast, Hiro-san?' the old Dragon asked.

Hiro glanced at the empty cushion beside him. He tried to smile, felt the ashes caked on his face crack and flake away. His voice was toneless. Formless.

'We beg your pardon, honourable Haruka-san. My beloved Aisha-chan is unnerved by the thought of the ceremony tomorrow, and bids me ask your indulgence. A bride can be forgiven her anxieties on the eve of her wedding, surely.'

Haruka looked to his own wife, nodded slowly. 'As you say. I recall the eve of my own betrothal. It is no small thing, to be bound to another for the rest of one's life.'

Lord Shou glanced at Hiro, the death-clad legion of Iron Samurai looming behind him.

'No matter how short that life may prove . . .' he muttered.

Hiro raised his cup, tapped one finger on the lip to call for silence. He looked to Second Bloom Kensai and his Lotusman retinue, seated at the far end of the table with empty plates and empty glasses, swathed in chi exhaust. The nobles of his own court assembled in all their finery, golden breather masks fashioned like tiger maws, pale, powdered faces and silk of bloody red. All of it so gaudy. So hollow and meaningless. He noted two empty cushions, consternation creasing his brow as he realized who was missing.

Where is Ichizo?

'Esteemed guests,' he began, speaking as if by rote. Metal in his mouth. 'Brothers of the Lotus Guild. Noble Daimyo and trusted friends. I am humbled and honoured to receive you on this, the eve of my wedding, and bid you welcome to the Tiger's palace.'

where once she lay in my arms
she who laid me low
she

'The thought of vengeance ever hangs in my mind, fills me with a thirst no cup can slake. The loss of this court's most favoured son hangs heavy on my shoulders, even in this time of . . .' he swallowed, ash-dry '. . . joy. And bound by oaths, we gather tonight, our mourning black shed but weeks ago. Though were my Lord Yoritomo-no-miya here—'

The ground rumbled, a low, furious vibration beneath his

feet, setting the tableware clinking, the lanterns in the rafters swaying. Hiro frowned, voice faltering, thinking another accursed earthquake had struck at this, of all hours. One of the guests gasped, eyes to the hall's high beach glass windows. Following her gaze, Hiro looked up into a night sky smeared with the colour of flame. Uneasy murmurs rippled among the attendees, serving girls glancing to each other with fearful eyes, stares turning to him at the table's head. Second Bloom Kensai stood, swift despite his bulk, his skin hissing. Brass fingers danced across the mechabacus on his chest, like a prodigy upon a shamisen's strings.

'Great Lord. Kigen city is under attack by Kagé rebels.'

Gasps and murmurs among the guests. A thrill of adrenaline in his gut. Iron hand snaking to the hilt of his chainkatana.

'Yukiko?'

'There is no sign of the Impure one, great Lord. Reports indicate multiple groups, striking with explosives through Docktown and Downside.'

'Honourless dogs,' Daimyo Haruka spat. 'They dare break peace on a night such as this?'

The Dragon clanlord stood swiftly, his retinue of Iron Samurai gathered about him. The Phoenix Daimyo stood with more languor, moving with that eerie synchronicity, narrowed eyes above ornate breather fans. Their retinue gathered and clung to them like painted leeches.

'Steel yourselves,' Hiro said, his voice rising above the growing clamour. 'This attack is a blessing. That these fools have dared enter Kigen on a night when my brother Daimyo are gathered with their hosts can be viewed as no less than providence. Lord Izanagi has surely blessed these celebrations and our vengeance. The fish have brought themselves to our nets.' He drew his chainkatana, arced the motor, vibration travelling up the iron in his arm and into his flesh. 'We need only gather them in.'

Haruka drew his chaindaishō, serrated teeth whirring and snarling. The Dragon Samurai about him did the same, the screech and growl of motors filling the air.

'We will defend First Daughter's city with our lives,' Haruka said. 'This I vow.'

The Phoenix clanlords turned to Hiro.

'We will return to the *Floating Palace*,' Shou said. 'Coordinate the assault from the sky, set our corvettes to the task of routing these rebels from their dens.'

'We place our personal retinue at your service, of course, Daimyo,' said Shin.

Hiro glanced at the ceremonial swords in the Phoenix lords' obi, the painted lips and powdered cheeks, the soft hands with manicured nails, utterly bereft of sword-grip callouses.

'An excellent notion. My thanks, honourable Daimyo.'

He turned to his Shikabane captain. 'Muster the Dead. Every man is to be ready to march in five minutes. Kensai.' He turned to the Second Bloom. 'Gather your Purifiers, any Lotusmen you can spare. We will purge these lice with purifying flame.'

'It shall be done.' Kensai bowed. 'Shōgun.'

All in the hall took note of the title. The three other clanlords shared knowing glances.

Hiro licked his lips, tasted ashes. 'You are charged to kill any Kagé you find on sight. If Yoritomo-no-miya's assassin dares show her face, I will offer substantial reward to any man who brings me her thunder tiger's head. But the girl herself is mine. Any man who kills that Impure whore robs me of my vengeance, and he shall know vengeance in kind. Is that understood?'

'Hai!' A cry from the legion of Samurai around the room,

underscored by the revving of chainblade motors, the clank and hiss of ō-yoroi.

'Draw your swords then, brothers. Draw your swords and march with me. Tonight, we restore our honour, and strike a blow that will live in the histories for ten thousand years. Tonight, we end this rebellion once and for all.'

'*Banzai!*' they cried. '*Banzai!*'

Hiro nodded.

'We move.'

46

One Hundred Degrees

A blossom of orange flame unfurled in the nighttime hush, a tiny sun daubing the chapterhouse walls in colours of the distant dawn. Long shadows stretched out from the sudden flare, dancing across splintered cobbles as the fire took hold. The night above was already choked and black – no winking stars, no weeping moon. Great billowing curtains of smoke rushed up to kiss the dark; a sweating, autumn evening overhung with the threat of storms.

The flames rose from burning barrels, stacked high on a wooden wagon outside the chapterhouse gates. Desiccated wood crackled amongst tongues of bright heat, sparks spiralling upwards like long-gone fireflies. A siren screamed inside the chapterhouse; a brittle, metallic wail rising over the fire's roar. A knot of blacklung beggars across the street curled down in their filthy rags and winced at the volume.

The great metal doors split apart with a squeal of dry hinges, just wide enough to allow four Guildsmen to march out into the firelight. Heat flickered across their atmos-suits; burnished brass dipped in flickering ochre. Insectoid helms, bio-mechanical lines of cold metal and snaking pipes, large tanks mounted on their backs. Three Shatei and a Kyodai captain, all wearing the white tabards of the Purifier Sect.

The Kyodai's eyes glowed blood-red as it scanned the street. The Shatei stepped forward, holding their hands towards the fire as if to warm them. Gouts of frothing white foam burst from their outstretched palms, engulfing the awning, wagon and broken barrels. Light and heat suffocated in the flood, leaving only charred wooden skeletons spattered in hissing foam, trailing clouds of reluctant smoke in the ember light.

The Shatei examined the wreckage under the frightened stares of the beggar-folk across the way. A few of the bolder wretches crept forward, watching the Purifiers stomp the last sparks beneath their boots. The Kyodai spoke, its voice a wasp-hive hymn.

'Accelerant?'

A Shatei knelt amidst the charcoal, looked up at its big brother. 'Chi.'

The Kyodai clicked several beads across the mechabacus on its chest. It stared around the street, luminous, bloody eyes coming to rest on the beggars creeping closer. They were swathed head to foot in dirty rags, black fingernails, scabbed knuckles. The closest one was a giant, only a few feet away and shuffling forward, limping slightly.

'Stay back, citizen.' Fire flared at the Purifier's wrist. 'This is Guild—'

The man hurled a clay bottle, filled with thick, sloshing red. It smashed on the Purifier's chest, coating its atmos-suit, and with a dull *whump,* burst into flame as it touched the fire burning at its wrist. The other beggars hurled more bottles, clay smashing on the stone at the Guildsmens' feet, across their suits, painting them with gleaming scarlet. A thunderous rush of heat, roaring around the four Guildsmen and withering the spaces between. The stench of burning chi rose amidst the sound of rasping curses, the Guildsmen staggering away and turning on each other with their foam, dousing the flames with gouts of hissing white.

A motor-rickshaw tore down the street, wheels screeching. It collided with two Purifiers, crushed one against the chapterhouse wall in a bright burst of sparks. The chi tank at the Guildsman's back split and exploded, the 'shaw's driver rolling out of the cabin just as the vehicle's snout burst into flame.

The beggars threw aside their black rags and drew weapons from within the folds, bearing down on the two remaining Guildsmen. The Kyodai raised its hand, skin still black and smoking, screeching a warning as the big man rushed it with his war club raised high.

Akihito pictured Kasumi lying in a puddle of blood on the floor of Kigen jail. He pictured Masaru's name etched upon a hundred spirit tablets around the Burning Stones. He pictured Yoritomo's face atop the burnished brass shoulders.

The Purifier's helm split at the seams, one glowing red eye spinning off into the dark, a leaden *whunggggggg* ringing out as the tetsubo connected. Wet crunching. A metallic rasp. The Purifier fell back, hands to its shattered face. Metal hit stone and it cried out, the sound all too human; a moan of fear and pain.

'No.' It held up its hand. 'Don't, wait—'

The tetsubo crashed down on the Kyodai's head, the crack of metal on metal ringing down the street. Akihito hefted the club, bringing it down onto the Guildsman's helm again. And again. And again. Until the faceplate buckled and the light in its eye cracked and died and thick red bubbled between the broken seams. The Kyodai twitched once and was still.

'Come on!'

The other Kagé had dispatched the remaining Purifiers, the fuses in the back of the still-burning motor-rickshaw were already lit. They grabbed Akihito's arm and tugged the big man away from his kill. Heavy metal footsteps could be heard beneath the wailing siren within the chapterhouse; a multitude approaching fast. The street was strewn with broken metal bodies, lit by the rickshaw fire, black, acrid smoke burning his throat and scratching at his eyes.

He nodded. Smiled.

The Kagé disappeared amongst the shadows.

*

An explosion tore across Downside, a bright bloom of flame lighting the clouds over Chapterhouse Kigen, smoke rushing skywards like a new bride into the arms of her groom. Daichi looked at the firelight sky, counting beneath his breath, one, two, three, and ah, there it went. A second explosion to the east, then a third; three dry-docked sky-ships bursting into flame and sinking slowly onto Spire Row, draping the boardwalk with burning skeletons. The Docktown fuel depot went up ten seconds later, and it seemed for a moment the sun had risen early, great feathered hands of fire stretching forth over the warehouse district, hard shadows and roiling smoke, screams of fear and pain, the reverb settling inside his bones. The night was filled with the drone of sky-ship propellers, Phoenix corvettes buzzing and slicing overhead, the belly of the *Floating Palace* lit with the lurid glow of Kigen's growing pyre.

Daichi put one hand to his mouth and coughed. Licked his teeth and spat. Hand pressed to tortured ribs, more bruise than skin beneath the bandages. Every breath was fire. Every word a trial. His speech to the Kagé had taken almost everything he had.

They were settled on the upper floor of a town house with a perfect view of the Shōgun's palace, waiting for the tigers to leave their den. Ayane knelt at a small table, head tilted, listening the chatter of the mechabacus in her head. The device hung around her neck, plugged into the jack at her collarbone, the beads chittering back and forth across her breast. Dirt still clung in the crevices, fingerprints of rust on the faceplate from its slumber beneath damp earth, a slight scratch from the shovel used to dig it free. She would lean close to the boy beside her, lips brushing his ear, and Kin would relay the incoming data about troop movements, numbers, disposition to the Kagé in the field via the shortwave transmitter on the table before him. There was intimacy to the pair, kneeling so close they almost touched – a kind of symbiosis Daichi found unsettling.

He could hear bells ringing, heavy feet, shouted orders. A cadre of Guild mercenaries spilled from the chapterhouse and stormed east over the Shiroi bridge, dozens more heading south to bolster the refinery defences. Firelight gleamed on their night-filter goggles and bulbous helms, like a hundred scarab beetles ready for war. Bushimen were taking position on the bridges, motor-rickshaws roaring through the streets, Iron Samurai mustering in the palace grounds. The fire spread across Docktown as the timber boardwalk caught and burned, cutting off access to most of the dry-docked Tiger fleet. Daichi smiled up at the black storm clouds overhead and whispered a prayer to Susano-ō, begging the Storm God to show his blessing to Lord Hiro's wedding and withhold the rain for just one more day.

'It's incredible,' Isao whispered.

The boy stood near the window, face lit with the flames, watching in awe as Kigen's peaceful facade began to blacken and curl.

'The music of chaos,' Daichi said. 'From a distance, it is beautiful. But consider for a moment how it would appear to an ordinary man down there in the street. Drenched in the sound of flame. Of fear. For yourself and the ones you love.'

He looked at the boy.

'Take no pride in this discord we now sow. It is an easy thing, to destroy. Be proud of the world you build after this is done.'

The old man coughed then, a long, wracking spasm that bent him double, one hand over his mouth, the other on his belly. His face twisted with the ache of it, teeth gritted, finally spitting black and viscous onto the boards beneath their feet. He wiped one hand across his mouth, turning his knuckles the colour of burnt oil. Isao placed a hand on his shoulder, expression pained.

'You should head outside and keep . . . watch with Atsushi and Takeshi. We will signal the strike on the palace after . . . the refinery is ablaze.'

'Hai.' The boy nodded, covered his fist, and stole down the stairwell.

Daichi turned to the pair who remained behind. The girl watching him, nervous hands and sunken eyes, machine chattering on her chest. Kin beside her, head down, stare locked with his. The boy looked old, worn thin, the skin on his bones almost translucent. Expressionless.

'Can you . . . feel it, Kin-san?'

'I feel it,' the boy replied.

Daichi turned back to the window, to the fire burning beyond the glass. He coughed once, hand over his mouth, watching the dancing flames.

'It has begun,' he said.

*

The Kagé dropped like falling leaves into the alley, flitted down cracking cobbles without a sound. Each wore black, only their eyes showing between cloth folds, straight-edged swords upon their backs. Kaori led them onto the levee, crouched low, eyes on the stone bridge crossing the river fifty feet away. Behind her crouched a lieutenant of the local cell; a thin, pock-faced man known as the Spider, who moved like wisps of clouds across moonlight.

The waters of the Junsei river were thick as mud, jet-black, reeking of excrement and caustic salt. Twelve shadows slid down the concrete bank and waded into the flow, quietly as they might. The sounds of flames and bells and marching boots masked the splashing and cursing, the smell growing so bad one man was forced to stop and tread water while he vomited.

They made the southern shore, crawled along the waterline until they reached the refinery outflow pipe; a four-foot-wide tunnel barred by a corroded iron grill. Reeking effluent dribbled between its rusted teeth. Kaori crouched at the tunnel mouth, drew a hacksaw and set to work on the corroded spot-welds. The Spider and the others gathered about her, crouched low, eyes never leaving the bushimen on the bridge.

Two dozen children were gathered on the northern banks, hurling stones and bottles at the guards. Kaori recognized the leader; a girl with the handle of Butcher, her shrill voice ringing across the water, rife with profanities that would make a cloudwalker gasp. She smiled, despite herself.

A sky-ship thundered overhead, the blast from its prop-blades whipping ash into her eyes. Speakers mounted on the ship's flank bellowed a warning for all law-abiding citizens to return to their homes, bright spotlights aimed at the gaggle of dissent near the footbridge. The children turned their rocks and bottles on the sky. Phoenix corvettes buzzed and dodged, letting off a few warning bursts of shuriken-thrower fire.

On a quieter night, the saw blade's rasp would have brought every bushiman in the city running, but it was lost beneath the engine's din. Kaori pulled a corroded bar away from the cross-piece, the space just narrow enough to squeeze through. She motioned the others forward, and one by one, the Kagé wriggled through the gap, down into near-darkness and a deathly chemical reek. Kaori found herself alone on the bank, slipping her wakizashi off her back and sparing one last glance to the clouds above. Rolling black, illuminated with thick fingers of firelight and floodlights from the shouting sky-ships.

She could smell it on the wind above the river's stench; the faint perfume of smoking timber and spice, the sharp tang of chi burning in the Docktown warehouses, spitting from the power units of the Iron Samurai marching to defend them.

The music of chaos.

Smiling, she turned and crawled into the black.

47

Crescendo

In years to come, Hana would remember the night the Kagé attacked Kigen city as one of the darkest in her life. Not the worst. Not by far. But dark enough to leave a scar that would never truly heal.

There she stood, just at the beginning of it, unaware of what lay coiled and waiting in the hours ahead. She could hear the crowds outside their apartment walls, the clash of steel, the war-drum rhythm of running feet. Yoshi was crouched in a corner, iron-thrower in hand. She hovered by the window, peering into the charcoal haze, the flickering glow of growing flames reflected on the goggles strapped across her brow.

Sick with fear. Hands shaking. Somehow, some tiny part of her sensing the tremors of the incoming hurt. And as the dread rose up inside her, a slick, ice-cold bellyful, so too did the memory. Just like always.

The pain of it. The taste of it. In a life full of awful, crushing days, the yardstick by which all days would be measured.

The Worst Day of Her Life.

It began like every other. Rising with the sun, washing in brackish water and slipping into threadbare, third-hand clothes. Hana shuffled to the kitchen, cold rice leftovers serving as breakfast. Yoshi sat opposite, told her a dirty joke he'd heard in town that made her spit a mouthful all over the table. He couldn't laugh with her, much as he wanted to; the inch-long split in his lip was still healing. The bruise under his eye was a toxic, sickly yellow, knuckles torn with the pattern of Father's teeth.

Funny thing was, Da had never laid a finger on her.

She could never figure out why. He beat their mother until she couldn't walk. Beat Yoshi like he was a pillow. But not once in her entire life had he ever raised his hand to her.

Not his little flower. Not his Hana.

It was autumn, and their pitiful lotus crop had already been stripped of blooms for the chi refineries. The ground was in terrible shape; blackening and beginning to crack in the worst of it. They stayed well away from the charred soil as they worked – Hana had tripped and fallen onto the dead ground the previous summer, spent an entire week vomiting and delirious, weeping black tears. The temperature was scalding, and the siblings were exhausted and filthy by sunset, creeping back to the house like kicked dogs slinking to their master's feet.

The table was set with cracked plates and a posy of dried grass. Their father knelt at the head, already halfway into his bottle, cheeks and nose aglow with broken capillaries. The stump where his right hand used to be was unwrapped, shiny and pink. Medals hung on the wall behind him, remnants of an old life, gleaming like seashells on a deserted beach. Trophies for the hero; the lowborn Burakumin translator who saved the lives of seventeen Kitsune bushimen. A platoon of blooded clansmen saved by the heroism of a clanless dog.

Their mother stood in the tiny kitchen, boiling rice with some seasoning she'd scrounged from gods knew where. Pale skin, vacant blue-eyed stare, black ink under her fingernails from when she'd last dyed her hair.

Just another trophy for the hero.

Hana washed up, knelt to await the meal in silence. The fear was there, always, hovering in the back of her mind. She listened to her father pour another shot, shadows in the room growing longer, the darkness at the head of the table slowly deepening. A weight sat on her shoulders, the question always hanging in the air waiting to be answered.

What will set him off tonight?

Yoshi knelt opposite her, shappo on his head, tied beneath his chin. He'd won the hat from a city boy in a game of oicho-kabu three days ago and he was terribly proud of it, strutting in front of her like an emerald crane in a courting dance, laughing as hard as split lips would let him.

'Take that thing off,' their father growled.

Here it comes.

'Why?' Yoshi asked.

'Because you look like a damned fool. That's a man's hat. It's too big for you.'

'Aren't you always telling me to be a man?'

No. Don't push it, Yoshi.

'I think he looks very handsome.'

Mother smiled as she placed a pot of steaming rice on the table. Tired blue eyes, full of love, crinkled at the edges as she stared at her son. Her Little Man.

Father glanced at her, and Hana saw the look on his face. Her heart sank into her belly, tongue cleaving to the roof of her mouth.

'What the hells would you know?'

Clenched teeth. A spray of spittle.

Oh, gods . . .

Mother turned paler still, bottom lip quivering. She took a half-step back, terrified and mute. To say anything at that point would be making it worse – to beg or apologize, even to whimper. As helpless as a field mouse in the shadow of black wings.

Da snatched up the saké bottle in his good hand, knuckles white as he rose to his feet.

'You worthless gaijin whore, I said what would you know?'

And just like that, just for that, he swung.

Hana saw the bottle connect with her mother's jaw, time slowing to a crawl, watching the spray of red and teeth. She felt something warm and sticky splash onto her cheek, saw her father's face twisted beyond reason or recognition. Screaming he should have left her there, in her accursed homeland with her bastard people, and he flourished the stump where his sword hand had been and roared.

'Look what they took from me!' Face purpling, skin taut and blood-flushed. 'Look at it! And all I have to show for it is you!'

He loomed over their mother, and for the first time in as long as she could remember, Hana saw rage burning in those brilliant blue eyes.

'You pig.' Mother's words were slurred around her broken jaw. 'You drunken slaver pig. Do you know who I am? Do you have any idea what I was?'

Spit on his lips as he raised the bottle again. 'I know what you're going to be . . .'

Yoshi opened his mouth to yell, rising from his knees, hands outstretched.

The bottle fell, a long, scything arc ending in her throat and a spray of blood, thick and hot and bright. And Hana did what any thirteen-year-old girl would have done at that moment.

She started screaming.

*

Explosions tore across the night, dragging Hana from her reverie, back into the world beyond the window glass. She saw the harbour was ablaze, firelight spray-painted across southern skies. Great walls of black cloud rumbled and crashed above the city, the smell of burning chi entwined with the growing promise of rain.

'Izanagi's balls,' Yoshi shook his head. 'Someone's riled about not getting invited to the Shōgun's wedding . . .'

Hana tried to shake off the dread, closed her eye, frowned. 'I can't see much. Can't feel many rats around.'

'Fire is making the little ones nervous. Big ones are opening shop on a fresh corpse two blocks north. Dinnertime.'

Hana left her vantage point near the window, knelt by the table, rocking a little, back and forth. She stared at Yoshi's straw hat, at the jagged, broken-bottle cut running through the brim. Refusing to remember.

'Where the hells is this boy?' Yoshi hissed.

'Maybe we could go look for him?'

'You fixing to go outside in all this?'

'Jurou's been gone all day, Yoshi. Aren't you worried?'

'Safe to say.'

Yoshi chewed a fingernail, falling mute. Hana looked towards the window again.

'Gods, it sounds like the whole city's coming apart . . .'

She reached out again with the Kenning, felt dozens of tiny sparks converging to the north. She could feel their hunger, taste their stink at the corners of her mouth. She reached towards

Daken, prowling western rooftops, just on the edge of word-range.

There's a group of rats north of the hotel.

... *so* ... ?

So be careful on the way back.

... *i am a cat* ...

There's a lot of them.

... *meow* .. ?

All right, fine. If you get eaten, don't bitch to me. What can you see?

... *people running fighting men in white iron with growling swords* ...

Can I use your eyes?

... *of course* ...

Lashes brushed her cheeks as she slipped behind Daken's pupils. He was looking down into a cramped alley three floors below his perch, and she clutched the table, fighting off a sudden rush of vertigo. The docks around Kigen Bay were ablaze, black smoke and seething flames. The clouds were full of Phoenix sky-ships, darting and weaving like swallows, occasionally opening up with barrages of shuriken-thrower fire into alleys and houses.

chug!chug!chug!chug!

They could smell stagnant water, urine and trash below, ripe with flies' eggs. Chi exhaust, ash and dust, the reek of pollution that had seeped into the city's skin. And high above it all, drifting arm in arm with the smoke came the stink of charred fat. The reek of burning hair.

Hana could hear the crowd through his ears, roaring flames, ringing bells.

Be careful out there, little brother.

... *still have one or two lives left* ...

She broke the contact with half a smile, mind drifting over the city. Feeling around one last time for corpse-rats, trying to catch a glimpse of the Kagé who *must* be behind these attacks. She found most of the Upside vermin gathered in that swarming knot two blocks north. They were a multitude, too grizzled to fear the flames, knuckle-deep in fresh meat and fighting amongst the guts. But a short spit from the edges of the feast, Hana felt a faint spark of distress.

The girl frowned. Pressed her lips into a bloodless line. Focusing tighter, she centred on the pain's source. Felt the tear of broken glass in his insides, rolling onto his back, tail tucked between his legs as he screeched. Tasted his blood on his tongue, lolling from their mouths, clawing at their own belly to make the agony go away.

She pulled back, felt more of them – other fading sparks crawling into storm drains and writhing in the gutters. Rolling over and clawing at the sky, twisting into little balls of mangy fur and slowly turning cold.

Something was wrong.

She could almost taste it now; a faint undercurrent of pain, little flares struggling away from their fellows and curling up on themselves, snuffed out like candles in a monsoon wind.

Bad meat.

'Yoshi . . .' She looked up from the floor and into his eyes.

'What?' He surfaced from his reverie, rose from his crouch. 'Did Daken see Jurou?'

'Yoshi, I think someone's poisoning our rats . . .'

The door slammed inward with a sharp crack, just as the window shattered. Four figures rushed in from the hallway, another tumbling through the broken pane, landing in a crouch amidst a shower of falling glass. Hana rolled aside as the lead door-crasher swung a tetsubo at her head, smashing onto the cushion where she'd knelt a moment before. The second man through the door raised a plain but functional-looking sword and took aim for Hana's throat.

Yoshi levelled his iron-thrower at the figure crouched amongst the broken glass. The man stood with a scowl. Hana caught a glimpse of small, piggy eyes, swollen, cauliflower ears.

'Gambler,' Yoshi hissed.

The pig-man lashed out with his war club, caught the iron-thrower across its nose and sent it spinning into the wall. A bright flash of light, a hollow boom as the shot in the chamber discharged, crossing the room to introduce itself to the door crasher's right eye. The man spun on the spot and collapsed onto the thug behind him, painting the man's face with gout of warm, fresh red. Yoshi landed a kick on the pig-man's thigh, tendons popping as the kneecap gave way.

Hana snatched up the fallen man's club as she scrambled onto her feet, taking in the assailants with a desperate glance. Just another alley fight, just another scrap over a crust of bread or a place to sleep, the kind of brawl she'd lived with since she could walk. She shrank back, a short feint, then dropped to her knees and drove her war club's haft into one assailant's groin. The man squealed like a stuck corpse-rat, and Hana's double-handed haymaker broke his jaw, teeth spilling across the piles of iron coins.

The pig-man lunged forward as his knee gave way, slamming his war club into Yoshi's ribs. Studded iron cracking bone, breath spraying from the boy's lungs. The pair fell into a tangle, flailing like children, all bloody knuckles and elbows. Yoshi gasped for breath, eyes full of tears. The pig-man locked his wrist and flipped him onto his belly, leaning into his shoulders with all his weight. The boy cried out, free hand scrabbling for the smoking iron-thrower laying just too far out of reach.

The blood-soaked gangster and his unstained comrade kicked aside their friend's corpse and brought their weapons to bear on Hana – another iron-shod tetsubo and a pair of punching daggers. She smashed one knife aside with her club before a blow sent her flying through the rice-paper wall. Her weapon spun from her grasp as she crashed to the floor, coming to rest in a tangle of bedclothes. She heard cruel laughter as a knee was planted between her shoulderblades, felt heavy weight on her back, a stunning blow to the blind side of her face, her good eye pressed into the pillow.

'Is this your bedroom, little girl?' Someone grabbed her arm, twisted it behind her back. 'Nice sheets.'

'The bitch broke my wrist!' The call came from the main room, hoarse with pain.

'Then come break hers.'

'Don't you touch her!' Yoshi roared, struggling against the pig-man's wrist-lock, spit flying between clenched teeth. 'Stay away from her or I'll kill you!'

The pig-man leaned close. Saké and sweat, damp breath on Yoshi's ear.

'Told you I'd see you soon, friend.'

Hana cried out as her arm was twisted up higher behind her back. The blood-soaked man was fumbling with her hakama, trying to tear them off. She heard footsteps, heavy breathing of the second man entering the bedroom.

'Help me get her clothes off,' the bloody man hissed.

'The Gentleman wants them alive.'

'She'll be alive.' A sharp smile; all teeth, no eyes. 'She'll just have trouble sitting for a while.'

'Who the hells are you people?' Hana cried.

She received another punch to the face in reply, stars bursting and spinning in her vision.

'Hold her down!'

'You want me to hold her down with a broken wrist?'

'Hurry up in there!' the pig-man roared.

'Get away from her!' Yoshi gasped, stretched towards the iron-thrower. 'You bastards, I'll kill you all!'

'Going to make you listen, friend,' the pig-man purred. 'Make you watch everything we do to her. Cut off your eyelids so you can't look away. It's going to make what we did to your sweetheart look like a holy day . . .'

Hana's screams were muffled in her pillow.

'No!' Yoshi roared.

'Listen, boy,' the pig-man hissed. 'Listen to her sing—'

A shape dropped in through the broken window, a blur of smoke-grey and scars and piss-yellow glittering like broken glass. It landed on the pig-man's shoulder, dug in with claws like katana. The man howled and reared back, flailing at the dervish of razors and dirty teeth. A paw brushed the surface of his eye, quicker than poison, so fast he didn't even feel the blow until something warm and gelatinous spilled down his cheek. He screamed then; a trembling, furious wail, clutching the bloody socket as he rolled away, tore the shape off his shoulder in a shower of blood and hurled it across the room.

It thudded into the wall, tumbled down and landed perfectly on its feet.

'*Mreowwwwwl*,' it said.

Pig-man lurched to his feet, blood spilling between his fingers, snarling with pain.

'My fucking *eye*—'

The shot popped his skull like a balloon full of red water, rocked what was left of his head back on his shoulders as it rang deafening in the room. Yoshi was already on his way to the bedroom as the man's body hit the floor, shattered skull cracking against polished boards, feet kicking as if he were swimming across the wood. A thin finger of smoke drifted from the hole in the back of his head.

Yoshi shot the broken-wrist man in the face as he rushed from the bedroom, iron-thrower bucking in his hand. The man crumpled like wax tossed into a fire. Stepping into the bedroom, Yoshi levelled the smoking weapon at the last intruder's head. The man stood and backed away, tried to simultaneously cover his face and put his hands into the air. Knees pressed together, hunched over, pleading eyes shining through splayed fingers.

'Don't,' he begged. 'Don't . . .'

Hana rose from the ruins of the bed, cheek purpling, hair tangled about her eye, leather patch askew on her face. Half breathing, half sobbing, she limped to her brother's side, holding her wrist, already bruised. Reaching out, she gently covered the barrel, pressed Yoshi's aim to the floor. He frowned at her as she took the 'thrower from his hands.

'Oh, thank you, girl,' the man said. 'Amaterasu bless you—'

Hana turned and fired into the man's crotch.

He dropped like a stone, screaming, clutching the bloody hole between his legs. Falling forward onto his face, he curled into a ball and screamed again; a high-pitched, vibrato wail that tore his throat raw. Hana kicked him onto his back, planted her foot on his chest and aimed the iron-thrower at his forehead. Daken prowled into the room, coiled around her leg. Her voice was a low-pitched growl.

'Who are you?'

'Gendo,' the man gasped. 'Gendo!'

'I didn't ask your name!' Hana yelled. 'I asked who you were!'

'Scorpion child.' The man pulled his uwagi off his shoulder, showed the duelling scorpions in the negative space between his tattoos. 'Scorpion-*chiiiiiild* . . .'

'Yakuza?' Hana blinked. 'I don't—'

Yoshi pushed past her, knelt beside the man and grabbed a fistful of collar, hauling him up into a clenched fist. Skin mashed against teeth, bright red paint on the gangster's mouth.

'How did you find us, bastard?' Yoshi spat.

And then Hana understood. Before he took another breath. Before another word escaped his lips. The piles of money, the late-night forays into the city, the wound on Yoshi's ribs . . .

'Gods, Yoshi . . . You clipped the fucking yakuza?'

Yoshi punched the man again, grabbed a handful of bloody crotch and squeezed.

'How did you find us?' Yoshi roared.

And Gendo told them.

*

Jurou's corpse was easier to look at than Yoshi's grief.

Tiny, bloody footprints and the bodies of poisoned rats on the cobbles all around it, shadows dancing in the light of Docktown flames. The earth trembled beneath them, an explosion lighting southern skies. Hana stared at the body and felt her stomach turn, the urge to look away almost overpowering. The pallor of its skin. The missing toes and fingers and teeth.

'Oh, gods,' she breathed. 'Jurou . . .'

Yoshi fell to his knees, hands over his mouth. Shapeless, gibbering grief spilled between his fingers, rocking back and forth, knees grinding into bloody dirt, tearing his hair and screwing his eyes shut. Spit and snot, gritted teeth and choking sobs, hands clenched into fists.

'Bastards.' He hugged himself and moaned. 'Oh, you mother*fuckers* . . .'

'Yoshi, we have to go.'

'Hana, look what they did to him . . .'

'I know.' She placed a gentle hand on his shoulder, heart aching. 'But there are bushi' everywhere and the yakuza are still after us. We have to go.'

. . . scorpion men . . .

'Yoshi, get up!'

. . . coming . . .

Hana hauled him to his feet, turned him away from Jurou's remains. She heard shouts, running feet getting closer. She glimpsed vicious, dark faces at one end of the alley. Sky-ships roaring overhead. She grabbed Yoshi's arm and ran.

Which way?

. . . down run down crowd noise hide . . .

She dragged her brother away, and he stumbled for the tears in his eyes and the weight in his chest. They tumbled from the alleyway into a blur of noise and colour and motion. A crowd flooded the street, bright silks and expensive breathers, possessions bundled in their arms; the well-to-do citizenry of Upside fleeing towards the palace like rats from the flames. Smoke thick in the air, sky-ships thundering, loudspeakers demanding all citizens return to their homes.

They lunged into the mob, tried to blend into the rolling sea of grime and colour. A motor-rickshaw sat in the middle of the street, blaring its horn. The driver finally broke, planted his foot, running down pedestrians in his hurry to escape.

Hana looked around at the mob, swelling and shifting about her. She could hear fighting down the way; truncheons and tetsubo and breaking glass. They were swept up in the current of flesh, Yoshi moving along in mute acquiescence, Hana's arms wrapped around him.

Daken's voice sang in her mind, tinged with mild anxiety.

. . . behind you scorpion men have seen you . . .

Which way do we go?

. . . left best way is left . . .

She turned in the crowd and dragged Yoshi away, struggling against the riptide. A glance behind revealed nothing, but she could hear struggles, angry commands.

. . . they are coming go go . . . !

They reached a squeezeway between two lopsided buildings, breaking away from the crush and heat. A shouted curse, a glimpse of tattooed flesh behind. The press of crooked walls all around them, stink of rot and waste, struggling through the shin-high filth. Yoshi's hand was slippery with perspiration and blood, and he stumbled along as if sleepwalking, dried tear tracks cutting through the dirt on his face.

'Come on, Yoshi,' she breathed. 'Run.'

Pounding footsteps, the scrape of inked flesh against the walls behind. The pair belted out onto a narrow street lined with empty merchant stalls, knocking aside a group of gutter-waifs beating on an overturned Guild crier, the machine spinning its tank tracks and clanging its bells in alarm. A backward glance revealed crooked faces, inked flesh, blades flashing in clenched fists. At least a dozen yakuza chasing them now, closing fast.

Yoshi crashed into an abandoned peddler's cart, old pots and children's toys cascading into the street as it upended. He stumbled, Hana grabbing his arm, pulled him upright.

. . . left go left now . . .

Daken bolted across the rooftops, a black shadow against the firelight glow. Corpse-rats squealed in the shadows, fleeing the growing mob, rising flames. Thunder rumbled overhead, mixing with the roar of sky-ship engines, spotlights cutting like lightning through the black.

... turn right alleyway ...

Breath burning in their lungs, sweat in their eyes.

... left left hurry ... !

'Faster!' Hana grabbed her brother's arm, dragging him along.

'I can't!'

... beware ...

Two tattooed lumps of muscle appeared at the alley mouth. Murder lit their eyes, split their lips into greedy grins. Hana tore the iron-thrower from her pants without thinking and aimed at the bigger man's face. She squeezed the trigger.

The weapon spat out a hollow, empty click.

A stout, brutish-looking man collided with her from behind, knocking the breath from her body. Hana screamed, clawing the man's eyes with broken fingernails. Tattooed arms grabbed her in a bear hug as she drove her knee into his crotch. Yoshi was on his feet, clubbing the man with a piece of rusty pipe, roaring at the top of his lungs. Two more men crash-tackled him, brought him down amidst a flurry of profanity. Boots danced on his ribs, his face. He struck back with his feet, connecting with one man's knee and inverting it. Snapping bone and bright, wide-eyed screaming. Blood. Kicks rained down on Yoshi's head.

The siblings were hauled to their feet, Hana still flailing with nails and teeth and fists, Yoshi's head lolling, nose and ears bleeding. She called his name, received no answer. Looking up, she saw a mangled silhouette peering over the ledge above. Stubby ears. Yellow eyes.

Daken, help us!

. . . Hana . . .

Please!

She felt the conflict within him, the desire to help overwhelmed by his fear, the certainty there was nothing he could actually do. One cat against half a dozen hardened thugs?

. . . too many . . .

Help!

. . . am sorry . . .

She felt him hovering as the Scorpion Children surrounded them. A sky-ship in Phoenix colours roared overhead, spraying the rooftop with shuriken fire. And then, heart sinking in her chest, she felt Daken running away. Over rooftops, away from the fire and smoke, soft as shadows. She screamed at him to stop, pleaded for help.

Don't leave us!

But he was gone.

The yakuza were a knot of inked muscle and curling, curdled faces. Hana looked up into the leader's eyes. A thin, angled scowl, teeth like a trash pile, tetsubo in his hand.

'You killed Hida.'

He raised his club into the air.

'You're going to wish it was the other way around, bitch.'

And down it came.

48

Stillness

Chaos ran through the Daimyo's palace, and the nightingale floors sang in time with its tread. The smell of distant flames mixed with the cooking fires, entrées lying cold on the feast tables. Panic at the Kagé attack was quickly replaced by outrage, vows of vengeance, drawn swords. And the Daimyo of the Tora clan led his Samurai out into the city, the Dragon Daimyo and his retinue falling into step behind these men with ash-streaked faces, these walking dead set once more like wolves amongst the flock on Kigen's streets.

A legion, almost one hundred strong, marching from the palace gates. Every one clad in great lumbering suits of iron, spitting chi smoke into the air, flags flying high in a scorching wind, tinged with the reek of burning skin. Michi watched them from an upper window of the servants' quarters, a grim smile on her face.

Soon, they will not know which way to seek the foe.

She stole amidst the corridors, down the servant's passages, Ichizo's package in her arms. Flitting through the abandoned kitchens, the cleaner's rooms, then down into the generator room, oiled rags and tongues of flame. The hum of quiet panic, fear amongst the remaining nobility suppressed beneath a stoic facade, the mask of honour, the notion of 'face.' It would be unseemly – indeed, *shameful* – to show anything but disdain for these Kagé dogs, anything but absolute faith in the Daimyo's ability to restore order to his capital. Trembling wives were rebuked. Guests returned to the dining hall, nervous glances still lingering on a fire-painted sky.

And then it began.

First, an explosion within the cellars, the Daimyo's generators splitting asunder, setting the bottom floor of the eastern wing ablaze. Cries of terror from the dining hall, courtiers running through the corridors. A hastily assembled line of bushimen gathered, stretching from the garden stream to the cellar doors, dashing buckets full of cloudy water and the occasional unfortunate koi fish onto the swelling inferno.

Guests fled the feast. Tiny, hurried steps within the hems of their robes, fearful expressions hidden behind beautiful breathers and fluttering fans. The families of the Dragon clanlord retreated to the guest quarters, personal house guards barring the doors. But all too soon, they were screaming; screaming and fleeing as the bleached cedar tiles above their heads caught fire, choking smoke and burning embers dancing in the air.

Heavy boots, running feet, shouted orders, iron bells. Smoke drifting through the corridors, seeping under the doorway of the room she slipped back inside. And finally, Michi stepped into the hallway and walked towards the royal wing.

If the sight of the pristine girl and her scarlet gift box seemed strange, the bushimen dashing past appeared to have more pressing concerns. Michi made her way around the veranda, away from the bucket line and the still-blazing cellar. She yelled at a passing bushi' brigade, telling them she saw rebels fleeing over the western walls, and they yelled thanks and charged away. Up the stairs, past the tearooms, the nightingale floor chirping beneath her sandals. Keeping her head bowed, eyes downturned from the guards who thundered past, crying for servants to bring water. The guest wing was a burning lotus field on a hot summer's day.

She heard combat somewhere out in the city, steel upon steel, the heavy thunder of shuriken-thrower fire. The *tickticktick* of a spider drone roaming the halls, perching on a balcony to watch the guest wing roof giving way, fire reflected in its tiny, glowing eye. She picked up her pace, small shuffling footsteps taking her across the mezzanine above the library, until she'd gone as far as she'd reasonably hoped to get.

'Halt!'

Four bushimen barred entry to the Daimyo's wing, huge double doors locked at their backs. Banded black across their chests, iron helms and face guards, nagamaki naked in their hands. This hallway was wider than those of the servants' wing; wide enough by far to wield the longblades. And for these men to have been stationed outside the Daimyo's halls at all meant they were no strangers to the art of steel.

'You girl,' barked the commander. 'What are you doing here?'

'I bring gifts,' she said, proffering the box in her hands.

'Gifts? What madness is this? Who are you?'

'Michi-san,' said another guard. 'I recognize her. She used to serve First Daughter.'

The bushiman commander stepped forward. 'No one is to see your mistress, Lady Michi. By orders of the Daimyo. Best to head downstairs and help with—'

She reached into the box and drew them out, scarlet card

falling to the floor. Four and three feet long, gentle curves and glittering saw-blade teeth. She thumbed the ignitions on the hilts and the motors roared to life, vibration traveling up her arms and into her chest, bringing a small smile to painted lips.

Michi gunned the throttles of Ichizo's chainkatana and wakizashi. Tearing away the intact layer of her jūnihitoe gown, she stepped out of her wooden sandals, wriggling her feet in split-toed socks. She took up her stance, flourishing the blades about her waist and head, a twirling, snarling dance of folded steel.

The commander looked incredulous. Several of the bushimen behind exchanged amused glances, wry smiles and short bursts of baffled laughter.

'Put those down before you hurt yourself, girl,' the commander said.

Michi dashed across the floorboards, narrowed eyes and gleaming teeth. The commander came to his senses first and stepped forward, bringing his nagamaki into some semblance of guard. She slipped down onto her knees, fine Kitsune silk and her momentum sending her into a skid across polished boards, blade passing harmlessly over her head. Cutting the commander's legs out from under him, a blinding spray of red, a shriek of agony as the chainsaw blades sheared through bone like butter. Spinning up to her feet, katana cleaving through another bushiman's forearm, wakizashi parrying a hasty thrust from a third as the soldiers at last registered the threat. Sparks in the air as steel crashed, the girl moving like smoke between the blades, swaying to the music she made.

A blade to a throat. A crimson spray on the walls. A parry. A wheel-kick. A thrust. Red mist in the air. Heart thundering in her chest.

Then stillness.

She blew stray hair from her eyes, idling chainswords dripping into the gore pooled at her feet, staring at the commander's corpse.

'I think I'll put you down instead,' she said.

She wiped her cheek on her forearm, smearing it with red, staring at the door before her. Sugi wood shod with cold iron. Rivets as fat as her fist. Six inches thick. Though she might have hacked her way through with enough time, the guards beyond would certainly hear her coming. And judging from the clamour behind her, more still had heard the screams of their dying comrades and were on their way to investigate.

She looked at the doors blocking the way she must go.

She looked back down the way she'd come.

And then she looked up at the ceiling.

49

Addition and Subtraction

Yoshi woke to the slap of ice-cold water in his face, followed by a real slap hard enough to rattle his teeth in his head. He could hear the swell of distant crowds, roaring flames and sky-ship engines. Sweat and old lotus and the stink of his own blood hung in the air. And he remembered Jurou lying dead on the alley floor, gnawed eyeless, stumps for fingers and toes, and he felt hatred burn so brightly inside him he feared he might catch fire.

Another slap to his face. Harder this time.

'Wake up, boy.' A lisping growl.

Tossing the hair from his eyes, he blinked in the gloom. He was dangling by his wrists from a hook and chain, just long enough for his toes to touch the ground. Naked save for his new hakama, now bloodied and covered in filth. The concrete was sticky, stained dark. A single globe threw a circle of light on the floor. On the periphery, he could see a dozen men and women, arms folded, watching him the way corpse-rats watch a death rattle. On each of their biceps, in the negative space between the tattoos, two scorpions were locked, claw to claw.

Yoshi's heart stilled inside his chest.

He saw Hana opposite him, hands bound, arms held by vicious-looking men with full-body irezumi. Her hair was draped around her face, nose bleeding, good eye closed, out cold.

Yoshi looked at the one who'd slapped him. Thin and hard and cruel, a street-sharp, angular face, dark, hateful eyes. He recognized him from their first rip; the Gambler's partner. The man held a pair of long-nosed pliers in his hands.

'Rise and shine, lazybones.'

'Fuck you,' Yoshi spat.

'Funny.' A broken yellow smile. 'Your boyfriend said much the same.'

Yoshi tried to lunge, succeeded only in making himself spin on his chain. The thin man laughed, all yellow, crumbling bone and dirty breath.

'My name is Seimi.' The man pressed the pliers against Yoshi's cheek. 'My face is the last thing you'll ever see. And for that, you have my apologies.'

'My sister had nothing to do with this. Let her go.'

'Nothing to do with it?' Seimi raised an eyebrow. 'Do tell . . .'

The man turned to a workbench on the edge of the light. It was arrayed with every tool Yoshi could imagine: hacksaws, screwdrivers, tin snips, drills, pliers. A bottle of saké. A bowl of salt. A chi-powered blowtorch. A hammer.

Seimi dashed water into Hana's face. He slapped her hard as she sputtered, head rising slowly, eye rolling around her bruised socket as she blinked and tried to focus.

'Hello, pretty one.' Seimi grabbed her face, fingers and thumb pressed into her cheeks, squeezing her thin lips into a pout.

'Yoshi?' His heart nearly broke at the terror in her voice. 'Yoshi, what's happening?'

'It's all right, sis.' He tried to keep his own voice from rising upwards towards hysteria. 'It's going to be all right.'

'Did you hear that, pretty one?' Seimi leaned close, stared into her good eye. 'Your thieving whoreson brother said it'll be all right. Does that still your pounding heart?'

'You bastards, you let her go! She has *nothing to do with this*!'

Hana was shaking so hard her teeth chattered. She struggled against the men holding her, but they were twice her size, all inked muscle and gap-toothed grins. Seimi ran one hand down her throat, parted the collar of her tunic. A hungry stare caught on the golden amulet draped around her neck. A tiny stag with three crescent horns. Glaring.

'Stop.'

The voice was low-pitched. Ironclad.

Soft footsteps. Measured breath. A man stepped into the light. Short. Tanned. Simply dressed. Greying hair swept back from sharp brows. Staring at Yoshi with empty, black eyes.

'Do you know who I am?'

'No.' Yoshi gasped for breath. 'No, I don't.'

He stepped closer, hovering just inches away. Yoshi could see the pores in his skin, the lines at the corners of those bottomless eyes. There was no anger – not even a hint of malice in the man's voice.

'I am the man who paid your rent. Paid the tailor who made your clothes. The artiste who inked your skin. I paid for your smoke. Your drink. I am the man whose face you spit in, every time you spent one of those stolen coins.'

'I'm sorry.' Yoshi swallowed. 'I'm sorry, but please, my sister didn't have anything to do with this, please just—'

'What is your name?'

'. . . Yoshi.'

'I am the Gentleman.' The man was staring at Yoshi's inkless arm. 'You are lowborn?'

'Hai.'

'It explains much.' The Gentleman paced in a long, slow circle around Yoshi. 'Do you know how we differ, Yoshi-san?'

'No . . .'

'I am Burakumin, just like you. A boy born with nothing, no clan, no family, no name. And like you, I was forced to do terrible things, just to survive this place.' The Gentleman shook his head. 'The things I have done, Yoshi-san. The things I will do . . .'

The man ceased pacing, looked Yoshi in the eye.

'But I am no thief. Everything I have, I bought with sweat and blood. I had the grace to look into men's eyes as I took everything they had. That is the difference between us. Why I stand here, and you hang there. Without your little hand-cannon.' As the Gentleman spoke, he moved his face an inch or two closer to Yoshi's with every word. 'You. Are. A. Coward.'

Yoshi said nothing, mind awhirl. Desperate. Looking for something. Anything. Some way out of this hole, this pit he'd dragged her into. Gods, not Hana, please . . .

'You say your sister is blameless?' The Gentleman looked at her, then back to Yoshi. 'That she knew nothing of your transgressions against the Scorpion Children?'

Sweat rolled down Yoshi's face, blood in his eyes. 'Nothing.'

'And you would have me let her go?'

'She doesn't deserve any of this.' He licked at split lips. 'Do what you want to me. I deserve it for what I did. But she doesn't deserve to see it.'

The Gentleman stared, head tilted as if listening to hidden voices.

'I suppose, Yoshi-san, you are right. She doesn't deserve to see this at all.'

Relief flooded through Yoshi and he almost sobbed, babbling thanks as the Gentleman turned away. And as he watched, the little man stepped up to Seimi and took the long-nosed pliers from his calloused hands, and in the space between one heartbeat and the next, the Gentleman leaned in close and plucked Hana's eye from her socket.

Her scream filled the air, louder than Yoshi could have thought possible. He found his own voice caught up with hers, a shapeless roar of hatred, thrashing against the ropes binding him, spitting and screaming and flailing. The Gentleman touched the men holding Hana and they dropped her to the floor. She brought her bound hands up to her face and curled into a ball and screamed, screamed until Yoshi thought his heart would break. Tears blurred his sight, his captors reduced to smudges in the glare, the scent of smoke filling his lungs.

'You *bastard*!' he screamed. '*You fucking bastard!*'

The Gentleman dropped the pliers as if disgusted by them. They hit concrete with a dull, metallic clang. He drew a kerchief from his uwagi, cleaned the blood off his hands as he spoke with a slow and measured voice to Seimi.

'Release the girl when you are done. But this one?' The Gentleman looked Yoshi up and down. 'I wish his suffering to be legendary. I wish Kigen to know, now and forever, the price of crossing the Scorpion Children. If you are an artiste, brother, let this boy's flesh be the canvas upon which you paint your masterpiece. And when you are finished, you hang him on a wall in the Market Square for all the world to see. Do you understand me, Seimi-san?'

The man covered his fist and bowed. 'Oyabun.'

A distant explosion tore the air. Marching boots. Steel and screams.

'If you brothers will excuse me, I have a wife and son to attend.'

The Gentleman spared a last glance for Hana, sobbing in a spatter of blood. Lips pursed, hands clasped behind his back. There was a brief flicker, just the tiniest moment of pity in his bottomless stare. But he blinked, and it was gone; the light of a single candle extinguished in a bottomless ocean of black. Motioning to the Scorpion Children on the spotlight's edge, he strolled from the room, taking eight yakuza with him. Yoshi heard heavy doors open and close, the chaos from the streets outside swelling momentarily, smoke-scent growing stronger still.

Seimi was watching him with narrowed eyes.

'You've got balls, street trash, I'll give you that.'

The yakuza walked to the table, picked up the chi-powered blowtorch, smiling faintly.

'But not for long.'

Yoshi drew a breath.

Held it for forever.

And there on the floor, amidst the anguish and the blood and the agony in the place where her eye had once been, Hana lay curled in a tiny ball and sobbed.

And shook.

And remembered.

*

The bottle fell, a long, scything arc ending in her throat and a spray of blood, thick and hot and bright. And Hana did what any thirteen-year-old girl would have done at that moment.

Yoshi crashed into their father, shapeless bellowing and flailing fists. He caught him on the cheek, the jaw, the pair falling on the table and smashing it to splinters. Hana stood and screamed over her mother's body, head throbbing like it might burst, looking at that open, grinning throat and those beautiful blue eyes, empty now and forever.

Her father slapped Yoshi aside, his face purple, sweat and veins and spittle and teeth.

'Little bastard, I'll kill you,' he growled.

Da raised the broken saké bottle in his good hand, leaned over Yoshi's crumpled form. Blood on the glass. Blood on his hands. Her mother's. Now her brother's too? Too little to stop him. Too small to make a difference. But in that moment, Hana found herself roaring anyway, thoughtless, heedless, throwing herself at his back, beating on him with her tiny fists, screaming, 'No, no, no,' as if all the storms in all the world lived inside her lungs. He spun around with horror etched on his face, as if he couldn't believe she would turn on him. Not his Hana. Not his little flower.

'My gods,' he said. 'Your eye . . .'

He pointed to her face with the blood-slicked bottle, features twisted in anguish.

'Gods above, no. No, not you . . .'

Yoshi leaped on Da's back with a roar, wrapping his arms around his throat. Father swung his elbow, connected with Yoshi's jaw. Teeth clapping together. Blood. Her brother fell amongst the table fragments, limp and senseless.

Da turned and slapped her, spun her like a top. She fell to her knees and he was on her, sitting on her chest and pinning her arms with his thighs. He was so heavy. So heavy she couldn't breathe. Sobbing. Pleading.

'No, Da. Don't!'

He pressed his stunted forearm to her throat, broken bottle still clutched in his hand.

'I should've known,' he hissed. 'I should've known it was in you. She's poisoned you.'

550

He pointed at their mother, irises glazed over like beach glass, the colour of dragon silk.

'It's in you,' her father was saying. 'You gaijin trash. The white devils are in you. But I can see them. I can get them out . . .'

He held the bottle to her face, inches from Hana's right eye, broken glass reflected in her iris.

'Da, no!' She shook her head, eyes closed tight. 'No, no!'

Then he dug the bottle in.

'I can get them out . . .'

50

Sensation

The world around her was so bright, so sharp, Ayane thought her eyes might bleed.

Faint breeze tickled her ankles and shins, clothing rasped against bare flesh, raising the new hair on her body in goosebumps. When Kin turned to look at her, she could feel his breath on her face, feather-soft. She shivered at the overload of sensation, all this *feeling*, so fresh and new. But more than that, as she watched the old man by the window, shaking and coughing and slipping towards his grave one breath at a time, she was surprised to feel pity swelling inside her chest. Pity for him, standing so close to the edge, blissfully unaware of what yawned beneath his toes. And pity for herself, that all this would end almost as soon as it began.

The mechabacus chattered on her chest. In her head. Orders. Movements. Questions.

Questions she longed to answer.

Kin was looking at her, a pointed stare, smooth and hard. And so she stood and asked for directions to the privy, bowing low to Daichi before stepping on quiet feet to the stairwell.

Three floors down into the Kagé basement, the battle plan spread on the table, chess pieces and charcoal sticks and rice-paper. Ayane knelt in the corner, face upturned to the ceiling. She ran one finger along her arm, delighting in the sensation, watching the tiny hairs stir and rise. The finger trailed up her shoulder, over the empty output jack at her collarbone, down her breast. And there she found it. Smooth metal and cold transistors. Chittering weight hanging on the cord around her neck. She touched a length of corrugated rubber cable spilling from the mechabacus's side, held it up to the light, staring at the bayonet studs at its head.

She closed her eyes and felt night air on her skin. Inhaling smoke and ash, listening to the swelling orchestra of the chaos outside. Holding her breath, as if she were about to dive into deep water. And then she plunged the cable into the output port at her collarbone, twisting it home with a sharp snap, exhalation drifting into a sigh.

Her fingers moved across the device's face, shifting counting beads back and forth in a tiny, intricate dance. She felt the chatter swell, shift focus to the new transmission, the signal that had been missing from the choir these past weeks. Their voices in her head, the nattering, clattering tumbling voices, sounds of the real world drifting away. And as the sensation of her flesh became nothing at all, tears slipped over fluttering lashes and down her cheeks, falling away from flesh almost too insensate to mark their passing.

Almost.

*

They crawled through the sewer, no louder than the rats around them, sleek, flea-bitten shapes baring crooked yellow fangs at their approach. Kaori in front, sweat soaking through her kerchief, a hand-cranked tungsten torch burning in her hand. The rest of the Kagé behind, single file, breathing heavy in the dank confines of the tunnel's gut.

They were half a dozen turns into the labyrinth when Kaori paused at a four-way junction, looked back the way they'd come. The Spider peered at her in the dark, eyes narrowed against the stink.

'Do you know where you're going?' The lieutenant's whisper was feather-light, almost inaudible behind the grubby cotton covering his mouth.

Kaori scowled, turned around, kept crawling.

They reached a four-way junction and Kaori paused again, looking left and right, chewing her lip. Her eyes were wide, pupils dilated.

'This makes no sense,' she whispered.

The Spider cursed beneath his breath, spat into the filth they crawled through.

'Raijin's drums, what's the problem?'

'We're looking for an emergency access shaft, up into the maintenance subbasement. But we should have hit a T-junction, not a crossroads.'

The Spider took Kin's map from Kaori's hand, smeared with filth but still legible. The Kagé lieutenant frowned in the stuttering light, looking back the way they'd come, even turning the paper upside down.

'This is wrong,' he said. 'We passed a five-way fork after the crossroads. But we shouldn't have hit that until *after* the T-junction.'

'That's what I just said,' Kaori hissed.

'Your Guildsman can't even draw a godsdamned map.' The paper crumpled in one sodden fist. 'Anyone would think the little bastard *wanted* us lost down here.'

Kaori looked at the Spider, he at her, watching her eyes grow wide.

'Oh gods . . .'

*

'What are you doing?'

The voice pulled Ayane from her trance, mechabacus fading to a whisper as she opened bloodshot eyes and saw Isao in the doorway. The boy's face was flushed, fist curled around the haft of a wickedly sharp kusarigama, muscles taut along his forearm. He advanced towards her.

'You're only supposed to be receiving, not transmitting. What are you doing?'

Ayane was on her feet, razored arms at her back unfolding with a bright, silver sound. The boy paused, one hand creeping up to his cheek; the thin red scar she'd given him on the bridge. Eyes on her fingers, still dancing on her mechabacus. He drew breath to shout for help.

A hand snaked over his mouth from behind and his eyes grew wide, a muffled, choking cry spilling through the fingers covering his lips. A knife gleamed red in the gloom.

'What's my name, Isao?' Kin whispered.

Isao bucked, clawing blindly at Kin's face. Kin stabbed again, red floods pouring down Isao's back as he crumpled to his knees and toppled forward onto dusty concrete. Kin fell upon him, plunging the knife down again and again, scarlet spraying across the walls. Chest heaving, sucking breath through clenched teeth, finally pushing himself away from the corpse and spraying it with a mouthful of spittle, hands painted red, face white as snow.

Ayane watched him as if hypnotized. The silver at her back gleamed, long, razored needles rippling like branches in a gentle breeze. She walked up beside him and peered at Isao's body, the blood pooling around him.

'You stabbed him in the back,' she said.

'So?'

Ayane reached out with one spider-limb to poke the meat cooling on the basement floor. Kin grabbed her arm, glaring.

'I'm just touching . . .' she said.

'Well, don't.'

'What was it like?' Head tilted, eyes a little too wide. 'To kill him? How did it *feel*?'

'This isn't the godsdamned time, Ayane.'

'Where are the others? Takeshi and Atsushi?'

'Already gone.' He gestured to the mechabacus on her chest. 'Is it done?'

'Hai.' Ayane reached out ever so slowly, touched the blood on Kin's cheek. 'It is done.'

Kin sheathed his knife, walked up the stairs. 'Then let's get this over with.'

Ayane lingered, watching the punctured carrion cooling on the ground in front of her. She looked at the droplets of blood, winding in random paths down the walls, smeared on her fingertips. Her tongue emerged from between bee-stung lips and she touched it to her fingers, just once, shivering as she tasted copper and salt.

Licking her lips, she turned and followed Kin up the stairs.

*

He hadn't moved from the window.

A silhouette against rising flames, sky-ships roaring over-head, the calls for calm, obedience, dispersal, hanging in the air with the smoke. He didn't even look at them as they entered the room; Kin standing in the doorway, smeared in blood, Ayane leaning into a corner, a halo of silver needles fanned out along the walls.

'I wonder how history will remember us, Kin-san,' Daichi said, voice frail with pain. 'I wonder what they will say.'

Kin's reply was flat. Dead.

'They'll probably call me traitor.'

Daichi nodded at the flames. 'Probably.'

'They won't call you anything at all.'

Daichi raised an eyebrow, turned towards the boy, and froze. He took in the unblinking eyes, the blood smeared across fingers and face, the dead-man expression.

'Nobody will remember your name, Daichi,' Kin said.

'What . . .' Daichi licked his lips, eyes fixed on those bloody hands, '. . . what have you done, Kin-san?'

'I told you,' Kin said. 'I found a way for all of it to end.'

The window exploded at Daichi's back, a rain of shattered glass and roar of blue-white flame. A Lotusman collided with the old man, knocked him off his feet, the pair crashing to the floor and tumbling across the boards. Another half-dozen suited shapes blasted in through the broken window, the roar of their burners almost deafening, filling the room with choking smoke.

Daichi kicked at the Guildsman tackling him, rolling away and drawing the old katana at his back from its battered scabbard, teeth gritted in agony. A second Lotusman advanced, brass fingers outstretched, and the old man struck with the blade, a dull note ringing out as folded steel connected with case-hardened brass. The hiss of breather bellows, the sound of metallic chuckling as the figures surrounded the old man, his sword raised high, gleaming in the light of bloody eyes.

They lunged and he moved; an ebb tide, flowing back then crashing forward, his katana's point skewering one Guildsman through the glowing red glass over his eye. The Lotusman screamed, a high-pitched, agonized squeal, thick with reverb as he fell, blood streaming down a blank, motionless face. A quick strike severed the breathing tubes of two more Lotusmen, and the old man staggered back, one hand pressed to his ribs, the other still clutching his blade, knuckles white upon the hilt. Gasping for breath. Blood at his lips.

Swordmaster the old man might have been, but he was one, beaten and sick, and they were six, hard and cold. More still rushing up the stairs now; heavily armed Guild mercenaries with Kobiashi needle-throwers. And they fell on him, just a dull weight of numbers without finesse or craft, bearing him down as he thrashed, stabbing and punching, cursing them with every ragged, gasping breath. Curling up under their blows and finally falling still as they plunged the blacksleep needles into his flesh, his stare locked on the boy who even now sat slumped at the table, bathed in blood, flames reflected in knife-bright eyes.

Kin heard his father's voice, the knowing rebuke amidst the workshop's thrum. The words he'd heard so many times, the simple rote that had been as much a part of his life as breathing. And in that moment, he finally understood their truth.

Skin is strong.

Flesh is weak.

'Godsdamn you, Kin,' the old man whispered. 'Godsdamn you to the hells.'

The boy watched the light in the old man's eyes fade as the blacksleep dragged Daichi down into unconsciousness. He felt pale hands on his shoulders, insectoid clicking as eight silver arms encircled him, holding him tight.

'I'm sure they will,' he said.

51

The Quiet Dark

Michi sheared through the ceiling of Aisha's chambers and down into a spray of bright red. Her chainkatana parted a head from its shoulders as she tumbled into a crouch, taking a second foe's legs off at the knees. Metallic screeching. Spattered walls. Rising into a faceful of silver needles.

The air about her sang, whipped into bright, cutting notes, pain behind it. Stepping backward, she lashed out with the chainwakizashi, heard jagged teeth sparking on metal, blinking the blood from her lashes. Gasping, eyes burning, sweat slick on her skin, gown weighing her down like the air in a tomb.

They had the seeming of demons: featureless faces, bodies clad in skintight, gleaming brown, long skirts studded with fat, gleaming buckles, eight impossibly thin arms arrayed about each in a gleaming halo. But Michi saw mechabacii on their chests, recognized them from the palanquin at the sky-docks, and she knew at last the hell they'd been spat from.

'Guildsmen,' she hissed.

The things lunged with those silver limbs, terrifyingly fast, cutting into her right arm and knocking the katana away. Michi's riposte with the wakizashi opened one along its belly, up into its chest, and the thing shrieked, distorted and metallic, stumbling backward and trying to staunch the glistening sausage-flow of innards bulging from the rend.

The final Guildsman filled the air with silver, Michi shifting onto her back foot as needles whipped and whistled about her. She crouched low, aimed a sweeping kick at its ankles, and hampered by the buckles and skirts, the Guildsman was forced backward. Its heel hit a puddle of blood, and with a squeak across polished pine, it lost balance. Spinning on the spot, Michi hurled the chainwakizashi at the thing's chest, punching through the mechabacus with the shrieking saw of steel teeth and a rain of brightly coloured sparks.

The Guildsman stared at the blade mutely, sinking to its knees. Retrieving her chainkatana from the bloody ground, Michi swung it without ceremony. The thing tumbled forwards, headless, silver limbs twitching as if in a fit.

'Michi,' said a voice. 'Thank the gods.'

She saw her then, throat seizing tight, and it was all she could do to choke out a reply.

'Aisha . . .'

She lay on a grand oaken bed, red silk pulled up to her chin, pillows all about her. Tomo, her small black-and-white terrier, sat beside her, growling even as his little tail wagged. Machines were arrayed on either side of her; towering contraptions set with dials and gauges and bellows, transistors and vacuum tubes. Michi dashed across the room, sheathing the blade at her waist, grabbing Aisha's hand.

'No time to explain, we have to move . . .'

She tugged hard, trying to drag Aisha from her bed. The Lady flopped forward, hair across her face, a deadweight sack of meat and bones. The silk sheet slipped away from her chin, bunched about her waist, and Michi realized with growing horror that the machines at her bedside, the cables spilling from their outputs . . . all of them were snaking across the floor, up onto the bed, and from there . . .

Into Aisha.

Into her arms. Into the bayonet studs puncturing her flesh. Into the device laid upon her chest, thin brass ribs and diodes, the bellows in the machine beside her moving up and down in time with her breath.

'My gods . . .' Michi whispered, pressing Aisha back into the pillows. 'What have they done to you?'

'Saved my life.'

Her voice was hollow, an almost imperceptible reverberation at the end of every word.

'Forcing my heart to beat, my lungs to breathe.' Her eyes gleamed with the beginnings of tears. 'Amaterasu, protect me . . .'

The tears broke, spilling over her lashes and down pallid cheeks.

'I can't feel anything, Michi.' Aisha's voice became a whisper, choked and tiny. 'My brother, he . . .' She screwed her eyes shut. 'I can't feel anything below my neck . . .'

'No,' Michi breathed. 'No, that can't be. I *saw you* at the sky-docks.'

'Propped up like a corpse in its box. Gagged behind my breather. Plugged into that accursed chair and the contraption beneath. All for show.'

'But you were seen on the balcony . . .'

Aisha's eyes flickered to one of the machines; a vertical trolley with a pyramid of wheels flanking either side, lined with gleaming buckles and belts.

'They take me out on the balcony in that,' she whispered. 'Strapping me in and trundling me into the sun. Just long enough that a stray courtier or bushiman could see me, to quash any rumours of my death. They were going to haul me to my wedding in it.'

'Good gods . . .'

Michi took Aisha's hand, but it was cold and limp as corpse flesh. The Lady's skin was pale, run through with blue veins, fingers so thin they looked like twigs. Michi looked up and down the bed, tears spilling down through powder and kohl and blood to patter upon the sheets like rain.

In the distance, a hollow boom rocked the city, screams ringing through the night. Aisha's eyes flickered to the window.

'What is happening out there?'

'I don't know. I think the Kagé are attacking Kigen. But they've drawn Hiro's forces away from the palace. I can get you out of here.'

'I cannot lift a finger, love.' Aisha looked into Michi's eyes. 'I cannot feel a thing.'

'No, it's these machines.' Michi whirled on the banks of equipment, desperate eyes roaming the impossible stretch of diode and cog and cable. 'They've stopped you moving. The Guild have tricked you. They've just made you think—'

'I felt it, Michi,' Aisha said. 'I felt it when Yoritomo broke my neck.'

'No. That's not true. It can't be.'

'She got away?' Light flared in Aisha's eyes, hot and desperate. 'Yukiko? She and the thunder tiger escaped?'

'Hai,' Michi nodded, blinked back burning tears. 'The people sing songs about her, Aisha. Arashi-no-odoriko, they call her.'

'Stormdancer,' Aisha breathed. 'It was worth it, then.'

A gurgling intake of breath tore Michi's eyes away, down to the Guildsman slumped against the wall. It held an armful of its own innards, spilling purple and wet from its torn gut, the sundered mechabacus coughing counting beads into its lap. Michi glanced from the Guildsman to the tubes in Aisha's chest and arms. She snatched up her chainkatana, murder in her eyes.

The Guildsman looked up at her approach, wet breath rattling in its lungs. It keeled over, choking, clawing at its back. And with a sound like breaking eggshells, the silver orb on its spine split open, and a fist-sized metallic object tumbled out onto the floorboards.

Michi stepped back, fearing some kind of explosive. But the object unfurled eight tiny clockwork legs, stared at her with a red, glowing eye.

'*Tang! Tang! Tang! Tang!*' sang the spider drone, as if outraged at the murder of its mother. Michi stepped forward and struck, scattering the floorboards with torn clockwork and a shower of bright blue sparks.

'They know,' Aisha whispered. 'They know you are here. They will be coming.'

'Let them,' Michi hissed.

'I will not have you die for me.'

'Who said anything about—'

Michi heard it before she felt it; a distant rumble, as if a long-slumbering giant was yawning and stretching in his cradle beneath the earth. The ground trembled, the whole palace shaking, dust drifting from the eaves. Little Tomo yowled at the sky, hopped in small circles on the bedclothes. Michi ran to the bed and threw herself over Aisha, holding her tight as the palace shook on its foundations, windows cracking at the corners. She lay there until the earthquake died, trying not to notice the smell of metal and grease seeping from her mistress's pores.

'The gods are angry,' Aisha breathed. 'The reckoning comes.'

'Aisha, I have to get you out of here.'

'Will you carry me, Michi-chan? All by yourself?'

They heard a distant booming; heavy weight pounding against the iron-shod doors to the bedchambers. Shouted demands to open in the name of various clanlords. Tiger. Phoenix. Dragon.

'You cannot bring these machines, Michi.' Aisha was looking at her now, tears gone. 'They are my lungs. They are my heart. Without them, I would have gone to the peace I earned long ago.'

'But I can't just leave you here!'

'No.'

Aisha looked into her eyes, a small, sad smile on her face.

'No, you cannot.'

Michi blinked, lips parted as she tried to breathe. 'You can't ask me that . . .'

'I would do it myself.' A bitter smile. 'But if I could wield the blade, there would be no call for its mercy.'

'Aisha, no . . .'

'No wedding. No Shōgun.' Aisha licked at dry, cracked lips. 'Do not leave me like this, love. They have picked over my bones enough. Dragged me from the quiet dark into wretched daylight. Show them I am theirs no longer, Michi. Tell them I am done.'

Michi couldn't breathe. Couldn't see for the tears.

'I can't . . .'

'The last of Kazumitsu's seed, that's what they called me. As if that's all I was. Just a womb to produce another heir for this cursed empire. And do you know what they did, Michi? Gods, could anyone begin to imagine?'

Aisha stared into space, her voice paling to a whisper.

'I was too fragile to receive Hiro's seed in the usual fashion. And he found no lust for me in my current condition. But the line of Kazumitsu needed its precious son. The Guild needed to cement their Shōgun's legitimacy. So do you know what they used?' She gritted her teeth, spit the words. 'A metal tube. A handful of lubricant. As if I were cattle, Michi. As if I were *livestock*.'

'My gods . . .'

'Lord Izanagi, deliver me.' Aisha turned her eyes to the ceiling, voice cracking. 'Have mercy upon me, great Maker. If never before this moment, take mercy upon me now.'

'Aisha, I can't . . .'

'You can.'

'I can't.'

'You *must*.'

Michi held her breath, squeezed her eyes shut, shaking her head over and over. She heard the distant sound of heavy blows on iron-shod doors. Splitting timbers.

'I asked when you raised your hand to me, remember?' Aisha said. 'I told you I would ask everything of you. I asked if you would give all. Do you remember?'

'I r-remember.'

'Don't make me beg, Michi. Give me that much.'

'Oh, gods . . .'

A breathless hush fell over the room, a stillness, broken only by the hiss and click of accursed machines. The machines that damned Aisha to this half-life, bid her languish in the gloom, violated by monstrosities. Michi clenched her teeth, forced herself to suck in one shuddering lungful, tasting smoke and blood, metal and grease, the bile of hatred.

Tears spilled from Aisha's eyes. 'I am so afraid . . .'

Michi cupped her cheek in one bloody palm, fingers trembling.

'It will be all right, Aisha.'

The woman closed her eyes, reached down and found a calm, long and quiet and deep. Just the slow rise and fall of her chest, the deep void behind her eyes, dark as the womb where first she slumbered. She opened her eyes, and Michi saw strength there, the old strength that had defied a nation.

'Tell me good-bye, Michi-chan.'

Michi leaned down and kissed her eyes, one after the other, salt on her lips. Aisha kept them closed, even after the kisses had ended, her face as serene as if she were sleeping.

'Good-bye, my Lady,' Michi said.

The hair needle sliced through Aisha's skin, the unfeeling flesh above her pale, blue-scrawled wrists. Once. Twice. A dozen times. No beauty to it. No art. But no pain either.

Blood welled and flowed, sluggish and thick, bright upon the gleaming gold in Michi's hand. The machines beside the bed shuddered, groaning as if unwilling to let her go. Aisha's eyes remained closed, a soft slippage from torture into peaceful slumber. Not the gentle deliverance of a woman passing in her bed, surrounded by loved ones after a life well-lived. Not a saviour's death. Not a hero's.

But at least it was quiet.

Quiet and dark.

Michi forced herself to watch, eyes locked on Aisha's face. And after an age, an eon, an eternity filled with the shudder and moans of those awful machines, there was a soft exhalation. Gentle as a mother's hands. And at last, in the end, there came stillness.

And tears.

52

Illumination

The snare was set, bait moving, quarry drawing close.

Akihito crouched behind a pile of packing crates, a clay bottle full of chi in one hand, tetsubo in the other. At the sound of approaching boots, he nodded to the other Kagé across the alley. Little Butcher dashed around the corner, a kaleidoscope of profanity spewing from her lips, half a dozen bushimen thundering behind her. A hissing, lumbering Iron Samurai followed, spewing chi from his power unit, ō-yoroi painted the white of old bones. Six Kagé dropped from their perches above, nagamaki spears pinning the bushimen to the floor. Akihito rose from his niche and hurled the chi bottle at the Samurai's chest.

Terror of the battlefield those ō-yoroi suits might be, but in the cramped confines of Kigen's labyrinth, the loss of peripheral vision under those bone-white helms was all the advantage the Shadows needed. The Iron Samurai stepped back, bringing his chainswords up to guard as a Kagé appeared from cover and tossed his hand flare.

The man screamed as he ignited, beating at the flames unfurling across his golden tabard, seething up under his faceplate and blistering the skin beneath. Akihito swung his tetsubo in a double-handed grip, nearly knocking the samurai's head off his shoulders. The soldier toppled backward, blood spraying between his helm's iron tusks.

Akihito leaned down with a wince, snatched up the fallen samurai's chainkatana as the Kagé gathered around. Two more of their number had fallen in the fight, neither one of them much more than boys. The guards were moving in bigger patrols, fighting harder – any advantage they had in surprise was fading fast. Akihito knew it wouldn't be long before they met Iron Samurai sweeping the streets in orderly phalanxes, and any edge the Kagé ambush tactics gave would be lost. Hopefully, they'd bought Daichi enough time.

'All right.' Akihito looked at the sky. 'Time to fall back. Everyone split up and make your way to the arena. Our ride will pick us up there. Go.'

The Kagé moved out, pausing at the alley mouth before slipping into the streets and scattering like dry leaves. Akihito was getting ready to move when a smoke-grey shape dropped from an awning overhead, peering at him with piss-yellow eyes.

'*Mreowwwwl,*' it said.

Akihito looked on in astonishment as the ugliest tomcat in Kigen city brushed up against his legs, purring like a tiny earthquake.

'Daken?'

*

Seimi raised the blowtorch in front of Yoshi's face, turned the fuel nozzle and sparked the flint, a burst of smoking heat flaring before their eyes. The boy was trying his best to hold his nerve, but Seimi could see it in the clenched jaw, the pupils dilated to pits, the way each breath made his whole body shake.

It was beautiful.

Seimi leaned close. 'I'm the one who did your boyfriend, you know.'

Yoshi lashed out with his forehead, but Seimi flinched back, sidestepping the spit sprayed in his direction.

'He lasted a *loooong* time, considering.' Seimi grinned like the cat with the cream. 'Must have really cared about you to stand tall that distance. The heart weeps.'

The few Scorpion Children who'd stayed to enjoy the show chuckled in the dark around him. Seimi was a master of the snip and clip; he'd once made an informer last six days in the shackles. Not out of any need, understand – the man had begun singing after thirty minutes. No, Seimi had done it just to see if he could.

He leaned close again, inhaling the fear, savouring it on teeth and tongue. And then he sat cross-legged at the boy's feet and lifted the blowtorch like an orchestra conductor before the music swelled.

'They're going to tell stories about you, boy. Stories to frighten their children.'

Seimi heard scuffling at his back. One of the brothers shouting a warning. And then there was only blinding pain, a knife of burning ice thrust into his neck. He turned with a cry and she stabbed him again, long-nosed pliers ripping his carotid wide, painting the air bright red.

Blood was smeared over her features, spilling from the ruined socket where her left eye had been. But she'd torn away the leather patch covering the other side of her face, and beneath the scarred brow, above the cheek bisected by a long, broken-bottle scar, burned a round, beautiful eye – luminous, glittering like rose-coloured quartz.

'Don't you touch my brother,' she said.

*

'It's in you,' her father was saying. 'You gaijin trash. The white devils are in you. But I can see them. I can get them out . . .'

He leaned in close, holding the broken bottle up to her right eye, jagged edge reflected in that gentle, glowing pink.

'Da, no!' She shook her head, eyes closed tight. 'No, no!'

'I can get them out,' he said.

She felt the bottle sink into her skin, broken glass scraping bone, and she screwed her eyes shut tighter and screamed as loud as she could. And then she heard him gasp, and something wet was falling on her face, and he was reeling off her and staggering to his feet, clutching the chopsticks protruding from his neck. And as he turned, Yoshi thrust another one like a dagger, burying it deep in his eye.

Da lurched forward and swung the bottle at Yoshi's face, ripping a four-inch tear through the brim of his new hat and missing his cheek by a hair's breadth. And then he fell, face forward onto the floor, amidst the ruin of their dinner and the ruin of their lives.

Yoshi stood above him, clenched and bloody fists, dragging in each broken gasp through gritted teeth. Staring down at the monster, the devil, the demon he'd finally conquered.

'Don't you touch my sister,' he said.

*

She'd learned to hide it, since the Worst Day of Her Life. The pale skin they could explain away with the fox blood that lay far back in their family tree. The blonde hair was easier still; just a coat of black cotton dye every few weeks to hide their golden roots.

But her eye?

Green was an oddity, but rose was an impossibility; a legacy of the gaijin blood flowing in her veins, impossible to deny. They had no idea why it had changed – whether it was trauma, age, something else entirely, and they had nobody to ask about it. In a

Downside saké bar, Yoshi overheard a drunken soldier returned fresh from the war, slurring a tale about gaijin witches striding amongst the round-eye hoardes, right eyes aglow with the hue of watered blood. The man spoke of them with horror and awe. And if Shima's people looked down on Burakumin trash, they looked with utter hatred on the eastern barbarians; the enemy that had butchered their colonies, fought their armies to a standstill these last twenty years.

Life for a clanless dog on Kigen's streets would have been hard enough.

But a half-breed gaijin witch-girl?

And so she hid it, even from poor Jurou, sleeping with her patch on, forgetting it herself as best she could; her brother alone knowing the secret behind the leather tied around her face.

Until now . . .

Hana lurched towards the tools on the table, snatching up a hammer as the yakuza closed in around her. She swung wildly, caught one across an outstretched hand, the man cursing and reeling back. But they circled behind, four of them now, closing in like thin and starving wolves, eyes narrowed, teeth bared.

'Hana, run!' Yoshi roared. 'Get out!'

His eyes on hers. Begging. Pleading.

'*Run,* godsdammit! Just leave me and go!'

She looked at him then, the wolves closing in, and despite everything he'd done, everything he'd dragged them into, she found herself smiling.

'Blood is blood,' she said.

One of the Scorpion Children tried to grapple her, and she caught him full in the face with the hammer, splitting his brow and dropping him like a brick. But another seized her from behind, wrapped two arms around her in a crushing, breathless hug, lifting her off the ground as she screamed and kicked and thrashed. The others closed in, all crooked smiles and empty eyes.

... Hana ...!

A grey shape pounced from the shadows, dug in with dirty razors and ran up her captor's legs. The yakuza howled and let her go, clutching at the spitting, hissing flurry of teeth and claws as Hana tumbled to the ground. He shrieked as Daken tore at his face, ripped his cheek and lips to shreds, yowling like an oni fresh from the Yomi gates. Hana crawled away from the yakuza, back towards the table. Hands seized her, tearing her hair as she screamed, a heavy weight bearing her to the ground.

... Hana ...!

She looked up and saw the bloodied yakuza seize Daken by the scruff, tearing him away in a spray of red and shaking him like a rag doll. She cried out as his hurt flowed into her, tearing muscle, popping bone. And as she watched, the man raised the cat high into the air and dashed him down onto the concrete.

Blinding pain, sending her reeling, fingernails clawing stone. Daken raised himself up, hissing, hurting, trying to crawl to safety.

... Hana ...

And as Hana watched, the gangster lifted his foot, spat a curse and stomped on Daken's head.

A scream. A scream of white pain and blackest hatred, a voice she didn't recognize as her own roaring as his spark flickered and died in her mind. She lurched to her feet, tore at the hands holding her, eye fixed on Daken's killer. But two other yakuza held her back, spitting, kicking as the grief tore her throat raw, Yoshi roaring with her, thrashing against his bonds.

She heard a heavy booming noise. A growling motor.

Bubbling screams. Blades chopping at bags of wet mud, splashing and plopping onto the floor. The hands released her and she sank to the ground, stare fixed on the little grey smudge upon the stone. She crawled through the blood, tears running down scarlet cheeks, reaching out to run trembling fingers through that scarred and matted mess.

She remembered the mewling little handful of fur they'd pulled from the storm drain. Those big round eyes blinking up at her as she held him in her palm. The life they'd saved. The life that had saved theirs in return.

'Daken . . .' she whispered.

There were hands on her shoulders, pulling her up, and she turned and screamed and flailed. Arms wrapped around her, holding tight, and the voice roaring over her cries was telling her it was all right, it was all right now, hush, hush now Hana, it's all right. The hands held her close, not hard, gentle and strong and warm. And over the rushing tide of the blood in her ears and the raw agony of loss, she finally recognized his voice.

Akihito . . .

She breathed his name, saw his face, grief plain in his eyes as he lowered her to the floor. He reached out with an unsteady hand, as if to smooth away the hurt where her left eye had been, fingers hovering just shy of her skin. And with tears in his eyes, he leaned forward and placed a gentle kiss on her bloody brow, and simply held her. Wrapped his arms about her and squeezed tight, whole and unmoving, until the cacophony of flames and cries and engines in the distance became too loud to ignore.

Minutes passed. Or hours. She didn't know which.

'I have to let you go,' he said.

'Don't.' She held tighter.

'I'll come back.'

573

'Promise?'

'I promise.'

She released her grip, felt as if she were letting go of driftwood in a raging, spinning sea, sinking down, down, down into nothing. Akihito stood and cut Yoshi off the hook, sliced the tethers at his ankles. And between the pair of them, they helped Hana to her feet, led her limping from the warehouse, stepping out into a hymn of chaos and seething flame that seemed to come from underwater, muted and pulsing with faint light. The city around them trembled, burned, skies filled with smoke and the thunder of sky-ships and the rumble of a distant storm. But all of it seemed so far away; as distant and faint as the pain in her eye, the pain inside her where Daken used to be, all of it drifting up like sparks off the burning city's skin and disappearing into the black above.

'Where are we going?' she asked with someone else's voice.

'North,' Akihito said. 'To the Iishi Mountains.'

'How will we get there?'

He squeezed her tight and the sound of his voice made her smile.

'We're going to fly.'

53

Phoenix Fire

The night sky was the colour of autumn days, a roll and swirl of reds and oranges and yellows, tasting of burning fuel and blackest smoke.

Michi retreated across the palace rooftops in only a silk slip, the thirty-odd pounds of her jûnihitoe abandoned before she'd made the climb. Little Tomo squirmed under one arm, her chainkatana clutched in her other hand. She listened to the chaos in the city beyond, the bushimen clambering up onto the roof after her. Their armour and weapons slowed them down, but it would only be a matter of time before they had her.

The guest wing was fully ablaze now, a flaming maw swallowing mouthfuls of tile and timber, creeping ever closer. Michi swung her chainkatana at a bushiman trying to scramble onto the roof, divesting him of his fingers, watching him scream and kiss the ground forty feet below.

The tiles shook, harder than the earthquake that had struck moments before, the vibrations accompanied by thunderous explosions. Michi looked towards the sky-docks, saw the *Floating Palace* of the Phoenix Daimyo looming above Docktown, spilling dozens upon dozens of barrage barrels from its innards onto the buildings below. Timber was reduced to kindling, metal to shrapnel as the Fushicho flagship emptied its payload onto the Tiger ships stranded at the sky-spires and the Dragon ships in the bay. The air was filled with Phoenix corvettes, firing with seeming abandon into the burning streets, strafing lines of Tiger bushi' with shards of spinning steel. It took Michi a moment to understand what was happening, and as realization dawned, she felt her lips curl into a grim smile.

The Phoenix clanlords have heard news of Aisha's death. No Kazumitsu. No oath.

'Treacherous bastards,' she whispered.

She tore her eyes from the carnage unfolding on the bay, back to her own world of hurt. Squinting through the roiling scrim of woodsmoke, she saw a half dozen bushimen pulling themselves onto the rooftops at the other end of the royal wing – too far away to intercept. She heard metal biting into cedar, four grappling hooks digging into the gutters, silk line pulling taut as more guards ascended. Too many to stop. Too many to fight.

Michi backed across the roof, towards the burning guest wing, hoping the smoke might give her some concealment. Her heart sank as more and more red tabards appeared over the rooftops around her, the bushimen gathering and marching forwards, one grim step at a time, naginata at the ready; a glittering wall of polished steel, gleaming with the light of the flames.

'I'm sorry, little Tomo.' Michi put down the puppy, raised her chainblades. 'You might have to make your own way home.'

Forty feet away, the guards halted at a shout from their commander. The front row fell to one knee, blades outthrust. Michi saw the rear line drawing crossbows, loading them with quarrels thick as broomsticks.

'Cowards!' she screamed. 'Come and get me!'

The commander raised his sword, and the crossbowmen took aim, expressions hidden behind black glass and red kerchiefs. Michi held her breath, stance spread, feeling the chaindaishō motors as a rumble in her chest. But as armoured fingers tightened on triggers, the rumble became a roar, a blast of wind and smoke from propeller blades, a black rain of arrows sailing through the air. She caught a glimpse of bold kanji running down a wooden prow, thick white letters on polished black: KUREA.

The sky-ship thundered down on the rooftop, the sound of her four great motors shaking the very skies. Splitting the tiles asunder, the *Kurea* interposed its hull between the girl and the bushimen's rain of crossbow bolts. Ropes were tossed and Michi thrust her chaindaishō into her obi, scrabbled about on the roof, trying to scoop up Aisha's terrified puppy. The crew above screamed at her to get aboard, the ship beginning to rise. Engines bellowed with the strain, compressors shuddering as they were pushed into the redline, her inflatable groaning like it was about to burst.

Michi finally seized the pup's scruff, grabbed hold of a swaying, knotted line with her free hand. The crew hauled her up as the sky-ship ascended, the air full of smoke and crossbow bolts. Hard, calloused hands dragged her over the railings and she slumped to the floor, breath burning in her lungs as the puppy scampered off across the deck. Propellers carved the air to ribbons, the ship trembling beneath them as they shed gravity's shackles, the light and noise of the burning capital fading away below.

Michi pulled herself to her feet, staring at the crew dashing to and fro.

'Who the hells are you people?'

'Michi-chan,' said a voice.

She turned and saw a tear-streaked face, pale with grief and anger, steel-grey eyes, a long scar cutting from brow to chin.

'Kaori?' Michi reached out as if the woman were an apparition. 'Gods . . .'

And they were in each other's arms, holding tight, as if the whole world might fall away beneath their feet. Michi blinked back the tears, looked at the smoke-stained faces of the folk around her, grim and drawn – faces that spoke of defeat, not victory. Her heart swelled in her chest as she caught sight of Akihito slumped against a far railing, a teenaged boy crouched beside him. Blood-soaked and exhausted, but the big man was alive at least, and for that, she closed her eyes and gave thanks. Aisha's puppy was snuffling about the boy's feet, the shell-shocked lad blinking, reaching down to him with one trembling hand.

'We were expecting to have to fight our way in for you.' Kaori stepped back, their hands still entwined. 'Where is Aisha?'

'Gone.' Michi shook her head. 'She's gone.'

Kaori closed her eyes, looking for a moment as if she might fall. She dragged a feeble breath through gritted teeth, shoulders slumping.

'Then it was all for nothing . . .'

'How did you know where to find me? That I was still in the palace?'

'I told them.'

A girl sat alone against the railing nearby, clothed in shadow and blood. A pale face, painted red. An unruly bob of ink-black hair, one eye covered by a blood-soaked bandage, the other glowing the colour of rose-quartz.

Michi blinked. 'Who are you?'

The girl managed to smile. 'Call me No One, Michi-chan.'

'You . . .' Michi knelt by the girl's side, concern and gratitude filling her with equal measure. The girl looked battered, bruised, bloody. But unbroken. Michi hugged her fiercely, a clumsy, feeble thanks forming on her lips.

'Guild!' A cry rang out from the crow's nest. 'Guild on our tail!'

Michi looked aft, squinting through the exhaust haze. The skies over Kigen were ablaze, a handful of Guild and Tiger sky-ships locked in deadly battle with the traitorous Phoenix fleet. The *Floating Palace* was laying down a wall of shuriken fire to stave off the assault, slowly cruising towards the Shōgun's palace, its retinue of corvettes blurring the sky around it. The entirety of Docktown seemed to be on fire. But a few Guild ships had somehow noticed the *Kurea* in the melee and had turned to pursue. Even with the capital of the Imperium in flames, the chi-mongers had set their sights on the Kagé and intended to run them to ground.

Michi released No One, ran up to the captain's deck, Kaori beside her. Cloudwalkers were gathered at the railing, cursing beneath their breath.

'Two dreadnoughts,' said one.

'Plus the corvettes to run us down,' another spat.

The *Kurea's* captain stood like a stone pillar at the pilot's wheel, tanned skin and sparkling eyes. He was tall and barrel-shaped, with an enormous braided beard and a long plait streaming out behind him. His voice was a drumming roar over the wind.

'All hands to stations! All hands!' He turned to his first mate, teeth clenched. 'Get below. Dump the ballast and any extra weight. Anything that's not nailed down. Go! Go!'

The crew scattered to their posts, half a dozen heading below decks, soon emerging with crates, furniture, ropes and tackle, heaving great handfuls over the side and out into the city below. Michi heard the engines pick up, the four great prop-blades churning the air, tethers and cables groaning with the strain.

'Can we outrun them?' Michi murmured.

The captain glanced at her, slammed the throttle to full ahead.

'Or die trying,' he said.

54

The Cruelest Storm

His bride? Murdered.

His allies? Traitors.

His capital? Ablaze.

All was undone.

Kigen thrashed below him, body charring, skin crawling. Thousands of people fleeing to the city walls, throwing themselves into the bay amidst the flaming ruins of the Dragon clan's tall ships. Empty motor-rickshaws rolling down the roads, burning as they went. Glass falling like rain. Bewildered bystanders, faces streaked with soot and blood. Stepping aside or crushed underfoot. Fire and dancing silhouettes, a tumult, a discord, arms held to the sky and swaying in the pulse.

Chaos.

Hiro stood aboard the flagship *Red Tigress,* watching his world crumble to ruin. After the Phoenix attack on the sky-docks, he'd mustered what defence he could, scrambling aboard his flagship as his city burned. Two Tiger dreadnoughts and three Guild ironclads had managed to intercept the *Floating Palace* on its way into Upside, cut off its assault on the palace proper. But the traitors Shin and Shou had already set fire to half of Docktown, their surprise assault incinerating most of Hiro's heavy ships and half the Guild fleet while still at berth. Worse yet, the Dragon clanlord and his Iron Samurai had quit the field immediately once news of Aisha's murder spread among the troops. Daimyo Haruka had returned to the palace to rescue his wife, but Hiro fully expected him to flee the city afterwards. He supposed he should be grateful the clanlord hadn't turned on him too.

This was their notion of honour? Of Bushido? Of the Way? Once the samurai of this nation had believed in something more than themselves. In courage. Service. Self-sacrifice. And yet quicker than lotusflies, both the Phoenix and the Dragons had turned and bared their fangs, their own dreams of rule burning brighter than the houses in Hiro's capital.

But was he so different?

How pure were his motives for accepting the throne Kensai had dangled before him?

The iron hand at his side clenched, the ashes of funeral offerings caked upon his lips.

'Treacherous bastards all of us . . .' he breathed.

The *Floating Palace* loomed above the slaughter, buoyed by swelling thermals rushing up from Kigen's blazing carcass. With a few more ships, Hiro felt he could have taken on the flying fortress and blown it from the clouds. But, incomprehensibly, Second Bloom Kensai had diverted two Guild ironclads from the battle and sent them chasing the Kagé rebels, now fleeing the city in some Dragon merchantman. Hiro had received reports that the leader of the Kagé had been captured by the Lotusmen – he was already *in their godsdamned hands*. But Kensai seemed intent on ending the rebellion tonight, once and for all. To the hells with Shima's capital. No matter if these effete Fushicho bastards turned Kigen into an inferno.

Shin and Shou had sat at his table. He had welcomed them into his city. And now they were burning that city to cinders. But if Kigen was truly *his*, if the throne, the mantle, the Way held any meaning for him at all, surely he owed it more than a token defence? Surely he owed the people below, *his* people, all he had to give?

Hiro clenched his teeth, enamel grinding, a burning glare set on the towering sky-ship laying all about it to waste. He turned to the *Tigress* captain.

'Send word to the *Kazumitsu's Honour.*' He nodded to the other Tiger vessel floating off their starboard. 'Send to the Guild ships also. Full attack.'

'Hai!' the captain barked.

Engines kicked into the red, the *Tigress* shuddering as she swung her snout around and lumbered towards the enemy. The Phoenix corvettes were swift to intercept, filling the sky between Hiro and his quarry. Crews manning the *Tigress*'s batteries opened up, and *chug!chug!chug!chug!* came the thunder of the shuriken-throwers. The corvettes returned fire, men on both sides became limp, lifeless meat, washing the decks with their insides, red as lotus blooms. Hiro ducked low, a shuriken whistling over his head, two more *spanging* off his spaulders and breastplate. A Phoenix corvette dropped from the sky, crashed into the walls of Kigen arena. Another collided with the Guild ship *Red Bloom,* clipping its inflatable and exploding into flame, the falling ironclad immolating a city block below.

Screams of pain from the streets beneath him. Prayers for mercy.

And there he stood, with none to give.

The Phoenix corvettes came about for a second attack as the Tiger fleet drew within range of the *Floating Palace*'s heavy 'throwers. The barrage hit Hiro's ships like hail in winter's bleakest hour, tearing holes through the *Honour* and littering its decks with dead. Another Phoenix corvette burst into flames and exploded in midair, momentum stringing its remnants out along the sky like fireworks on a feast day. Engines roaring, men around Hiro screaming for coordinates, for ammunition, for their mothers, lying in puddles of their own guts and clutching the places their limbs were supposed to be. The air filled with gleaming, hissing death, a tempo and percussion of razor-sharp steel and *chug!chug!chug!chug!* went the music they all danced to, and when it stopped there was only roaring propellers and cries of pain and lifeless shapes staring at starless skies. Eyes and mouths open. Seeing and saying nothing at all.

'We can't get close, my Lord!' the captain cried. 'Our inflatable is already ruptured! I can't keep her aloft for long!'

'Get on the radio to Kensai!' Hiro roared. 'We need those ironclads back here!'

'They're pursuing the Kagé, great Lord!'

'To the Endsinger with the Kagé! If these Phoenix bastards decide to destroy Kigen rather than claim it as their own—'

As if bidden, the *Floating Palace* changed course, swinging away from the Tiger palace and bringing itself to bear on the smoking chimney stacks to the west of the blazing bay.

The refinery . . .

The ground around the chi refinery glittered with blood-red eyes and firelight reflections, gleaming on the suits of dozens of Guild Purifiers. The Lotusmen were dousing everything in sight with flame-retardant foam, Guild marines spraying burning buildings with black water pumped in from the bay, beating back the inferno from the refinery storage tanks. But if the *Floating Palace* had any fire-barrage munitions in reserve . . .

The captain of *Kazumitsu's Honour* had sent his ship on a roaring collision course with the *Palace*, but as she drew close, her inflatable was riddled with heavy 'thrower fire. The ironclad's return salvo tore great, heaving gouges in the *Palace*'s own balloon, but its sheer size and number of hydrogen compartments kept the behemoth afloat, droning towards its target. The air was filled with half a dozen Phoenix corvettes, cutting through the rolling smoke, airborne sparks dancing like fireflies.

In a minute, maybe less, the Phoenix would be directly over the refinery.

One barrel would be all it took.

'Captain,' Hiro said. 'Set course for the *Palace*. Ramming speed.'

'. . . Hai!'

Hiro cursed, licked ashes from his lips. Be this his last breath, he'd take those honourless dogs down to walk with him in the hells. The iron fist at his side clenched, involuntary, thoughts turning to the vengeance he'd now be forever denied. The murder he'd dreamed of, her face upturned to his, terror in her eyes as he closed iron fingers around that pretty throat and squeezed the very life from her body.

And then thunder tore the skies.

The reverb rolling down his spine, familiar as a lover's fingertips, goosebumps rippling across his skin. Running to the railing. Ashes cracking on his cheeks as he narrowed his eyes, squinted into the fire-clad pall filled with sparks and smoke and screams of the dying.

Looking for them.

Looking for *her*.

And like a dream, there she was.

'Yukiko . . .'

*

Buruu's roar cut the sky, talons tearing through the inflatable of a swift Phoenix corvette, sending it tumbling to the earth. Yukiko was pressed low to his back, katana drawn, hair streaming behind her in a cinder wind. The air was filled with shuriken fire, burning sky-ships, Tiger and Guild and Phoenix, all hammering at each other with every 'thrower they had. The city below was ablaze, folk fleeing in screaming droves, the night almost as bright as the day. Chaos. Absolute bloody chaos.

LOVELY WEDDING.

Buruu's thoughts echoed in the Kenning, underscored with the reverb of psychic trauma in the city below and fatigue from their frantic eight-day flight here. Yukiko's eyes were full of sand, head heavy as lead, bruised face and pounding skull. Every muscle aching. Every breath burning. Buruu and Kaiah had both given almost everything to get here, but at least they'd made it in time to see. The sight filled her with horror and joy, the fury and bedlam of it all. She had no idea where they'd even begun, but somehow Kin and Daichi and Kaori had done it. Set the wolves upon each other. Torn the wedding night to tatters and Hiro's dreams of dominion to ruins. She could taste smoke through her grin.

Reaching out through the Kenning's heat, she felt for the thunder of Kaiah's psyche, pulled the female arashitora's thoughts into herself, wincing at the volume. Beneath a pulsing rush of pain against her wall, blood on her lips, she could feel both thunder tigers inside her mind, her thoughts a conduit between each, her skull echoing with the pair's bloodlust and awe.

I don't know what the hells is going on here. But unless I'm mad, those Phoenix ships are attacking the city.

– LEAVE MONKEY-CHILDREN TO THEIR SLAUGHTER? –

Buruu growled in response.

THERE ARE INNOCENTS IN THE CITY BELOW.

Buruu is right, we can't just—

A burst of 'thrower fire gleamed through the smoke towards them, Buruu and Kaiah splitting apart and weaving through the shards. The Tiger and Guild vessels had spotted them, opening up with their batteries alongside the Phoenix ships. Whatever enmity had sprung up between the two clans, it seemed to vaporize in the presence of Yoritomo's assassin and two full-grown thunder tigers. But glancing at the deck of the monstrous Fushicho flagship, Yukiko could see her crews loading barrage-barrels into firing tubes, priming ignition charges. Picturing the bombardment of the Iishi forest in her mind's eye, looking at the course they were on, Yukiko felt a cold dread in her gut beside the two burning sparks of life she could now feel with every part of –

They're going to attack the refinery chi reserves! Kaiah, you keep the smaller ships off our tails long enough for us to deal with the big one!

A low growl was her only response, and Buruu was swooping and rolling through the withering hail of shuriken spewing from the flagship's flanks. The Tiger and Guild vessels were still pouring on the fire too, a stray burst cutting one pursuing corvette to shreds. Yukiko slipped into the heat behind Buruu's eyes, felt the thunder of his pulse inside her own chest, clinging to him with all her strength as they wove through the silver rain. She felt herself falling inside him, that familiar totality stretching out to envelope her, infant lightning playing at the tips of her fingers as he opened her mouth and roared. And there in the fire-torn black, the air around her filled with whistling death, his heat beneath her skin and her thoughts within his mind, they felt the warmth of them, the *four* of them, and found a oneness no other could ever know.

Crashing through a corvette's inflatable, canvas torn to ribbons, the screeching of propeller blades across the sky. Falling and flying and spinning and swooping, her beak open as he roared and clapped their wings together, blue-white flaring across the severed beauty of their feathers and Raijin Song, *Raijin Song*, stretching out and taking hold of the night's hem, tearing it to tatters and the ships filling it alongside, a shock wave from the heart of them smashing the tiny flying things as if they were wrought of glass. Through the spinning fragments, towards the hulking shape of the death writ large over Kigen skies, the Phoenix and their palace of pleasures, now sowing death in great flaming handfuls through the streets below. Kaiah's roar thrilling them, electricity rippling along her hackles, bellowing in response, the cry for war, the call for blood, blood, blood like rain as they tore another wingless fly from the air.

But to sink in it?

To drown?

Down through the hail, a strike to his shoulder, blood on her feathers, shrieking in rage. Swooping under the belly of the colossal ship, a brief moment of stillness in the shadow below, gravity clutching them cold and trembling as they dragged themselves up the other side, momentum and mass and beautiful, thunderous will ripping them up past the astonished faces of the Phoenix crews, the open howling mouths of two men with painted eyes and beautiful, perfect faces, resplendent in sunflower silk fine enough to die in. Riding a beast of metal and wood and canvas – the dream of monkeys crawled down from the trees, looking to the skies since the day they were born and filled with yearning. To feel the clouds kiss their faces and the wind in their hair and the weak slip of gravity as it fell away like a tiny, mewling thing. A question. Always.

Why not, my friend?

Why not fly?

And they screamed it – the two (four) who were one (one), there at the last, talons outstretched and rending deep, compartment after compartment, the skin of the false-flyer peeled open like ripe fruit and spilling the squeal of escaping hydrogen out in the flooded night. Screamed their throat raw. Screamed for all the world to hear and feel and know. The answer why not, my friend, why not fly.

Because the skies are ours.

Because the sky is mine.

And the fire bloomed in their talons, reflected in their eyes, gleaming amber and bottomless black, trembling in their grip. The tiny handheld flare, just a spark unworthy of the name of flame. How easy would it be to hurl it towards the vapour, like a lover heartsick from a day of solitude, back into its beloved's arms? And in that marriage, that love, that lust, conflagration would bloom, a shattering as wide and bright as a god's eye, searing and blistering and mushroom-shaped. An unmaking filled with the scream of Phoenix lords, princelings undone by flame's bright kiss, their *Palace* blown to splinters and shards of iron, raining down on fair Kigen like the cruelest storm. Ashes to scatter on the screaming wind, falling like fine snow, swirling amidst the smoke and char and soot and dusting the gutters with all they had been and ever would be.

Not enough left for even a Phoenix to rise from.

How easy would it be?

They dug their knuckles into her temples. Bloodlust pounding in their (her) skull. They had been here before. The sight of three ironclads tumbling from the sky in her (their) mind's eye. Ayane's terrified gaze. Takeo's letter. Her own tears. Kin's voice echoing in their thoughts.

'And piece by piece I see the Yukiko I know falling away . . .'

They blinked.

Too easy.

And they saw true. The hundreds of lives aboard the Phoenix flagship. The men and women who were not soldiers or clanlords, samurai or butchers. The servants and engineers, the cabin boys and deckhands. The people who dreamed of beloveds' arms or children's smiles, not growling swords and empty thrones – all of them would die if she let the flare fall. If she let herself slip beneath the flood. If she gave anger its head.

Is that what she was? Is that what she'd become?

What her father had died for?

The *Floating Palace* groaned, her inflatable crumpling under its own weight as hydrogen hissed into the burning night. And with a fierce cry they hurled the flare, not towards the sinking sky-ship, but out into the bay, down into the black water beneath them, the tiny trembling spark swallowed in the dark. The flagship fell, slow if not graceful, the bladder that had once kept her afloat now streaming behind her in tatters. And their voice echoed in their own minds, uncertain where hers ended and his began, his gentle smile on her lips.

LET US HOPE THIS FLOATING PALACE *LIVES UP TO ITS NAME.*

Kaiah called, a roar filling the empty space before the ship's thunderous impact into the mouth of the Junsei, the black foaming flow gushing up over the banks in a great rushing wave and dousing the smouldering houses at the water's edge. The *Palace* sank down to its railings, scummed water flooding the decks and streaming back out in a hundred waterfalls as the hulk resurfaced, her balloon falling over her like a shroud, steam rising from the banks. Wallowing in her own ruins as the Phoenix corvettes scattered like rats when the corpse runs out. The Phoenix princelings on their knees, smeared in black and screaming with impotent rage. But alive.

Alive.

Through the smoke and billowing flames they wheeled, falling back inside one another again, Buruu and Yukiko, Yukiko and Buruu, the city's pyre setting their eyes aglow. Lightning flickered in the clouds overhead, through the haze of bitter-black smoke, a pulse setting their own pulses to quickening. The remaining Guild ships had gathered in tight formation, bristling with death – awaiting the girl they all feared. Bated breath, bellows falling still, dry mouths and sweat-soaked flesh hidden beneath skins of gleaming brass. Chattering mechabacii. Chattering mouths. Setting their teeth on edge.

Hackles rising. Smoke in their mouths. Decks crawling with chi-mongers. Bloodlust pulsing, swelling, *wanting,* spilling from each thunder tiger into the Kenning, amplified and purified, doubling and trebling and feeding upon itself. They stared at this tiny pack of metal insects, blind grubs who thought themselves so far above the hell they forged that its flames would never reach them. Each ship crewed by soldiers and Lotusmen; no innocents here, just killers, all. And through the smoke, they saw it, saw it for the first time – the hulking ironclad daubed in Tiger red, three flags streaming from its stern marked with the Daimyo's seal.

Through his eyes they gazed, sharp as new pins and twice as bright, onto the choked deck. Through the crowd of little boys in their smoking armour, stained with the colour of death, there, *there* to the littlest boy of all. The boy they had given themselves to. The boy they had loved (she had loved) and the sight of him, daubed corpse-white with his ashen face set the bloodlust swelling again, gripping her tight, dragging her in. Buruu's need to kill, pure and primal, rushing over her like a flood. Filling her. Fighting her. Dragging her down to drown.

But she kicked. Fought. Seethed. To pull herself free, rip herself out, back from the oneness and into herself, the taste of her own blood on her lips and the pain flooding through the cracks in her wall. Just herself again. Just Yukiko.

Unwhole.

Buruu reared up into the air, metal wings spread wide, Yukiko sitting up tall on his back. Delirium and vertigo, the sense of her own body for a moment utterly alien, her flesh shivering and cold. The thunder tiger beneath her roared, time slowing to a crawl as she felt the blood flee her face, lips parted as she struggled for breath. Eyes fixed on the tall figure standing on the bow, even now drawing his swords, pointing his chainkatana at her, screaming challenge.

'Hiro,' she breathed.

Lips peeled back from her teeth. Eyes locked with his. The green of Kitsune jade. The green of lotus fronds. But not the green of the sea, no, not the green she had named them for. Because the seas around this island she called home were red, red as lotus, red as blood, poisoned scarlet by these bastards and their stinking, wretched weed.

She could see Hiro's face, twisted with rage, gesturing for his samurai to clear a space on the foredeck. To back away, let him stand alone. His words were lost in the drone of the engines, the howl of the flames, but his gestures made his intent clear. Calling Yukiko out. Demanding a duel. Satisfaction. Vengeance. He beat one fist upon his chest – an *iron* fist – gestured for his samurai to step farther back. Holding his arms wide, eyes locked on the girl and her thunder tiger. Actions speaking louder than any words.

Come on.

He bellowed, pointing his chainkatana at her again.

Come and get me.

Buruu growled, low and long, their hatred spilling into each other and gleaming in his eyes. It could all end. The Guild's ambitions for Hiro's rule. The threat of war still looming large over Shima. The stormclouds gathering on distant horizons. All of it could end, here and now.

WHY DO WE FALTER?

Buruu's thoughts in her head, as always, echoing the deepest recesses of her own.

THE PHOENIX I UNDERSTAND. THERE WERE INNO-CENTS ABOARD THAT SHIP. BUT HIRO WANTS YOU DEAD. THE GUILD BACK HIM TO THE HILT. THIS IS KILL OR BE KILLED, YUKIKO.

She struggled for breath, clawing her hair from her eyes.

And then what? If we kill him, the Guild will just choose another puppet. Another thrall.

THIS IS THE PATH YOU CHOSE. THIS IS THE RIVER OF BLOOD I PROMISED.

And weren't you afraid I would drown in it?

ALL YOU NEED DO IS DIVE IN AND SWIM.

I . . .

She wiped her fist across her nose, brought it away bloody.

Kaiah wheeled through the sky, circling them, roaring again, fairly trembling with anticipation.

Her hand strayed to her belly.

I don't think I can, brother . . .

WE KILLED HIM ONCE. WE CAN DO IT AGAIN.

Yukiko sat tall on his back, katana clutched in her hand.

I let anger and vengeance cloud my judgement before. We've killed hundreds of people and what has it gotten us? Where has it led us? We killed Yoritomo and simply made more chaos. We had a hand in all of this, Buruu. We helped set this city, this whole nation, on fire.

We have to be more than this. More than rage. More than revenge. Or else we will *drown, Buruu. You. Me. All of us. Just like you said.*

The beast growled, hackles rippling.

HE DESERVES IT FOR WHAT HE DID TO YOU. THIS BOY DESERVES TO DIE.

Yukiko sank down on his shoulders, a fire wind whipping hair across her eyes.

Everything dies, brother.

She stared at the boy on the deck of his ship, watching him roar and rage and rev his blades. All that was. That could have been. That would never be again. The memory of a tablet in a garden of stone, marked with her own father's name. The memory of his loss, real and sharp in her mind. Hand slipping from her belly to the blade he'd given her, all she had left of him save fading memories. And she stared at the boy whom once she loved, the arms that had once encircled her waist as he pressed his lips to hers – one of flesh, and one of cold, dead iron. She reached across the gulf between them, into the burning fire of his thoughts, acutely aware of how little effort it would take to simply

. . . squeeze. And there, amidst that impossible tangle, curled at the edges by rage and despair, she caught an impression. A single revelation. A fragment of knowledge, consuming, inundating, immolating all he was.

Aisha gone.

Dead.

So much blood.

And looking down on the ruins of the city below, the smoke and the bodies, the scarlet in the streets deep enough to sink in, the thought of adding one more drop filled her to sickening.

What we came here to do has been done for us.

WHAT?

The wedding has been stopped, Buruu. The dynasty is in ruins. The Guild's plan is undone.

She ran one hand through his fur.

Enough for today.

She sheathed the katana at her back. Put away her anger and tossed her head. The boy in his ash-pale iron roared and spat and screamed, and her hands drifted once more to her stomach, to the dread and horror and enormity she felt swelling there. Fire burning in her mind. The city burning below. The Shōgun's peace in tatters, the civil war inevitable now. Tiger against Dragon. Dragon against Fox. Fox against Tiger. The Guild amongst it all.

'Good-bye Hiro . . .'

And as they turned away from Kigen, cutting through the air back to the north, a single thought burned like a star in her mind. A promise on a not-too-distant horizon, so close she could taste it in the very air. A certainty, light as iron, warm as ice, that Buruu's river would swallow them all now, no matter what they did.

The Lotus War has begun.

55

Army of the Sun

The wolves had almost run them to ground.

Michi hovered by the railing on the captain's deck, watching the pursuing floodlights grow larger. The running lights of the corvettes were smaller, brighter, the drone of their engines of a higher pitch. She fancied she could make out something of their shape in the glow of their floods and the hint of a distant dawn; sleek and sharp, like knives flung through the air, speeding right towards them.

The *Kurea*'s captain stood by the wheel, occasionally looking back over his shoulder and spitting, knuckles white on the controls. The ship's engines were at full-burn, temperature gauges hovering in the red, her aft shuddering with the strain. Smoke poured from her exhaust, her four propellers making the sound of thunder. But no matter how hard her captain willed it, no matter how loud her engines bellowed, she simply wasn't fast enough to outrun the hounds on her tail.

'What happens when the corvettes catch us?' Kaori asked.

'They'll hit our engines to wound us, slow us down enough for the ironclads to catch up. Then they'll board. They'll want to take us alive.'

'That can't happen,' Kaori said.

'I know,' he nodded. 'I know.'

'What is your name, Captain-san?' Michi said.

'They call me the Blackbird.' He tipped his hat.

Michi nodded. 'A pleasure to die with you, Blackbird-san.'

She could see the corvettes clearly now; a pair, just a few hundred feet off their stern. Their inflatables were flattened, shaped like the leaves of a beech tree or an arrowhead, hulls streamlined to cut through the wind like blades. Their small crews were gathered on deck; brass suits and glowing eyes, peering at them through the lenses of telescoping spyglasses. She drew in a shuddering, hateful breath at the sight of the Guildsmen, remembering Aisha chained to those wretched machines, that wretched life.

The Kagé gathered their weapons, Kaori beside her, Daichi's wakizashi in her hand. The older woman looked at Michi, nodded once, loose strands of raven hair whipping about her eyes. As good a place as any, she supposed. And better company, she couldn't hope to find.

The corvettes closed in, the claw heads of their fore-mounted net-throwers springing open as if fingers on iron hands, heavy wire cable slung between each digit like strands of spiderweb. The Guild gunners bent low over their sights, thumbs poised on firing studs.

Michi licked her lips, tasted the wind, thick with chi-stink. She looked down at the land below, vast stretches of lotus fields barely visible in the predawn light. She imagined sleepy farmers rising from their beds, wives cooking breakfast, men heading out into crops choking the very life from the soil. Too busy with their tiny lives to realize what they were doing, who they were robbing, where the road they walked would lead. And in the skies above their heads, men and women who'd decided to stand up, to resist, were about to die for their sakes, and none of them would ever know they had lived at all.

She thought of poor Ichizo. Of the choice he'd offered. Of the life she could have lived. And then she looked at the people beside her, her brothers and her sisters; the family she had chosen to stand beside in defiance of the Guild and its tyranny.

The wrench among the gears. The buzzing in their ears. The sum of all their fears: that no matter how much they smothered, how much they lied, how much they owned, there would still be people willing to defy, to stand tall, to fight and bleed and die for the sake of the strangers below, the tiny lives, the people who would never know their names, the children yet unborn.

And Michi held her chainkatana high and screamed; a single clear note of challenge, taken up by the men and women around her, until *Kurea*'s deck was nothing but open mouths and bared teeth and raised, glittering blades. Fists in the air. Cries roiling in altitude's chill, each breath taken freely in the sunlight worth a thousand drawn in the shadow of slavery.

And their scream was answered.

A harsh cry, a shriek of winter wind, high and fierce. A second joining it, underscored with the rumble of thunder across autumn skies. And the hair on Michi's arms stood up and her eyes grew wide, and the breath caught in her lungs as her heart began singing inside her chest.

'I know that sound . . .' she breathed.

A white shape streaked out of the clouds, down the *Kurea*'s starboard side; the rumble of a storm in its wake. Wings as broad as houses, feathers as white as Iishi snow. A second shape followed down the port side, floodlights glinting on iridescent metal, highlighting the figure on its back; a pale girl in mourning black, a dark ribbon of hair whipping in the wind behind her. And Michi screamed again, screamed at the top of her lungs, eyes full of tears as the arashitora thundered past, circled back around and bore down on the Guild ships like lighting hurled from the hands of the Storm God.

'Yukiko!' she screamed. '*Yukiko!*'

The decks of the corvettes moved like insect hives kicked from their perches, the Guildsmen rushing about as panic took hold, pointing towards the shapes swooping towards them, the nightmare that woke them sweating in the dark. Slayer of Shōguns. Ender of empires.

The Girl all Guildsmen Feared.

The net-throwers fired, spools of metal singing in the air, the arashitora moving like poetry between the wailing cables. Buruu and Yukiko swept beneath the keel of the right corvette, coming up on her port side and tearing her engine loose in a bright plume of rolling flame. The sky-ship spun on its axis, listing hard to one side, her crew leaping out into the dark, rocket packs arcing in the brightening night as their vessel tumbled earthwards. The second arashitora sailed over the inflatable of the sister corvette, reaching down with ebony claws and shredding the canvas; peeling it away from the framework spine like bloated corpse-skin. Hydrogen shrieked as it escaped into the dark, the corvette plummeting from the sky like a broken bird, spiralling down towards its end, Lotusmen fleeing its ruins amidst plumes of blue-white flame.

The Kagé roared in triumph, weapons raised to the sky as the white shapes wheeled about and returned to the *Kurea*'s flank. Yukiko sat up straight, held her hand high in the air, fingers curled into a fist. Dozens of fists were raised in answer, Akihito leaning over the railing and bellowing Yukiko's name, hand outstretched. Buruu roaring like colliding thunderheads, his cry echoed by the second thunder tiger on their starboard side as the light of Lady Sun finally cleared the eastern horizon and set the skies aflame.

Michi sheathed the chainkatana at her waist, exhaustion and relief and bitter, black sorrow, Aisha's passing weighing heavy on her heart. But at the sound of the Kagé cheers, the joy shining on Akihito's face, the sight of fists rising into the air as the Guild ships fell back, she found a faint smile blooming on her lips. Breathing just a little easier. Happy for a moment just to be alive, in the space where death had loomed just moments before. When all had seemed lost. When all hope was gone.

The second thunder tiger bellowed loud enough to set the *Kurea*'s rivets chattering, descending in a broad spiral around the sky-ship, the Kagé's eyes alight with wonderment. And as Yukiko and Buruu swept around the stern amidst their triumphant cries, fingers balled tight and thrust in the sky, as their eyes met across that howling trail of blue-black smoke and Yukiko called her name, Michi found herself grinning, raising her fist into the air.

And together, the arashitora and the *Kurea* turned north, towards the shadow of the Iishi on the horizon, bathed in the light of a dawn long overdue.

Not a victory. Not even close.

But perhaps . . .

Michi nodded.

Perhaps soon.

56

Womb

The cage stank of dried blood. Of failure and fear. The soup-thick reek of lotus smoke and stale human waste made Kin's eyes water, the boiling thrum of the chapterhouse above reverberating into tired bones. The manacles were cutting off his circulation, and he wriggled the numbness from his fingers. Sweat burning his eyes, fumes burning his lungs, he hung his head and waited in the aching dark.

His cage was one of hundreds, row upon row of iron bars, running the ribs of a vast, gloom-soaked room. The wall at his back was dirty yellow, armpit-moist with condensation, slick and warm to the touch. Not so long ago, the chapterhouse cells would have been filled with flesh – the old and the infirm, women and children with fair skin and wide, round eyes and blonde and red and auburn hair, all waiting their turn to shuffle meekly into the inochi vats and meet their boiling end. But now the cages were empty, one after another, bare, sweating stone picked out by pinpricks of flickering halogen.

He closed his eyes, sought his centre, the emptiness of self he'd found in the workshop, the long silence within the press of his metal shell. He could feel sweat creeping into the plugs studding his flesh, the pull of cable beneath. He tried to block out the half-remembered echo of the mechabacus in his head, the stink of the smoke and the shit, to remember why he'd come here. Why he'd chosen this.

He thought of the girl, felt the lead-lined wings of butterflies in his stomach, heart thumping in his chest. He pictured her standing on a rope footbridge in the Iishi village, a silhouette etched against ancient trees as the moon took his throne, wind running its fingers through her hair.

To be the wind . . .

He remembered the kiss in the dark, shrouded in wisteria perfume. He could still feel her body against him, the soft, insistent press of her lips against his. He remembered how she'd looked, crying in the gloom, moonlight glittering in her tears. He remembered the taste of them. The heartbroken sigh.

'We don't belong here.'

Guilt tied his stomach in knots, and choked his butterflies one by one.

Kin felt him before he heard him, more an absence than a presence; a dead-blossom scent or the empty in an echo's wake. He opened his eyes and saw the figure lurking at the halogen's cusp, serene as a sleepwalker. Small and slender, sun-starved skin, shaved head, loose dark cloth. Sleek black filters of a mechanical breather, bottomless eyes so scrawled with capillaries there was nothing but red around his irises. Hands clasped, long, clever fingers intertwined like a penitent before a shrine. If it were not for the soft rise and fall of his chest, the chi smoke spilling from his mask with every exhalation, Kin would have thought him a statue.

His voice was soft as lullabies, a metallic whisper behind the breather.

'Do you know who I am?'

'No,' Kin said.

'Do you know *what* I am?'

'Of course, Inquisitor.'

And so they began to speak.

Epilogue

Now witness the beginning of the end.

A ghost-pale boy, seventeen years old, tendrils of blue-black vapour and drying scarlet scrawled across his face. A motionless figure, swathed in black, the boy's fate held in the palm of his hand. The pair speaking in the chapterhouse bowels as countless hours swirl and dance in the gulf between them. And the Inquisitor finally nods, and opens his mouth, and speaks the words the boy has longed to hear.

'Welcome home, young brother.'

So here I sit. Back again. The Lotus Guildsman who betrayed all he knew, and all he was. Who gifted his brethren with the leader of the Kagé cabal. Who helped a lone girl undo the rebellion, and drag this nation back from the tempest. Traitor is the name I will wear in the histories. Kioshi was the name I inherited after my father died.

But in truth, my name is Kin.

I remember what it was to be encased in metal skin. To see the world through blood-red glass. To stand apart and above and beyond and know there was so much more. And even now, here in the depths of the chapterhouse that birthed me, the only home I have ever truly known, I can hear the whispers of the mechabacus in my head, feel the phantom weight of that skin on my back and on my bones, and part of me misses it so badly it makes my chest hurt.

I remember the night I learned the truth of myself – my future laid bare in the Chamber of Smoke. I remember the Inquisitors coming for me, swathed in black and soundless as cats, telling me it was time to see my What Will Be. I try to recall the certainty I felt as I walked from that chamber, try to recall what it was like to be proud of who I was. To feel the flesh tingle beneath my skin as I accepted my Truth. Stepping into a new life. A bright and gleaming future.

The What Will Be.

My What Will Be.

Thirteen years old and they call you a man.

I had never watched the sun kiss the horizon, setting the sky on fire as it sank below the lip of the world. Never felt the whisper-gentle press of a night wind on my face. Never known the feel of her skin against mine, the touch of her lips lighting fires on my own. Never known what it was to belong or betray. To refuse or resist. To love or to lose.

But I knew who I was. I knew who I was supposed to be.

Skin was strong.

Flesh was weak.

I wonder now, how that boy could have been so blind.

Glossary

GENERAL TERMS

Arashitora – literally 'stormtiger'. A mythical creature with the head, forelegs and wings of an eagle, and the hindquarters of a tiger. Thought to be long extinct, these beasts were traditionally used as flying mounts by the caste of legendary Shima heroes known as 'Stormdancers'. These beasts are also referred to as 'thunder tigers'.

Arashi-no-odoriko – literally 'Stormdancer'. Legendary heroes of Shima's past, who rode arashitora into battle. The most well-known are Kitsune no Akira (who slew the great sea dragon Boukyaku) and Tora Takehiko (who sacrificed his life to close Devil Gate and stop the Yomi hoardes escaping into Shima).

Blood Lotus – a toxic flowering plant cultivated by the people of Shima. Blood lotus poisons the soil in which it grows, rendering it incapable of sustaining life. The blood lotus plant is utilized in the production of teas, medicines, narcotics and fabrics. The seeds of the bloom are processed by the Lotus Guild to produce 'chi'; the fuel that drives the machines of the Shima Shōgunate.

Burakumin – a low-born citizen who does not belong to any of the four zaibatsu clans.

Bushido – literally 'the Way of the Warrior'. A code of conduct adhered to by the samurai caste. The tenets of Bushido are: rectitude, courage, benevolence, respect, honesty, honour and loyalty. The life of a Bushido follower is spent in constant preparation for death; to die with honour intact in the service of their Lord is their ultimate goal.

Bushiman – a common-born soldier who has sworn to follow the Way of Bushido.

Chan – a diminutive suffix applied to a person's name. It expresses that the speaker finds the person endearing. Usually reserved for children and young women.

Chi – literally 'blood'. The combustible fuel which drives the machines of the Shima Shōgunate. The fuel is derived from the seeds of the blood lotus plant.

Daimyo – a powerful territorial Lord that rules one of the Shima zaibatsu. The title is usually passed on through heredity.

Fushicho – literally 'Phoenix'. One of the four zaibatsu clans of Shima. The Phoenix clan live on the island of Yotaku (Blessings) and venerate Amaterasu, Goddess of the Sun. Traditionally, the greatest artists and artisans in Shima come from the Phoenix clan. Also: the kami guardian of the same zaibatsu, an elemental force closely tied to the concepts of enlightenment, inspiration and creativity.

Gaijin – literally 'foreigner'. A person not of Shimanese decent. The Shima Shōgunate has been embroiled in a war of conquest in the gaijin country of Morcheba for over twenty years.

Inochi – literally 'life'. A fertilizer which, when applied to crops of blood lotus, delays the onset of soil degradation caused by the plant's toxicity.

Irezumi – a tattoo, created by inserting ink beneath the skin with steel or bamboo needles. Members of all Shima clans wear the totem of their clan on their right shoulder. City dwellers will often mark their left shoulder with a symbol to denote their profession. The complexity of the design communicates the wealth of the bearer – larger, more elaborate designs can take months or even years to complete and cost many hundreds of kouka.

Kami – spirits, natural forces or universal essences. This word can refer to personified deities, such as Izanagi or Raijin, or broader elemental forces, such as fire or water. Each clan in Shima also has a guardian kami, from which the clan draws its name.

Kazumitsu Dynasty – the hereditary line of Shōgun that rule the Shima Imperium. Named for the first of the line to claim the title – Kazumitsu I – who led a successful revolt against the corrupt Tenma Emperors.

Kitsune – literally 'Fox'. One of the four zaibatsu clans of Shima, known for stealth and good fortune. The Kitsune clan live close to the haunted Iishi Mountains, and venerate Tsukiyomi, the God of the Moon. Also: the kami guardian of the same zaibatsu, said to bring good fortune to those who bear his mark. The saying 'Kitsune looks after his own' is often used to account for inexplicable good luck.

Kouka – the currency of Shima. Coins are flat and rectangular, made of two strips of plaited metal; more valuable iron, and less valuable copper. Coins are often cut into smaller pieces to conduct minor transactions. These small pieces are known as 'bits'. Ten copper kouka buys one iron kouka.

Lotus Guild – a cabal of zealots who oversee the production of chi and the distribution of inochi fertilizer in Shima. Referred to collectively as 'Guildsmen', the Lotus Guild is comprised of three parts; rank-and-file 'Lotusmen', the engineers of the 'Artificer' sect, and the religious arm known as 'Purifiers'. 'False-Lifers' are a sub-sect of the Artificer caste.

Oni – A demon of the Yomi underworld, reputedly born to the Goddess Izanami after she was corrupted by the Land of the Dead. Old legends report that their legion is one thousand and one strong. They are a living embodiment of evil, delighting in slaughter and the misfortune of man.

Ryu – literally 'Dragon'. One of the four zaibatsu clans of Shima, renowned as great explorers and traders. In the early days before Empire, the Ryu were a seafaring clan of raiders who pillaged among the northern clans. They venerate Susano-ō, God of Storms. Also: the kami guardian of the same zaibatsu, a powerful spirit beast and elemental force associated with random destruction, bravery and mastery of the seas.

Sama – a suffix applied to a person's name. This is a far more respectful version of 'san'. Used to refer to one of much higher rank than the speaker.

Samurai – a member of the military nobility who adheres to the Bushido Code. Each samurai must be sworn to the service of a Lord – either a clan Daimyo, or the Shōgun himself. To die honourably in service to one's Lord is the greatest aspiration of any samurai's life. The most accomplished and wealthy amongst these warriors wear chi-powered suits of heavy armour called 'ō-yoroi', earning them the name 'Iron Samurai'.

San – a suffix applied to a person's name. This is a common honorific, used to indicate respect to a peer, similar to 'Mr' or 'Mrs'. Usually used when referring to males.

Sensei – a teacher.

Seppuku – a form of ritualized suicide in which the practitioner disembowels himself and is then beheaded by a kaishakunin (a 'second', usually a close and trusted comrade). Death by seppuku is thought to alleviate loss of face, and can spare the family of the practitioner shame by association. An alternative version of seppuku, called 'jumonji giri' is also practised to atone for particularly shameful acts. The practitioner is not beheaded – instead he performs a second vertical cut in his belly and is left to bear his suffering quietly until dying from blood loss.

Shōgun – literally 'Commander of a force'. The title of the hereditary military dictator of the Shima Imperium. The current line of rulers is descended from Tora Kazumitsu, an army commander who led a bloody uprising against Shima's former hereditary rulers, the Tenma Emperors.

Seii Taishōgun – literally 'great general who subdues eastern barbarians'.

Tora – literally 'Tiger'. The greatest of the four zaibatsu of Shima, and the clan from which the Kazumitsu Dynasty originates. The Tora are a warrior clan, who venerate Hachiman, the God of War. Also: the kami guardian of the same zaibatsu, closely associated with the concept of ferocity, hunger and physical desire.

Yōkai – a blanket term for preternatural creatures thought to originate in the spirit realms. These include arashitora, sea dragons and the dreaded oni.

Zaibatsu – literally 'plutocrats'. The four conglomerate clans of the Shima Imperium. After the rebellion against the Tenma Emperors, Shōgun Kazumitsu rewarded his lieutenants with stewardship over vast territories. The clans to which the new Daimyo belonged (Tiger, Phoenix, Dragon and Fox) slowly consumed the clans of the surrounding territories through economic and military warfare, and became known as 'zaibatsu'.

CLOTHING

Hakama – a divided skirt that resembles a wide-legged pair of trousers, tied tight into a narrow waist. Hakama have seven deep pleats – five in front, two at the back – to represent the seven virtues of Bushido. An undivided variant of hakama exists (i.e. a single leg, more like a skirt) intended for wear over a kimono.

Jin-haori – a kimono-style tabard worn by samurai.

Jûnihitoe – an extraordinarily complex and elegant style of kimono, worn by courtly ladies.

Kimono – an ankle-length, T-shaped robe with long, wide sleeves, worn by both men and women. A younger woman's kimono will have longer sleeves, signifying that she is unmarried. The styles range from casual to extremely formal. Elaborate kimono designs can consist of more than twelve separate pieces and incorporate up to sixty square feet of cloth.

Mempō – a face mask, one component of the armour worn by samurai. Mempō are often crafted to resemble fantastical creatures, or made in twisted designs intended to strike fear into the enemy.

Obi – a sash, usually worn with kimono. Men's obi are usually narrow; no more than four inches wide. A formal woman's obi can measure a foot in width and up to twelve feet in length. Obi are worn in various elaborate styles and tied in decorative bows and knots.

Uwagi – a kimono-like jacket that extends no lower than

mid-thigh. Uwagi can have long, wide sleeves, or be cut in sleeveless fashion to display the wearer's irezumi.

WEAPONS

Daishō – A paired set of swords, consisting of a katana and wakizashi. The weapons will usually be constructed by the same artisan, and have matching designs on the blades, hilts and scabbards. The daishō is a status symbol, marking the wearer as a member of the samurai caste.

Katana – A sword with a single-edged, curved, slender blade over two feet in length, and a long hilt bound in criss-crossed cord, allowing for a double-handed grip. Katana are usually worn with shorter blades known as wakizashi.

Nagamaki – a pole weapon with a large and heavy blade. The handle measures close to three feet, with the blade measuring the same. It closely resembles a naginata, but the weapon's handle is bound in similar fashion to a katana hilt – cords wrapped in criss-crossed manner.

Naginata – a pole weapon, similar to a spear, with a curved, single-edged blade at the end. The haft typically measures between five and seven feet. The blade can be up to three feet long, and is similar to a katana.

Ō-yoroi – suits of heavy samurai armour powered by chi-fuelled engines. The armour augments the wearer's strength, and is impenetrable to most conventional weaponry.

Tantō – a short, single- or double-edged dagger, between six and twelve inches in length. Women often carry tantō for self-defence, as the knife can easily be concealed inside an obi.

Tetsubo – a long war club, made of wood or solid iron, with iron spikes or studs at one end, used to crush armour, horses or other weapons in battle. The use of a tetsubo requires great balance and strength – a miss with the club can leave the wielder open to counter-attack.

Wakizashi – a sword with a single-edged, curved, slender blade between one and two feet in length, with a short, single-handed hilt bound in criss-crossed cord. It is usually worn with a longer blade, known as a katana.

RELIGION

Amaterasu – Goddess of the Sun. Daughter of Izanagi, she was born along with Tsukiyomi, God of the Moon, and Susano-ō, God of Storms, when her father returned from Yomi and washed to purify himself of Yomi's taint. She is a benevolent deity, a bringer of life, although in recent decades has become seen as a harsh and unforgiving Goddess. She is not fond of either of her brothers, refusing to speak to Tsukiyomi, and constantly tormented by Susano-ō. She is patron of the Phoenix zaibatsu, and is also often venerated by women.

Enma-ō – one of the nine Yama Kings, and chief judge of all the hells. Enma-ō is the final arbiter of where a soul will reside after death, and how soon it will be allowed to rejoin the wheel of life.

Izanagi (Lord) – also called Izanagi-no-Mikoto, literally 'He who Invites', the Maker God of Shima. He is a benevolent deity who, with his wife Izanami, is responsible for creating the Shima Isles, their pantheon of Gods and all the life therein. After the death of his wife in childbirth, Izanagi travelled to Yomi to retrieve her soul, but failed to return her to the land of the living.

Izanami (Lady) – also called the Dark Mother, and the Endsinger, wife to Izanagi, the Maker God. Izanami died giving birth to the Shima Isles, and was consigned to dwell in the Yomi underworld. Izanagi sought to reclaim his wife, but she was corrupted by Yomi's dark power, becoming a malevolent force and hater of the living. She is mother to the thousand and one oni, a legion of demons who exist to plague the people of Shima.

Hachiman – the God of War. Originally a scholarly deity, thought of more as a tutor in the ways of war, Hachiman has become re-personified in recent decades to reflect the more violent warlike ways of the Shima government. He is now seen as the embodiment of war, often depicted with a weapon in one hand and a white dove in the other, signifying desire for peace, but readiness to act. He is patron of the Tiger zaibatsu.

The hells – a collective term for the nine planes of existence where a soul can be sent after death. Many of the hells are places where souls are sent temporarily to suffer for transgressions in life, before moving back to the cycle of rebirth. Before Lord Izanagi commanded the Yama Kings to take stewardship over the souls of the damned in order to help usher them towards enlightenment, Shima had but a single hell – the dark, rotting pit of Yomi.

The Hungry Dead – the restless residents of the Underworld. Spirits of wicked people consigned to hunger and thirst in Yomi's dark for all eternity.

Raijin – God of Thunder and Lightning, son of Susano-ō. Raijin is seen as a cruel God, fond of chaos and random destruction. He creates thunder by pounding his drums across the sky. He is the creator of arashitora, the thunder tigers.

Susano-ō – the God of Storms. Son of Izanagi, he was born along with Amaterasu, Goddess of the Sun and Tsukiyomi, God of the Moon, when his father returned from Yomi and washed to purify himself of Yomi's taint. Susano-ō is generally seen as a benevolent God, but he constantly torments his sister, Amaterasu, Lady of the Sun, causing her to hide her face. He is father to the Thunder God, Raijin, the deity who created arashitora – the thunder tigers. He is patron of the Ryu zaibatsu.

Tsukiyomi – the God of the Moon. Son of Izanagi, he was born along with Amaterasu, Goddess of the Sun, and Susano-ō, God of Storms, when his father returned from Yomi and washed to purify himself of Yomi's taint. Tsukiyomi angered his sister, Amaterasu, when he slaughtered Uke Mochi, the Goddess of Food. Amaterasu has refused to speak to him since, which is why the Sun and Moon never share the same sky. He is a quiet God, fond of stillness and learning. He is the patron of the Kitsune zaibatsu.

Yomi – the deepest level of the hells, where the evil dead are sent to rot and suffer for all eternity. Home of demons, and the Dark Mother, Lady Izanami.

ACKNOWLEDGEMENTS

Jay Kristoff would like to offer Big Scary Hugs to the following outstanding human beings:

Amanda, for the throwaway line that planted the seed for the entire book, reading it seventeen thousand times, being generally wonderful and forgiving of my silence, surliness and sarcasm.

Pete Wolverton, Julie Crisp and Anne Brewer, for handing me the hacksaw and blowtorch, and helping make this book something I'm truly proud of.

Brunch Bitch, Sharkgrrl, KK and The KitKat for telling me the parts that sucked and saying OMFG in all the right places. I love youse guys.

Matt Bialer and LT Ribar for shooting straight, changing my diapers and wiping the dribble away from my bubbling lips.

The fantabulous Cassie Galante, Rachel Howard and the PR/Marketing posse at St Martins Press, Bella Pagan, Louise Buckley and all @ Tor UK, Charlotte 'Don't call me Reetard' Ree, Hayley Crandell, Praveen Naidoo and crew @ PanMacMillan Aus. You people are awesome, and the energy you put into pimping my sorry ass is nothing short of amazing. Much love.

Scott Westerfeld, Pat Rothfuss, KW Jeter, Stephen Hunt, Marissa Meyer and Kevin 'Droogie' Hearne for not only reading but pimping my warez.

Lance Hewett, Narita Misaki, Sudayama Aki and Paul Cechner for being my gurus in all things Japanese.

The mighty Kira Ostrovska for laying the smackdown on my Russki. 'Imperatritsa dvenatseti stolits!'

Brad Carpenter, the web-mastah of disastah, the ayatollah of rock and rollah.

Marc, B-Money, Rafe, Weez, Surly Jim, Burglar, Eli, Beiber, The Dread Pirate Glouftis, Bertie, Tom, Steve, Mini, Chris, Gav and all other members of my nerd posse, past and present, for getting me out of the godsdamn house occasionally.

The inimitable Doctor Sam Bowden, for the hasty class on tension pneumothorax, and dragging his fiiiine self all the way across the country for my book launch.

Eamon Kenny, for setting me straight on all things radio (even though we cut 90% of it in edits).

Kristy Echeverria for *allllll* the gory details.

Araki Miho, once again, for her beautiful calligraphy.

Jimmy the Orrsome for our clan logos (shoulda charged a percentage, man), and Sir Christopher Tovo for the lurrrve on film.

Jason Chan, holy shit, dude. You can be my wingman any time.

The book bloggers – too many to mention, never too many to remember – who did so much to get this thing's clockwork wings off the ground. You people are so very, very metal. You know who you are. I know who you are. Never stop being awesome.

The incredible people who made me poetry or music or paintings or reviews, who took this thing I created and created something themselves. That, more than anything on this strange little ride, has struck me as extraordinary.

My family for never really changing, despite the distance and the years.

And last but far from least:

You.

www.panmacmillan.com